About the Book

Tony Glover is a writer and film-m:
His first film, **Posh Monkeys**, won a ʀoyɑɩ ɪeɪevɪsɪon Society award
and was promoted by the British Council at the Angers, Munich
and New York film festivals. **Year of the Tiger**, set in Newcastle's
Chinatown, was filmed for Yorkshire Tyne Tees. **Just A Trim** won
Tony a **Sony Radio Award** and the title of BBC North Playwright
of the Year. He is working on a script for a feature film, **The Curse
of Anaïs**. His first novel in the Kitty Lockwood series was **Cars Just
Want to be Rust**.
www.tonyglover.net

About **Cars Just Want to be Rust**

By the bottom of the first page I knew I had found an exceptionally
good writer. Tony Glover takes you straight into the story and
grabs the reader almost instantly. This is a real page turner and I
can't wait for the next in the series. The characters are beautifully
fleshed out but the writing remains taught, constantly pulling you
forward. *John Simon*

I give this book a well deserved Five star rating and would
recommend it to all those who enjoy crime novels by such
esteemed authors as, for instance , Ian Rankin or Ed McBain.
Edward M. Frais

Gripping stuff! The characters are interesting and well developed
and the Northumberland countryside is beautifully portrayed.
The plot weaves its way along at a good pace with plenty of twists
and turns. But best of all, it really builds up the suspense and keeps
the reader guessing. *Artemisia*

Can't wait to see what happens in the next book! The story really
developed in front of your eyes. Brilliant. *R. W.*

Gripping from the first chapter, in the way that Vinnie Jones
gripped Gazza. *Sinderhope Clarion*

About **The Luxury of Murder**

The wife of a nightclub owner is attacked while sunbathing by her pool. There's a quick arrest but Kitty Lockwood is certain the wrong man is in custody. How far is she prepared to risk her own life to find the real culprit?

The Luxury of Murder

Tony Glover

First published 2015 by
Rudham Books

13 Horsley Wood Cottages
Horsley
Northumberland
NE15 0NR

United Kingdom

rudhambooks@gmailcom

© Tony Glover 2015 www.tonyglover.net

British Library Cataloguing in Publication Data:
A catalogue record for this book is available from the British Library.

ISBN 978-0-9934003-0-8

Cover image : Leanne Pearce
Typeset: Jade Hays
Cover design: Wayne Gamble

RUDHAM BOOKS

To Kofi and Jake and to Chris, my brother.

With special thanks to Stevie Glover and Ailsa Mason.

Who knows their heart's true desire: for we are strangers, even to ourselves.

CHAPTER ONE

YOU WAKE AT SIX, eyes wide, staring at the ceiling.

You dress without thinking, drive on autopilot. For the first hour you keep busy. On the outside, everything looks the same. Your face is a mask. Inside your head, it's quite different. Your mind is miles away, dwelling on this other matter.

You're just not the kind of person who can allow something like that to happen. You have too much pride. If a problem can be fixed, then you *do* that. You take control. You feel the fear then do it anyway. Feel the fear and do it.

Just do it.

So you pull on your gloves, the Madovas. You get in the car and drive out to her house in suburban dreamland, the bitch's kennel. You park on the side of the road, in front of her mansion. Switch off the engine.

The sun beats down on the windscreen. You close your eyes. For a moment there is a chance you will change your mind. Then you think about the two of them together.

You breathe. In and out, filling your lungs. Thinking about your happy place, seeing the pictures, little clips of the times when you loved and felt loved.

When you open your eyes the first thing you see is a squirrel. The creature watches from the trunk of a Scot's Pine. It skitters down the tree and bobbles across the road. It stops, tilts its head, turning one eye, a button of black glass. You think about her. How it has always been the same. When you climb out of the car, everything changes. As you walk across the drive, you glance down, watch your feet crunch gravel. Every stone, every pebble shifts beneath your feet. Everything is so far away, shimmering in the heat of the sun.

This isn't you.
You reach out your hand and ring the bell.

CHAPTER TWO

BARRY LIU DANGLED the keys to his lavender Lexus, holding the fob between his thumb and index finger.

'Your usual space, sir?' said the concierge, as the keys dropped into his palm.

Mr Liu peeled a banknote from a clip and tucked it into the man's palm. The concierge closed the door of room 922 and headed towards the lift. Mr Liu hung his jacket in the wardrobe. He flicked a speck of lint from the lapel with a manicured nail. He closed the mirrored door and studied his reflection. He was a young man, old enough to know he would not be young forever. Liu passed his fingers down his cheek, pulling the skin taut. He ran his fingers through spiky black hair.

Rolling up the sleeves of his white shirt, he opened a bottle of sparkling water and half filled a glass. Mr Liu carried his drink to the window. He watched the rush hour traffic on the street below. The lights turned green and the cars moved away. Evening light shone down the valley, glinting on the surface of the river.

It was almost five. Mr Liu planned on taking a nap. At seven he would take dinner in the hotel dining room, where he would meet Mr Lumley. Afterwards they would return to this room and shake hands on the deal. It was a formality. Mr Liu did not foresee a problem. At the start of their negotiations Mr Lumley had been less agreeable, his face red, his eyes flashing white around the iris. But Mr Liu had stated the case, explaining how things would be. Mr Lumley had seen sense. Honour was satisfied. The men had mutual respect. They had moved beyond the stage of conflict.

Mr Liu yawned. He sat on the bed and removed his shoes, Pakersons, Italian ostrich leather. He placed them side by side in front of the wardrobe. As he removed his silk tie he studied his reflection in the mirror. Each time we look in the mirror it may be for the last time. But Mr Liu had no concerns. Everything was going well. Tonight he would close the deal. In the morning he would return to Manchester.

There was a knock. As Mr Liu strolled to the door he wrapped his tie around his fingers. He expected to see the concierge, returning with the keys to his Lexus. He saw a young man with pale skin. Tufts of light red hair escaped from the hood of his jacket. The young man took a step inside the room. Mr Liu was about to speak when he saw a flash of silver as his head flew across the room.

'*This* one has his own...erm. Dog hoist!' Jacqui Speed struggled to get her tongue around the word 'veterinary'. 'He's a *vet*!' She prodded the screen with an unsteady finger. 'Look! There's a lovely picture of the hoist...' Kitty sat at her side, sipping a glass of Merlot.

'A vet?'

'They make good money. Vets.'

'Would *you* go out with a man who's just had his hands up a cow?'

'Of course!' Kitty saw her friend slyly fill her glass. 'Think of the saving if little Merlin gets ill!'

Kitty scrolled through the catalogue of single men. 'A lot of loneliness in the world, isn't there?'

You're getting drunk, Lockwood.

Kitty struggled to fill in the details of her on line profile. In the end she settled on 'slim, with reddy brown hair.' She omitted her work profile. Admitting she was a police officer would be a mistake. It might deter some men while attracting others best avoided.

'What was wrong with your last one?'

'Can't remember!' Kitty shuddered. 'Oh yes! Too much butter. He slathered it all over his toast, great chunks. I wanted him out of the house before Molly woke up. Great thick slabs of butter.'

'The utter, utter bastard. Too much butter...'

'It's timing, Jacqui. It's all about timing.' Kitty stretched her arms, keen to change the subject. 'Molly's not right. There's something at school. And I've just started a new job. My mother is going loopy. I can't take my eye off the ball. Not now.'

'It's never the right time, is it, Katherine Lockwood? You're chicken.'

'I'm embarrassed. Deeply awkward. I'll admit that!'

'It's a waste, Kitty. You. A waste. You'd make someone happy.'

'You didn't say 'very.''

'You're right.' Jacqui shook her head. 'I didn't...'

One thousand and sixty two days have passed since Kitty Lockwood felt the cool touch of a gun barrel against her neck. Three years. When she looks in the mirror she sees another faint line at the side of her mouth when she smiles. Her red brown hair has grown a shade darker. Her eyes are a little wiser, a little sadder. She wrinkles her nose and turns away.

Her daughter Molly has grown five inches. She has become more distant, more moody - if that were possible. Kitty still goes to her weekly Wado-Ryu class in the church hall, every Wednesday evening, if her shift permits. She has risen from a white to a green belt, from tenth kyu to sixth. If the class is full the teacher, Master Raphael, trusts her to teach the youngsters and new recruits. She enjoys sparring with Raphael, not least because his teaching saved her life.

Her career has moved on. A few months after returning to work as a Neighbourhood Beat constable, Kitty passed her OSPRE exams. She is newly promoted - a detective sergeant.

Sometimes, when she's tired, or lonely, Kitty imagines she hears the voice of her dead father speaking to her. It no longer worries her. The dead are ghosts we carry around in our heads.

Life moves on: life remains the same.

Kitty put the screen to sleep and joins her friend Jacqui at the window. They have been close friends since the High School. Kitty was bridesmaid, when Jacqui married Trevor. Shoulder to shoulder they sip their wine, watching the sun sink towards the edge of the valley.

'I'm on my own, Jacqui. That's my choice. You get to the point where...you have everything just the way you want it. A routine.'

'A rut,' Jacqui whispers, into her glass.

Kitty bites her lip. Their friendship has weathered plenty of arguments. She has no desire to start another. 'Why would I risk all that? For some bloke? Even if he has got a beautiful dog hoist.'

The light has almost gone when Kitty walks home, weaving down the lane, through the small town of Belfordham, towards her cottage in Cloud Street. The evening air in Northumberland is cool in May. As she turns into the cobbled lane a grey shape separates itself from the surrounding darkness and slinks towards her.

'Hello cat!' Merlin winds himself around her leg. '*You* love me, don't you?' She picks up Merlin and tickles his chin. The old cat purrs deep in his throat. 'My tin opener, anyway.'

CHAPTER THREE

'CAN YOU TURN that down?'

When Greta Lumley arrived home her husband Clive was stretched out on the sofa, watching the racing on Channel 4. Clive lay in the usual spot, his legs spread, his eyes glazing as they flicked over the screen. His phone lay in easy reach. He scratched at the racing page with the stub of a pencil stashed behind his ear. A slab of belly fat flopped over the waistband of his all-day leisure suit. Clive's mouth fell open as he studied the runners and riders circling the paddock.

'You eaten, Gret?'

His voice was gruff but whiny, like a pug pretending to be a ridgeback. As Greta disappeared into the kitchen he tried again, shouting at her back. 'I said, you eaten?'

Twelve years ago, when Greta met Clive, the man had presence. He was six feet four, bright eyed, with shoulders like a steel joist. When Clive entered a room eyes turned. Since his spell in Durham, he seemed less of a man. His hair was straggly, wispy tufts sprouting from his ears. No longer a sharp dresser, Clive shuffled around the house in his tracky and slippers.

Before the bust, Clive's nickname was Dial-a-Dealer. He was the top drugs bunny south of the Scottish Border. He built a huge network to shift cocaine, cannabis and sulphate. Just spreading the love. Anyone who whispered against Clive Lumley ended up missing or elsewhere. For years the police could only look on. Kitty Lockwood's mentor, Bryson Prudhoe, pieced together a case against him, only to see it fall at the last fence. When the case fell apart Bryson started all over again. Biding his time, Bryson watched Clive for months before nailing him on a minor possession offence. So Clive spent time in Durham Prison, then HMP Acklington. He still held a grudge against Bryson Prudhoe. Kitty Lockwood had been a member of the team that raided Clive and Greta's country home, Kyloe House. That was the start of Clive's troubles. It was something he would never forget, never forgive.

'People who cross Clive get hurt,' it was said.

Clive Lumley had been out on licence for three months but a piece of him was still caged between the yellow gloss walls of Durham nick. It took him a while to adjust to life on the out. For the first week he was still on jail time, sleeping during the day and pacing the floor at night. Prison had got into his bones.

Greta had taken over running the family firm while Clive was inside. She sold Kyloe House and moved into a modern home on the Callerton Lodge estate. The old place was filled with bad memories and she was happy to leave it behind. The new house was everything she wanted - a drawing room with a Chesney stone fireplace, granite worktops and a Kohler tub bath. And it was only ten miles from the city. Greta enjoyed having complete control over their business. She was more cautious than Clive, yet more methodical. Now and then Clive dragged himself to his office in town but the outside world seemed to trouble him.

Every day had the same shape. Breakfast. Exercise - a shuffle around the garden. Lunch. Sleep. Racing on the telly. Supper. Telly. Bed. Lights out. The routine was comforting, Greta guessed.

In the first days after his release, their sex life was spectacular. On the day Greta picked him up Clive made her stop the BMW by the Angel of the North so he could have her on the back seat. For the first few days he was like a man in his twenties. The sex tapered off, then stopped altogether. Sometimes, in the middle of the night, he would mumble in her ear and take her from behind, grinding away like a sweating boar. Afterwards he would fall asleep and snore. She knew it took him six minutes because she watched the seconds flip away the on the digital clock by her bed. Who was he with, she wondered. Was it her, or someone inside his head?

Kitty stared at the ceiling, waiting for the alarm. It sounded just as she fell asleep, the honking *dive dive dive* of a submarine going under the waves. She kicked off the covers, vaulted from the bed and got dressed. She missed her footing as she tumbled down the narrow stairs. It was early May, light at half five, though the staircase of the cottage in Cloud Street was always gloomy.

'Fuck, fuck, FUCK! ' She hobbled into the kitchen and lit the gas beneath the porridge. She stirred with one hand and switched on the radio with the other.

'Molly!' Her shout rang around the walls of the tiny kitchen. 'Porridge or cereal?'

The letterbox clattered. There were two bills and a flyer from the council which she dropped in the pedal bin. But it was the fat ivory coloured envelope which worried her. Nobody sends a letter unless they need to talk about love or death. She wafted the envelope, feeling the heft of the twenty five per cent cotton stationery. The watermark said it was printed by G.Lalo and made 'according to traditional methods but with modern techniques.' A grid of translucent lines was etched into the paper. The envelope smelled like newly minted banknotes. It came from Molly's dad, she was certain. Whatever it contained, it would stir up memories she preferred to forget.

She placed the letter on the kitchen table and stared at it as she ate her porridge. Molly drifted into the kitchen, dragging a brush through her dark hair. She picked up the envelope then tossed it aside. The movement was too sudden.

Gave yourself away, there, my darling.

Kitty scooped up her post and pushed the letters into her bag. She couldn't face opening bills this early. Nor that letter. Better to pretend it didn't exist.

They were in the Saab by quarter to seven, rattling down the lanes.

'If that little madam says anything to you, Mollusc, just walk away.'

'Don't call me that, mum.'

Kitty bit her lip. Least said, soonest mended.

They bimbled along the lane in silence. As they reached the school gate Kitty tried again.

'If that little bitch tries it on...'

'I know,' sighed Molly. 'Walk away...' Molly slammed the door and sauntered into school, her bag slung over her shoulder. Kitty watched her go. She was right. She wasn't a kid.

When did that happen?

Molly vanished in the throng of girls. Kitty strained to see who was talking to her daughter but they all looked so similar. Kitty glanced at her watch. She was late.

Cathy Fletcher caught the nine o'clock bus from the stand at the Haymarket. She took her usual seat at the back of the X77, kerb side, next to the window. The air in the bus was scented with diesel and fabric rinse. As the bus rolled up Claremont Terrace Cathy opened her *Daily Mail* and finished the crossword with 25 across, '*Muppet pal of Elmo, three letters.*'

The bus rocked her though the familiar stops, Kenton, Bank Foot, the leafy suburb of Wolsington, before leaving the city behind. She stared out of the window at the fields, the grass so fresh and green, the trees heavy with blossom, the petals drifting like confetti. Cathy had always wanted to move away from the Town, but they would never have the money for that. She and Mike had enough to pay the bills and buy food. They would always live in their flat in the West End. They had a beautiful kitchen but they would never afford foreign holidays. 'It's not all doom and gloom,' Cathy whispered to herself.

She counted her blessings. She worked in a beautiful house, surrounded by gorgeous things. The furnishings, the art, the pictures, though not to her own taste, took her breath away. The view from any of the twenty two windows was stunning. She knew there were twenty two because she counted them every morning as she polished the glass. If she looked up from her work there was greenery everywhere, the lawn sloping down to the river, the line of trees along the banks. Her employers were so... For a moment, she was stuck for the word. *One across. Seven letters.*

Devoted.

Jack and Marisa Lyndon were such a *devoted* couple.

Cathy folded the newspaper and lay it on the seat, in case anyone else wanted to read it. She closed her eyes, knowing it was safe to doze for the next quarter of an hour.

Sometimes the memories return. You hear the bell ringing, echoing inside the house. No answer. You walk back, out from the portico and you look up at the windows. Nothing. No sound but for the birds and the hiss of the fountain, the droplets of water glittering like crystal.

You walk around the side of the house. She's lying by the pool. Stretched out on her lounger beneath a clear blue sky. Her body like white gold in the sun. She's almost naked, the sheen of oil on her skin.

Pods dangle from her ears and she's humming along with some tune. That's why she didn't hear the bell. She doesn't know you're here. One of her feet taps on the stone flags around the pool. A small, perfect foot. Scarlet nails. Your pulse quickens as you walk towards her. You have something you need to say but as you approach her, the words vanish, floating away like May blossom in the breeze.

CHAPTER FOUR

KITTY LOCKWOOD'S DOODLING skills were improving. She drew a perfect circle on the crossword section.

'Is that a sign of madness?' she wondered. She embroidered a kind of Arabic script around the inside rim, then shaded the space, enjoying the way the sharpy tip glided across the newsprint.

Getting high on the ink.

Kitty sat alone in the deserted canteen. Stillness was a rare and guilty pleasure. The best strategy at headquarters was to keep moving. Management consultants lurked everywhere. The Thin Blue Line was being stretched as thin as it would go. 'Frontline services are safe,' was the management mantra. It was a lie, of course. They were closing local stations and replacing them with a 'police presence in fire stations.' No-one told the truth anymore - better to finesse a lie than tell the truth. Our world is all about presentation, telling pretty lies.

'Look busy when you're at headquarters,' Bryson Prudhoe counselled. 'A police officer who's moving looks more productive than one staring through the window.'

Over the last two weeks, Kitty had become used to her own company. In April she had been posted to Headquarters, a collection of prefabs set in farmland north of the city. News came through that the place was being sold for housing, part of the 'restructuring.' Kitty lifted her gaze to gaze across the rolling fields that would soon be covered with newly built houses. Headquarters was being sold - the site would soon become another 'executive estate.'

Her flat white grew cold. She nibbled her pastry and pushed it aside. It was typical of Vipond. He summoned her as if there was an emergency, then left her waiting. For the last two weeks the morning routine had been the same. She rose at half six, dropped Molly at school, then drove eighteen miles to Headquarters, where she signed in and checked her duty for the day. Each day she waited in the canteen while DI Tony Vipond held strategy meetings. Vipond worked the big cases, but she was only on the edge of things. It was a little like being a chauffeur, she decided. Or was it 'chauffeuse?' Whatever the word, she was his driver.

She was not sure whether she hated Vipond or merely disliked him - it changed from day to day. Most of the time he baffled her. Vipond never thanked anyone. He never praised anyone. He never spoke unless it was absolutely necessary. He possessed none of the skills which eased everyday life between human beings yet he had the gift of making all around him submit to his will.

Her mobile buzzed.

'Bryson? How are you?'

'Good, Locky. Considering...'

She imagined him twirling his coffee cup on the desk at Shaftoe Leazes, running his fingers down the walrus moustache.

'Making steady progress...'

'In the fight against crime?'

'In the master bedroom. Finished on Saturday. *French Gray*.'

'Lovely! I expect...'

'It's like *Mouse Back*, but half a shade lighter. Closer to *Elephant's Breath*.'

'Sounds like a hangover.'

Kitty realised how much she missed the old sod.

'Everyone well? Eileen keeping you busy?'

'She's fine.' Bryson rarely mentioned his wife and sons. He never revealed any details of their lives. 'The gloss is *Wimborne White*. Beautiful finish! Perfect.'

She could not recall the last time she'd decorated her own house. Most of the rooms were the same as when she and Molly moved into Cloud Street. Molly was six then, twelve now. A dangerous time. The start of all the trouble to come. 'How's everyone at Shaftoe?

'We struggle on without you, Locky. Somehow...'

It was a tease, though she sensed he missed her. Since passing her OSPRE exams, she had bounced around the county. Her first posting was close to the Scottish border, followed by a stint in the ancient and battered nick in the port of Blyth. Now she was attached Vipond, her new mentor, at HQ. She glanced around the canteen.

'It's early days.' Her voice dropped to a whisper. 'I'm 'attached' to Tony V.'

'Vipond.' Bryson's voice was as flat as his chalk based emulsion. 'You've worked with him?'

There was a pause before Bryson answered. 'That is correct. I have worked with Tony Vipond.'

She glanced over her shoulder, checking she was alone.

'Prat, isn't he?'

'His career has been marked by a considerable degree of success, DS Lockwood. More than mine...'

She smiled, gazing across the fields. That he did not approve of her new boss was no surprise - Bryson Prudhoe rarely approved of anyone. A flock of black face ewes skittered through a clump of hawthorns.

'Sheep,' she murmured.

'What did you say?

'Sleep.' She yawned. 'Could do with a sleep. I'm bored rigid! Wish I was back on the Neighbourhood Beat team.'

'Lies,' said Bryson.

There was dead air for a moment. Kitty could hear talk in the background. It seemed Bryson had his hand over the phone. When he spoke again there was an edge to his voice.

'Got to go, Locky. We have a shout. Something nasty in the Jury's Inn. See? When it kicks off, you'll pine for these lovely, tedious days!'

'Which service do you require, Mrs Fletcher?'

Cathy Fletcher's knuckles blanched as she gripped the phone. 'I don't know! Everything! Ambulance?' Her fingertips traced her brow as she stared at the scene by the pool. Blood was spreading across the stone flags and dripping from the edge, clouding the water. Sunlight danced on the Persia Blue tiles that lined the pool. Marisa Lyndon's body lay by the lounger. Her face was half covered by a towel. If it had not been for the matted blood in her hair, she might have been sleeping. 'Police too. Quickly please! She looks really awful!'

Cathy Fletcher pushed her fingers through the hair at the back of her neck. She twisted the strands, pulling them taut until she felt pain. Tears rolled down her face.

'Tell me the postcode, Mrs Fletcher?'

Vipond's greying pelt of buzz cut hair stood on end. Kitty watched him thread his way between the tables. His hands were thrust deep in the pockets of his North Face jacket. A haze of cigarette smoke hung around his face.

'We have a shout,' he barked. 'Chop chop!' Kitty slipped her phone into her bag as she struggled to keep up.

Vipond bleeped the car as they ran across the tarmac. For the last few days Kitty had driven while Vipond sat in the back seat, making calls or playing with his phone. Now he jumped behind the wheel, folding his body into the driver's seat. They were rolling before Kitty closed the door.

'What's the shout? The Jury's Inn?'

'Eh? No! Violent assault, possible homicide. Meadow Lane.' The car leaped forward as they hit the main road.

'Where's Meadow Lane?' Kitty fumbled, searching for her belt.

'Callerton Chase estate. Five minutes away.'

Vipond put his foot to the floor and flashed blues. Kitty was pressed back as the car roared past the church and into the centre of the nearby village. Heads turned as they shot past the Seven Stars pub. He flipped the wheel to the left and they were in the Callerton Chase estate, tyres squealing as they flashed past the tennis club. They hurtled along quiet roads lined with beech hedges. She glimpsed luxury cars parked in the gated driveways. This was no sink estate : the Callerton Chase was a ghetto of a different kind - a haven for the wealthy. The houses were vast, the gardens full of mature trees and rolling lawns. It was a foreign land to Kitty, who took in the view as the car hurtled up Meadow Lane.

'They call this 'Millionaires' Row,' said Vipond. The narrow road curved into the distance, lined with tall beech hedges, clothed in the fresh green of early summer.

'Victim's called Marisa Lyndon.'

'Right.' The name meant nothing to Kitty. 'I think I know the name,' she lied.

'Married to Jack Lyndon,' said Vipond. 'He runs bars in the Town.'

Kitty was only twenty miles from home, yet this was a different part of the forest. Kitty wasn't in Belfordham anymore. They rounded a curve and she saw an ambulance, parked at the side of the road, the motor running. A few yards further along the road a battered pick up was parked. Vipond drove thirty yards beyond the ambulance, squeezing his car between whitewashed stones on the tightly clipped verge.

'Eyes open,' Vipond muttered as he slammed the door. 'Mouth shut.'

They hurried past the ambulance to enter a pebbled gateway. A brass sign on the gatepost revealed that the house was called *The Fox Covert.* It was a two storey mansion in terra cotta, fronted by a Classical portico supported by eight marble columns. It was about the size of a Roman temple. Kitty guessed there were at least twenty windows on the front of the place. The house was framed by tall trees, silver birch and native oaks. A rotator hissed in the sunlight, arcing jets of water across the bright green lawn. To the right stood a triple garage, fronted by blond hardwood doors. To the left the gravel path snaked around the side of the house.

The front door lay open. Kitty followed Vipond into a hallway which might double as a small ballroom. She glimpsed bright airy rooms to the left and right.

'Hello? Police?' Vipond's shout echoed through the house. There was no answer. A staircase, wider than a country road, led to the upper floor. They skirted the stairs and down a corridor which led towards the rear of the building. As they reached an oak panelled door Kitty heard voices from somewhere beyond. Vipond opened it to reveal a spacious sitting room. The far wall was a window which ranged along the whole room. Kitty could see people huddled around a body by a small outdoor swimming pool. The group was still, a tableau of figures gathered around a body on the sandstone flags. Kitty followed Vipond through a sliding door.

At the edge of the group a woman with tired blond hair was weeping, a crumpled tissue pressed to her lips. bordering the pool. Her blond hair was matted with blood. To the side stood a young man, his broad shoulders barely contained by a sleeveless leather jerkin. He stared at the ground, his hand over his mouth. Every few moments he steeled himself to look at the body before turning away. Two paramedics, a man and a woman, kneeled by the body. The dark haired woman was tending to the victim. She pushed red framed glasses up her nose as she worked. The victim was a young woman, mid to late twenties, Kitty guessed. Her head lay at the centre of a dark stain which had spread across the flagstones the left side of her head was scarred by a dark wound. Drops of blood spattered her neck and shoulders. She wore only sunglasses and a yellow bikini bottom. The top of the costume lay at the edge of the pool, the fabric splashed with blood.

Vipond pulled his id from his pocket a held it out. Nobody so much as glanced at him. As the seconds ticked by, Kitty realised how foolish he looked.

'OK.' The dark haired woman nodded to her partner. They eased the victim onto the stretcher and moved towards the house.

'No,' said the paramedic, slinging her stethoscope around her neck. 'Let's take her around the side. It's quicker.'

Kitty and Vipond trailed after them. For the first time the paramedic glanced at them. 'Who are you?'

'DI Vipond.' He waved his id in her face. 'What's the situation?'

'She has a severe trauma to her head.'

Vipond hurried ahead, blocking the narrow path.

'When did she die?'

The paramedic shook her head. 'Could you move out of the way please?'

Vipond held up his hand as if stopping traffic.

'This is a crime scene.'

'Out of the way!' said the paramedic. 'I need to get this woman to hospital now. End of story.'

Vipond's mouth fell open. 'Hospital?'

The woman stared at him as if he had crawled from beneath a stone. 'She's not dead! Now piss off out of my way! *SHIFT!*'

Vipond rocked on his heels. Kitty shivered with guilty pleasure. As they lifted Marisa Lyndon into the ambulance, Kitty scribbled down the plate number. The dark haired paramedic climbed inside and leaned over her patient. The doors slammed and the ambulance rolled away, the siren wailing as it took the bend.

'Fuck a sodding duck!' Vipond shouted. 'We need someone on board! Get on the phone and make sure they're met at the other end!' He kicked the gravel as he stomped inside the house, leaving Kitty to call in his request to Market Street station. By the time she finished the call the siren had faded away. The only sound was the burble of birdsong and the breeze blowing through the beech hedge. She touched a fingertip to her cheek as the first drop of rain splashed her face.

CHAPTER FIVE

KIRK 'WHITEY' WHITE is twenty two. Six foot three, thin as a streak of piss. His hair is red, cut short on his skull but tufts of it sprout on his chin. Whitey wears sports clothes, though he never plays sport. He wears trainers - Rockports or Wallabees, tracky bottoms, a white tee, a grey hoodie or a Helly Hanson if the weather is inclement. His favourite is either a Tog 24 or a Berghaus. He used to like anything Burberry - these days he's more discreet. Everything is man made fibre, all box fresh, shiny as steel wire. It's fair to say that Whitey's clothes generate enough static to power a small radio.

Once upon a time Whitey spent all his cash on 'White Shite' - White Lightning cider and tack. Those childhood pleasures are long gone. Back then his limbs were thin as string, the skin as pale as white bread. Whitey's teenage body looked like a strand of damp tagliatelle. In those years all of Whitey's moist, intimate crannies carried their own micro climate. They grew their own flora - a cocktail of Dhobies Itch, genital warts and thrush. His father teased him about it. These days, Kirk White is a different proposition. Whitey is a changed man.

His skin is still almost translucent, though the muscles are firm, the shoulders broad. His eyelashes are pale, a shade of sandy red, like those of a pig. Whitey has pale blue eyes. Even when at rest he's on the move, popping his knuckles or bouncing from foot to foot: when walking he swings his arms, loping along, rocking the Gartree Roll.

You would find Whitey's inner life disturbing. It's a mash up of carnival horror show and butcher's slab. His mind runs down one narrow track - the way of the warrior - violence and blood, severed flesh and splintered bone. Along with his weakling teenage body, Whitey has left laughter behind in his transition to manhood. He knows there's little to laugh about. His personality was forged by parental neglect and physical injury. His mother never hugged him. His father dropped him on his head when he was two. Whitey wriggled and twisted, tumbling out of his father's drunken grasp. There followed months of hospital time while his neural pathways reconnected, but in a damaged, dangerous way.

The doctors told his father that Kirk had BPD - Borderline Personality Disorder. Not one fuck did his daddy give. So none of this is Whitey's fault. I blame the parents. Brutalised, he became a brute. Bullied, he became an utter bastard.

Nature AND nurture - it's a bugger, isn't it?

CHAPTER SIX

THEY TOLD KITTY that shadowing Tony V would be a great opportunity. He was sharp, had presence and he handled the media well - a rarity in the police. If she wanted to progress, she was in the right place.

On her first day Vipond climbed into the back seat of her car, muttered their destination and spent the journey reading his papers or playing with his phone. Guessing he was taciturn by nature, Kitty did not force the conversation. But as the days went by she found it hard to work in near silence. Simple remarks were met with a chilly stare. It seemed Vipond wanted to be elsewhere, doing something different, with other people.

On the fourth morning she remarked that he smelled nice. It was innocent - there was nothing calculated about it. She was certainly not flirting with him. In the awkward silence that followed she made it worse by asking what cologne he wore. 'Spanish Leather,' he murmured before returning to his papers.

'Lovely!' She cringed as the word left her lips. They did not speak for the next thirty miles, which was why it gave her such pleasure to hear the paramedic give him a tongue lashing. Vipond had it coming.

She found him in the garden, pacing back and forth by the pool. The spring shower had passed and the garden smelled sweet and fresh. Vipond crooked his finger, beckoning her over.

'So. We jumped the gun a bit. It's not a murder,' he said. 'Yet...'

'Sir.' She noted the 'we.' It seemed she was part of his team now, if only because he'd screwed up. Through the kitchen window Kitty glimpsed the housekeeper and gardener. The woman had her hand to her face, wiping tears. The gardener was shaking his head.

Vipond kept his voice low. 'We're on our own here for a minute. This is way I run things, OK? We identify, secure and protect the physical evidence. We find the routes to and from the scene taken by the suspect and victim.'

'Do you have a suspect?' Kitty's surprise was genuine. Vipond glanced at the figures behind the window.

'Maybe. That doesn't matter for now. Keep everyone out. No-one is to walk anywhere near the place she was found. Same with the SIO - in any case I expect that I'll be the Senior Investigating Officer, so... When uniform arrive, put them on the doors. Tell 'em I need the house, garden and drive taped off. They *must* keep any nosy sods out. Set them to knocking up the neighbours and anyone working in the street. All those plumbers, builders, whatever - names and numbers. What did they see? What did they hear? What do they know about this house and the people who live here.'

Kitty scratched notes in her pad, nodding as she wrote.

'*Everyone* who enters the scene needs to suit up. Gloves, bootees - at the very least. No ifs, no buts. Make sure those two,' here he tipped his head towards the kitchen window - 'are swabbed for DNA. And I want *you* to start the log, as of this moment. Jot down names, times. When we got here. What happened. Who said what. Everything.' Again he nodded towards the window. 'Their details too. Log anything I tell you. Log anything I *don't* tell you. Notes on everything. Got that?'

'Sir.'

Vipond rocked back and forth, his hand on his cheek.

'Right now I want you to call the Control Room and give them the gen. After that...'

He stared at the ground, passing his fingertips across his cheek. She watched him, the nib of her pen hovering over her pad. Close up his tanned skin had the texture of crepe paper.

'After that *you* take the woman. I'll talk to him. We need an initial account. What's happened here? What do they know? Did they call anyone? Who was it? Names, numbers, times.'

He waited until she finished writing, then moved closer. He looked straight into Kitty's eyes, his voice low.

'This is the Golden Hour. I know they tell you that on the course and you probably think it's bollocks.' He waited until she nodded. 'It's not. We do this carefully. We work in a methodical way and we get a result. Usually with whatever we find in the next fifty minutes or so.' He rested his hand on her shoulder. 'You with me?'

Kitty nodded. 'Of course, sir.'

He slapped her shoulder and half smiled. She smiled back.

Inside, she bloomed. She laughed at herself, the way she fell for his first kind word, a desert flower opening to a single drop of rain. His temper tantrum had passed. Vipond exuded calm, a quiet sense of purpose. Perhaps she had been wrong about him. Perhaps all of this would work out well. He paused, speaking over his shoulder.

'What was that about the Jury's Inn? Earlier?'

'There's a shout there. Something very nasty.'

'Like what?'

'I don't know. Sorry.'

Kitty followed him as he entered the house through the sliding window. They found the door into the kitchen. Vipond approached the young man.

'Can we have a word? What's your name?'

'Kemp. Saul Kemp.'

'OK Saul. Let's go outside, eh?' Vipond led the man out to the garden. Kitty watched him pass, tanned arms swinging at his side, his legs apart. He was a big man, an inch taller than Vipond. His shoulders were broad and he looked like a gym addict. She wondered if he owed his body to hard work or steroids.

Kitty noticed that the woman was shaking as she moved around the room, lifting plates and wiping surfaces with kitchen roll, her face blank, eggshell pale.

'Hi.' It seemed that she had not heard. She ran the cloth over a mark, rubbing hard as she tried to wipe it away. 'I'm sorry. Can I ask you to stop doing that?'

Cathy Fletcher stared at Kitty, as if seeing her for the first time. Her lips parted. 'Why?'

'This is a crime scene. You might destroy evidence.'

The woman peered at the cloth in her hand. She dropped the rag and backed away, putting a hand to her brow.

'Could you tell me your full name?'

'Cathy. Catherine Anne Fletcher.'

'Is it OK if I call you Cathy?' The woman nodded.

'I'm Kitty. Kitty Lockwood.'

Cathy Fletcher tried to smile.

'The rain's stopped, Cathy. Let's go into the garden?'

Cathy nodded. As they walked out onto the stone terrace behind the house she leaned on Kitty, averting her eyes from the blood beside the pool. Kitty wondered if the woman was about to faint.

'You OK?'

Cathy Fletcher nodded. She leaned on Kitty as they crossed the lawn. Kitty caught the aroma of cleaning spray and buttered toast. The grass sloped away from the house towards the river. A thin mist rose from the grass as the sun warmed the earth. Vipond sat on the stone steps, the young man at his side. Kitty earwigged the chat as they passed.

'Kemp. Saul Kemp.' The young man was spelling his name for Vipond, his voice a hoarse whisper. He plucked at the lapel of his leather jerkin and stared at the ground between his boots.

'Saul will take it badly,' Cathy whispered.

'Is he a relative?'

'No.' Cathy dabbed her nose with the tissue. 'Saul works on the garden.'

Kitty sat Cathy on a garden bench near the edge of the property, in the lee of a tall hedge. 'Sure you're OK?'

Cathy nodded. Kitty opened her notes. 'Who rang this in? You?' Another nod.

'Finding her must have been a terrible shock?'

The woman reached for a tissue to dab her nose.

'Are you a relative?'

Cathy shook her head, pressing the tissue to her nose. 'No. I'm...' She stopped, shaking her head, her blue eyes unfocussed. 'I work here.'

Kitty took her phone number and address, noting it was in the west end of the city, a dozen miles away.

'I need to make a timeline of what happened this morning. Take your time. Just tell me what happened.'

Cathy Fletcher recalled the sequence of events. Kitty made notes without looking at her pad, her gaze fixed on Cathy's face. The 'tells' - micro-expressions that flashed across the face for a fraction of a second - were as important as the words the witness uttered.

'I got off the bus,' Cathy began. 'It drops me about ten to ten. I just walked up the road,' she pointed her thumb over her shoulder. 'As per usual.'

'You work here how often?'

'Every day. Except weekends.'

'Did you see anyone on the road? Cars parked?'

Cathy shook her head.

'Just a few vans going up and down. It's really quiet around here. So peaceful...'

Kitty nodded.

'Marisa gave me a key. So I let myself in - if she's gone out, or whatever. So in I comes, just as per usual. Put my pinny on. Then I was looking through the window, as I tied the...'

Cathy mimed tying the strings. Her eyes were haunted as she replayed the scene.

'How did the house look?'

'Normal! Everything was just the same.'

'Did you *hear* anything unusual?'

'It was quiet. Not a sound.'

'Was the radio on? The telly?'

'No. I don't think so. It's always quiet out here!'

Kitty glanced towards the house. Further up the garden Vipond and Saul Kemp were talking in low voices.

'OK, Cath. Will you try something for me? Close your eyes.'

Cathy Fletcher stared at Kitty, blinking. She closed her eyes.

'Tell me about the moment you came in. You came through the front door?'

'I came through the front door.'

Kitty waited, watching the woman's eyes flicker back and forth beneath the lids. 'I called out.'

'What did you say?'

'Just *'Marisa? Would you like a coffee!* Just as I always do.'

'What happened?'

'Nothing. Not a sound. Just the birds singing.' Cathy shook her head, opened her eyes. 'Usually she's up and about. In the kitchen or upstairs in the office. She doesn't usually have a coffee but I always ask. That's just my way of saying I'm here.'

'So she's not in bed when you get here?'

'Never!' Cath's eyes opened wider and she shook her head. Kitty clocked the micro flash of indignation. 'Marisa is *always* up and about. She's on the phone or the computer. Even if she's walking around the garden she's working.'

Cathy Fletcher seemed affronted at the suggestion her employer might enjoy a lie in.

'What does Mrs Lyndon do?'

'PR? What do they call it? Public relations or whatever. She'll be organising one of her events. A charity do or whatever. She's very busy! Always very busy...'

'OK. But what does she actually *do*?'

'She does things for artists. Arranges them. Shows. What do they call them?'

'Exhibitions? Openings?'

'Openings. Promotions. Receptions. They're just parties really, aren't they? Drinks and bits of nibbles and so on.'

'So she's making calls? Organising stuff? Caterers, booking rooms?'

'Yes! All that. Calling the printers. Phoning the papers and what have you!'

'But *this* morning...the house was silent?'

Cathy Fletcher gazed at Kitty, her face blank.

'Try closing your eyes again, Cathy.'

When she had done so Kitty noticed the lines around her lids, the fine hairs on her skin. A soft breeze bent the tops of the trees. 'Tell me what you hear.'

'The birds are singing. I'm pottering about, getting myself sorted, but I can hear the birds. A cuckoo. In the garden.'

'So...a door was open?'

Beneath the lids, Cathy moved her eyes from side to side.

'Must have been. Yes, because I went through to the sitting room to close it. They have those doors, sliding window things, opening onto the patio.'

'Was there any mess?'

'No more than usual. A couple of wineglasses. An empty bottle.'

'Was anything missing?'

'You mean like, a burglary?'

Kitty nodded.

'No. I don't think so. It was all normal.'

'So. You're at the window? That's when you see Marisa?'

She shook her head.

'No. I see Saul first.' Cath opened her eyes and tipped her head towards the young man who sat on the stone steps. The man's fingertips are pressed to his temples as he listens to Vipond.

'Saul's here every day?'

'No. Twice a week. Though I haven't seen him so often lately. Don't know whether he's been ill, or...' She shrugged. 'We don't talk much. I mean, he's outside, I'm busy in here. He gets his own coffee. I don't really know him that well, to be honest.'

'When did Saul start working here?'

'Early April.'

'And you?'

'I've been here for ages. Three years? Four maybe?'

'So where was Saul when you first saw him this morning?'

'Standing there.' Cathy pointed to a spot on the lawn, halfway between the pool and the hedge at the side of the garden.

'What was he doing?'

Cath Fletcher dutifully closed her eyes. She chewed her bottom lip as she pictured the scene. 'Staring at the side of the pool. I wondered what he was looking at. I thought it might be a bird, or something. There's a lot of nature out here. Rabbits. Foxes. Squirrels. Whatever.'

'So...'

'So I looked as well. I saw her leg. And I just thought. 'Oh, Marisa's lying by the pool.' At the same time it seemed odd! Because she was lying by the lounger and I thought, why lie on the stone? She'll be freezing! Then I see there's a towel over her head. Covering her face. I thought 'Why's she lying under a towel?' I thought maybe she'd had a dip then nodded off, or something. And her earphone things. They were there, but all tangled. Then I saw the blood. On the tiles by the pool. Everywhere.'

'What did Saul do?'

'We ran towards her! Both at the same time.'

'What happened next?'

Cathy put her hand to her brow. 'It's a bit of a blur.' She stared at the ground. 'I peeled the towel off, slowly, because I still thought she was asleep. There was blood in her hair. And I screamed then. I just screamed.'

She stared at Kitty, wide eyed, desperate to find some meaning in what had happened.

'Does Saul say anything?' Kitty glanced towards the house. Vipond was leaning in, his mouth inches from Saul Kemp's face. Kemp sat on the stone step, resting his sturdy arms on his knees.

Kitty turned back to the housekeeper.

'Saul kept saying 'God. My God!' And shaking his head.'

'Did either of you touch Marisa?'

'Just to move the towel away. I could see she was breathing. There were bubbles of stuff...bubbles of blood coming out of her nose. Popping, sort of thing. I just kept thinking, '*She'd hate anyone to see her like this.*'

Kitty glanced towards the men, sitting on the far side of the pool. The gardener looked at the ground as Vipond whispered something. Kitty's voice was low as she asked her next question.

'What did Saul do?'

'He was standing there. Watching. Great soft lump! I felt for her pulse. The wound was still bleeding. So I started to mop up the blood with the towel. I could see it dripping into the pool and all I could think was, '*She'll not want that! Messing up her pool. She'll be vexed about that!*' After a bit I ran inside and fetched out a wad of tissue to mop up the blood.'

Tears fell from Cathy Fletcher's eyes, streaking her pale cheeks. Kitty touched Cath's shoulder, feeling the shudder at each sob. Kitty looked towards the trees to see the rooks wheeling, a black circus in the air. At last Cathy Fletcher fell quiet. She dabbed her nose, crunching the tissue into a tight ball.

'You called the ambulance?'

'Who would *do* that?' Cathy shook her head. 'Marisa wouldn't hurt a soul!'

Behind them, Saul Kemp's voice rose. 'Ask her bloody husband! *Ask* him!'

Cathy's hand flew to her mouth.

'Has anyone called Mr Lyndon?'

'Give me his number,' said Kitty. She glanced across the garden. Vipond looked up and nodded. Kitty dialled the number.

'Jack Lyndon.' His tone was curt. Kitty walked across the grass, the phone pressed to her ear.

'This is DS Kitty Lockwood, Mr Lyndon. Northumbria Police. I'm at your home at the moment. There's been an incident.'

'Is Marisa OK?'

'As I say there's been...'

'I'm on my way.'

'Where are you now, Mr Lyndon?'

The phone went dead. Kitty redialled, but the call went straight to answerphone. It seemed an odd response - shock is unpredictable, yet the normal reaction, if there were such a thing, would be to hear what she had to say. Kitty laid her hand on Cathy's arm.

'Where is Mr Lyndon this morning?'

'At one of his places. The *Diamond Strip*. No!' Cathy's hand flew to her mouth. 'Marisa said he was driving to Edinburgh today. He'll be on the road somewhere.' Kitty scribbled notes into her pad. Cath Fletcher twisted her tissue into a point and ran it along her upper lip, back and forth. Kitty sat beside her.

'You mentioned her headphones. Where were they?'

'Up here,' said Cathy, her hand circling her head. 'All tangled around her neck.'

'The pods were still in her ears?'

'I think so. Yes.' She glanced at Kitty, her eyes wide, pleading for reassurance. 'Will she be alright?'

'I just don't know, Cathy. That was a serious wound.' Kitty looked up. 'Fingers crossed she's OK, eh?'

Cathy Fletcher turned to gaze down the slope, towards the line of oak and Scot's Pine at the far end of the Lyndons' property. As Kitty finished writing her notes she tuned in to the voices behind her. Kitty could only make out the odd word. Tony Vipond's tone was gentle, cajoling. But Saul said little, shaking his head and staring at the ground.

There was movement at the house as the police photographer arrived, along with two uniformed officers. Vipond was still occupied, so Kitty moved indoors to greet the new arrivals. She knew the photographer by sight, Paul Moss.

'OK to put stuff here?' Moss said, indicating a space on the lawn. Kitty nodded. He rested a gloved hand on the door frame as he pulled plastic bootees over his trainers.

'What's to do?'

Kitty pointed at the drying blood by the pool.

'The pool and everything around it. Position of the lounger. Tanning lotion. The towel. Her iPod. Earphones. All her bits and bobs. The blood, obviously. And general views of the back garden and exterior of the house, so we can get a sense of the geography.'

'Okey cokey.' As Moss unpacked his kit, two beat officers

arrived. As Kitty led them to the front gate she relayed Vipond's instructions.

'Tape the front drive, lads. One of you stay out front to secure the entrance.' She nodded towards the tradesmen's vans scattered along the length of the road. 'Get the details of those guys. Ask them if they've seen anyone walking around, driving away, anything suspicious. And knock on doors too. A dozen houses each side, to start with.'

The younger of the pair trotted up the road. She turned to the officer who remained.

'No-one comes in or out unless it's Mr Lyndon - he's the owner. Let him come straight through. I don't know that anyone *will* poke their noses in. But the press might get a sniff, so keep an eye out.'

Kitty watched the officer don a hi-viz waistcoat and stretch crime scene tape across the entrance. In any other estate a small crowd might have gathered. On Callerton Chase, it seemed, the residents kept themselves to themselves. As she returned to the house Kitty looked up to see the cold, dark eye of a CCTV camera aimed at the front door. Kitty stared up at the lens. Perhaps the whole crime was caught on tape. She found Paul Moss kneeling beside the pool, framing up on the dried blood stain.

'There's CCTV out the front door.'

The shutter clicked and Moss smiled. 'Your lucky day!'

'Maybe...' The rain clouds had gone and heat haze shimmered over the garden as the sun climbed higher. Kitty watched Paul Moss work. After a while he beckoned Kitty to his side. His voice was soft as he pointed into the turquoise water.

'Is that important? At all?'

They leaned over the edge, peering into the depths. It was a small pool, no larger than ten metres by five. Sunlight shimmered on the surface, throwing a mesh of light and shadow over the bottom of the pool, the lines bending and flexing as the surface moved. Kitty was mesmerised by the stretching, swaying pattern. A pair of dark shapes lay on the bottom of the pool, in the shadow of the rim. Kitty leaned closer, her face inches above the surface. The larger shape was a hand axe, the silver blade fixed to a matt black handle - rubber, she guessed. The other shape glittered when the sun caught the edge. It looked like a phone - a black oblong, the water clear enough to reveal the Apple logo.

'I suppose they just *might* be relevant...'

CHAPTER SEVEN

DITA KRAKOWSKI DID not reach room 922 until 11.45 that morning. There had been a stag party in her first four rooms and there was vomit in one of the bathrooms. On a normal morning she reached the 920s before eleven am. She knocked on the door of 922. A 'Do Not Disturb' sign hung from the doorhandle.

When she knocked a second time there was no answer. She stifled a yawn as she leaned against her trolley. She blinked as she consulted her room list. The occupant, a Mr Liu, was due to check out that morning. Checkout was eleven am so the room should be vacant. Dita knocked again and pressed her ear to the door. Silence. The door felt so cool and smooth against her cheek. She wanted to sleep.

Dita slipped the pass key into the lock. When she leaned on the door she felt resistance. She pushed harder. The door gave way and she tumbled into the room. It took her a moment to make sense of the scene. A man was staring at her from the floor. His eyes were wide and there was a look of surprise on his face. His head seemed to be poking through from the floor below. The head was surrounded by a dark stain, forming a circle on the carpet. Dita's first reaction was distress. Heavy staining like that was almost impossible to remove. Mr Liu's torso lay behind the door. His once white shirt was now claret. 'Sorry,' mumbled Dita, looking at the head. It was a reflex. She closed the door. She blinked, then reached for her mobile phone.

Whitey was never going to be an asset to society. A career as a doctor, a nurse, a banker or lawyer was not an option. So it was a while before Whitey discovered his particular skill.

His mother left when Whitey was six. His father was a drinker and never had enough money to slake his thirst. That was one of the reasons Whitey gave up drink.

Dad used little Kirk White as an inside man, getting him to walk along the yard walls to peer through windows. If Whitey saw a likely gaff, a student flat, he would find a way inside.

Student flats were easy to spot - they never had curtains and they left the windows open on warm nights. Whitey would point out a likely prospect. His dad would nod and Whitey would pop a window while Dad kept toot. Sometimes Whitey squeezed through the cat flap. He was slight as a kid - there was never much to eat around the house. Once inside, he would open the door and let his father in to sniff out the valuables.

When Whitey grew a little and knew what he was looking for, he would creep the house on his own. That meant he could pocket some of the gear for himself. He gave it away at school, or spend it on tabs or White Lightning.

Whitey had no fear, except for two things - dogs and wasps. He never did houses with dogs after sticking his hand through a cat flap and having his fingers skinned by a Doberman. His instincts were so sharp he could smell a dog from ten yards. If he saw a hound he moved on. His other fear was wasps. He legged it if he ever spotted a wasp buzzing around a gaff.

Everyone's frightened of something, aren't they? And wasps *are* bastards.

Kitty glanced over her shoulder. Tony Vipond and Saul Kemp were still sitting on the stone steps, their heads together. She leaned close to Paul Moss. They peered at the phone at the bottom of the pool.

'Get a shot of it there.' Kitty kept her voice low. 'Then we'll need to fish it out.' She turned to find Vipond at her side.

'Is the husband on his way?'

Kitty nodded. 'The daily says he drove to Edinburgh this morning. I've no idea how long he'll take to get back.'

'Why not ask him?'

'His phone's switched off, sir.'

'He's driving from Edinburgh? What's that? Two and a half hours?' Vipond closed his eyes and passed a finger along his brow. Kitty moved closer.

'Sir?'

Vipond lifted his head. He yawned and stretched his arms.

'We do have a possible weapon.' She indicated the pool. 'And perhaps the victim's phone.' Vipond moved to the edge and peered into the water. She watched him, his long, thin body stooped, a heron hunting a fish. Their shadows fell across the water.

'The DNA will be compromised on that,' he murmured.

'Doesn't every contact leaves a trace?'

He snorted. 'You're an optimist, Lockwood.' Vipond leaned closer, his voice a whisper. 'I don't want laddo to hear, but the phone will be fucked.'

'But...'

'Fish it out. Bag it with some rice. Maybe we can have a listen in a week or so, if it dries out.'

'Rice?'

'Ask the daily. Must be some Uncle Ben's in the kitchen.'

'Right...'

'As I say, the technical term for a phone that's been fished out of a chlorinated pool is 'fucked.' It doesn't matter much - we can get the call records - but it would have saved time.' With a tilt of his head, Vipond beckoned her to follow. He returned to his perch beside the gardener.

'Saul? This is my colleague. DS Lockwood.' Kitty perched on the step beside Saul Kemp. She and Vipond sat on either side of the young man. Kitty noted his green eyes, the light golden tan on his forearms.

'Tell Kitty what you told me, Saul,' said Vipond. He leaned away as he lit a cigarette.

'I don't get here till twelve, usually. But I'd had a bit of a row, so...'

'A row?'

'With the wife. I had some catching up to do here. So I thought I might as well get out of the house.'

'What did you row about?'

Kemp's leg bobbed up and down. 'She's not too happy with me working here.'

'What's the problem?'

Saul Kemp knotted his fingers and popped the knuckles. He jerked his chin towards a dense hedge that ran alongside the garden. 'Leylandii. Previous owner planted 'em. Forty foot weeds, those fuckers!' Kemp reddened. 'Sorry.' Kitty smiled, putting him at ease. She needed him to talk. 'Marisa wanted 'em down.'

Kitty slowly shook her head, turned her lips down.

'Why would that upset your wife?'

She saw the shake in his head, the tremor in his hands.

'It's a big job. And the wife didn't like me working here.'

Saul Kemp rubbed his palms across his face. Above his bowed head, Kitty glanced at Vipond, who blew a plume of smoke into the air.

'Does this wife have a name, Saul?'

Saul Kemp glanced at her, then at the ground beneath his feet.

'Wendy.'

'So you had a row with Wendy, about work. I still don't get that part. But you drove off and got here early?'

'Yup.'

Kitty nodded. Waiting. Kemp rubbed his palm across his face. The meaty slab came to rest over his lips. He spoke through his fingers.

'I parked the pick-up on the road. I usually ring the door bell, to let the client know I've started. That I'm not a burglar. Let 'em know the clock's ticking, as it were. And sometimes clients on this estate need to switch off their alarms.'

'They all have alarms?'

'People on this estate have cameras, infra red beams, trip wires, all sorts. This place is a target, isn't it? Lots of rich folk live here. That paedo Lottery winner has a house up the road! Footballers, what have you. The rich. Best to let the client know you're here. So I ring the bell.'

'That's what you did?'

'Yup. No answer.'

'Did that worry you?'

Kemp shook his head.

'Marisa's usually in but... I figured she'd popped to the shops, or the town. If she's not here Cath lets me in.'

'Cathy Fletcher?' He nodded. Kitty wondered why Saul needed to be let into the house. 'So there was no answer?' Saul Kemp rubbed his huge hands across his face, as if washing away the memory.

'Cathy hadn't arrived.'

Kitty studied his face.

'Went back to the pick up. Got me tools together and came round the side of the house. I was still in a mood. I just wanted to get cracking. To work it off.'

'Your bad mood?'

'I were furious!' He glared at Kitty, shaking his head.

'What happened next?'

'I dumped my tool bag over there.' Kitty glanced over to see a tangle of shears, saws and clippers spilling from a green canvas bag in the shadow of the hedge.

'What did you do then?'

He darted a glance at her, as if suspecting she was leading him into a trap. He tilted his head, challenging her.

'I didn't kill her. If that's what you're thinking!'

Kitty bit her lip, aware that Vipond had turned away. She looked at Saul Kemp, fixing her gaze at the bridge of his nose. 'And?'

'I saw her lying there.'

'What did you think?'

'I was pissed off.'

'You were angry?'

'Saw her lying beside the pool and I thought, '*You lazy fucking cow!*'

Kitty's gaze never left his face. He rubbed his hands together. 'Like I said. I wasn't in a great mood.'

Kitty nodded, aware that Vipond was staring at her, seeking eye contact.

'And she was sort of covered,' said Kemp. 'Her face were covered, and the top of her body.'

'Her breasts?'

Saul nodded, avoiding her eyes.

'Covered with what?'

'This towel. Sort of a beach thing. I shouted her name.'

Sweat ran down his brow. Saul Kemp ran a meaty hand across his face. 'Then I saw the blood.' His head fell forward and he stared at the ground.

'Thought she'd had a fall. Maybe cracked her head on the side of the pool and tried to stop it with the towel.'

Vipond leaned in. 'But you knew it wasn't an accident, Saul.'

The gardener spread his fingers over his face. Kitty saw tears slide between his fingers, running over the calloused skin. Kemp's shoulders lifted and fell, though he made no sound. It was a full minute before he spoke again.

'She could be a right bitch, you know?' He rubbed the back of his hand across his face, smearing the tears. 'A right little cow.' His turned his gaze towards Kitty. His eyes were red. 'I didn't kill her.'

Kitty nodded. 'She's not dead, Saul.' Saul Kemp stared at her, his eyes searching her face. 'Let's hope it stays that way.'

'She's going to be OK?'

Vipond stood. He tapped Kitty on the shoulder, beckoning her to follow him. She closed her eyes. Vipond's timing was appalling. In another moment, she was certain, Saul Kemp would have opened up. She followed Vipond to the side of the pool. He leaned over the water, peering into the depths. He pursed his lips and straightened.

'Got shots of everything?'

Kitty glanced at Paul Moss, now taking wide shots of the whole terrace.

'Sir.'

Vipond stubbed out his cigarette on a stone. He checked it was out, nipping the end before tucking the stub into the packet. He rubbed his thumb across his watch, a fat Tag Heuer.

'SOCOs should be here any minute. When they arrive, fish it out,' said Vipond. 'The water's compromised the DNA but let's see. Make sure you get plenty of pictures, yeah?'

Kitty nodded. Vipond nodded in the direction of the gardener. His voice dropped to a whisper. 'Laddo's about to cough. So I'll stay close to him.' He turned to walk away.

'Sir?'

Vipond paused, putting his head on one side, as if listening to a child.

'Isn't it a bit odd? The weapon being just there. In the pool?'

'I don't see why.'

'It suggests this was spontaneous. Unplanned. I mean, there's a river just down there,' she pointed to the trees. 'It's only a couple of hundred metres away. That's a better place to dump the weapon. But it's just been dropped, or has fallen, into the pool.'

Vipond shrugged. 'A man who does this is high as a kite. Adrenaline's pumping. It's a dynamic situation. There's no 'plan.' He just does it. He's in shock, or excited. He flings the weapon away.'

'The lizard brain takes over?'

'Eh?'

'It's reflex?'

'Yes. Whatever.'

'What about the towel?'

Vipond sighed. 'What about it?'

'It seems pretty unlikely she covered *herself* with a towel. She'd be out cold. Cathy Fletcher said the towel was wrapped around her face. Why would the attacker do that?'

'I have no idea, Lockwood.' Vipond glanced at Saul Kemp. 'I'll ask him if you like.'

'And her pods, her headphones - they were still in her ears.'

'What's your point?'

'She didn't hear her attacker. If there was some sort of conversation, she'd have taken them out. And he covered her face.'

Vipond looked towards the trees. 'So?'

'I don't know. Pity, perhaps?'

The silence stretched. Vipond raised his eyebrows, tilted his head to the side. 'Thank you, Lockwood. All these things I'll bear in mind. Include them in your log.'

'Sir.'

Vipond coughed then raised his voice so that Saul Kemp could hear. 'I'm taking Saul along with me, to North Road. Just to get a quick statement.' Kemp looked up. 'That OK with you, Saul?'

Kemp nodded. 'I need to put my tools in the van.' His voice was dead.

'Just leave 'em for now, Saul. We'll get someone to drive your pick up back. We'll handle all that. Won't you, Lockwood?' In a softer voice he whispered, 'Hang on to 'em. They all need testing. And the pick up, while we're on.'

Kitty nodded. Vipond turned back to Kemp.

'They'll be safe, Saul. Let's you and me get all of this down on paper, eh? While it's fresh in our minds?'

Kemp thumbed the corner of his eye but said nothing. His chin dipped as he fixed his gaze on the ground. Vipond took Kitty's elbow and steered her towards the house.

'Stay here. Keep an eye on Forensics. Handle the husband when he arrives. I know him - he's sound as a pound. Get a first statement from him. Be gentle. Log everything. Make a note of what we discussed there. I'll send a car back for the woman, the daily. What's her name again?'

'Cathy, sir. Cathy Fletcher.'

'Have another chat with her then send her along to me at North Road. And keep her away from her phone. I don't want any contact between these two. Just in case.'

When he arrived at Room 922 at the Jury's Inn, it was the stillness which fascinated Bryson Prudhoe. The forensic examination of the scene was complete. Iain 'Leapy' Lee stood in the corridor, packing his kit into a case. He nodded at Bryson.

'All done, Leapy?'

'It's all yours. Have fun.'

'Find anything?'

Leapy Lee peeled off his gloves and rubbed his eyes. 'I assume you are being humorous, Mr Prudhoe. It's early days, but there's plenty of material from the victim. I don't know there will be much else. Don't think your attacker came far inside the room - just enough to swing the blade. The attack happened here, as you might surmise...' He pointed at the circular stain on the carpet. 'The room looks virtually unused. There's the glass. Apart from that...Someone was seriously pissed off at the guest.'

'Room service leaves a lot to be desired...'

Leapy Lee shrugged. 'Sorry. Got to run. Another job - over at Callerton Chase.'

'Posh,' murmured Bryson.

'Absolutely,' grinned Leapy. 'Toodle pip!' He donned his aviator shades, hoisted his bag onto his shoulder and left.

For the first time since the murder of Mr Liu, Room 922 was empty. Bryson stood in the middle of the floor and slowly turned. He stared at the spray of arterial blood on the wall. He gazed at the untouched bed, the blank television screen. The room seemed as if it were waiting. The air conditioning sighed, the noise so faint it was on the edge of his hearing. A buzz of traffic rose from the street, nine stories below. Bryson scratched his chin. Had he escaped his fate, Mr Liu might have been lying on that bed now. Watching television perhaps. Making calls. The sudden end to his life made no sense.

Bryson stood in the centre of the room, turning slowly, as if something might be revealed. It was an empty hotel room. It had never possessed any atmosphere. It was a blank, dead space. Hundreds of souls had passed through this room. They had slept in that bed. They had looked in that mirror, washed in that basin. They left no trace. Bryson shivered. Life is a stroll on a sheet of thin glass.

He went down to the manager's office to review the CCTV footage.

'Can I get you a drink?' The manager was a plump young man in a shiny blue suit. His nametag read 'Colin Bland.' He flapped about, fetching a tray of coffee and biscuits. Colin sat beside Bryson and they watched the screen. There was nothing untoward, nothing unusual. After a few minutes Colin confessed that the camera on the ninth floor had been switched off.

'I'm sorry. Things are a bit tight and Head Office doesn't want to fork out for non emergencies.' Colin munched his biscuit. 'The camera developed a fault last week. They're coming out on Thursday. To fix it...'

Bryson nodded. He dunked his biscuit into his coffee. The soggy end fell into the depths. He put the cup on the desk and turned back to the screen. The camera covering the lobby showed a flurry of activity that morning. Guests arriving, checking in and out. Ghostly figures returned keys and collected newspapers. The footage was grainy, the figures silhouetted against sunlight flooding in from the windows at the far side of the lobby. There was nothing which indicated a hitman. What would a hitman look like, Bryson wondered. He had no idea what he was looking for. He stroked the walrus moustache which graced his upper lip. Then something on the screen caught his attention. A young man entered the lobby from the street. Bryson leaned forward to peer at the screen. The young man was tall and walked with a loping swagger as he swung around the crowd at the desk. This brought him close to the camera - so close that most of his body was out of frame. Bryson could see his head, in profile. His tracky hood was pulled over a cap with a broad brim. His face passed in a blur of white, a shadow of stubble on his cheeks. There was little unusual about him. He might have been delivering pizza. If pizza was delivered in a cardboard box a yard long.

CHAPTER EIGHT

HIS DAD CAME to depend on him. For this Whitey got a cut of the proceeds - and avoided a smack. But inside his anger was growing. Cider and tack dulled the rage, though never washed it away. It was too late for that.

Whitey felt anger towards his mother and hatred towards his dad. He raged against his teachers, the social workers who wanted to take him into care and the bizzies who locked him up. He raged against the world.

The violence started when he was eleven. He was mooching about the cut, a stream that ran through a field at the edge of the estate. Whitey was building a dam, patting mud onto a skeleton of sticks they had laid across the water. Davy Clark teased him about his mother, calling her a 'hoor.' Davy said everyone knew about her. They all laughed about it. They'd all fucked her too. Whitey knew that probably wasn't true but he hit Davy across the head with a stick he was holding. Davy fell in the water and Whitey punched his face and chased him through the brambles. But Whitey tripped on a root and by the time he got to his feet, Davy Clark had gone.

He sat by the stream for a long time, watching the water flow. He could not forget the images that swirled around his head. He picked up a stone and hurled it into the water. Something shifted in the long grass. Whitey searched the bank, parting the reeds until he found the frog. The animal blinked as it clambered over his fingers. Whitey stared into the creature's eyes for a long time. He could do anything, it seemed, at that moment. The frog made no sound as he killed it. He dropped the body in the water and watched it float away, twisting in the current. He felt calm afterwards. The fire inside was dead. The rage had gone. Whitey rinsed the blood from his fingers and walked home.

He would think about that moment many times as he grew older. It calmed him, the thought of it. That quiet rush of power when he had control over life and death.

Kitty watched Vipond's car disappear. Shielding her eyes against the sun, she peered up and down the lane, hoping to see Jack Lyndon's car. She dreaded that meeting. The road was empty. The vans had vanished, the workmen gone for their lunch. She wandered along to Saul Kemp's van and peered inside. A few CD cases were scattered on the passenger seat beside a high protein snack bar and a pair of gloves. She made a note in her pad then leaned against the door of the pick up. The road was quiet. It could have been a country lane in Surrey. She wondered about the people who lived behind the beech hedges, the solid oak doors. Wealthy people - football stars, property magnates and lottery winners - people who wanted privacy, yet were keen to show they enjoyed their wealth. In the distance she saw Addy, her eager constable, leave one driveway and hurry up the next.

Word about the attack on Marisa Lyndon would spread. She imagined the residents hitting their phones as soon as they closed the door. 'You'll never guess...' It would not be long before the media arrived, sniffing out the story. For the moment, this place seemed so peaceful. Meadow Lane was a tunnel of green, the road dappled by sunlight shining through the leaves.

Every garden was crammed with mature trees. They towered above the houses, the branches of Scots Pines and Silver Birch almost touching, high above the tarmac. Beneath this canopy there were splashes of vivid colour - blousy rhododendrons in purple and deep red, the pinky white flowers of the magnolia and rowans laden with blossom. Callerton Chase was like an exotic forest in which tacky but expensive mansions lay hidden.

These people must think they've bought a ticket to heaven.

As Kitty turned back to the house, a red squirrel bobbled across the front lawn and vanished beneath the hedge. The sprinkler played over the lawn, beating a steady rhythm as the silver droplets swished across the grass.

It was cool inside the house. Sunlight streamed through the window, turning the applewood floor golden. A Persian rug ran up the centre of the hallway, leading to the foot of the wide staircase. Kitty walked through to the back of the house.

Cathy Fletcher sat by the pool, dabbing her lips with a twist of tissue paper.

'My boss is sending a car for you, 'said Kitty. 'He'd like you to make a formal statement.'

'I can't leave! I have things to do.'

'Not today. We'll pop you down to the cop shop. In the village.'

'It's Thursday. I have the upstairs to sort.'

'This is a crime scene, Cathy. We have to leave things as they are. It won't take long. Someone will drive you home afterwards.'

Cathy nodded. 'Bring your bag,' said Kitty. 'You won't be coming back here today. '

Cathy dabbed her eyes and tucked the tissue in the sleeve of her cardigan.

They waited by the front gate. Kitty nodded to Addy, the uniform waiting in the patrol car. He shook his head. Kitty took this to mean he had discovered nothing in his house to house. She nodded in reply. Addy lay back, tilting his seat to recline.

A black Maserati drove down the road and swept past the house, tyres hissing over melting tar. The driver, a blond woman wearing shades, glanced at them, then stared straight ahead. The car drifted out of sight.

'People keep themselves to themselves around here?'

Cathy tapped her hand against her lips. Kitty noticed she was shivering.

'Who did it?' said Cathy Fletcher, tucking a wisp of hair behind her ear.

'I don't know, Cathy.' Kitty saw that the woman's eyes were wide, the white visible around the green iris. 'Most likely it was a burglary which went wrong.'

Lie.

By hinting this was a 'hot' burglary, Kitty was being kind. Such a random event was easier to accept than planned malice. The truth was more unsettling. The stats for aggravated burglaries - those featuring violence - had been falling for years. Most burglars want to enter and leave in moments. They worry about finding a dog. They hate finding people. Edgy, buzzing with adrenaline, they panic when they meet another human being. Kitty knew that it was unlikely that a burglar who had come across Marisa Lyndon would hurt her. In any case, Marisa had been sunbathing, with pods in her ears. She had no idea there was anyone there. Someone had sought her out. Someone had chosen to attack her.

It was clear that Cathy Fletcher was fragile. The truth would terrify her. Two women a week were killed by a partner - current or past. The most likely scenario was that Marisa Lyndon knew her attacker - someone who hated her enough to kill.

A police car rounded the bend, the garish paintwork clashing with the leafy gardens. Kitty recalled the way one of her crims described a police car as 'a caked up bizzy wagon' - a slab of Battenburg on wheels. As Kitty nodded at the driver, her smile faded. At the wheel of the Volvo Estate sat her old colleague from Shaftoe Leazes, Des Tucker. Kitty saw a grin spread across Tucker's shiny face as he recognised her. He lowered the window and stuck out his head.

'Locky! Long time!'

Kitty was thrown. It had taken Kitty a long while to understand that Des was unlike other men. He was good hearted but had a filthy mind.

'Like a bad penny, Des.'

'Like a floater in a bog, eh? What's occurring?'

Kitty turned to Cathy Fletcher.

'Cathy? Constable Tucker will take you down to the village to see Mr Vipond.'

In an instant Des Tucker was all business, leaping out to open the door and shepherd Cathy Fletcher into the back seat. Kitty made sure her lips were hidden behind Tucker's lanky frame.

'Serious assault. Victim's in the Royal Victoria. This lady's employer. I'm waiting for the husband to arrive home. But SOCOs have gone missing.'

'That'll be the hotel job.'

'Sorry?'

'Someone's chopped up a businessman,' Des Tucker whispered. 'In the Jury's Inn. A murder takes priority, doesn't it?'

'When did it happen?'

'This morning. Well, last night, word is. They found him this morning when they came to clean the room. It'll take more than a tin of Pledge...'

Kitty realised why no media were outside Fox Covert House. And the Scene of Crimes Officers had not arrived because they were needed elsewhere. Resources only stretched so far.

'It's chop suey over there! Shredded duck!'

Kitty frowned, unsure of his meaning.

'He was a ch...' Des Tucker stopped, catching himself. 'The victim was of Oriental origin.'

'We need to crack on here.'

'The Golden Hour, eh? Or the Golden Shower, as I call it.'

'I'm sure you do, Des...'

Tucker raised his eyebrows, pleased he'd managed to wedge a double entendre into the conversation. 'Just saying. Effective deployment of limited resources and all that bollocks. This isn't a homicide. Murder trumps everything, bar your terrorist attack. So you may have to hang about.'

Kitty closed her eyes.

'Anyway. Your lady is Cathy Fletcher. She's Mrs Lyndon's daily. She was one of the first on the scene. The other was the gardener. Saul Kemp. Ring any bells?'

Des Tucker curled his bottom lip and shook his head. 'Nope.'

'OK. Take Cathy to North Road shop. Put her in an interview room and stay with her until someone arrives. Make sure she doesn't meet the gardener. Make her a cup of tea and be nice. She's a bit wobbly, OK?'

Tucker nodded.

'Then I'd like you to do something else for me, Des?'

Tucker pursed his lips and waggled his eyebrows. A part of him had never left the playground. He was still a little boy, in short trousers, with something nasty in his pocket to frighten the girls. But Kitty outranked him. She watched his face as that dawned on him. Things had changed. His face took on a look of bland attentiveness, which she knew was just another pose.

'I need you to come back here and knock on doors. Speak to Addy. Ask if anyone has seen or heard anything. Find out if they have CCTV. If it *was* a hot burglary, maybe the villain tried a few doors before he reached this one. Maybe there's something on a surveillance tape. They all seem to have cameras.'

'Tape? It'll be on a hard drive!'

'Whatever.'

She glanced up and down the deserted road as they walked to the car. Kitty leaned on the open window so that Cathy Fletcher could hear.

'When Cathy's made her statement see she gets a lift home. OK?' She bit her lip as Tucker made a sarky salute, one finger to his brow.

'If you fancy a drink sometime, Locky, I'm at North Road.'

'If I ever get that thirsty, Des, you'll be the first I call.'

As Tucker climbed in, Cathy Fletcher beckoned Kitty to the open window.

'I've been having a think. About what you said. I know where everything is in that house. If I don't dust it I wash it. There's nothing missing. Pictures or jewels or whatever.'

'Thanks Cathy.'

'Is there a safe?'

'If there is, nobody told me.'

'Thanks. I'll ask Mr Lyndon to take a look when he gets here.'

'There's nothing missing from that house, dear. Nothing.'

The Volvo took Cathy Fletcher away. Kitty walked back towards the Lyndon house, one eye out for that red squirrel.

CHAPTER NINE

THE FIRST MAN he cut was his father.

One night in late summer his dad returned from the *Raby* popped up and furious. The barman told him to pay his tab but Peter White was seven quid short. Peter flung a handful of coins across the bar and stumped out. When he got home he clattered up the stairs, screaming Kirk's name in the darkness. Peter pulled his son out of bed and told him they needed to go on the rob. When Whitey protested, Peter slapped him. Whitey fell on the floor beside the bed and Peter took the opportunity to kick him in the ribs, calling him a little twat and saying he should have been aborted.

'We go on the rob. Or I kill ya. Choice is yours.'

Whitey dressed in the dark. When they stepped out into the night the town was silent. They walked along the lane in the moonlight. Whitey was boiling with rage. His rib hurt every time he took a breath. He looked at his father, hating everything about him. Whitey slipped his blade from his pocket and shouted for his dad to stop.

'Got to tie me laces.'

'Waste of fuck'n space!' After ten seconds the old man lost his rag. Whitey was bent over his shoe when his father raised his fist. Peter swung but missed. Whitey opened his blade and reached up, grabbing a fistful of hair. The old sod was so pissed he never twigged. Whitey made a sweet job, cutting from the ear to the point of the chin, the blade slipping and sliding through flesh. The cut bloomed like a flower, blood flooding the line, pouring out as if it would never stop. It spattered the ground, glistening in the moonlight. Peter White sank to his knees. He groaned, a deep, animal bellow. By then Whitey was gone, his footsteps echoing down the street.

Thrilled by what he had done, heart fluttering, he turned back to look. His father was kneeling, a hand to his throat. Peter White fell forward, stretched out in the lane. A woman came out of her yard door, tugging her dressing gown.

Whitey never saw his father again. That was one off the list. It made him feel better, for a day or two. He wanted to kill. He thought about that a lot. He knew it would happen, he just didn't know when.

The van squealed to a halt by the incident tape. A tired looking man slithered down from the passenger seat. Ian 'Leapy' Lee pulled off his aviator shades and tucked them into his breast pocket. He stretched his arms, yawned and rubbed his eyes, twisting his fists in the sockets. Kitty knew 'Leapy' well. They had gone to the same school, though Leapy was two years older. He tugged a sports bag from the van and limped towards her, a wan smile on his face.

'I'm knackered, Locky. This take long?'

'*You're* asking *me*, Ian? I have no idea, to be honest.'

Ian 'Leapy' Lee blinked and rubbed his eye as he looked up and down the road. 'If we're being honest, I should confess I may not be offering you my pristine, award winning, five star service.' Kitty heard the faint, asthmatic wheeze in his voice. Leapy hated the pollen season. His flesh had a grey pallor and Kitty worried about him. He was a gentle soul with a dark sense of humour.

'I've been to the Jury's Inn.'

'Sounds nasty.'

Lee closed his eyes and shook his head, trying to wipe the memory.

'This will be a stroll in the park then,' said Kitty, trying to walk and talk him to her crime scene.

'That room...' He was till shaking his head. 'Anyway. Harris has spared me for an hour. Kind, isn't he?'

'So...'

'What do we have here?'

'A woman. The householder. Attacked in her own garden.'

Leapy dropped his bag on the grass verge and sat on the tailgate of his van. Kitty told him all she knew. Pushing a finger into his ear, Leapy scratched around. 'So it's assault. You haven't got the luxury of murder, have you?'

'I suppose not.'

'But we'll do what we can, eh?' He unzipped his bag and pulled out a new body suit and a fresh packet of lilac coloured gloves.

'Give me a minute to kit up, then you can lead the way.'

When Leapy was suited and booted she walked him around the crime scene. He pursed his lips, whistling softly. He sighed and shook his head at the bloody footprints smeared around the edge of the pool.

'Nasty.'

'I don't have the medical report yet but it looks like a single blow to the head.'

'I didn't mean the wound,' said Lee. 'I meant the clown army you've had traipsing through my crime scene.' He pointed a lilac finger at the footmarks. 'Who's done this? All this bloody... *walking*?'

'The daily and the gardener found the victim. The paramedics picked her up. Then DI Vipond and me arrived.'

'That's six. Not counting the victim and the assailant.'

Kitty liked the way Leapy used the word 'assailant', stretching it out into a whisper, the hiss of a snake.

'And it's been raining?'

'Just a shower,' said Kitty. Leapy shook his head. 'But we may have a weapon,' said Kitty, pointing at the pool. Leapy leaned over to peer into the water. He pursed his lips.

'Is that going to be a problem?'

'I don't know, yet, sighed Lee. 'The enemies of DNA are sunshine and water. Not looking great, is it, Sherlock?'

Picking his way around the blood stains, Leapy Lee moved closer to the edge of the pool. He squatted down. 'You've pictures of all of this?'

Kitty nodded.

'So I can fish out the axe?' He pointed into the pool.

'Yes.'

'The longer it's in there, the more any trace is degraded.'

'Go for it.'

Leapy returned from his van with a set of pincers. He crouched by the pool and slid the tool into the water. Opening the pincers with the button, he tried to grab the shaft of the axe.

'Reminds me of those funfair games.' Kitty heard the wheeze in his voice. 'Where you grab sweets.' He grunted in triumph. As the axe broke the surface Leapy shook it, allowing the drips of water to fall. The blade shimmered in the sunlight. As the metal dried the weapon seemed to shrink, the silver turning dull. There's nothing glamorous about violence, thought Kitty. It is always the same - dreary. Banal.

'What can you do with it?'

'I'll process it for contact DNA. Go through the motions, anyway.' He read the disappointment on her face. 'I'm joking, Locky! We'll do what we can. I use the M-VAC system. It's handy when there's been limited contact. Or when the sample has been submerged in water, like this.' Leapy Lee was about to slide the axe into a bag when Kitty stopped him.

'Hang on a tick.'

She squatted beside him and pointed her finger at the handle. Smudged, stencilled letters in white spray paint were visible on the rubber haft. 'What's that?'

A minute later, Kitty called Vipond. His voice echoed, as if he were walking down a corridor. Kitty found him hard to hear, so she walked across the lawn, leaving Leapy Lee by the pool.

'The axe is made by a company called Gränsfors Bruks of Sweden, sir. It's their smallest model. It's called a Belt Hatchet. Designed for trekkers and campers. Gardeners too. It's around two seventy millimetres long - ten and a half inches in old money. Rubber handle. The blade is so sharp you could shave your legs with it. Well, I mean...*I* could. Seventy quid, so it's a proper tool. Battered. Well used. '

'You know a lot about axes, Lockwood?'

'I have Google on my phone, sir.'

'Of course you do...' Vipond did not disguise the sneer.

'It comes with a leather thing. A holster? Guard?'

'A sheath?'

'Sheath. It clips over the blade when you're not using it. It was blocking the filter. Leapy's here. Ian Lee. He's bagged it.'

'Good for Leapy,' said Vipond. He sounded weary.

Miserable git.

His stock was falling again. Kitty wanted to know how he was getting along with Saul Kemp. Vipond, of course, would never say.

'I want you at the Infirmary, Lockwood. I need someone I can trust on the bedside vigil.'

'Sir.'

Kitty tried to keep the surprise out of her voice. That he trusted her came as a shock.

'But stay where you are until the husband arrives. I've posted a uniform by the bed for now.' His voice trailed away. 'When you do get there, stay close. Anything she says, or does, I need to know.'

'Sir.'

'Try to charm the doctors. I want to know what was happening when the paramedics arrived at the house. I need a statement from her.'

'I was wondering...'

Vipond's impatience crackled through the ether.

'Quickly, Lockwood.'

'Maybe that sheath saved her life? Instead of the blade, she was hit by a lump of steel. Heavy, but blunt.'

The silence lengthened. Kitty started to count the rooks in the woods along the river, dotted like musical notes in the treetops. She reached five as Vipond replied.

'Right. So you've logged everything? Got pictures?'

'The initials 'SKLS' are stencilled on the handle...'

'Are they indeed. And what do you think they stand for?'

'Saul Kemp Landscape Services? That's what appears on his van. And the other tools in his bag.'

'All turning out sweet. Isn't it?'

Kitty sat on the stone steps and watched Leapy Lee. His young assistant, Kevin, arrived. They crouched over the stone flags beside the pool, moving on all fours as they combed through the scene. She watched them pick up Marisa Lyndon's belongings. Her iPod, the bottle of sun oil, the bloody towel that had covered her face. That morning the victim had picked up those things, carried them out to the side of the pool. What had she been thinking at that moment? Not that they would be packed into evidence bags an hour later.

For twenty minutes Kitty scribbled in her notebook, expanding the brief notes she'd made over the last hour, adding times and names. She sketched the details of the scene from memory. After a while she glanced at her watch. While Vipond wanted her at Marisa's bedside, she knew that meeting the husband took priority.

She closed her eyes and turned her face to the sun, feeling the warmth spread through her skin. A gentle breeze sighed through the trees along the distant riverbank. The rooks fussed by the river, cawing and clattering through the treetops. Somewhere a cuckoo was calling, she thought. Kitty wondered about Molly. What was she doing, at that very moment?

'Skank!'

Molly Lockwood wiped a fleck of spittle from her cheek. Her gaze flicked back and forth, looking anywhere but into the eyes of her tormentor. Midge, a dark haired girl with green eyes, leaned closer. Molly pushed herself against the corridor wall, willing the brickwork to open so she could vanish. She was lined up with the rest of her Year 9 set as they waited to go into Mrs Loveridge's English class. Midge's forehead touched hers. Her sharp green eyes blurred into one. Molly stared at the floor, seeing every fibre in the grey carpet.

Kitty sensed, rather than heard, Lorelle Ferrier's arrival. A ripple of fear moved along the corridor, the class like startled birds. Lorelle moved along the line, sniffing the air.

'I can *smell* something.'

Heads turned, eyes peeping at Lorelle, then flicking away. Midge moved aside to allow Lorelle Ferrier to see her prey. Molly tugged a book from her bag. She lifted it in front of her face as Lorelle approached. Molly heard the whispering, the sniggers running along the line. In her edge vision she glimpsed Lorelle's dark hair. She caught a whiff of the expensive scent which Lorelle always wore. School rules never applied to Lorelle Ferrier.

'What *is* that stink?' Lorelle wrinkled her nose in distaste. More giggles. She tilted her head, looking down at Molly.

'Something really *mings* around here!'

Molly prayed that Mrs Loveridge would open her door and let them into the classroom. She stared at her book, reading the same phrase over and over again.

'It's the Snail,' said Midge. 'You can smell her trail.'

Lorelle was flanked by Midge on one side and Becky, her gangly enforcer, at the other.

'Reading, Snaily? What's the book?'

Molly swallowed, her throat tight.

'Is it about personal hygiene?'

The laughter was edgy. They fell silent as Lorelle's fingers snaked around the book. Her nails, immaculate as ever, whitened as her grip tightened. Molly steeled herself to look up. Their eyes locked. A slow smile spread across Lorelle's Cupid bow lips.

'Let me see?' Her voice was sweet, wheedling as she prised the book from Molly's grasp. Her smile broadened as her eyes flicked back and forth. She read aloud.

'I look a lot prettier when I'm not standing next to Rose...'

Lorelle lowered the book and stared into Molly's eyes. The tremor began in Molly's neck, then spread to her face. A drop of sweat formed on her brow. The silence lengthened.

'*Do* you, Snail?'

Molly swallowed, her mouth dry. 'Do I what?' There was a catch in her voice. 'Do you feel pretty?' Lorelle's smile was so close. She leaned in so that her mouth was an inch from Molly's face. 'Ever?'

The words cut, a knife twisting in flesh. The bead of sweat rolled down Molly's brow and slid down the side of her nose. Lorelle saw it and pulled back, curling her lips. She held out the book. As Molly reached out, Lorelle flicked her wrist, tossing it over her shoulder. The book clattered against the far wall. Molly's eyes burned. Becky tore her bag from her shoulder and tossed the contents across the floor. Lorelle's smile never wavered. The bell rang, a buzzsaw cutting the air. Molly jumped and the corridor filled with laughter. Lorelle Ferrier sauntered into the classroom, a sweet smile on her face. Molly stood alone. She scrabbled around the carpet, gathering her stuff, stuffing it into her bag. Mrs Loveridge stood in the doorway, shaking her head.

'Molly Lockwood. What *are* we going to do with you?'

CHAPTER TEN

KITTY DOZED, THE sun on her skin, orange light glowing through her eyelids. Leapy Lee cleared his throat and she awoke. He stood beside her, dabbing his nose with a tissue.

'Wakey wakey!'

'I may have nodded off there, Leapy.'

'Your secret is safe.'

'Beautiful, this sun, isn't it?'

'Murder!' Kitty heard the wheeze in his throat, squeezing the airway. 'Not good for the old asthma. Got to love you and leave you, Locky. Back to the hotel. Might be back late afternoon. Don't hold your breath.'

'What do we do if it rains?'

'Kevin's tented the edge of the pool. That will keep everything ticketty boo.'

Ask him about the DNA.

'What do you reckon? DNA?'

Leapy yawned until his jaw cracked. 'Continuing today's theme of honesty, I'm not optimistic. The scene's contaminated to buggery, what with your herd of buffalo trampling everywhere. I'll get Kev to swab them for DNA. Make sure he gets contact details for everyone. As for the integrity of the material we've got, time will tell. We've only done the basics. We've blood samples. Likely to be the victim's but...you never know. We have footprints. Probably the paramedics.'

'That doesn't sound great.'

'Take a goosy at the National Injuries Database. Compare the wound and the weapon.'

'Any other tips?'

He rested his hand on her arm and leaned closer. 'Let's be honest, Locky. You've got the gardener - first on the scene. Significant witness, at the very least. You've got the likely weapon. *His* axe, with *his* name on it. Maybe DNA...'

'Even in water?'

'This happened mid morning. So there *might* be victim DNA, reasonable amount, maybe. It's likely to have *his* - since it's his axe.' He spread his palms wide. 'Let's hope it's that simple. Bish bash bosh!'

Kitty stood, following him towards the house.

'How long before the report?'

He paused by the French windows, scratching his chin. 'A week?'

'Are you weaving it in tapestry?'

Leapy shrugged. 'Best I can do. I've a mountain to do on the hotel job. Absolute bloodbath...'

North Road nick was little more than a country police station, a two storey villa squeezed between the Methodist chapel and an estate agent. Open for a hundred years, it had three months to live, being one of the stations due to close in the latest round of cuts. The thin blue line was stretched to a raggy thread. The PR spin was that this was 'a much needed shake-up' for the force. The word 'cuts' was taboo.

Tony Vipond made himself a brew and climbed the stairs to the tiny office, tucked beneath the eaves. He made a call and asked for the sound file of the incident calls to be pinged over. While he waited he sipped his drink and watched the rolling news. It seemed he was on the wrong case. The media wanted to know about the killing in room 922 of the Jury's Inn. The nationals were there already and had dubbed it the 'Horror Hotel'. The attack on Marisa Lyndon was not mentioned at all. The Lyndons were not close friends, but he was on nodding acquaintance with the couple. It was never a good idea to work on a case where you knew the victim. Unless this became a murder, Vipond planned to stay at arm's length. Lockwood could dep on this. To him she was a mystery, like all women, but he was sure she could handle it. The sooner he could escape the Lyndon case and take charge of the Horror Hotel, the better.

Vipond dragged the audio clips of the emergency calls onto his screen. Hoisting his feet onto the desk, he sipped his tea and listened.

'Is there anyone with Mrs Lyndon now?'

Cath Fletcher's voice was tight, keening. *'Kemp. Saul Kemp's with her. Can you hurry? Please!'*

Vipond had listened to many calls in his time. It was his way of tuning into the incident. Some callers were hysterical, while others sounded calm, their voices dead. Cath Fletcher's voice was shaky, as if she was seeing something she could barely believe. But Vipond heard nothing out of the ordinary. He finished his tea and returned to the rolling news. Exterior shots of the 'Horror Hotel,' showed the growing media presence. He looked at the familiar image - a woodentop standing outside the main entrance, hands behind his back. The officer was performing for the cameras, making a play of scanning the street, as if the killer might return at any moment. Incident tape flapped in the breeze. The attack on Marisa Lyndon did not make the news at all. He had been in the wrong place at the wrong time. Vipond called the Chief Constable.

'Tony!' Her voice was cheery, always a notch too loud, as if she were addressing a press conference. 'How's things?'

'All good, thanks Ma'am.'

'That Lyndon thing looks bad. How is she?'

'Not great. She's in the Victoria. Intensive Therapy Unit. But I think we'll have things sewn up in a few hours.'

'That's quick!'

'I have a face that fits. We're making steady progress.'

Vipond heard the breeze at the other end. He suspected she was on the golf course.

'Good.'

'If you'd like me to have a look at the other job? The hotel?'

'I was hoping you'd offer.' The phone crackled.

'I have a very able officer who can dep. A woman. Kitty Lockwood. I'll keep a watching brief of course.'

'Well then. Everybody's happy!'

'Ma'am.'

Vipond placed his phone on the desk. He switched off the news and gazed through the window. The slate roofs in the village shone like silver. It was all looking sweet.

Kirk White had done very little prison time, considering the amount of misery he brought into the world. He spent a year in Aycliffe when he was fourteen. To a visitor, the place seemed charming, the atmosphere relaxed, like a finishing school for the sons of criminal gentlefolk. Everything was clean and bright and modern. The pads were furnished to look like bedrooms in suburbia. There were no bars, just plexiglass windows overlooking open fields. Outside sheep grazed and barley waved in the summer breeze. The gardens were filled with flowers. Damaged children would have a fresh start.

The inmates weren't fooled. The windows were bulletproof. Kick off and the screws put you 'in restraint' in a heartbeat, pressing your cheek to the cold tiles, pinning your arms behind your back. Do anything other than breathe in that position and your thumbs snapped like twigs. Whitey sussed it out in a week or two. He kept his head down. 'Smile at them,' was his motto.

It wasn't a complete waste of life. He learned how to etch borstal spots into his cheek with a pin and marker ink. He tattooed CAF into his arm. One summer night, on 'Association', Whitey rolled up his sleeves to play pool. A screw saw his tattoo and asked what the letters meant. After a bit of prodding Whitey explained that it was the name of his girlfriend. The screw couldn't help laughing. He couldn't help bleeding either, when Whitey cracked his cheekbone with a pool cue.

Kitty popped her head through the flap of the tent. Leapy's young assistant, Kevin, was scraping a tile at the edge of the pool.

'How's it going, Kev?'

He did not look up. 'Be a late one.'

'If you need me, I'm inside,' she said. Kevin returned to his scratching. Kitty pulled on a fresh pair of evidence gloves and bootees and entered the Lyndon's house by the patio doors. She walked through to the entrance hall. She closed her eyes and listened to the house. It was silent, but for the slow tick of a grandfather clock across the wide hall. Birdsong drifted through from the open doors. A drowzy bumble bee buzzed around, stotting off the window panes in a bid for freedom.

Kitty breathed in, filling her lungs. She caught the waxy tang of furniture polish, but there was something else - cologne, or scent. She closed her eyes and took another breath. sensing a mossy, musky perfume. She tilted her head, catching the tang of lemon, or chypre. It was something fresh, something expensive. But the trace was so faint, so elusive, that Kitty wondered if it was her imagination. She opened her eyes and the light flickered, shimmering like hummingbird wings. The bumble bee bounced against the window pane and fell to the floor.

Kitty padded up the hallway, her bootees squeaking on the applewood tiles. The house was filled with light. Whoever designed the place had used a palette of beige, white and yellow. She trailed a fingertip along a table top. Not a grain of dust clung to her glove. Cathy Fletcher did a thorough job. This house contained only grown ups. No toys, no balls or bikes cluttered the hall : no coats or hats heaped on pegs by the door. This house was immaculate - almost sterile.

The kitchen was filled with sunshine. Light bounced around the gleaming surfaces. A telephone hung on the wall by the fridge. A neat, typed list of numbers was slotted behind the perspex above the keys. Kitty flashed her own kitchen, the cloud of notes and numbers scribbled on the wall, in crayon and lipstick. The Lyndons lived in a tidy, ordered world.

A Smeg fridge hummed in the corner. Kitty opened the door to find hummus, venison, champagne and several bottles of nail varnish. It was clean and smelled fresh. Kitty recalled something Bryson once said - 'The working class have clean fridges, Locky. It's only the middle class who let their fridge fester.' Perhaps this was Cathy Fletcher's work.

The sitting room was big enough to host a game of badminton. The rear wall was glass, the windows polished to such clarity they were invisible. Kitty crossed to the window and looked over the garden. She could make out the silhouette of Kevin, hunched over as he scratched at the ground beneath his tent. Beyond the pool and the stone terrace, a lawn sloped away for a quarter of a mile, ending in a line of trees which marked the course of the river. The wood was an old one - oak and silver birch and Scots Pine. It was beautiful, yet there was something melancholy about that view, even in early summer.

She turned to look at the room. The sofas were tan suede, the leather soft. Yellow, white and beige were everywhere. Most houses contain a hotch potch of furniture - the new and the old, the bought and the bequeathed. The Lyndons' stuff looked as if it had all been delivered from a showroom that very morning. Everything was toned and balanced and placed in the perfect position. The surfaces gleamed. The room was immaculate and as sterile as a room in an hotel.

Kitty leafed through the magazines on the coffee table. There was a mixture of sporting titles and art porn - *Aesthetica*, *Metronome* and *Sculpture* were stacked with well thumbed copies of *Racing Ahead* and *Equiworld*.

The fireplace was primed with sticks of blond wood, artfully arranged and ready to light. Hardwood logs, each the same size and colour, lay in a tidy stack on the hearth. A plasma TV the size of a pool table was mounted above the fire.

On the wall to the right hung an oil painting, kitsch but expensive. A young woman lay on a chaise longue, dressed in a gold evening dress, her shoulders bare. Her gaze was enigmatic, a half smile aimed at the viewer. There was a hint of defiance in her smile, as if she knew the portrait was tacky, yet was enjoying herself all the same. In her hand she held an open fan. On the table by her side lay a perfume atomiser. Kitty guessed the subject was Marisa Lyndon - her green eyes, her beguiling face framed by tumbling blond hair.

Beautiful bone structure.

Not so beautiful, now...

Kitty shuddered at the thought of the injury to Marisa Lyndon's face. What might provoke such violence? She looked away from the painting, unable to bear the sadness any longer. That face was so perfect, so unaware of what would happen. A woman walking through life, mistaking ice for solid ground. As we all must do.

Kitty glanced at her watch. It was over two hours since she had called Jack Lyndon. If he was on the outskirts of Edinburgh when he took her call, he would arrive at any moment. She returned to the hall and stood at the foot of the broad staircase. She tilted her head on the side, listening for the sound of his car. She heard only the faint rasp of metal on stone as Kevin, Leapy Lee's assistant, scratched at the tiles on the terrace. A blackbird was singing, such a joyful, innocent song. She turned towards the staircase, searching for the Lyndons' bedroom.

CHAPTER ELEVEN

MOLLY LOCKWOOD DRIFTED along Eilansgate, her schoolbag slung low, skimming her knees. The afternoon was warm and her school shirt clung to her skin. She had forty minutes to kill before the next bus for Belfordham. She wandered up Eastgate, shielding her eyes to peer into shop windows.

This town is minging. I need a beautiful place to shop! I want money - NOW! Hungry hungry hungry.

She peered into the window of *Get The Look*. It was the same old rags. The clothes looked hideous and years out of date. She studied her reflection, hating what she saw.

Why is my hair so shit?

When she was old enough she would leave here. She would fling her door key into the river, run to the station and jump on a train to London. Life would begin, in a city where no-one knew her name or her face. She would go somewhere her mother would never find her, be who she wanted to be.

Molly pushed open the glass door of Rutherfords, the town's department store. The young women behind the counter were in their twenties. She envied them.

They have money. They don't live with a sad police-bitch mother.

Molly lolled against the lipstick counter, her toe tapping the floor. Her gaze wandered over the colours in the rack. The snooty blonde behind the counter glanced at her, then looked away. Molly felt the insult, the implication that the pink lipped bitch thought she was too young to be a customer. As Pink Lips kneeled to slide a tray beneath the counter, Molly saw a Mac lipstick, dark satin, blood red in black and silver. She wrapped her fingers around the tube and slipped it into her bag. As the assistant stood up Molly tapped her fingertip against her chin, as if deciding what to buy. Feeling her pulse race, she worried a guilty blush had spread to her face.

'Need any help?' said Pink Lips, her smile fake. Molly shook her head. She weaved between the stands, drifting ever closer to the exit. She fingered the lipstick, feeling the glossy sheen of the casing. The glass doors parted and she stepped into the street. A shadow fell on the side of her face. Bony fingers circled her wrist.

'Excuse me?' The voice was polite.

'I believe your bag may contain items which have not been paid for.'

Molly looked up at the woman. She was in her forties, in Molly's eyes a crone in a fawn cardigan. A tortoise in a woollen shell. There was no warmth in her smile. Molly shook her head.

'No.' Her voice was too weak to escape her throat.

'Let's go back inside, shall we?'

Molly blushed, the blood rushing to her face.

'No!'

Fawn Cardigan tightened her grip. She glanced over Molly's shoulder and nodded. As Molly turned a burly man gripped her shoulder, squeezing the flesh to the bone. Molly turned to shout at him but he avoided her gaze, his eyes glassy. His eyebrows were black, the tips of his hair silver. Though clean shaven, the man's beard shadowed his skin. In silence, without fuss, the pair steered Molly into a tiny office at the back of the shop.

'Sit,' said the man, pushing her into a chair. He stood in front of the door, his feet apart, his hands clasped in front of his groin.

'Turn out your bag, dear,' said Fawn Cardigan.

Why do ladgeful things always happen to me?

Molly dropped the lipstick on the desk.

'And the rest,' said Burly Man.

'There isn't any 'rest.''

Fawn Cardigan picked up Molly's bag and shook it. The contents clattered across the desk.

'I think we need a word with your mother, dear,' she said, picking up the phone. 'What's her number?'

When he was nineteen, Kirk White opened a man's cheek with his razor. 'Gave the sod an extra mouth,' he told Davy Clark, when Clarky came to visit. Whitey grinned, slapping the table. Davy Clark laughed, though it unsettled him.

Whitey served a year in Castington Young Offenders Institution, way out in the wilds. Every night he lay in his cell, listening to the keen of the North Sea wind through the wire. Sometimes he wept, though nobody would ever know that.

Whitey ached to feel the sun on his back, so he asked to work in the gardens. He cut the grass, weeded the flower beds, raked the leaves in the autumn. When his supervisor found out Whitey couldn't read he persuaded him to take classes. Whitey hated the thought that anyone knew more than he did, so it was a struggle persuading him to go to the Education Department. He switched it around when he told the lads what he was doing.

It'll be a fucking doss, man! There's fit teachers! They're crazy for cock. Why else would a fucking woman be in a man's prison, man?'

But Whitey was scared when he joined the class. He glared at anyone who laughed at his mistakes. They knew his reputation and wound their necks in when his stare fixed upon them. Over the next few months Whitey learned to read. He read anything and everything. It was a way to escape those four tight walls. A way to do his time and stay sane. He borrowed all kinds of books from the prison library - anything to take him out of his pad and into another world. Reading blocked out the wind howling through the razor wire. After a while he felt better about doing his time. He could hack it. Prison was safe. It was the closest thing to home he had ever known.

The master bedroom in the Lyndon house reminded Kitty of a small barn. The vaulted ceiling was supported by beams of hand cut walnut. The emperor sized bed lay unmade, the cream coloured duvet in a soft tangle. As on the floor below, one entire wall of the room was glass. Kitty imagined the Lyndons lying in bed, listening to the rooks wheeling above the tree lined stream. She smoothed her gloved hand over the cotton bedding, wanting to straighten it, to make everything right again.

Here they sleep. Here they make love.

What do they talk about as they stare up into the darkness?

Kitty moved to the window. She watched the rooks twisting in the air, squabbling, settling on their nests in the treetops. This morning, Marisa Lyndon had looked through this window. She had seen the clear blue sky and decided to lie by the pool.

Every day we walk on glass.

She turned to see a painting hung above the bed. In this Marisa was naked, reclining on a green chaise longue, her arms wide, her wrists turned upwards, her back arched.

An open door led to a walk-in wardrobe. Kitty peered inside, pursing her lips as she saw the racks of dresses, gowns and coats. She touched a Vivienne Westwood evening dress, her lavender gloves touching the red silk. She riffled the gowns by Jane Norman and Gina Bacconi. She felt dowdy amongst such luxury. Everything seemed brand new, a confection of froth and lace which would have cost ten years of her wages.

The far wall of the dressing room was a custom built rack for shoes. She picked up a pair of stilettos by Cesare Paciotti, black and red, the dagger logo shaped to the heel. Kitty shook her head in wonder. The collection would have paid for Kitty's house in Cloud Street.

She glanced at her watch. Where was Jack Lyndon? She imagined him roaring down the A68, desperate to see his wife. As Kitty crossed the landing she looked through the circular window above the front door. The breeze wafted the incident tape stretched across the drive. There was no sign of Lyndon's car.

She walked along the landing and peered into the next room. Files were stacked neatly along a low bookcase. A new Mac lay on a leather topped desk by the open window. The screen was dark, though a light pulsed on the monitor. In her mind, she heard Bryson's voice.

When you find the computer, look for the porn.

She tapped the keyboard with gloved fingers.

If you can't find any, you're not looking hard enough...

The screen came to life, revealing the website of something called *The Sculpture Center,* in New York. She moved the cursor to the top of the screen and clicked *Recent Items.* There was only one document in the list, called *untitled.pages.* Kitty clicked on the document, then on the 'Get Info' tab. Her eyes flicked over the screen. Whoever had used the machine had created the document at 09.40 that morning. It was information on flight times from a website called Budget Air. She speed read the print. 'New York (JFK, EWR, LGA) (NYC) - Newcastle (NCL) / Deutsche Lufthansa: 2.25 pm on Wednesday - 20/05 Deutsche Lufthansa LH409 LH3456, Stopovers: 1.'

If Marisa Lyndon had used the computer that morning, this

suggested she'd been attacked after 9.40, when the document was saved. As Cathy Fletcher had arrived at ten that morning, the window in the timeline was narrow. She imagined Marisa leaving the computer, running downstairs, fitting her pods in her ears, arranging herself on the lounger. That must have taken five or six minutes. The intruder had entered, attacked and left in less than fifteen minutes. Kitty jotted the times in her notebook, her eyes flicking between the screen and her note pad.

She froze as she heard a sound on the landing. In that instant she realised there had been other sounds, on the edge of her hearing - tyres on gravel, a murmured conversation.

'What are you doing?'

The voice was deep, edged with rage. Kitty turned to see a man in the doorway. He was mid forties, slim, his dark hair swept back. His suit was tan linen. A neat tuft of beard sprouted beneath his bottom lip. His eyes were hidden behind Raybans.

'Are you Mr Lyndon?' Kitty reached for her id, giving herself a moment to compose herself. 'I'm DS Kitty Lockwood.' She breathed in, taking time.

'What do you think you're doing?'

'This is a crime scene, Mr Lyndon.'

'That doesn't give you the right to snoop around.' He moved to the desk, edging her aside.

'I don't need your permission, Mr Lyndon. I'm securing the property. There's been a serious incident.'

Kitty saw his hand tremble as his finger stabbed the keyboard. The screen went dark.

'Where's Marisa?'

'*Are* you Mr Lyndon?'

'Of course!'

'We think your wife has been the victim of an assault.'

'Where *IS* she? I need to see her *NOW*!'

Kitty counted to three before she replied, keeping her voice low and slow. 'She's in the Infirmary. The Royal Victoria.'

Lyndon slumped against the desk. He pulled off his sunglasses and pushed the heels of his hands into his eyes.

'I know this is difficult, Mr Lyndon. We need to work together to find out what happened. We need to make a tour of the house to see if anything is missing.'

Lyndon's hands fell to his lap. He glared at her.

'When can I see Marisa?'

'Soon. If we find out what happened, it helps us to know *why*. If it was a burglary, or...'

Jack Lyndon stared at the floor, his head moving from side to side.

'Let's take a look, Mr Lyndon. Together?'

Molly twisted her fingers into a tight knot and watched the knuckles whiten.

'Done this before, pet?' Fawn Cardigan said, leaning forward. Her voice was sweet, though there was flint in her eyes. Molly shook her head.

'What will your parents think?'

Molly opened her mouth but no words came. She stared at her lap, twisting one thumb around the other.

'What sort of things do you usually steal?' said the Burly Man.

'I don't,' said Molly.

'Speak up!' said Fawn Cardigan. 'I couldn't hear *that* behind a bus ticket!'

The Burly Man sat by Molly's side. 'It's better to tell us the truth.'

Fawn Cardigan leaned over the desk. She was so close that Molly could smell violets, and beneath that, something sour. 'You've done this before, haven't you?'

Molly shook her head. A tear splashed her hand.

'It's our policy to prosecute,' said the Burly Man, savouring each syllable 'In *all* cases.'

Molly squeezed her eyes shut.

'What's your dad do?' said Fawn Cardigan.

'I don't know,' said Molly.

'You don't *know*?'

'He doesn't live with us...'

'There's a surprise,' said the man, sitting back. The woman rested her fingers on Molly's arm.

'What does your mum do, dear?' The woman tugged a tissue from a box on the desk and thrust it into Molly's fingers.

'She's in the police. She's a detective.'

Molly saw the two exchange a glance. The woman spoke more softly. 'Would you like to give us your mum's address? Her mobile number? Then she can come here and take you home?'

Molly pressed the tissue to her eyes. She tried to meet the gaze of Fawn Cardigan but had to look away. She nodded.

Jack Lyndon wandered from room to room. He looked dazed as they checked his safe, his wife's jewellery, the laptops. Nothing was missing. They went outside to the double garage. Marisa Lyndon's white Range Rover stood in the shadows. Kitty touched the bonnet, feeling the cool metal. Nothing had been touched. Nothing was missing. Jack Lyndon rubbed his mouth, listening as Kitty recounted the sequence of events. He held up a hand to stop her.

'I don't care about any of this. Just Marisa.' He flipped the fob of his car keys against his hand, slapping the leather against the skin. 'I need to see my wife!'

'Of course. I'll ask one of the officers to drive you to the hospital. I'll come along for the ride.'

'Where's Cathy?'

'She's with my colleague, at the station in the village. Making a statement. '

'Where's Kemp? He's the one you need.'

'Is he?' said Kitty. 'Why?'

But Lyndon said nothing, rubbing his hand over his face as he paced the floor. 'DI Vipond is the Senior Investigating Officer. He'll interview both of them. As witnesses.'

'Vipond? Tony Vipond?'

Kitty nodded. 'I'm sure he'll find out all they know.'

He paced back and forth, expensive shoes crunching the gravel on the drive. 'Who's going to look after our house?' He put on his sunglasses, hiding his red rimmed eyes.

'It's OK, Mr Lyndon. There's a Scene of Crime officer here. One of the uniform guys will remain on the gate. We'll lock the house as we leave. Everything will be safe.'

Lyndon stared at the ground. All the fight had left him. Kitty's voice was soft. 'Does Marisa have any family we should tell?' Jack Lyndon looked up. 'Her parents?'

'Dead. Marisa's parents are both dead.'

'Right. What will happen is that you'll be given a Family Liaison Officer, someone to talk to. But if there are any relatives who need to be told perhaps we should do that now? It would be better if the news came from you.'

'Right.'

'So...Any brothers or sisters?'

Jack Lyndon's gaze was so direct she was unnerved. 'Nobody. Marisa had no-one. Except for me.'

'She's alive, Mr Lyndon.' She led him through his house and out of the front door. He stumbled as they crossed the threshold and Kitty took his arm, fearing he would keel over. His face was blank, all the colour leeched from the skin.

As Kitty closed the front door she glanced up to the CCTV camera mounted beneath the edge of the portico. The lens was trained on the front door.

'You have CCTV?'

He narrowed his eyes. 'Everyone round here has cameras.'

Kitty steered him towards the gate. She would let Vipond know about the CCTV. He would look at the recordings. Given the narrow time frame of the attack, and the position of the camera, it was all looking good.

Lyndon allowed Des Tucker to usher him into the back seat of the police Vauxhall. Kitty walked to the rear of the car, pulled off her overall and gloves and dropped them in the boot. She climbed into the back seat. She tried to give a reassuring smile. But Jack Lyndon's eyes were dead as he stared through the windscreen at the road ahead.

CHAPTER TWELVE

AFTER A YEAR inside, Whitey was freed. Inside Castington, the shape of the day was always the same. Wake, stretch, brek, education, lunch, exercise, tea, telly, bed. The clink of the keys, the smell of the kitchens, the tread of the screws' boots along the landings - these were always the same. They were the sounds and smells of home. Back on the streets, he floundered. On the out, life has no shape at all.

He hit the low point when he spent a month in a hostel in the west end of the city. The other lags were strangers, old men stinking of drink and desperation. He stayed in his room as much as he could. On the window sill he found a battered copy of *Shogun*, by James Clavell. One drowsy afternoon, lying on his cot, beneath the window, he began to read. A breeze puffed the net curtain. The sound of evening traffic drifted through the opening. But Whitey was in another world. Two days later he was still reading. Whitey was living inside the book - his body in a pad in a bail hostel, his mind in feudal Japan. The worlds were not so different - except that the samurai warrior had a reason to live. They had a code. When Whitey finished the final page he closed his eyes. He wanted the story to continue. His own world, the hostel with the drab curtains and the battered furniture, the smell of Pot Noodles rising from the downstairs kitchen - all of that seemed grey and shabby.

He read everything he could find about samurai, stealing the books on his walks around town. He devoured *Rashomon and Other Stories* by Rynosuke Akutagawa. He moved on to stories of other warriors, reading *Stalingrad*, then a biography of Hitler, then *Anatomy of the SS State*. But the world of the samurai was his favourite. There was something about the code that appealed to him. He liked the discipline. The life of a warrior had structure. They had a code. Warriors had a reason for living. He could see no point in his own life. He decided to change that. He would become clean. He would turn his world around.

Kicking the civvies was easy. He crumpled the pack in his fist, smelling the tobacco for the last time before he tossed it over a wall. Giving up the booze was more of a sacrifice. He made it into a ritual, buying a bottle of White Lightning, unscrewing the top and pouring it down the drain. It made him feel strong. Those simple changes gave him a new outlook. But it wasn't enough. Whitey was like a weary stray looking for a master. He wanted a reason to live. He wanted a code to live by. His ambition was to be a warrior for hire. He dreamed about becoming a mercenary but had no idea where to start. No contacts. He tried joining the Army but they kicked him out of the office when he admitted he'd been inside. He wandered the streets for hours, picking away at his problem. As the days passed he lost weight, shedding the prison flab, walking until his body was lean and taut.

One day Whitey paused at the window of a sporting goods shop on Clayton Street. He saw his reflection in the window. His skin was pale and he could do nothing about his ginger hair, but he looked different. He looked fit, hard, like a warrior. He stared at the swords that hung in the window. The one he wanted was a Samurai Katana, hand forged, forty inches long. The blade was carbon steel with a lion stamped onto the edge. The handle was gray leather ray skin, the scabbard black lacquer. Whitey admired the gentle curve of the sheath, the 'Thai silk' tassle that dangled from the pommel.

Hang it above the fire. When I get my own place.

A friend he met inside gave him a cash in hand job fitting carpets. The work was hard but the money was sweet. After a month he found a tiny flat near the football ground. He was living in a part of town the feds called the Swamp. And he finally had saved enough money to buy that sword.

'Take a pew, Saul. I need to take a few notes.'

Tony Vipond slurped his coffee. The matey, 'just an ordinary bloke' routine was well honed. He set his mug on the table and smiled across the desk at Saul Kemp. They sat in the cramped interview room in the North Road cop shop. A uniformed WPC sat beside Vipond.

'Like a drink before we start? Kelly here wouldn't mind finding someone to make you a brew, I'm sure.' He glanced at the WPC, who stared straight ahead.

'I'm fine,' said Kemp.

'Okey dokey. If you change your mind, just shout.'

Vipond grinned. Saul Kemp watched him, his face stony.

'We'll crack on then.'

They ran over the details of Saul Kemp's morning - the time he awoke, his breakfast, the time he left home. Vipond kept it light. It had the desired effect. As they chatted about the cost of diesel Vipond saw Kemp relax. The gardener sat back, his body softened, his clenched limbs uncoiled.

'Sure you don't want a coffee, Saul?'

'No thanks.'

'Tea? It's no bother!'

'I need to get back to Wendy. She'll be worried.'

'Best not keep her waiting, eh?'

Vipond flipped the pages of his small black pad. He peered at his own writing, leaning back to focus. Vipond needed reading glasses, but felt that wearing them would be an admission of weakness.

'Maybe you can help with this, Saul. One of our officers found something in the swimming pool.' He raised his eyes to look at Kemp. When the gardener said nothing, he went on.

'I *say* swimming pool. Not exactly Olympic standard, is it?' He grinned. 'Bigger than mine, though! Eh? And yours...'

Saul Kemp looked straight through him, the skin around his mouth taut.

'Any idea what they found there, Saul? In the pool?'

A crease appeared on Kemp's brow. He shook his head.

'Sure about that?'

Vipond peered at his pad. He flipped a page, making it clear he was reading. Turning down the corners of his mouth, he nodded to himself. 'My officer says she found an axe.' Vipond looked up at Saul Kemp. He looked back at his pad and nodded, as if answering a question. 'Yup. An axe. An axe made by...' Here his voice became hesitant. He narrowed his eyes as he peered at his notes. Pretence of course - he knew every detail. '...made by Gransfors Bruks. Swedish mob, apparently. Names they have, eh? Gransfors Bruks. '

The notches in Kemp's brow deepened. 'So..?'

'Rubber handle,' Vipond went on. 'Black, I think.' He shook

his head. 'Can't read my own bloody writing! Yes! Black. With a leather sheath sort of thing. A holster.'

'In the pool?'

Vipond looked at his notes, raised an eyebrow and nodded.

'Apparently so. In the pool. At the bottom.' He smiled, shaking his head at his own stupidity. 'Have to be, wouldn't it? Axes don't float!' Vipond leaned back, still smiling. 'Do they, Saul?' He scratched his chin.

'That's my axe.'

'I *did* think, to be honest, that it *might* be yours. Must be. Specially as she says it has the initials SKLS painted on the handle.' Vipond shook his head, touching a thumb and forefinger to his chin. He looked at his notebook. 'Because SKLS...That would be Saul Kemp...erm...?'

'...Landscape Services.'

'Saul Kemp Landscape Services!' Vipond leaned back in his chair. Watching. Waiting.

'I don't understand.'

'It's a puzzle, Saul. A right puzzle! Because *you* arrived there just before ten, you say. And when you got there, you took your tools from the van? You walked around the side of the house to the back garden. And there you found Mrs Lyndon.' Vipond paused. His head was still, his eyes fixed on Kemp's face. A cat, moving in on his prey. 'You found Marisa Lyndon. Bleeding. By the side of the pool.' Another pause. 'And Marisa Lyndon had been attacked by somebody using an axe.'

Saul Kemp stared at the surface of the desk, his eyes unfocussed. Vipond allowed the silence to stretch, certain that he was close now. But Kemp could only shake his head, bewildered. 'And later on,' said Vipond, 'bugger me if we don't find an *axe* in the pool...' He turned his hands to the ceiling. Vipond's eyes never left Kemp's face. The silence lengthened. The room was still.

'It's not a magic axe, is it, Saul?'

There was a moment before Saul Kemp heard the question.

'*What?*'

'Well if - in some way - the axe got there before *you* did. And if it started attacking people on it's own, as it were. If it did *that*...'

Saul Kemp just stared at him, his brow creased. But Vipond was unstoppable. 'Perhaps your axe was making it's own travel arrangements. Maybe it was leading a life of it's own and attacking people. Then it would *have* to be a magical axe.'

Kemp stared at him, shaking his head.

'Wouldn't it? Saul?'

'I just don't understand...'

Tony Vipond pursed his lips.

'Are you *sure* you don't want a coffee, Saul?' Vipond sat back and folded his arms. 'It's no bother.'

They travelled in silence. The air conditioning sighed as they rolled through the estate. Kitty peered beyond the hedges, glimpsing houses with Palladian columns, houses shaped like windmills, houses with ten, twenty or thirty windows. Each mansion seemed bigger than the last, protected by gates of cedar, galvanised iron or steel.

Empty rooms. What do they do in all those rooms?

As they paused at a junction an SUV swept by, a yummy mummy at the wheel, driving her children home from school. Through tinted glass Kitty glimpsed giggling children dressed in private school blazers. The woman behind the wheel was smiling, her eyes hidden behind designer shades. Kitty's school run was always fraught, Molly sulking while they squabbled over forgotten books or clothing. Glancing at her watch, Kitty pictured Molly on the school bus, trundling along the lanes to their cottage in Cloud Street.

The patrol car left the estate and hit the long sweep of Rotary Way. Oaks and ancient limes towered over the road. They drove through open countryside, the atmosphere in the car charged. By the airport Des Tucker put his foot to the floor. Kitty gazed at a line of white clouds ranged in the perfect blue sky. She asked no questions. At some point Lyndon would ask about his wife. The excitement of the day was taking its toll. She closed her eyes. The car thrummed along the road, rising and falling like a boat crossing a lake. She dozed.

'It's my fault,' said Jack Lyndon. Her eyes flicked open. Lyndon scratched the window glass with his finger nail.

'I'm sorry?'

A tear glistened on his cheek. His hand fell to his lap as he closed his eyes. Kitty glanced at Des Tucker, catching his eye in the mirror. He arched an eyebrow.

'Are you feeling OK, Mr Lyndon?'

They travelled half a mile. Lyndon pushed himself into the corner of the back seat. He shook his head, rubbing his palms across his face. When no answer came, Kitty turned to look at the clouds.

'Is it OK if I call you by your first name, Jack?'

She realised they were not clouds at all, but the vapour trail of a jet, fragmenting and fading away, dissolving into the blue. 'I know this is a terrible shock.' There was no reply. 'Is there anything you know that may help us find out who did this?'

'Why *would* anyone do this?'

He passed his fingers over his brow then doubled up, his face on his knees. Lyndon straightened, wiping his face. Kitty saw Des Tucker glance in the mirror.

'*Everyone* loved Marisa!'

She rested her hand on Lyndon's arm. Tears were taboo. They broke the bubble and allowed reality to flood inside. That was too much for most men. In the past such tears would have melted her, dissolved any doubts. A year ago she would have accepted his grief without question. These days there was a part of her which remained cold, watching, needing more to be convinced.

'Can you think of anyone who had a reason to hurt Marisa?'

Lyndon shook his head, pushed his knuckles into his eyes. He tugged a linen handkerchief from his pocket.

'How did you find her?' His voice was hoarse.

Not, 'How badly is she hurt?'

'Your cleaner found her. By the pool.'

They climbed the rise towards Kenton Bar, the edge of the city. Kitty felt the car slow. Lyndon's eyes were on the road, judging the angle, the distance, the speed, as if he were the driver.

'Was she alone?'

Not 'Is she going to be OK?'

'Where were you this morning, Jack?'

'Edinburgh. I told you. I had to be there for a meeting.'

Kitty flipped the cover of her notebook.

'I left the house just after eight.'

'Your wife was where? When you left?'

'In bed. She was still sleepy.'

They took the roundabout, into the city traffic.

'You had no concerns when you left?'

'She was fine!' He shrugged his shoulders. 'She's an owl. I'm a lark. I need to be up and about. I made her a cup of coffee. Put it on the table beside her bed. I kissed her forehead. Then I left.'

'Did you talk?'

Lyndon ran his fingers across his brow. Kitty watched his face, looking for 'tells,' tiny movements that might give him away. She knew that right handed people move their eyes up and to the right when they invent a lie. But Lyndon was staring at his fingers.

'What were her plans for today?'

'I don't know! What does it matter?'

'It helps me work out the timeline. That makes it easier to find whoever was involved.' He nodded as he dabbed his eyes. 'So. You talked?'

'I can't *remember*! OK?'

'One memory triggers another.'

Lyndon blew air between his lips. 'I put the coffee down. She thanked me. I kissed her.' He glanced forward, towards the driver.

'OK. You kissed her.'

'I said I was off to Edinburgh. She said 'Drive carefully.' She was still asleep.' His eyes flicked back and forth. 'I said I'd be there two or three hours, then straight home.'

'Anything else?'

'I said I'd ring her later. But she'd drifted off.'

They hit heavy traffic. Des Tucker drummed his fingers on the wheel while Kitty scribbled notes.

'Did you call her?'

'I made a few calls. No. I don't believe I called Marisa.'

'We'll request a look at your phone records, Jack. How would you feel about that?'

'You don't think I would have anything to do with this?'

'It's just procedure, Mr Lyndon.'

He turned away, seeming to accept this. 'I was on the road by ten past eight. I heard the interview with the Prime Minister.'

'Edinburgh is what, from your place? A hundred, hundred and ten?'

'Ninety six miles.'

'Tell me about the drive.'

Lyndon glanced at her. 'You must have driven there?'

'I need *you* to tell me, Jack.'

Lyndon sighed. He prodded the back of the car seat, jabbing the leather with his index finger. 'I go down Fox Covert Lane. Turn onto the A68. Belsay. Otterburn. The road rises. Crossed the Border at Carter Bar. Then Jedburgh, Newtown St Boswell's... Straight on till the City Bypass at Edinburgh. I do it on autopilot.'

'Did you stop?'

'No.'

'Did anyone call you?'

'No.' He shook his head. Kitty was quiet for a while, pausing to wonder about a businessman who gets no calls in the first hour of the day.

'Who did you meet?'

'Nobody. I just got there when...'

'Who were you planning to meet?'

'People from the brewery. They were taking me out to lunch.'

'Can you give me the details?'

'Yes! Of course! Do you think I'd make all of this up?'

Kitty held eye contact while she waited for his anger to cool. Her voice was low. 'I'd like the details.'

Lyndon breathed in, filling his lungs. He exhaled.

'Of course.'

'Thank you, Jack.'

The patrol car swung into the gates of the Infirmary and braked by the main door. Des Tucker left the engine running. No one made a move to get out.

'Where were you when you got my call?'

'The multi storey,' said Lyndon. 'On Castle Terrace. The car park near the castle. I was buying the ticket when I got your call.'

'What did you do?'

'Got back in the car and drove home, of course! Probably got speeding points.'

Kitty imagined him, standing in front of the ticket machine, credit card in hand as his mobile rang. She tried to imagine his face as he got the news.

'At some point, Jack, we'd like to view the tapes.'

'Which tapes?'

'From your security cameras. At home.'

'No.'

'I'm sorry?'

'I won't allow that.'

'There's no point.'

'Nonetheless, we need to see them.'

'I don't give you my permission.'

Kitty pursed her lips. There was no point in a row. Vipond would persuade Jack Lyndon to give up the footage. If not, they would use Section 19 of PACE, the Police and Criminal Evidence Act, to seize his hard drive. One way or another, they would see those recordings.

'Thanks, Des.' She patted his shoulder. 'We'll hop out here.'

'Have fun,' murmured Tucker, winking at her in his mirror.

CHAPTER THIRTEEN

FAWN CARDIGAN SIGHED and lay her mobile on the desk. She gave Molly the hard stare. 'I can't reach your mother, dear.'

'Busy catching robbers, I expect,' said the Burly Man.

Fawn Cardigan tapped her nail on the desk. 'I'll try the school. Maybe the head is still there. Someone needs to take you away, dear.'

Molly stared at her lap.

Kitty hurried to the hospital Reception. She flashed her id and asked about Marisa Lyndon. They told her that Mrs Lyndon had been in Surgery. Now she was on Ward 18, the Intensive Therapy Unit. They took the lift. Jack Lyndon's face was reflected in the glass panel of the door. He leaned back, his chin on his chest. As Kitty studied his expression, empathy battled with suspicion.

Is this the way a loving husband behaves?

'Correct procedure' decreed she stay with the spouse throughout the visit. More than one violent partner tried to finish the job during a bedside vigil. She wondered if Lyndon was such a man. It seemed unlikely. The way he displayed his grief might be odd, but she had the feeling he loved Marisa. Yet his refusal to show the CCTV footage was suspicious.

At the nurse's station Kitty saw a doctor writing on a clipboard, her red framed glasses perched on the tip of her nose. She pushed the tip of her tongue into her cheek as she scribbled. Kitty clocked her name tag - Doctor Hobart.

'I was wondering if you treated Marisa Lyndon this morning, doctor?'

Doctor Hobart frowned, as if listening to a puzzling cough. She had dark brown eyes, wide lips and a sharp, foxy nose.

'Yup.'

'I was one of the officers at the scene. Kitty Lockwood.'

Hobart rewarded Kitty's smile with a cool stare, as if this might be the least interesting news she had ever heard.

Bitch!

Kitty took her time, opening her id. She laid it on the surface, beside the doctor's clip board. Doctor Hobart ignored this, finishing her note writing with a flourish. She raised her eyebrows, pushing out her lip like a sulky kid.

'This is Jack Lyndon, Doctor Hobart. Marisa's husband. I think he would like some information?'

A tiny shift in the doctor's expression hinted that what Kitty was asking for might just be arranged.

'Your wife, Mr Lyndon, suffered a blow to her head. She was admitted to theatre and underwent an emergency operation. She's now in the Recovery Unit.'

'She'll be OK?'

'It's difficult, at this stage, to know. The issue is not whether the blow penetrates the skull. Luckily, it didn't. But the brain is a very soft, squishy organ, surrounded by fluid. When the head takes a hit, the brain moves around. If it moves hard enough, what happens is that it slams into the other side of the head, which can cause bruising and tearing, sometimes shearing off blood vessels. The bruising causes the brain to swell, which increases the pressure in the head. The brain may have a lot of cell death, which leads to more swelling.' Kitty saw Jack Lyndon's face drain of colour. But Doctor Hobart ploughed on. 'That can result in the brain pushing everywhere to get out. Eventually it pushes down to the spinal cord. That's called herniation of the brain. That is the worst case.'

'That would be fatal?'

'I've seen patients suffer similar injuries and make a full recovery,' said Doctor Hobart. She glanced at Kitty, asking if she had said enough. 'It all depends...'

'When will Marisa wake up?'

'She's in for a long haul, Mr Lyndon. She's in a coma. We don't know.' Doctor Hobart waited until Jack Lyndon nodded. 'I'm sorry. That's about as much as I can tell you.' She bit her lip, stifling a yawn. 'If there's no more, I've been on duty since early this morning. I'm away for my bed.'

Kitty stepped forward. 'Did you take a blood sample? Before the operation?'

'She was taken straight to theatre. But I expect so. Why?'

'It would help us put together a picture of what happened. If she was intoxicated, or under the influence of drugs.'

'I can't say, for certain. They were busy saving her life.'

The sample was vital. Kitty knew she would have to put in a request for the result. She turned to Jack Lyndon.

'I need to take Marisa's personal items, Jack. I'm sorry. It's procedure.'

'What do you mean?'

'Her clothing. Mobile...' Kitty bit her lip, remembering that Marisa's phone was, at that moment, drying out in a bag of rice.

'Do what you have to do. Not my problem.'

Doctor Hobart walked away. 'The Nurses Station can help.'

Kitty followed the doctor to the door.

'Just one more thing, doctor? Jack wants to stay as close to his wife as possible. Where would be best?'

'Look. I'm knackered. Ask at the desk, would you?' She glanced over Kitty's shoulder then held up her hand, as if stopping traffic. Kitty turned to look but Jack Lyndon was nowhere to be seen.

'Where is he?'

The corridor was empty.

'Where's Marisa?' said Kitty, her voice tight. They hurried down the hall, peering into the single bed wards on each side. Kitty's heart was in her throat. When they reached the room where Marisa Lyndon lay, her husband was slumped across her bed. He held his wife's hand, pressing the skin to his lips. Above him, Marisa Lyndon lay, her face waxy, her body still.

Doctor Hobart whispered in Kitty's ear.

'I don't like to see a crowd around a bed.' She rested her hand on Jack Lyndon's shoulder. 'Your wife is unconscious, Mr Lyndon. She'll be like that for quite a while.'

With a nod to Kitty, Doctor Hobart slipped away, her trainers padding softly down the corridor.

Jack Lyndon stirred sugar into his coffee. Kitty stared at the spoon going around, transfixed by the movement. Steam rose, coiling upwards from the hot sludge. The spell was broken when he tapped the spoon on the side of the mug.

'They don't want anyone at the bedside, Jack. For the moment.'

Lyndon looked up, as if seeing her for the first time. The bag by Kitty's foot held Marisa's effects - her yellow bikini, her wrap,

Wayfarers, a book that she was reading when she was attacked - *Sculpture Now*. Her mobile phone should have been part of the cache but that languished in an evidence bag along with a handful of white rice. Muffled sounds drifted from the hospital corridor - trolleys squeaking across rubber flooring, doors swinging closed. The smell was haunting - the over heated air, laden with the scent of Sterilox and canteen food.

Fear and gravy.

'Don't you have anything better to do?' asked Lyndon.

'We need someone at the bedside on this sort of...' Kitty's voice faded. 'At the bedside.'

Lyndon stared at the surface of the table. 'She looked worse than I expected.' Lyndon tugged at his cuffs, twisting his expensive watch around his wrist. He seemed unable to stay still. His eyes darted around the canteen.

'I can't stop thinking. Who would do that? Why would anyone do something like that?'

Sex. Money.

While so many people in the world had nothing, Lyndon had everything most men could want - an attractive wife and a beautiful home. Yet none of it saved him from this pain. Kitty wanted to touch him, to soothe his pain.

'Marisa's in the best hands. In the best place. Everything that can be done...' But she fell silent. It sounded lame. In any case, Jack Lyndon was not listening.

At six in the evening another officer arrived at the Intensive Therapy Unit. For a moment Kitty wondered whether she should stay. There was a slim chance Marisa might talk, whisper a name, or a description - something which might be admissible in court as a 'dying declaration.'

But Kitty was done. She wanted to be home for Molly and she had a Wado Ryu session that evening. She briefed the officer who replaced her, then took a taxi back to headquarters to pick up her own car. Checking her messages, she discovered the mobile was flat. She plugged in the charger in her own car and set off for Belfordham. She was a mile from home when the phone buzzed. When she pulled over she saw 'School' come up on the screen. She had a moment of panic before the phone connected.

'Is that Mrs Lockwood?'

'Yes?' said Kitty. She had long since given up protesting that she was single and was not 'Mrs' anything.

'It's Marianne Loveridge, Mrs Lockwood. 'There's no easy way to say this...'

No!

'...Molly's in a spot of trouble.'

'Right.' Her pulse slowed. 'We need to have a word about it.'

'Do we? Right. OK.'

'Is she home yet?'

'I don't know. I expect so. I'm on my way back from work.'

The moment of silence was long enough for Kitty to feel a twinge of Bad Mother guilt.

'She was caught shoplifting in the town. This afternoon. In Rutherfords.'

'She found something worth stealing in *there*?'

'Apparently so, Mrs Lockwood.'

Kitty felt only relief that that Molly had not been hurt. But she had that hot, giddy feeling, as if it was *she* who had been caught.

'When would you like me to come in?'

'Now would be good, Mrs Lockwood. She's sitting across the desk from me at this moment. And I'd like to go home myself, at some point this evening.'

CHAPTER FOURTEEN

WHEN WHITEY GOT his own place the first thing he did was to rip out the manky oatmeal carpet and fit a roll of Karastan New Zealand white wool. Lush, expensive stuff. It was a scrap left over from a job in Callerton Lodge. His new pad was almost empty, just a few lamps and sticks of furniture he'd chorred from a skip behind World of Leather.

Whitey bought the sword and hung it on the wall. The blade curved like an inky line in a Japanese painting. He liked the way the light glinted on the black lacquer scabbard. It felt good that his room was so bare - cream walls, white carpet, sword - just like the cell of a monk, or a knight.

Whitey could have taken any direction when they let him out. If he'd wandered into a church or a mosque, he would have been happy to go that route, following a spiritual path. If those knobheads in the Recruitment Office had let him, he would have joined the army. If he'd met a member of a far right sect he might have swallowed their poison. Whitey needed a shape to his life, a code to follow. He just wanted someone to tell him what to think and what to do. Don't we all, at one time or another?

As it happened, he picked up that battered paperback about feudal Japan. So Whitey was destined to follow the way of the samurai. A carpet fitter by day, a soldier of fortune by night. A wool rich warrior. The samurai of the Stanley knife.

The sigh of the ventilator morphed into surf breaking on a shore. Marisa Lyndon's vision flooded with blue light, tiles of different shades, moving in from above and below, slotting together to form a seascape. Waves lapped the sand. She felt the heat of the sun on her skin.

In her dream, Marisa fell towards the surface of the water. The icy coldness of the sea was a shock. She gasped, then laughed. She moved over the sea bed, gliding through the water without effort. The sea bed became the tiles in her pool.

Persian Blue.

Marisa had chosen the colour. This pool was vast, its distant edge a sandy beach which ran in front of her house. Her own house, the one she shared with Jack, lay a dozen miles from the sea. She understood that. This was a dream. Marisa rose to the surface, kicking an arc of silver droplets across the pool.

Friends lined the shore, clapping, urging her on as she swam towards them. Jack, dressed in his suit, his face solemn. His hands met and parted in a languid motion. Cathy stood at his side. Marisa saw her tired smile, the tears running down her cheeks as Cathy beckoned her to the shore, shouting encouragement. Saul was there too, his hands beating a heavy rhythm, as she kicked towards the shore. The sight of Saul made her anxious and she avoided his eyes.

Marisa's arms scythed the water in a steady, regular crawl, pulling her towards home. There were others on the shore - a man with copper curls falling to his shoulders, a golden light around his head. A woman, dressed in black, a woman whose face gleamed like the sun. Their names slipped from her mind, just out of reach. Beyond her stood a nurse, an Asian woman, reaching out to take her wrist as she studied the watch pinned to her tunic.

The ground beneath Marisa's feet became firm. Her toes pushed into the sand. She strode through the water, the waves breaking over her thighs. She heard a rushing roar as the wave sucked her back. Marisa looked down, giddy as she watched the wave retreat, the rushing water tumbling pebbles along the beach.

When she looked up she was alone. The sea had vanished. Now she gazed at the same view she saw every day, the lawn sloping down to the riverbank, the rooks wheeling above the tree tops.

'He' would arrive in a little while. She sprayed Ambre Solaire over her shoulders, breathing in the scent. 'It's changed.' She smoothed it over her chest and shoulders.

Oil dripped from her fingertips, falling onto hot stone. A skylark rose into the sky. The song faded as the bird soared higher. 'Why did they change the scent?' The bottle slid between her fingers and bounced on the stone flags beside the lounger. A breeze riffled the surface of the pool, chilling her skin.

She slipped the pods of her phones into her ears and lay back. *One more week.*

A voice behind her. 'It's time.' She knew that voice. The flash of red across her eyes. She felt searing pain, heard the hollow beat of her heart as she sank into darkness.

Kitty rocked from foot to foot, circling her opponent. She moved on the balls of her feet, her head still, eyes locked on her sparring partner. Kicking the slats out of her opponent was the only way she could relax. This evening her partner was a determined young man called Neville. They were practising *Seishan*, a set of movements known as 13 Hands. They moved around in an elaborate dance, mixing Karate kicks with jujitsu throws.

In summer it was usual for her teacher, Master Raphael, to open the doors of the village hall. This evening was different - a gale howled down the valley and the wooden hall in the wind. The only sound inside the room was the scuffle of bare feet skidding across the mats. Raphael narrowed his eyes, stepping in when he saw a fault.

Kitty had made steady progress in the class, moving from a white belt to a green, rising from the 10th kyu to the 6th. Now she was one of the senior group, trusted to practise routines while Raphael gave his attention to the youngsters. This evening something was wrong. Her rhythm was fitful, her moves clumsy. She was aware of Raphael's critical eye. She felt uneasy as he hovered nearby, scrutinising every move.

There was an edge to her sparring with Neville. Kitty could see he was eager to impress the teacher and she felt a pang of jealousy. As Raphael arrived by their side, Neville raised the pace. He landed a kick on her wrist which jarred her whole body. She glimpsed a smirk of triumph in the young man's eyes. When he tried the same move again she lashed out. The next moment she lay on her back, staring at the ceiling. Neville smiled down, barely concealing his triumph.

Raphael pulled Kitty to her feet and clapped his hands as he moved the class into the relaxation phase. For once, Kitty felt no sense of calm when the session was over. As the other fighters drifted away, she sat down with Raphael. Outside, the tips of the trees tapped the roof.

'You seem distracted.'

She put her hand to her brow. 'Molly's in trouble at school.

Shoplifting.' Kitty fiddled with the cap on her bottle of water. 'I suspect there's more to it. But she'll never tell me.'

His calm, gentle gaze never left her face. She smiled, realising this was a technique she used with a suspect. She sipped her drink.

'Children,' said Raphael, 'are little buggers sometimes, aren't they?'

Kitty laughed, blowing water through her nose. She had expected him to say that they were butterflies, or flowers of the future - some mystical whimsy.

'But it's true!'

She saw him in a new light. Raphael was in his fifties. It was possible there were many little, or not so little, Raphaels running around.

'All we can do is bring them up right and hope, in time, they come to their senses.'

'Some people are expected to have immaculate children. Teachers. Police officers. Child psychologists. Molly calls me her 'crazy police bitch mother'. It's a joke. I think.'

'When she's older she'll understand.' He shrugged. 'Or maybe not...'

She took another sip of water. It felt good, having someone to talk to.

'And I'm working with someone I can't stand.'

'He bullies you?'

'He's not a *bad* man. As far as I know. A bit weird. Very ambitious, but...' She searched for the word. 'Cynical, I suppose. He just doesn't care any more.'

 nodded, the corners of his mouth turning down.

'His problem is not *your* problem.'

'I need to get on with him.'

'Why?'

Kitty listened to the wind howling around the hall. Outside, leaves and twigs clattered against the windows.

'Because I decided to do this, I suppose. I have to try to make it work.'

'You want to be perfect.'

'I need to do things right. I think I got that from my dad.' Kitty had studied hard for the OSPRE exams, desperate to prove she was worthy.

'Perfection is a destination. Nobody gets there. Just follow the road. It's about acceptance.'

'I've never felt comfortable about that.'

'You took out your frustration on Neville.'

'Poor Neville.'

Raphael passed a thumb along his chin.

'Here…in this class, we go with the flow. The idea in Wado-Ryu is to work *with* nature.'

He raised his eyebrows, seeking a response.

'Yup. I know that…'

'Your technique should be flexible. A flow of movement. There's no such thing as perfect technique. Techniques must be infinitely changeable.'

'So I just go along with it? Do what I'm told?'

'Be open to change. Don't use unnecessary force. Don't make unnecessary movement.'

'Don't knacker myself…'

Raphael grinned.

'You might say. Don't knacker yourself…'

'We should talk about this.'

Molly sat at the kitchen table, her pasta lay untouched. She rocked, ever so slightly, back and forth.

'Anything you want to say?'

There was always a part of Molly which remained out of reach. Kitty wadded a sheet of kitchen towel and ran it along the surface. 'Look, if *you* don't need to talk about it, *I* bloody do!'

Molly raised her shoulders and let them fall.

'What's that supposed to mean?'

Molly shook her head. 'Doesn't mean anything.'

Kitty crunched the tissue into a ball and hurled it into the bin. The crash of the lid echoed around the room. She tore another sheet from the roll.

'I give you money. Your father sends you money. Why steal?'

Molly was silent.

'Was this something you needed?'

Molly rocked on her chair.

'Did you ever, for one second, stop to think how embarrassing this would be for me?'

Molly rolled her eyes. Kitty wanted to swallow her words. She saw the contempt, the sly curl of Molly's lip.

Kitty leaned against the counter and closed her eyes. A chair leg scraped the floor and Kitty realised her daughter was about to slip away.

'Sit!' After a moment Molly sat. 'What's the problem?'

'Why does there have to be a problem?' Molly's voice was filled with sweet reason.

'You've never done anything like this.'

'Loads of girls do it.'

'Not you.' Kitty looked up. 'Am I wrong?'

For the first time they looked at each other. Molly blinked. 'No,' she said, her voice a whisper.

'So.' Kitty moved her palm across the surface of the table. 'Let's talk...'

'You won't understand.'

'Is it to do with, you know...what happened to us? '

Molly snorted and shook her head.

'You know, sometimes the shock comes later.'

She watched Molly pick up a fork and twist it between her fingers.

Kitty still dreamed about the psychopath who had held them hostage. Sometimes her flashbacks were triggered by a scent - the whiff of smoke or the stench of petrol. Her senses were open to that ghost from her past. She would 'see' the flash as the petrol burst into flame, hear the crackle of burning timbers. Her dreams of dying in the fire came less often, but she knew the fear would never leave her. Kitty had often wondered if the experience would emerge in her daughter's psyche. Molly found the idea ridiculous.

'I hate the way...' She bit her lip. Kitty remained still, anxious not to close this small chink in her daughter's armour. 'I hate the way I look.'

'What? But...'

'Don't.' Molly's glare silenced Kitty. She wanted to hug her daughter, to kiss away the pain. Only yesterday, it seemed, would she have been able to do that.

'I don't *know* why I did it.' Molly jumped from her chair and threw her arms around Kitty. Molly's tears fell on her shoulder. They stood in silence, their arms around each other. At last Molly broke free. 'This is kind of weird.'

'I don't think so.' Kitty smiled.

'There was a letter. This morning.'

'Yes,' said Kitty. She sensed what was coming. 'It was from your father,' said Kitty. 'I expect.'

'You haven't opened it?'

'Not yet.'

Later that evening they watched television. A man was talking about the history of the perfume industry. 'The history of fragrance is a chequered one,' he droned, picking up a bottle of scent and sniffing it.

'I'd like to meet him,' said Molly. 'My father.'

Kitty turned to look at Molly. Her daughter's eyes never left the screen.

CHAPTER FIFTEEN

AS SHE DROVE to work the next day Kitty felt a tug of stiffness in her calves. Her mobile bleeped and she pulled over to take the call. It was Vipond.

'Go to the Infirmary. Now. Stay by the bedside. OK?'

'Boss.'

'I'll be along shortly. If anyone talks, I need to know. OK?' Without waiting for a reply he was gone.

Prat.

It wasn't single minded dedication, nor lovable eccentricity. She would make no more excuses for him. Tony Vipond was the rudest man she had ever met.

Kitty headed for the Infirmary. She drummed the steering wheel with her fingers as she replayed the conversation. Vipond knew he was on the wrong case. The Horror Hotel job had it all. Blood and blades were a reporter's wet dream. Room 922 was the lead story on the local news and had made the national press. The attack on Marisa Lyndon lacked the same 'glamour'. In his rush to get his mug on a sexy job Vipond had missed out.

Kitty flashed her id at the Nurses' Station. A nurse with vivid red hair looked up at her.

'Hi. How's Mrs Lyndon?'

The nurse swivelled in her chair and glanced at a whiteboard fixed to the wall. The names of patients were inked onto a hand drawn grid.

'She's stable. But unconscious. Were you hoping to talk to her?'

Kitty nodded.

'No chance at the moment, I'm afraid. Even if she were awake I'm not sure they'd allow that.'

'Her husband's still here?'

'He's with your officer.'

Kitty found Jack Lyndon stretched out on an easy chair in the Family Room. His head had fallen to one side and a soft light from the window fell on his face. Lyndon's frame was too big for the chair, his arms and legs spilling over the sides.

Across the room Des Tucker was reading a copy of the *Sun*. Kitty tipped her head, beckoning him outside. Tucker followed her into the corridor.

'What's happening, Desi?'

'He's been out since four this morning. Sometimes he opens his eyes and peers around. Then he's off again.'

'Did he talk in his sleep?'

'He whimpered a bit. Like my dog. Chasing rabbits.'

'He hasn't *said* anything?'

'Not a dicky. Not about the incident, anyway. We talked about his clubs. Just general chit chat. Cocktails they sell. Who gets in, you know. Footballers. Singers and that. All sorts. But his heart wasn't in it.'

'Did he cry, Des?'

'Nope. Not one tear has fallen.' Des Tucker shook his head, curling his lip. 'He wasn't full of the joys of Spring either. Seemed a bit glum. Like he was remembering what had happened.'

'What about the victim?'

Des Tucker glanced down the corridor to the room where Marisa Lyndon lay. 'She's out. Not a peep while we were there.'

'Anyone other visitors?'

'A couple of press. Locals. Said I thought DI Vipond would make a statement this morning. I didn't let on the husband was here.'

'Good.'

'They're more interested in the hotel hit, to be honest. Banging on about that! Wanted the low down on 'The Horror Hotel.' I told them to piss off.'

'Very diplomatic...'

Kitty looked along the corridor. Striplights shone their cold, blue light.

'Any family turn up?'

Des shook his head. 'Husband said her mother died years ago. Father's long gone.'

'Get off and have your breakfast.'

Tucker trudged up the corridor.

Everyone has someone.

No neighbours, no family, no friends. Only her husband and a couple of reporters. Kitty wandered to the Nurses Station, where Red Head was bent over the desk, scribbling on her clipboard.

'Hi.'

Red Head looked up. Kitty glimpsed her badge - Jayde.

'Just wondering, Jayde. Has anyone visited Mrs Lyndon?'

'Not while I've been on. There were a couple of calls. When I explained the way things were...' Jayde turned to her notes. Kitty wandered back to the waiting room. Jack Lyndon was still sleeping. She crept across the floor, picking up a magazine on the way. Settling into a recliner, she licked her thumb and turned the page. The paper crackled and Jack Lyndon stirred. His face was crumpled, the skin marked with frown lines.

Kitty wondered if Molly was enjoying her Saturday lie in. Perhaps her daughter had lain awake all night, full of guilt. Kitty dropped the magazine by the side of her chair and reached for her bag. She pulled out the letter from Paris and tapped it against her palm. Lyndon slept on. The postmark revealed it had been posted two days earlier. Taking great care, she peeled open the envelope.

Something about expensive stationery commanded respect. Two A4 sheets of Vergé De France Ivory writing paper lay inside the envelope. She glanced at the pages, steeling herself, picking out words like 'careful' and 'baby.' Gerard's hand writing was as beautiful as ever, the loops expansive and relaxed. His English was impeccable, the phrasing well formed and precise, as it had been on all of his love letters. As it had been in his leaving note.

'Dear Kitty,

Forgive me - it is a while since I wrote. It did not seem right to telephone, nor send an e-mail. After much thought I decided to write in the 'old fashioned' way. I want you to consider this proposal. You should feel no pressure to reply in haste.

Although we have not seen each other for some time there is a connection between us which endures - Molly. I see from photos you post that she is growing into a beauty - much like her mother.

Kitty broke off. She stared through the window, shaking her head. Lyndon stirred. Kitty waited a moment before returning to the letter.

I regret that I left you 'holding the baby.' Though I have never met our daughter, I hope this might change.'

Kitty walked to the window and leaned on it, watching the traffic shuffle along Queen Victoria Road.

'I ran away. I was an idiot - that much you know! When I look back at that privileged, arrogant young man I feel ashamed. We are all fools when young, though that is not an excuse. I cannot ever make that right. I am not asking for forgiveness.

I would like you and Molly to be my guests, here in Paris. If you feel that is possible I will arrange everything. your hotel and travel.

I hope the money I send each month has been of some use. I would dearly love to meet her in person. It would also be my greatest pleasure to see you once again.

With respect
Gerard

Kitty wafted the paper beneath her nose. What did she expect? It did not smell of him. It smelled of money.

A chaffinch dapped around the bird feeder in the patients' garden below. Kitty stuffed the letter back into the envelope and tossed it into her bag.

'Cheeky little bollock!'

She glanced at Jack Lyndon, his eyelids flickering as he sought to stay asleep. His beautiful, expensive suit was creased. His lips parted as his head fell onto his chest. He seemed so innocent, so vulnerable as he settled back into his dreams. Kitty wondered if they were as innocent as they seemed. Was he dreaming of Marisa as she once was - still whole, still alive?

'How would you respond, Saul, if I told you that we found one of your tools close to the place where Marisa was attacked?'

Saul's lips parted. He shook his head.

'I have no idea what you're talking about.'

Vipond smiled. His patience was slipping away. He needed to wrap this up so that he could move onto the Horror Hotel job. While this was a serious case it held no mystery for him. He was searching for a short cut to a confession.

'I'm talking about attempted murder, Saul. Or worse.'

Kemp's head swung from side to side, his gaze unfocussed.

'No idea...'

'You admit it's your axe?'

'Yes. It sounds like.' Saul Kemp fell silent. He blinked and looked into Tony Vipond's cold eyes. 'I want a solicitor.'

'My officer found it in the pool, Saul.' Vipond pushed one of Paul Moss's stills across the table. Saul stared at the picture. 'It's very likely we'll pick up forensic evidence from it.'

Saul Kemp looked up, his eyes wide. 'I need to speak to my wife.'

The hiss of traffic on Queen Victoria Road became a low rumble. Kitty listened to the hospital waking up - the clatter of trolleys, the squeak of rubber wheels on vinyl flooring, the chatter around the Nurses Station.

Jack Lyndon's eyes flicked once, twice, then opened. He blanched as he remembered where he was. He licked his lips, straightened and stared at her.

'Right...' he said, stretching his arms and legs. 'I need coffee.' He stood. 'Marisa?'

'Stable. She's no worse.'

'Is she awake?'

'No. Not yet.' Kitty had no idea whether Marisa would ever open her eyes, but she pitied Jack Lyndon. 'Come on,' she said. 'Let's see if there's any news.'

'I feel rough.'

'I'll buy you a coffee.'

Jayde, the red haired nurse, had gone. Her replacement had no news about Marisa's condition, so Kitty led Jack Lyndon towards the canteen. They trudged along the corridor in silence. Lyndon insisted that he would buy the drinks. Kitty gave him her order and found a table by the wall. She watched Lyndon shuffle along the counter, filling his tray, fumbling for cash. He seemed stunned.

'I'm sorry it has to be like this.'

He sipped his coffee, then set it down. 'I'm the last person who would hurt my wife.'

'Perhaps,' said Kitty. 'But we can't take that risk.'

White teeth sparkled, spike heels speared red velvet. The air was heavy with scent - Tom Ford's *Black Orchid*, *Royal Oud* by Creed.

There was jazz playing on the sound system - nothing too

challenging - *Éthiopiques*, gentle loping beats from the North Africa of the nineteen sixties, a time when the North Africa seemed glamorous and exotic. The room filled with excited chatter as the crowd swelled, new guests meeting old friends. This was the sound of busy ants stroking feelers, the buzz of networking. This was the sound of money.

Marisa and Jack Lyndon walked into their own party an hour late. Their smiles were tight as they pushed through the crowd. During their drive to town their minor spat had escalated to a war. It was Jack's fault. His meeting had run on and he arrived home late. An apology was not enough. Marisa had been planning this opening for two months.

'It was out of my hands.'

'I've told you over and *over*, Jack! I need to greet in person!'

This was an art event held twice a year - spring and autumn. Marisa's input was to select the five artists who were showing. Jack let them host the show in one of his bars, closed to the public for one night. It brought new people inside and gave the place a touch of class. He had done everything she asked. Yet he let her down at the last minute.

'You need a better balance in your life, Jack. We both do...'

Marisa checked her coat while Jack found her a glass of wine. His forfeit for screwing up was to drive home at the end of the evening. She was sipping her glass of chilled Montrachet when the stranger appeared. He stood in front of her, his feet apart, sipping his drink. He was an odd, puckish man, slight and wiry, with thick, copper coloured curls which tumbled to his shoulders.

'Hello,' said Marisa, thinking she must know him from somewhere. He grinned and took another sip of champagne. His dark suit was well cut but he wore new Converse trainers. The face seemed familiar, though no name came to mind. She glanced around, looking for Jack. When she turned back, Puck was still there, still smiling, a few inches closer. 'I'm sorry. Have we met?'

He leaned a little closer. 'If we had, I would remember.'

'Right...' Marisa glanced around the room. 'I wonder where Jack's got to?'

'Jack?'

'My husband. He promised to get me a drink.'

'But you have a drink.'

She blushed, caught out. He inched closer. 'This is my show.'

'Is that so?' Marisa smiled. She had ammunition now. He moved closer still. She held her ground.

'There are several artists showing tonight,' she said. 'I have to say I don't recall you being one of them.'

'My show.'

'I don't think so. I *would* remember. Since I'm one of the organisers...'

The corners of his mouth turned down. 'Oops!' He seemed relaxed about being caught out. He linked his fingers around her wrist. 'Let me show you something.' He towed her into the crowd. Marisa looked around, anxious to locate Jack. She teetered on her heels as the stranger squeezed through the mob.

They emerged near the rear wall, where he steered her into a lofty alcove off the main room. It was quiet in here, the noise of the crowd a faint murmur. A plinth stood in the centre of the space. A jagged bronze shape, spotlit, rested on top. The stranger released her hand.

'What do you think?'

At first sight it was a tangle of twisted, rusting metal. It looked like a strange, alien plant. Sharp fronds sprouted from the heart, as if shooting towards the corners of the space. The longer Marisa stared at the shape, the more she was intrigued. She circled the piece, her lips parted. It was hard to resist the urge to touch the surface. She wanted to run her fingers along the sensuous curves, to trace the fronds of steel to their barbed tips.

'It's striking,' she murmured. 'I mean, it's not really my thing but it *is* quite...'

'Sexy?'

She laughed, amused by his total lack of modesty. 'What's it called?'

There was a moment before he answered. '*Sweet Spot.*' Anything less sweet it was difficult to imagine. She heard the mocking laughter in his voice. 'It's not really *my* thing, this kind of event. But I asked if I could enter this piece, and...'

'You never asked *me*!'

'No.' He pursed his lips. 'Honor had a word. So Jack squeezed me in.'

'Did she? Honor had a word. Did she, indeed...'

Marisa moved around the piece and stood by the stranger once more. 'Good old Honor...' she murmured.

'Honor knows the guy who owns this place. They go back. Apparently.'

'I know,' she said. 'I know they do...'

He held out his hand. 'I'm Caspar.' As she moved to take his hand her heel caught and she stumbled, half falling into his arms. Their faces were an inch apart. He smiled, his lips brushed hers, teasing. She pulled herself free, feigning interest in the sculpture. The metal coiled into the air, arcing like stock whips..

'It's amazing.' She was aware of his gaze. 'I hope the floor is strong enough.'

'Hope so. It's staying.'

'Where?'

'Gives the place tone, don't you think?'

This was another voice - Jack - standing at her shoulder. They were no longer alone.

'I wondered where you'd got to,' he said. 'Let me introduce Caspar Greene.'

'We've met,' said Marisa, slipping her hand in Jack's arm. The smile stayed on Caspar's lips.

'I bought it,' whispered Jack, as they moved into the crowd.

'Why?'

'For you. Beautiful, isn't it?'

'It's something,' Marisa said, taking a glass from a passing tray.

'It'll be a conversation piece. If nothing else, the punters can drape their handbags on it.'

The rest of the night passed in a blur. Marisa hit her stride as she worked the room, flattering the artists, greeting old friends. Her quarrel with Jack was forgotten.

'I see you've met Caspar,' whispered Helen Brooker. Helen was a good friend - they organised the event together. Helen flicked her dark hair aside and raised her glass in a toast to Caspar, who watched them from across the room. He was at the centre of a group of admirers.

'Where did *he* come from?' said Marisa, her voice low.

'Caspar sort of charms his way in. Don't ask me how. When Jack mentioned it I assumed he'd okayed it with you.'

'He never said a word.'

'That's the way Caspar works. I saw a small bronze by him in Edinburgh. In the Red Door. I lusted after it then.'

'I don't trust him.'

'God no!' Helen laughed. 'I suspect he's a little beast. Though Honor seems smitten.'

Looking again at the group that surrounded Caspar Marisa saw the familiar mane of ash blond hair. Honor Blackett hovered at Caspar's shoulder.

'She's 'managing' him.'

At that moment Honor looked over. She caught Marisa's eye and smiled, showing teeth.

'You still love each other, then,' said Helen, smirking.

'Like sisters,' said Marisa, raising her glass.

After an hour Marisa rejoined her husband. Jack was flipping his car keys against his palm, a sure sign he wanted to leave. Marisa said her goodbyes and went to collect her coat. As she waited by the counter, she realised Caspar had appeared at her side.

'Come home with me?' He ran his finger along her arm.

'I'm married, Mr Greene.'

'Caspar.'

'*Still* married.'

He leaned closer, pushing his lips through her hair until he found her ear. His skin had a scent, the tang of sweet chestnuts.

'I want you to do something for me, Marisa.'

She pulled away, glancing over her shoulder to see if Jack was nearby. Caspar nuzzled her ear once more. 'I want you to go home with your husband.'

'Don't you worry. I will.'

'When you get home...' He held her arm now, pulling her tight, his lips by her ear. 'I want you to fuck him. And when you do - think about me.'

The next instant Caspar Greene had gone, melting into the crowd. Marisa was stunned. She realised the cloakroom attendant was watching her, holding her coat. The woman smiled at Marisa, her smile cool and distant and very, very knowing.

CHAPTER SIXTEEN

'WHY WOULD I hurt her?' said Saul Kemp. He glared at Vipond. 'I loved her, for fuck's sake!'

The duty solicitor was Vanita Mistry, an ambitious woman in her early thirties, of Indian descent. Mistry glanced at her client, then tapped the keyboard on her laptop.

'We all hurt people we love, Saul.' Vipond's eyes were glassy. 'We do things we don't mean to. Sometimes it's love that makes us do them.'

'I didn't '*do*' anything.'

The room was warm, the air stale. Vipond stifled a yawn. The lights on the recorder pulsed red. 'Saul. I've had conversations like this many, many times. A lot of folk were in the same boat as you. None of this was on your 'To Do' list, was it?'

Vanita Mistry a flicked a swatch of dark hair over her shoulder and leaned forward. 'I think it's time we took a break, Mr Vipond?'

'Most people I charge with murder don't get up in the morning planning to hurt anyone. It's just another day.'

'I don't know what you mean.'

'Sometimes people have a quarrel. It gets out of hand. Becomes something else.'

Saul Kemp cupped his fingers over his mouth. Vipond waited. 'You had a row. You were angry.'

'With Wendy! I had a row with my fucking wife!'

Vipond reared back, in mock fright. 'Rows happen. Arguments happen.' Vipond spread his hands. There was a faint smile on his lips. 'Things get out of hand.' Vipond looked at the recorder, watching the LED pulse, red, black, red. Saul Kemp shook his head. The air around him buzzed with static. 'Most people who kill aren't killers,' said Vipond. 'Sometimes, it just happens.'

Saul Kemp's knee bounced up and down. 'I don't know what you want me to say.'

Vipond leaned over the desk, lowering his head so that he looked up, peering into Kemp's eyes. 'I'm a police officer, Saul. I've heard thousands of lies.' He shook his head. 'It's a sad thing. But I recognise them...'

Vanita Mistry peered at her watch. 'Can I get clarification here, DI Vipond?'

Vipond sighed. He leaned back, spreading his hands.

'My client has been here for eighteen hours...'

Vipond knew the clock was ticking down. Saul Kemp would have to be charged, or released, by four o'clock that afternoon.

'At this point Mrs Lyndon is unconscious, but stable?'

'That's the latest information I have.'

'So this is not a murder inquiry.'

'A serious assault has been committed.'

'But not murder.' Mistry spaced the words, locking eyes with Vipond. After a moment he smiled.

'No murder has been committed.'

'Thank you, DI Vipond.'

Vipond turned to Saul Kemp. 'My pleasure.'

'I can't believe this is happening.' Jack Lyndon rubbed his face. He blinked and looked around the cafe. 'When I left her she was fine. I wanted to get going, just get on the road so I could get back. Get home.' Kitty watched his eyes fill. This time he made no attempt to hide the tears.

'How long have you been married, Jack?'

'Five years.'

'Where did you meet Marisa?'

'In a shop. She worked on a perfume concession.'

'A sniper?'

He frowned.

'A perfume assassin, I call them,' said Kitty. 'They lie in wait as you pass through the shop. They aim the spray.' Kitty mimed a handgun. 'Anyway...' She waved her hand. 'What was she selling?'

'I can't remember. Black something or other.' He shook his head. 'It's all coloured water, isn't it? It's fantasy. Selling dreams. It's a bit like my business. Doesn't look so glamorous when they're hosing down the streets on Sunday morning.'

'We're all suckers for dreams.'

He clicked his fingers. '*Creed*, I think. *Creed*. Perfume. The brand.'

Kitty nodded and pursed her lips, as if impressed. 'Not cheap rubbish then!'

'She knew her stuff! Any idea what 'sillage' means?'

'Tell me.'

'It's the rate at which a perfume fades from the skin.' He shrugged, smiling with pride. 'She knew the business! Always.' He tapped the side of his head with a fingertip. 'Clever, as well as beautiful.'

'But she had her mind on higher things?'

'Marisa has a degree in art. The History of Art. Open University. She turned me on to all that. We had our honeymoon in Florence. Took me around the Uffizi Gallery - she knows so *much*!' He shook his head in admiration. 'I knew I would marry her, the moment I saw her.'

Kitty was surprised at the gap between Jack Lyndon's public image and the reality. This lounge lizard gushed about his wife like a love struck boy. There was a warmth in his eyes, a gentleness in his voice when he mentioned her name.

'Marisa moved in and never went home. I bought a loft apartment on the Quayside. I'd lived there since I opened the first bar.' He shrugged. 'It was a bachelor pad, you know? Bare brick walls! Telly. Sofa. Empties. Pizza boxes. I didn't know anything about art, so I hung mirrors everywhere. It was only yards from the Strip. It took me less than a minute to walk to work. I liked hard edges. Simple. Clean. Marisa changed all that.'

'Whose idea was it to move to Callerton Chase?'

He shrugged. 'I don't remember, to be honest.'

Marisa's idea, then.

'I was thirty five? Thirty six? Time to be a grown up. It was the right time for a change. For both of us. Though Marisa's a kid, in many ways - which I love.'

Kitty found it was easy to get him to talk about Marisa. He had relaxed, forgotten Kitty was police. He ran his fingers through his hair.

'I'd finished with the night life. Poker. Boozing all night.' A dark lock fell across his brow. ' I had a wild time! My first two bars were going great. The last thing to suffer around here is the nightlife. The city was opening up. Back then, people had money. None of this 'austerity.' Life was sweet. But there comes a point. You need to share it. Otherwise life seems a little empty.'

His smile vanished. Two floors above, Marisa Lyndon lay in a coma. She floated on the edge, the borderland between life and death. Kitty saw that he knew Marisa might die. He would face that emptiness once again. He stared ahead, his eyes unfocussed.

'So you moved out of the city?' There was a moment before he replied.

'I put the loft on the market. The timing was perfect. Marisa wanted somewhere close to the city but which felt like the countryside. Callerton Chase was perfect.'

'So, you moved four years ago? Five?' He nodded. 'When did Cathy start to work for you?'

'Almost as soon as we moved there.'

'And Saul Kemp?'

'He's been around a few weeks?'

'And you like it? Where you live?'

His easy openness vanished. 'Callerton Chase is quiet. It's private. You can meet people if you want, or you can keep yourself to yourself.' He shrugged. 'Meadow Lane is beautiful. It's where people like us live.'

Once again, he stared into the distance. Kitty let him be for a moment. She cradled her cup in both hands. 'You have cameras above the door. Are they elsewhere?' She knew the answer, but wanted to hear it from Lyndon.

'Most people on the estate have cameras.'

'I think you should change your mind, Jack. Let us see the footage. If you don't do it willingly, you can be compelled to show us.'

He nodded. His face was stony. 'I'm not sure it will help.'

'Why's that?'

'It was disconnected.' He sipped his drink. 'I switched everything off. A few weeks ago.'

'Why?'

His cup chinked against the saucer as he set it down.

'Foxes. We have a lot of them cross the garden. We were woken up every time a fox tripped the beams.'

She took her time. 'That must be annoying.'

'Every night! I find it hard to sleep at the best of times. It goes with the job. I get home late. I need to unwind.'

'So, there's no footage?'

'It wasn't recording.'

He turned towards her. There was a hint of defiance in his eyes - steel beneath the velvet. They would take his kit - the cameras, the hard drive - and search for evidence. But that took time. The last thing she wanted was for him to make that difficult, so she let it drop.

'We'll do what we can to find whoever did this.' Her own touch of defiance.

Don't say it.

'We'll find whoever did this.'

Never make promises.

It was as if she could hear Bryson's voice, see him tapping the desk.

Promises return to bite your arse!

'That's all I want!' Jack Lyndon reached across the table and held her hand. 'Marisa means everything to me!'

Marisa could not recall the moment she decided to surrender. It was more that she fell into the affair than chose it. Two days after the party, Caspar called, inviting her to his studio.

'Why would I do that, Mr Greene?'

'To see my work.' After a moment he added, 'To talk about art.'

She could hear the smile in his voice. On the third call she agreed. She was not naive. She knew why Caspar Greene wanted her to call by. But she did not tell Jack that she was going, which was a bad sign.

Caspar Greene's studio was an industrial unit on the edge of the city. She parked in a side street and picked her way along the dusty lane. Spring sunlight glinted on the river. Caspar was working when she arrived. He washed his hands and made coffee. They never got to drink it. As she walked back to her car she could taste him on her lips, catch traces of his scent on her skin.

'What *traces*?' Vanita Mistry's show of anger was impressive. Vipond yawned, to show her he was not rattled.

'I've spoken to the lab,' he lied. 'They gave me the usual gobbledygook. But this is what matters. There are latent prints on the blade. Saul's - your client's - prints. And male DNA on the handle - contact DNA. A very strong match to your client.'

'Of course there is! The axe belongs to him!'

Tony Vipond stretched his arms above his head and let them fall. His smile was rueful.

'Vanita. Let's stay friends, eh? I'm stacking up some very strong evidence here. The CPS will bite my hand off. But...' Tony Vipond ran his finger along the edge of the table. 'Maybe we can try to work something out?'

It was like being fifteen again. Marisa could not stop thinking about Caspar. She knew it was another mistake. If Saul Kemp was a disaster then Caspar was something much worse. She could handle Saul. He was in love with her, which meant she had some control. But Caspar was something else: he was just out of reach.

Thinking of her lover sent a shiver of pleasure through her body. But at times she questioned her sanity. Any other woman would be happy with Jack Lyndon. He was caring and attentive. He was good looking. He was rich. But Marisa knew Jack was not the man she needed. She remembered something Helen said to her - 'Who wants Prince Charming when you can have the wolf?' Caspar was slippery. He was wicked. That was a flaw she found irresistible. She waited as long as she could before she called him.

'It's me.'

'Hello, you.'

'What are you doing tomorrow?'

Jack had bought the beach house two years earlier. It lay on a remote stretch of coast an hour's drive to the north. Though it was little more than a wooden chalet when they found it, Jack had it rebuilt. He added a sun room and a new bathroom but it still looked, from the outside, like a clapboard cottage. The shingles were weathered and battered by the North Sea winds but the inside was beautiful.

Jack was in London, on business. Marisa picked up Caspar at his studio and they drove north. They reached the beach house around eleven. She made a pretence of showing him around but they never got beyond the sitting room.

Afterwards they lay on the floor, listening to the waves breaking down on the shore. Caspar was asleep. She studied his face, her fingers tangled in his long, coppery hair. She felt such tenderness, such peace.

When he woke they ate her picnic of champagne and olives. Then they dressed and walked along the deserted beach. She looked up at the gulls wheeling above the dunes, hanging in the air. She felt so happy, yet she knew this would never last. When they returned to the house she was wearing a sun hat and her white linen dress. He moved her to face the wall and lifted the hem. She moved to take off her hat but he shouted 'No!' She giggled. She leaned her forearms against the wall and he was inside her.

They lay on the floor. She traced her fingertip along his neck, smiling to herself. She pushed her fingers through his hair, raking her nails against the skin at the back of his head. He watched her through half closed eyes.

As dusk fell he lit a fire. They watched the flames curling and twisting as the driftwood caught. Marisa realised what was missing from her life with Jack. He would never know how to touch her. He was too eager, too clumsy. With Jack it would always be wrong.

'Why don't you leave him?' It seemed Caspar read her mind.

'I'm a coward.'

'That's not true, is it?'

He was right, of course. She had remade herself more than once. 'Well, I never know what's good for me. Maybe that's what I mean.'

'Let me show you.' He held her, turning her face to his. The fire crackled in the grate, the driftwood spitting and hissing as the flames took hold.

CHAPTER SEVENTEEN

JACK LYNDON TWISTING the cup in his fingers.

'I'll see if there's any news,' said Kitty.' She slipped away, leaving him at the table. She squirted gel on her hands before entering the Therapy Unit. They were still moist as she approached the Nurses' Station, where a woman with ash blond hair was leaning on the counter. Jayde and the stranger were giggling, their heads together. Jayde held a small package in her hand.

'It's a *freebie!*'

'That's so kind !' said Jayde. Aware of Kitty's presence, she slid the gift beneath the counter.

'Got to spread the love around, haven't we?' the blond woman purred, her voice like chocolate. She beamed at Kitty. Beneath the glare of the striplights this woman seemed exotic. She wore a black tailored suit, spike heels and silver earrings. It was clear she intended to spend the evening somewhere more glamorous than the Intensive Therapy Unit. She pulled a glove from her hand.

'Honor Blackett.' Her eyes were lasers, her smile dazzling. This was clearly a well practised routine, designed to ensure that nobody would ever forget Honor's name. Kitty took her hand, soft skin warming into her own, chapped fingers. A silver ring glittered on the third finger.

'I'm a friend of Marisa's.' A crease appeared on Honor's brow. 'I'm devastated to hear she's unconscious...' She glanced at Jayde, who put on her sad face, nodding agreement. Honor held Kitty's wrist.

'This is dreadful, isn't it?' She raised her eyebrows, looking deep into Kitty's eyes. She seemed anything but stunned - Kitty guessed it would need a Taser to achieve that.

'I'm Kitty Lockwood. One of the investigating officers.'

'Lovely to meet you, Kitty. A shame it's in such circumstances.' Honor sighed, shaking her head. 'What sort of man would do this?'

'We're following several lines of inquiry,' Kitty lied.

Honor shook her head again. 'But everyone *loved* Marisa!' She dabbed the corner of her eye with a fingertip. 'She didn't have an enemy in the world!'

'You're a close friend?'

'I hope so!'

Kitty nodded. Kitty looked away. Something in those smoky eyes unsettled her. 'A *close* friend?'

Honor's bottom lip turned down. 'We weren't 'besties,' or anything! My friendship with Marisa was...' She looked away, as if she might find inspiration on the wall of the corridor. 'I'm closer to Jack, really. We've known each other since forever! But *everyone* knows Marisa, don't they? Everyone *loves* her.' She turned to the desk and wafted her hand. 'Jayde, do you have a tissue?' Her slender fingers moved like wands. Jayde jumped to her bidding, offering her box of tissues. Honor dabbed the corner of her eye. 'What a mess. I just hope you get him.' Her voice was husky. 'Just find the *animal* who did this!' Honor pulled a silver compact from her purse, flipped it open and fixed her face.

Kitty remembered not to make a promise she could not keep. Honor clicked her compact and pulled out a business card which she slid across the desk.

'Jaydey? If there's any change, darling, *please* let me know?' She tapped the card. 'I switch off the mobile at weekends, so leave a message or better still - email me - that always gets through.' She lifted her fingers and 'Jaydey' tucked the card beneath the counter. Honor glanced at her watch. 'Sorry! Right now I need to be somewhere else.' She threw the strap of her purse over her shoulder. 'Good to meet you Kitty.' She leaned forward, pinching the fabric of Kitty's jacket. 'That's intriguing! I could never get away with that.'

Honor fell silent. Kitty realised that she was looking over her shoulder, towards someone in the corridor. Jack Lyndon stood in the doorway. The pair stared at each other for a moment. Honor rushed forward, as if to go to him, then stopped. After a moment Jack took her hands and kissed her on each cheek.

'If you need anything, you know where I am, darling,' said Honor. With a wave to 'Jaydey,' she was gone, heels clicking on the vinyl floor. The doors of the unit swished shut. A hint of her scent hung in the air.

Kitty followed Jack Lyndon into the Visitor's Room. He lay on the beige recliner, staring into space.

'Old friends?'

Jack nodded. He closed his eyes. Kitty wandered back to the Nurse's Station.

'I wonder, Jayde,' she said, leaning on the desk, 'if you'd do me a favour?'

Jayde was scribbling on a pad, suddenly keen to catch up on her paperwork. She stopped writing, though her head remained down. 'Would you pop your head into Marisa's room and let me know if there's any change?'

Jayde stared at Kitty for a moment, then opened her fingers, allowing her pen to drop. The impact seemed to clatter around the room. Jayde's ponytail swished as she trotted down the corridor. As soon as she was out of sight, Kitty ducked her head beneath the counter. She found Honor's card. Matte black, the lettering etched silver, it read *Honor Blackett. ceo honor/bright. PR. Branding. Promotion. Inspiration.*

There was a landline number and a website address. The office was in a business park by the river. Hearing the slip slop of Jayde's shoes, Kitty replaced the card. She just had time to read the branding on Honor's 'freebie.' *Black Phoenix Alchemy Lab.*

Jayde delivered her news in a monotone. 'Unconscious. Stable.' She flopped onto her chair and resumed her scribbling.

'Thanks,' said Kitty. 'I'm with Mr Lyndon, if there's any change.'

Jack Lyndon stood at the window of the Family Room.

'Honor seems very fond of your wife?' Lyndon did not turn around. She tried another tack. 'She said you were old friends?'

'Honor says a lot of things. It's her job. Talking.'

'Is she closer to you, or to your wife? Would you say?'

Lyndon sighed. 'We grew up in the same town, Honor and I. That seems like a very long time ago.'

Jack Lyndon was done talking. He remained at the window, staring out at the city.

Lyndon made his money in the nightworld. When he drove home in the small hours he wanted to leave it behind. His house was his sanctuary. Like so many of his neighbours he wanted to keep the world at bay. So many of them had security cameras, alarms, electric gates, dogs. Jack Lyndon had built a golden cage for Marisa, yet his wife was attacked in her own home on a fine, bright spring morning.

Kitty delved into her bag, seeking the emergency paperback she always carried for situations like this - stakeouts, court waiting rooms, bedside vigils. That was when she noticed the letter she had received that morning, postmarked Paris. Now was not the moment. She tucked the letter between pages 79 and 80 of *The Red and the Black*.

When I reach page 79, I'll decide.

Bryson Prudhoe dunked a two finger Kit Kat in his tea. The pile of witness statements lay on his desk, fat as a bible. His mood, never sunny, was sinking. He pushed the last wedge of biscuit between his lips and licked his fingers. At least he had escaped the 'Horror Hotel'. He had seen a lot of ugliness in his time, but the thought of what the victim had endured haunted Bryson. Each night he woke in the small hours, covered in sweat, haunted by glistening blades and blood fountains.

There were not enough bodies to cover this case. All the PR guff about 'smart policing' couldn't paper the cracks.

Bryson had been dragged in to the city to plug a gap, but his mind drifted back to Shaftoe Leazes. There he enjoyed the comfort of a quiet office at the end of a corridor. Back there Bryson had a view of the hills. His view here was a wall of grubby red brick. The view matched his mood. He gazed at the bricks, letting his mind wander over the case.

Sex.

The autopsy revealed Liu had only been in the room a few minutes before he was killed. The bed was untouched. There was no sign of sexual activity.

Money.

Liu's wallet contained credit cards and £535 in cash.

Drugs.

No drugs or paraphernalia were found. The autopsy stated the only stimulant in the victim's system was caffeine.

Bryson read through the notes from Greater Manchester Police. Liu was a single man. He had no known girlfriend. His family had moved to Manchester from the New Territories in 1990. He made his living importing wedding dresses from sweatshops in mainland China. His PA claimed that Liu was in the city seeking retail outlets for his gowns. Mr Liu had no criminal record. He appeared to have led a completely blameless life. Bryson tried a Google search. After ten minutes he came up with a press report which mentioned a Manchester man with the same name.

A man sustained a fractured eye socket after he was attacked outside a takeaway in George Street. At about 12.10am on Saturday 7 March, Liu Xiang was waiting for a taxi outside a takeaway on George Street with three friends. A group of men approached and the encounter escalated into a brawl, which spilled into the road. The young men involved were fighting amongst moving traffic. They knocked the victim to the floor and repeatedly punched and kicked him in the head, before running away towards Nicholas Street. As a result of the attack the 25-year-old victim received a fractured eye socket.

Bryson checked the autopsy report. In the notes he read '*Victim had historical blowout fracture of the walls of the orbit.*' He logged on to the Greater Manchester Police database. Mr Liu had been questioned - as a witness about the fight in Nicholas Street.

Bryson's heart skipped. Liu's fractured eye socket was the most serious injury but five young men had been injured as two groups clashed. Several were given short sentences, six or eight months. It was alleged that one of the groups included members of the Wo Shing Wo gang. Liu was questioned as a victim. He was not suspected of being a gang member. Yet it was an intriguing fragment. And it was the only thing Bryson had.

Molly sat at the dining table, bent over her homework. Kitty propped the laptop on her thighs, a glass of red within reach as she Google-stalked Honor Blackett. The top search item was an article in *North East Life* from January.

'*Honor Blackett often sings the praises of her clients. But we turn the spotlight for a rare interview with this charismatic entrepreneur.*'

Kitty suspected it was concocted from one of Honor's own press releases. The entrepreneur was quizzed about her 'Loves and Hates.'

'*Shoes! I've got a pair from Alexander McQueen in leopard print with enormous heels, a pair of Manolo Blahniks for special occasions and a pair of Vivienne Westwood's, with toes in the shape of a lion cub. Even my wellies have heels!'*

But Honor Blackett is anything but shallow. A glance along the shelves of the library in her chic riverside loft reveals her tastes are eclectic - almost highbrow. The Black Swan: The Impact of the Highly Improbable by the epistemologist, Nassim Nicholas Taleb, nestles alongside works on philosophy, poetry and art. It's clear she has an active mind as well as a healthy body.

'I believe in self improvement. I'm hungry for life!'

We ask why there's no pc on the desk.

'The net has turned us into tethered goats. I've lately returned to books. We're not short of data Ñ we're drowning in the stuff. Most of it is clickbait!'

The hack wondered how she handled business without technology.

'I delegate! That's the secret of success in any business.

I don't own a mobile so my PA fields my calls. I like to keep life simple. Uncluttered. I need to think! '

Honor showed us around her beautiful apartment.

'It's open plan and the bath stands on a marble plinth, right in the middle of the room. A friend said it was a good place for orgies! When boyfriends see it, they're either impressed or frightened off. It's a useful test,' she laughs. We ask her to list her favourite things. She muses for a moment before coming back with an impressive list.

'I love games - all kinds!' she says with a wink.

'Playing chess with my good friend, Caspar. We have backgammon nights. Poker too, if I'm in the mood!'

My favourite scent is called Whoso List To Hunt. Made by a little company called Black Phoenix Alchemy Lab. Sex and money distilled into one gorgeous bottle!

We wonder how she finds time to relax.

'Walking my dog, Spike. A dog will never let you down.' She laughs again. 'Whereas a man...'

Kitty could almost hear Honor's voice, smooth and deep, honey dripping from a silver spoon. She admired the energy of the woman, while flinching at the self obsession.

'My favourite view? Grisedale Pike from my home town, Cockermouth, in Cumbria. I don't go back often, but roots are important, aren't they? Part of me is that little girl who looked up and said to herself, one day I'll see what's beyond those hills.'

The way Honor Blackett worked brand names into the interview was impressive. It was *her* gym, *her* favourite scent. No doubt all of them were her clients. She never stopped working, thought Kitty.

Just like me...

CHAPTER EIGHTEEN

YOU RARELY TOUCH drugs, knowing they might topple you into madness, like your crazy mother. And that would be such a waste. But this is a new kind of thrill. The knowledge that you are beyond the law gives a dizzy freedom. The danger is intoxicating. A feeling of real power. Of invincibility.

So you start to get reckless.

The SIO on the Horror Hotel was Colin Harris. A wiry man in his mid thirties, Harris cropped his hair so close that his scalp peeked through the prickles. He teased the hair on his brow into a Tintin quiff. To Bryson Prudhoe his head looked like a coconut. Harris spread his hands wide and leaned on Bryson's desk.

'Progress?'

Bryson Prudhoe pursed his lips.

'Maybe.'

'Specifics?'

What Bryson should have done was to reveal the fragment he had learned about Liu's past. But there was something about the way Harris leaned across his desk, the way he barked that word 'Specifics?' which boiled Bryson's piss. So he kept it to himself.

'I'm working my way through these witness statements.' Bryson shrugged. 'There's a hell of a lot of information.'

Harris leaned closer, resting his forearms on Bryson's desk. 'You know Bry, there are some people - no names - who wonder if your best years are behind you.' He pushed his specs to the bridge of his nose. 'I'm not one of them. But that's the way some people think...'

Bryson dreamed of vaulting the desk and taking Harris by the throat.

'It's always easy to find reasons to *not* do something, Bry. Bring me solutions, old son, not problems.'

'Soon as I find one, I will,' was what Bryson replied. 'At the moment, sir, we're searching for the motive.'

Harris tapped the pile of paper on Bryson's desk. 'The answer's in there.' Harris walked away. 'Sniff it out Bry,' he called over his shoulder. 'Like a big old truffle hound. Sniff it out!'

Bryson returned to the pile. He wanted to go home, to have a kickabout in the garden with his boys. He wanted to clip the hedge and listen to Maureen bitch about someone at work, someone he would never know. He wanted to do normal stuff in the normal world. People did such terrible things to each other. Bryson wanted to remember that human life wasn't just appetite and viciousness. He needed to know that people were more than lizards in monkey suits.

He picked up another statement. Each statement was part of the picture, but the key to this lay elsewhere. He teased that one slender thread, the brawl related to the Wo Shing Wo triad. What did the Triads do? Prostitution? Protection? Drugs, perhaps? He reached for his mobile, scrolling through the names until he found Greta Lumley. He lay the phone on the desk and stared at the screen.

Caspar Greene strode into the lobby of the HSBC Bank on Grey Street. It was a warm day in May and the long shadow of Grey's Monument stretched across the stone flagged plaza.

'Honkers and Shankers,' Caspar murmured as the doors opened to allow him inside.

His personal account at the branch contained just twenty seven pounds and eighteen pence. The amount had not varied in the last four months. Caspar had accounts in all the major banks. Whenever he received a grant, or sold a piece of work he would move the funds around, shifting them from one account to another, a little sleight of hand designed to keep the Revenue guessing.

A young woman with a clipboard stood in the centre of the lobby, greeting new customers. 'Can I help?' she smiled, rocking on one heel. Caspar's eyes flicked over her body, imagining several ways she might 'help'.

'Need to pay a cheque in.' He looked over her shoulder, towards the Paying In machines.

'Are you OK with that?'

Red lips. Perfect white teeth.

He wanted more of her. More lips, more silky, shiny hair. More help. Her name badge read '*Keri-Ann.*' He rooted inside his jacket and plucked out a crumpled wad of Marisa's cheques.

'It's just, erm...what do I do with 'em?' His little-boy-lost act always worked.

'The machines are over here.' She pointed at the boxes that lined one wall. 'Let me talk you through it.' She walked him to the podium. Paying in slips were stacked in perspex dispensers. She ran her fingers over the paper, smoothing imaginary creases.

'Do you know your account number?'

He pursed his lips, as if this was baffling him. She moved closer, her arm touching his.

'Is it OK if I start?' Keri-Ann mimed writing the cheques. 'What's the name?'

'Caspar.'

'Really?' Her voice sparkled like tinsel. 'That's so unusual! I've never heard that before!' This was going so well. He would have her number by the time the cheques were paid in. She tapped the slip with her pen. 'Your surname?'

'Greene. With an e at the end.'

'So...' The tip of her tongue peeped between her lips as she wrote. 'Your name goes *here*...' He leaned against her, pretending to get a better look, enjoying the warmth of her body.

'And down here, we write the amount...' She looked up at him from beneath long, thick lashes. He smiled and handed her the cheques. She was very still, her eyes flicking over the cheque. He drank in her perfume, listened to her breathe. Caspar was slow to realise the change in the atmosphere. She moved a cheque to the bottom of the pile and peered at the next. 'Right.' She tapped her pen against her lip. 'These cheques are for large amounts.'

'Aren't they *just*? He grinned. 'Fucking *huge* amounts!'

She straightened, rocking on her heel. 'Can I ask you to wait here, Mr Greene? For just one moment?'

He watched her walk to the rear of the lobby where booths were separated by panels of frosted glass. Keri-Ann's hips swayed as she walked between them. She whispered to a young man whose neck seemed too slender for his shirt collar. The man glanced at Caspar, then tilted his head to listen. Keri-Ann placed the cheques in front of him, one by one. Together they approached Caspar.

'I'm going to pass you over to Neil, Mr Greene.'

'What's up, Neil?' Caspar noted the rash around the young man's collar. There was a tuft of fluff on Neil's upper lip and he smelled of cheap soap.

'It's just that we have a policy.' Neil's voice dropped to a discreet whisper. 'When amounts are over ten thousand sterling, we require some additional information.' He spread his hands. 'Sorry - we're obliged to do that. These days.' He flashed his 'world's gone mad' smile of regret.

'I'm sorry about this, Caspar,' whispered Keri-Ann as they waited. 'Banking regulations. Neil won't be long.' She shepherded him to the seating area.

'Can I get you a coffee?'

'Yes,' growled Caspar. If they wanted to dick him about he would return the favour. 'Strong. Black. Two sugars.' He watched her arse as she walked away.

'Fucking Shonkers and Wankers,' Caspar muttered. A pair of Chinese students, their gaze fixed on the screens of their mobile phones, looked up. Caspar flung one leg over the arm of his chair and raised his middle finger.

Bryson reached the *Falcon's Nest* early. He parked his Galaxy in the shade of a lime tree. He called the switchboard and lied, claiming he was confirming some details on a witness statement. He peered at his watch. Greta had agreed to meet at twelve. The pub lay five miles north of the city, standing alone on a country lane, surrounded by parkland and open fields.

A honeysuckle clung to the ricketty trellis around the door. The hanging baskets had not been watered for weeks and the lobelia hung in a withered tangle. Bryson left dazzle outside for the gloom of the bar. For a moment he could see nothing. He tucked his sunglasses into his jacket pocket and leaned against the zinc.

'D'you keep Wylam Bitter?'

The young barmaid pointed at a pump.

'Is there a beer garden?'

She tilted her head towards an open door. 'Out the back.'

As he watched her pouring his pint Bryson chinked the column of £2 coins he always carried in his pocket. The barmaid's flip flops slapped the flagstones as she brought his ale.

'I'm meeting someone.' She raised an eyebrow. 'A lady. A woman,' stuttered Bryson. She stared at him, waiting. 'If she arrives, tell her I'm in the garden?'

She slammed the till. Bryson glimpsed a smirk on her lips. 'Would you like a peek at our menu?' She slid a laminated card across the bar. Bryson carried his pint outside. The Beer Garden was a dusty paddock surrounded by a low wall. A clematis snaked along the stonework. Aubretia spilled over the top of the wall, the purple blooms turning their faces to the sun.

The place was empty. Bryson sat at one of the 'rustic' picnic tables beneath a Scots Pine and sipped his ale. He closed his eyes, listening to the drowsy hum of bumble bees. The heat was stupefying. The city seemed far away. The Horror Hotel was in another world. He tilted his sunglasses to scan the menu. His appetite was returning. Bryson dabbed his brow with a clean handkerchief.

Maureen ironed that.

He was meeting a source, that was all. She had to remain anonymous, for her own safety. Bryson might claim that this was legitimate intel but he would be lying to himself. This meeting was dangerous. If Harris found out, he would be in trouble. If Maureen Prudhoe or Clive Lumley found out he had met Greta, he would be dead. He glanced at his watch. Seven minutes past twelve.

She's not coming.

He felt a rush of sweet relief. If he was to spend the next hour alone, then he decided to enjoy it. He admired the battered roses struggling to climb the back wall. A flock of spuggies frolicked through the honeysuckle. His pint was delicious, cool, firm bodied and hoppy. This felt good - a stolen moment, away from the bleakness of that job.

Enjoy this.

Contentment is a fleeting emotion. Bryson picked up his mobile and found Kitty Lockwood's number. He punched the keys, then stopped. If Kitty was getting on with her boss, he didn't want to know. He placed his phone on the table and looked across the empty fields. The Cheviot Hills shimmered on the horizon.

'If you can see the hills, it's going to rain...'

Bryson sipped his pint and thought about work. He was following a legitimate line of inquiry. Mr Liu had been attacked with a brutality that was far beyond what was needed to kill. Someone believed that such violence was justified. Villains rarely saw themselves as the bad guys. The hit might have been done for revenge, or as part of a gang war. The Triad connection was slender, but intriguing. It all came back to sex or money. Money often meant drugs money. So his attempted meeting with Greta was legitimate.

Another half. A small one...

As he walked towards the open door of the pub he heard the sound of voices. When he stepped inside Greta Lumley stood at the bar. Bryson recognised her silhouette - the long straight nose, the high cheekbones, the chignon of ash blond hair. Greta saw him and smiled.

No escape.

Bryson could not leave a woman at the bar, buying her own drink. 'What can I get you?' He avoided using her name in front of the barmaid.

'A mineral water. Thank you.'

The barmaid glanced from one to the other. No doubt, thought Bryson, wondering what the glamorous woman is doing with the fat fool. Bryson carried the tray of drinks into the garden. Greta followed, her heels spiking the turf.

'Thanks for this, Greta.'

Bryson sipped his beer. Greta's drink lay untouched. She glanced towards the pub doorway.

'You're not wired are you, Mr Prudhoe? You're not recording this?'

'I'm lucky to get a crack at the bloody photocopier!'

'Take off your jacket. You must be the last man in England wearing a suit!'

Bryson did as he as told. He draped his jacket on the back of his chair. He rolled up his sleeves, taking care to keep the cuffs neat, equal on each side. Greta watched all of this. He rested his elbows on the table.

'Ready?' She seemed amused.

'I need your help, Greta.'

'When you had my husband put away?'

'How is Clive?'

She sipped her drink, the ice cubes chinking the glass.

'Watching a lot of television.'

Bryson had spent months building a case against Clive Lumley, only for it to fall apart. His mistake had been to think that Clive ran the show. Greta was the strategist, Clive the public face. She owned the brains in the partnership, as well as the beauty. It was a reminder that women too, can play rough.

'You've helped me in the past, Greta.' She had given Bryson vital information on the day that Kitty Lockwood was taken hostage. It was not through a new found sense of public duty: she had traded the information - something she would dread Clive hearing.

'I'm not asking too much.'

Greta smiled. She pushed her fingers through her hair. He watched it fall on her shoulders.

'You know what Clive would do? If he knew we were here?'

'You didn't tell him?'

He saw he'd scored a point. Greta smiled, her fingernails clicking as she tapped the surface of the table, the ticking of a time bomb.

'Let me tell you what I want,' said Bryson.

The caller id read 'Chief Con'.

'Sue.' Tony Vipond's voice dripped honey. 'How can I help?'

'Know how much it costs to keep officers by a hospital bed?'

'I planned to drop by in the morning to update you, Ma'am. This is good timing.'

Vipond imagined the Chief reclining on a beige sofa, stroking a Persian cat. 'I'm charging the chief suspect this afternoon. Once he's tucked away we can step down the surveillance.'

'I think you meant to say 'end,' didn't you?'

'Of course. *End* the surveillance...'

'Then you'll be free for the Hotel job?'

'Steve Harris is working very hard.'

'He always does.'

'Once my suspect is charged I'll offer Steve any assistance he needs. If that's really what you would like, Ma'am?'

The call ended. Vipond stared at the flickering screen. He had his own ideas about the Horror Hotel. If Harris was out of the way he'd have a free hand. Bryson Prudhoe was a pain, but the rumour was he was on the way out. It was all working out well.

The Red and the Black slid from her lap and clattered to the floor.

Kitty looked around the room, relieved to see that she was alone. She rang Jacqui Speed, who was minding Molly.

'Did Molly mention anything about school?'

'Not a peep.'

'Some kid is giving her grief. I'll tell you later. Thanks, Jacqui.' Kitty rang off. She stretched, glanced at the mirror and wandered into the corridor. Jayde sat behind the desk at the Nurses' Station.

'Any news?'

Jayde shook her head.

'OK if I look in on her?'

Marisa Lyndon's face was waxy, though her bruises were yellowing around the edge. The pulse on the monitor was regular. Kitty sat for a while and watched Marisa's chest rise and fall. She flashed a memory of the time she had seen her father's body. She recalled the sense of his absence. Wherever he was, it was elsewhere. Kitty closed her eyes, felt her father's hand on her shoulder. She heard his voice.

Katherine.

Eyes closed, she listened to the pulse of the monitors, letting the hiss of the ventilator wash over her, each breath like a wave lapping the shore. She heard her father's voice once more.

She seems so innocent.

Kitty prayed that Marisa's dreams were sweet. Perhaps she was frozen in the moment when she was attacked, the sun on her skin, the scent of a new spring on the breeze.

At nine that evening Des Tucker arrived to take over. Kitty gave him her home number. 'Text or call if there's any change, Des. Doesn't matter what time.'

'Okey doke.' Des Tucker studied the figure in the bed.

'But I don't think I'll be bothering you.'

Kitty had a long drive home ahead. She made her way to the cafe, bought tea and a muesli bar and sat near the escalators, watching the steady trickle of people moving in and out of the hospital. She struggled with the milk carton, squirting it down her top. A woman at the far corner of the cafe was watching her. Kitty recognised the doctor sitting with a couple of white coated colleagues. When she left the table Kitty followed. The doctor's whites flapped like wings as she hurried down the corridor. Kitty called out.

'Doctor Hobart?'

The doctor glanced over her shoulder, without breaking her stride. 'Hi.' Kitty broke into a jog to catch up.

'Can we have a word?'

'Not a good time.'

'It will only take a moment.'

'Walk and talk. I need my bed.'

Hobart punched the keypad to open her office. She pulled off her coat and flopped into a swivel chair. The doctor rubbed her eyes and tapped a keyboard. Peering at the screen, her lips moved as she skimmed her report.

'Patient suffered a severe trauma to the left cranium blah blah... Resulting in a serious bleed...'

'We think the weapon was an axe.'

'She was lucky, in that case.'

'We found a leather sheath in the pool.'

'If it had been the blade itself - the edge - death would have been instantaneous.'

'So the axe was in the sheath when it struck Marisa Lyndon? Or the *side* of the axe made the impact?'

'Maybe...'

As the doctor leaned closer to the screen, Kitty glanced around the room. There was little to see, apart from framed certificates on the wall. It seemed Doctor Hobart's first name was Caroline. A framed photograph sat on the desk, in the doctor's eyeline, though not Kitty's. Caroline Hobart leaned back.

'As I said to the husband, it's a serious injury. Once there's internal bleeding there are inevitable consequences.'

'What are her chances?'

'She's a fit young woman. Or was.' Doctor Hobart shrugged. 'Off the record, and *don't* quote me - her chance of a full recovery is about thirty per cent.'

'So this might become a murder inquiry?'

'That's your department. But yes, she may well not make it.' Caroline Hobart shrugged her shoulders. 'She might wake up tomorrow. We just don't know.'

'Was there any sign of sexual activity?'

Hobart's eyes flicked back and forth as she read the screen.

'No sign of sexual assault. No sign of sexual penetration. We carried out serological testing which revealed no sign of semen or spermatozoa.'

'I didn't know there was an either/or option,' said Kitty.

Caroline Hobart's smile vanished. Humour, it seemed, was certainly not an option. 'So...No sperm or semen. Which - for you - is bad news. Nobody,' said Caroline Hobart, 'would want the poor woman to be raped or sexually assaulted. But if she had, you would find DNA.'

Kitty nodded.

'She's not pregnant. Which again, would have helped on the DNA front.'

'Sex might have been a motive.'

Doctor Hobart waited for silence, like a snippy school teacher. Kitty knew the woman took her for a thick plod.

Play the part.

The framed photo by the monitor showed Caroline Hobart, her arms wrapped around a little girl.

'She's lovely. Is she yours?'

Hobart looked puzzled. She turned the frame so that the image was hidden.

'My daughter.'

'She's beautiful! What's her name?'

'Eva,' said Caroline Hobart.

'She's beautiful!'

'Thank you.'

'I have a daughter.' said Kitty.

Not that you asked.

'Molly. A little older than Eva.'

That was moment that Kitty's ploy backfired. 'Molly's...' She heard the flutter in her own voice. 'She's just been cautioned for shoplifting.' Kitty found herself on the verge of tears. 'Not great when your mum's a copper, is it?'

Doctor Hobart watched with a cool, professional gaze as Kitty struggled.

'Well. Thanks for seeing me, doctor. I'll let you go.' As Kitty reached the door Caroline Hobart spoke.

'Perhaps she's being bullied? At school.'

Kitty paused, her fingers on the handle.

'Girls can be vicious at that age,' said Caroline Hobart. 'At any age. She'll get through it. Most of us do.'

As she unlocked her car Kitty realised the doctor was not the dragon she seemed. Like everyone, she wore a mask to help her get through the day. There was a word for that survival mechanism but it eluded her.

Kitty had dropped out of the final year of a Psychology course when she fell pregnant with Molly. It was her intention, one day, to finish that degree.

She started her battered Saab. The evening traffic was heavy, giving her plenty of time to think. Something about Marisa Lyndon's wound puzzled her. Why cover her face with a towel? Why use an axe which was still sheathed? Did that suggest they lashed out in passion, or that they felt pity? Perhaps the attacker was unused to handling the axe - or had grabbed the first thing that came to hand. The idea hovered on the edge of Kitty's thoughts, always just out of reach. As the lights changed from red to green beside the *Double Diner,* she slapped the steering wheel.

Doubling!

Doubling. Caroline Hobart split herself into two people : the no nonsense professional and the caring mother. At work she was the doctor - able to deal with blood and guts, someone who doled out strong medicine and broke bad news. Her double was the caring mother, able to read fairy stories to Eva and pretend that life was fair and that the world wasn't cruel.

Kitty recalled something she had read, a piece by some Swiss author. She drummed her fingers on the rim of the wheel.

Door knob? Doormat?

'Dürrenmatt!' She spoke the name aloud, relishing the Germanic tang of the name. 'Friedrich Dürrenmatt.' She glanced over at the car to her right. The driver, a middle aged man, grinned and winked. Kitty smiled back.

Any of us...

The sentence slipped out of her mind. Two miles along she caught the fragment again.

'Any of us could be the man who encounters his double.'

Dürrenmatt argued that the only way Nazi doctors were able to work in Auschwitz was through doubling. They split themselves into two people, switching between their selves as circumstance required - both the family man and the heartless butcher. She would discuss it with Bryson Prudhoe, next time they met. She missed the old buffalo. But now she had to drive home and work out how to deal with Molly.

Good cop? Or bad cop...?

CHAPTER NINETEEN

'YOU'RE LATE,' SAID Clive Lumley. His eyes never left the television screen. Greta dropped her keys on a side table.

'I was busy.'

'Doing what?'

'Shopping.'

'Where?'

The edge in Clive's voice raised the hairs on her skin.

'I went to town.'

'What did you buy?'

She took a moment to answer. 'Nothing. As it happens.'

'Nothing?' He sounded incredulous. Clive had not been this animated for months.

'No. I tried everywhere.' She moved through to the kitchen. 'I couldn't find anything I liked. Have you eaten?'

Her attempt to change the subject was too sudden. Clive was there, at her shoulder. She filled the kettle, reached into the cupboard for a mug. Clive nuzzled her neck, breathing in her scent.

'What are you doing?' She laughed, teasing him, shrugging him off. He scared her.

'Sniffing you.' He held her around the waist as he pushed his face into her neck. His voice was low, a growl. 'Breathing you in.'

He was smiling, but there was no warmth in that smile, no twinkle in those cold eyes. 'Wondering if I can smell another man.'

Caspar remembered lying on the bed, naked, staring at the ceiling. He hummed softly to himself while Marisa faffed around the room, chirping away, telling him how their new life would be. His eyes closed then, just as now.

'I don't care about money.'

'Everyone cares about money,' he said.

'I don't.' said Marisa. 'I'm just not materialistic.'

Caspar pulled the sheet up to his chin. He drifted along the edge of sleep, barely listening as she werritted on.

'Jack and I have a joint account.'

'Sounds good,' he mumbled.

'That's what worries me!' she said. 'I'm frightened he'll freeze the account. When he finds out about us.'

Caspar was tempted to remark that, for someone who was not materialistic, she spent a lot of time talking about money.

'Half that money is mine! I don't want to start our new life with nothing!'

She moved to the bed and hovered above him, butterfly kissing his face. Caspar was on the point of telling her to shut the fuck up when she said, 'Would you mind if we transfer some of my money to your account?' He managed to bite his tongue.

'No,' he said. 'I guess not.' He imagined cash falling from the sky, could see banknotes fluttering down on the bed. She was kissing him, wanting more but right now he needed sleep. She was wearing him out. He slept, a smile on his lips.

When he woke she had her back to him.. Her head was bent over the dressing table as she wrote. He knew she kept a diary and he dozed, listening as her nib scratched away. She leaned back and tore a cheque from her book. A small pile of them was building up by her elbow.

'What are you doing?'

'You need to pay these into your account. We don't know how much we'll need over there. When you speak to the bank make sure you can transfer the money to the States. OK?'

'Marisa?' She turned to face him.

'Shut up and come back to bed.'

That afternoon seemed an age ago. Caspar stretched his arms and legs and yawned. He turned his chair so that it faced the street. The Chinese students glanced at him but Caspar flicked them two fingers. He settled in his chair and watched the shoppers drift up and down Grey Street. A band of Peruvian buskers were setting up on the plinth in front of Grey's Monument.

Neil, the young man in the ill fitting suit, grinned and cleared his throat.

'Would you like to come over to the desk, Mr Greene? Keri-Ann is bringing your coffee.'

He led Caspar to one of the frosted glass booths. Neil tapped his screen. Keri-Ann put his coffee on the desk and scurried away.

'So, Neil. What's the fucking problem?' Faking rage was something Caspar enjoyed.

'No problem at all, Mr Greene. It's just that ninety five thousand pounds is rather a lot for a current account. We just wondered if you had plans for the money?'

'Yes,' Caspar growled. 'I have. I plan to spend it on cocaine and prostitutes. Now put the money in my account, Neil. Chop chop. I'm in a hurry...'

Greta's black Porsche 911S bumped and rolled along the narrow track between hawthorn hedges. The incident with Clive worried her. Since leaving the house that morning she had checked the mirror a dozen times to make sure she was not being followed.

After a half mile she saw the farm house. Buildings of honeyed stone formed three sides of a square. To the right was an open byre, stacked to the roof with egg boxes. Some of the stone slates had fallen and shafts of sunlight pierced the gloom, glinting on a rusty tractor with flat tyres. To the left stood a tall barn. Chickens pecked the grit between the cobbles. Greta pushed her Ray Bans up to her brow and locked the car.

The farm house was shabby. Paintwork on the windows was cracked and peeling, exposing the rotten wood. Cobwebs fogged the window panes. Greta raised the knocker with her fingertips and let it fall.

Moorlands Farm was owned by a shell company Clive used to cover his tracks. The Lumleys had survived for so long because they avoided dealing with the foot soldiers in person. Greta kept herself at one remove from the couriers and dealers, distancing herself from the grubby day to day trafficking. The farm was a new enterprise, one she had set up herself. It made business sense to create the merchandise as well as trade it. The terms of Clive's early release meant he had to report to his probation officer once a day. His movements were restricted and he seemed content to let Greta run the operation. But the events of last night showed he was far from becoming an old man.

Greta had appointed a Vietnamese manager, Lê Van Bính, to run the farm. Moorlands had always been a sheep farm but Lê Van Bính looked nothing like a shepherd. He was a spare, small man, about fifty years old. He wore a charcoal grey shirt and chinos. His shoes were shiny leather, a gold bar across the top. His greying hair was cut to the skull. He emerged from the barn, carrying a chicken by the feet. The bird flapped and screamed but Lê Van Bính took no notice. Though he was quiet and unfailingly polite, Greta felt uneasy in his company. They nodded at each other.

'Shall we go inside?'

Holding the still flapping chicken away from his guest, Lê Van Bính opened the door. She watched from the doorway as he carried the bird across the yard to a tree stump. A hatchet was buried in the wood. Lê Van Bính flipped the bird onto the stump and with a deft move, brought the hatchet down. Carrying the twitching body in his free hand, he followed Greta inside.

On the ancient stove a pan lay, the metal scorched where rice had burned dry. A tap dripped into a bowl of dirty crockery. It was clear that only men lived at Moorlands Farm.

Lê Van Bính laid the chicken by the sink. The legs twitched, the wings fluttered and were still. Blood oozed from the headless neck. He rinsed his hands beneath the tap turned to Greta.

'Can I offer you some tea, Madame?' He spoke English with a French accent.

Greta shook her head. 'I can't stay long.'

'Would you care to see the crop?' said Lê Van Bính.

'I want to discuss another matter.'

'We may talk, perhaps, as we look?' said Lê Van Bính. He led her out of the farmhouse. They crossed the yard. The light inside the barn was blinding. Greta pulled her shades over her eyes. A hard white glare bounced off silvered walls. The light streamed down from racks of lamps in the rafters. Black binliners were taped over the windows. The air was filled with a scent like warm tar. A dense green jungle covered the entire floor. Each cannabis plant stood in its own tub of dark soil. The pungent aroma caught in Greta's throat. Towards the rear of the barn stood the 'mother plant', which would provide seeds for the next crop. It was the size of a Christmas tree.

The delicate, spear shaped leaves fluttered as Lê Van Bính led Greta along the walkway. They came to a halt beside a rack of shelving. A rat's nest of metal ducts and cabling covered the wall. The space was crammed with misty propagator trays and tubs of

Supernatural Bud Blaster.

'They grow tall,' said Lê Van Bính. 'Strong!' He looked proud as he surveyed the crop.

'Yes.' Greta pressed a silk handkerchief to her nose. 'You've been working hard.' She crumpled the handkerchief into a ball in the palm of her hand. 'A man was killed,' she said.

Lê Van Bính turned to her. His smile was frozen.

'Yes?'

'You must have seen it? It was on the news?' she went on.

His head dipped, a tiny nod. He waited for the next question.

'I need to know who did it.'

When he got back to the office Bryson slipped his jacket onto the back of the chair. At the far end of the open plan office Harris sat at his desk. Bryson found a battered packet of mints in his drawer and slid a couple between his lips. Pulling a witness statement from the top of his pile, he flipped it open. He rested his head on his hand as he read. Grinding his way through a statement of half remembered, half invented facts, Bryson's mind soon wandered.

In his mind, he saw the curve of Greta's neck as she turned to look around the beer garden. Bryson closed his file, placed it on the 'done' pile and reached out to take another.

He stared at the first page but the words slid from his mind. He gazed through the window at the dingy brick wall and remembered those moment he spent with Greta. A strand of her hair touching the skin on her shoulders. Her scent.

'Winning, Bry?' The jokey, blokey rasp of Harris shocked him back to the real world.

'Getting there.'

The answer did not lie in this pile of paper. He hoped Greta would discover something. He pulled his jacket from the back of the chair and strolled towards the door. Harris was perched on a desk, leafing through a report.

'If you're going to the shop get me a Twix, there's a good lad.' Harris fished in his pocket and pulled out a handful of change, dropping the coins on his desk. For a moment both men were still. Harris smiled as he looked up at the older man.

'I'm not.'

'Not what?'

'Going to the shop.'

'Then where the fuck *are* you going?'

'I've had a whisper. I'm following it up.'

Harris watched him, the smile still on his lips. Bryson knew it did not come from the heart. Harris tilted his coconut head towards Bryson's desk. 'That pile looks as big as ever.'

'I have a tip. From a credible source.'

'Care to share with your Senior Investigating Officer?'

'I'd rather wait, sir. If you don't mind.'

Harris reached up and tapped his finger on Bryson's chest.

'You're not helping yourself, old son. There's people who want you out. See me when you get back. I want to hear what this 'credible source' has to say.'

His mobile chirped. As Bryson moved away Harris raised his finger, commanding him to wait. Harris tapped the screen. As Harris listened to the call, his finger dropped, falling like a lowered flag. Bryson watched the colour drain from his face. Harris placed his phone on the desk.

'Change of plan,' he said. Bryson waited. 'When you come back, report to Tony Vipond. Seems he's the Senior Investigating Officer. As of this moment.' Steve Harris pushed back his chair and stood. He walked into his office and closed the door. Bryson felt almost sorry for him.

Molly Lockwood's salad lay untouched. She pressed her fingers over the page of her book, flattening the spine. Around her the chatter of the dining hall faded into the background. Without raising her eyes she reached for her glass of juice. A shadow fell across the page. Lorelle Ferrier sat beside her. Molly read on, the words sliding off the page. Lorelle pushed her face into Molly's hair.

'Good book, Snail?'

'It's OK.'

Lorelle snorted with laughter. She sat beside her victim.

'I hear you've been a bad girl?'

Molly sipped her drink. She could think of nothing to say. Lorelle bumped her shoulder. It hurt, though Molly tried not to show it. 'Robbing shops? I'm shocked.'

Lorelle closed Molly's book. 'I'll tell you a better story. Want to hear it?' Lorelle dug her elbow into Molly's ribs. 'I *said*, 'Do you want to hear it?'

Molly nodded.

'You're going back to that shop. Back to that trampy, minging shop you love so much.' At the edge of her vision, Molly glimpsed Lorelle's sly grin. 'And find me a present.'

'What are you two up to?'

Both girls started at the sound of Mrs Loveridge's voice. Lorelle slid her arm around Molly's shoulder.

'Molly's upset, miss.' The teacher squinted down her nose. 'I was giving her a hug?'

As Loveridge drifted away Lorelle's grip tightened. Her lips brushed Molly's ear. 'A lipstick. It's called *Angel*. For tomorrow.' She leaned closer, seeming to kiss Molly's ear while nipping the lobe with her teeth. 'If you *don't* get it, don't bother coming in.' Lorelle stood. 'Maybe we'll let you hang out.' Lorelle slapped the back of Molly's head. 'This is as a test, Snail.'

Lorelle Ferrier sauntered off, looking for her next new best friend.

Driving home, Greta wondered what she should tell Clive about her visit to Moorlands Farm. Her talk with Lê Van Bính left her unsettled.

He was quiet, relentless and efficient operator. He built the shelving, wired up the lighting and found the seed and fertiliser. The plants grew quickly. Cash flooded in. Greta gave him the freedom to run things in his own way. But while she trusted him with her business, she wondered where his loyalty lay. He seemed evasive in his dealings with her, as if holding something back.

When she arrived home one Clive was standing at the window, lifting weights.

'Busy day?' His face was flushed, sweat glistening on his cheeks and forming dark stains on his T shirt.

'I called by the farm. To see how they're getting on.'

'I know,' he said. Clive's arms pumped as he raised the weights to his chin in a steady rhythm.

'What's with the weights?'

'What does it look like?'

She walked through to the kitchen. 'I'm hungry!' Clive bellowed from the living room. Greta leaned her brow against the door of one of the units. She closed her eyes.

'I wish you'd die,' she whispered. The thought shocked her. For so long she had done whatever Clive wanted.

'What?' He stood in the doorway, mopping his brow with a towel.

'What are you doing, Clive?'

'Getting fit.' He patted his arms, flexing the muscles. 'I thought you'd be pleased.' He rubbed his face with the towel draped around his neck.

'Yes. I'm dizzy with happiness.'

'What?'

'What would you like to eat?'

He shrugged. 'Whatever.'

'I'll cook that then, should I?'

As she prepared the meal she glanced at Clive through the kitchen door. While flesh of his belly still spilled over his waistband there was no denying he was looking slimmer. His heavy lidded eyes flickered across the screen, the glow reflected in his cheeks. Clive dropped the weights on the hardwood floor, pushed his hand into his crotch and scratched.

'If Bryson Prudhoe could see you now,' murmured Greta.

Clive never took his eyes from the screen. 'Why are you talking about that fat cunt?' Greta hid her face in a cupboard, stacking the tins. Clive picked up his weights and turned to the screen, his grunts drowned the thunder of hooves as the race began.

CHAPTER TWENTY

BRYSON WAS UNEASY. A coffee shop was not his natural habitat, despite the tempting displays of fuschia tinted tarts and cupcakes in and lemon yellow. When Kitty arrived he was sitting at the back of the Cafe Royal, in a chair facing the door. He seemed pleased to see her. She was wearing her hair up, and she saw his mouth fall open as she tucked a loose strand into place.

'You've ordered? I'm late. Sorry.'

Two wedges of walnut cake lay beside his coffee.

'The first slice was tiny. I said as much, so she brought another.'

'How's the diet going, Bry?'

'The quack said I should avoid beige food. This cake's more of a *Raw Umber*, wouldn't you say?'

'It's more about what it's made from. Sugar. Fat. Rather than the shade.'

She ordered tea and raspberry cheesecake. 'Been busy?'

'Painting the stairwell, as it happens.'

'Exciting...'

'How's little Molly?'

'Not so little.' Kitty looked away for a moment, unable to meet his gaze. 'Not so good, either. She was caught shoplifting. Makeup from Rutherfords.'

Bryson's fork chinked against the plate. 'A one off?'

'I hope so. I feel so guilty. Bad mother. So - as punishment - I'm taking her to Paris. To see her father.'

Bryson raised an eyebrow.

'I know. I must be mad. But Molly's never met him. She's seen photos, they've talked on the phone. Skyped. But never actually met. Maybe the scales will fall from her eyes when she they do. And maybe I can find out what's been going on.'

Bryson nodded.

'How's Mr Vipond?'

'Tricky, isn't he?'

'A glamour chaser,' said Bryson.

Kitty relaxed. Talking about work was safe. Bryson had been her mentor since the early days. She often wondered how he saw their relationship and knew he would never say.

'Tony V likes flashbulbs. Press conferences,' said Bryson. 'He likes to tip the press. Likes to be their contact on the inside. Vipond wants to see heads on sticks, preferably with his name scribbled all over their faces.'

It was clear Bryson had passed this judgement before - to others, or inside his own head.

'He gets things done.'

'I detect a change in your attitude, Locky. A mellowing.'

She prodded her cake with a fork, lifted a piece to her mouth, set it down again. 'You think?'

'He's ambitious - you're right there. He rates cases on how many column inches he'll get.'

'He should be working with you then. On the 'Horror Hotel'.'

'He is.'

Kitty's jaw dropped.

'But we haven't closed the case! Wow...He never mentioned it.'

'You're surprised? The Horror Hotel is a murder. Whereas Mrs Lyndon...'

'But she's had her head stoved in! She could die.' Aware that other customers were tuning in, she lowered her voice. 'Nothing's missing from the house. No sexual assault. So Vipond thinks it's a crime of passion.'

'You don't?'

'I'm not convinced.'

'So he's going for jealousy? As the motive?'

Kitty nodded.

'Which puts one face straight into the frame.'

'The lover?'

'There's a lover?'

'There is.'

'I was thinking of the husband.' He stirred his coffee with his fork, skewering another cube of walnut cake. 'So. The lover. The husband. Two faces.' His jaws rolled, the cake bulging his cheek. 'It's usually one of the Golden Three. Sex. Money. Or revenge.' He wafted his fork.

'Of course,' said Kitty.

'Anything interesting on her phone?'

'It ended up in the bottom of the pool. Though we're getting the record of calls and texts.'

Bryson nodded. 'So, her laptop?'

'Didn't have one. She used her phone, or the Mac in the house.'

'What do her friends say?'

'That's the strange thing. She doesn't seem to have many.'

Bryson scooped the last of his cake into his mouth. Kitty watched the relentless grind of his jaws. 'Why is that strange?'

'Women - maybe I should say 'most women'- have a close friend. Someone they can trust. But Marisa Lyndon seems to be different.'

'Betty No Mates?'

'Everyone says 'We love Marisa!' Maybe it's true. So who did she talk to? Who knows her secrets?'

'Her husband?'

'Hah!' Kitty snorted with laughter, then chewed her lip, realising that Bryson was serious. 'Well, maybe some of her secrets. Though I know things about my friends that their husbands will *never* know.' Bryson looked uneasy. Perhaps he was wondering about Maureen Prudhoe's secrets.

'Who do you trust?'

Kitty watched a pigeon waddle along the flagstones, pecking at cigarette butts. 'Jacqui, I suppose. I've known her since school. If I was at work, I'd talk to Elayne Hawes. Even you, Bryson. You know where *some* of the bodies lie...'

Bryson covered a blush by swigging his tea.

'But if Marisa Lyndon has a best friend, she hasn't surfaced.'

'It's the Callerton Chase estate, isn't it? It's a funny place. Nobody there pops next door for a cup of sugar. That's exactly the kind of thing they've paid to avoid. People keep themselves to themselves. It's exclusive. That means other people are excluded.'

'There has to be *someone* who's close to her. Maybe it's the daily. She knows more than she's letting on.'

Kitty sensed that Bryson's thoughts were elsewhere. One part of him was mulling over her case, the other chewing on something closer to home. She watched the pigeon work the gutter, pecking at scraps then dropping them.

'Vipond says it's a jealous lover?'

'He's sure it's Saul Kemp.'

'That name rings a bell...'

'The Lyndons hired Kemp to do some landscape work. His axe was used in the attack.'

'An axe. Classy!' Bryson squinted in the sun. 'Anything else against this Kemp?'

'Kemp had been sleeping with her. She finished it.

'Not so good.'

'Gets worse. His axe matches the wound. I found it in the pool.'

Bryson closed his eyes. 'His *axe*? Which you found in the pool?' She watched his shoulders shake with laughter. 'You're right. It got worse.'

'But Vipond's wrong. I just don't buy it.'

Bryson nodded but she felt he was no longer listening.

He looks haunted.

Before she could stop herself, the words spilled out.

'What's up, Bry?'

She saw the guilt flicker across his face.

'Nothing!'

Her phone thrummed across the table. The caller ID was Tony Vipond. She wandered along the pavement to take the call.

'I need you here. Now. I'm charging Saul Kemp.'

'Give me twenty minutes.'

'Sooner.'

He ended the call. She hurried back to their table.

'Sorry, Bryson. Got to run.'

'Not a problem!' Bryson seemed relieved. He circled the debris with a plump finger. 'I'll get these.'

Molly drifted along the aisle, her eyes darting from side to side, checking out each assistant she passed. They were busy with their afternoon routine - filling shelves, stacking the product high. She was just another customer, a girl bunking off school, window shopping for stuff she could not afford. She glanced up at the surveillance camera, the shiny black eye in the sky.

They're watching.

On the lipstick counter the glittering tubes were arrayed like howitzer barrels. The assistant was chatting on the phone. Molly found the lipstick Lorelle wanted. She reached out to touch it, her eyes on the assistant. The woman was laughing now, gossiping about some customer. Molly's fingers closed around the smooth barrel. At that moment she sensed a movement of the air. A woman stood at her side. Molly opened her fingers, dropping the lipstick. The tube clattered on the glass surface and rolled across the floor. Molly hurried through the store. In a moment she was walking down the High Street. Her heart was pounding but a smile spread across her lips. She had made the choice. Whatever happened, whatever punishment those witches meted out, she was free. She would never steal for Lorelle Ferrier.

Tony Vipond paced the tarmac in the car park as he made a call on his mobile. He nodded at Kitty and finished his call.

'I'm heading up the Horror Hotel job. As of now.'

'Really?' Kitty tried to look surprised.

'That's why I need you here. We need to wrap up this Lyndon thing. I'm charging Kemp so you'll be my eyes and ears on this case. I think it would be good experience for you.' He strode towards the station. She followed. 'I'll charge him. You take over from there.'

'Sir?' They turned the corner of the corridor. 'You're sure this is the right man?'

Vipond paused. 'You're not?'

'I just wondered if there might be more to it.'

'Like what?' He frowned.

Kitty knew there was no room for havering. She could hardly say her doubts were based on instinct. Yet that was all she had - a feeling that they were making a mistake.

'Kemp didn't run. Why not, when he had the chance?'

'Because the daily was there. Either in the house or just outside. Cathy whatsername. Perhaps he heard her arrive. Or shock? A hundred reasons. Who knows?' He shook his head.' Kemp had the means - the axe. She dumped him, so that's his motive. And he had the opportunity. He was alone - or thought he was.'

'But that's a guess.'

'No. It's fact. I know you're playing the Devil's Advocate. Which I understand. But there's no need to look too closely at this, Lockwood. And if, by some incredible misfortune, I've got this wrong, the lawyers will sort it out.'

'OK.' Kitty forced a smile. They walked shoulder to shoulder as they approached the room where Saul Kemp was waiting.

'The answer is not always elsewhere, Lockwood.' Vipond paused, his hand on the door. 'Sometimes it's right in your face.' They went in.

A sliver of sun shone through the slit window high on the wall of Interview Room 3. A patina of scuffs and stains covered every surface in the room. The air was scented with the aroma of milky coffee and digestive biscuits. Tony Vipond rested his elbows on the desk.

'Afternoon Saul. I'm going to record this?' Kemp shrugged. Tony Vipond switched on the recorder. The buttons glowed, spider eyes in the gloom as he announced the date and time, then the names of all present - Kitty, Kemp and his brief, Vanita Mistry. A chronograph watch glittered on her slender wrist.

'Tell us about your relationship with Marisa Lyndon,' said Vipond. Kemp slumped in his chair. He tilted his head, rolling his eyes to stare at the ceiling.

'No comment.'

The silence lengthened. Kemp was still, the only movement the rise and fall of his knee. Vipond opened a Black and Red note pad. He ran his thumb along the seam, flattening the page, breaking the spine. Kitty watched him pull a Fineliner from his jacket pocket. The cap popped as Vipond pulled it free. He pushed the cap onto the blunt end of the pen. He wrote the date on the top of a clean page, the tip of his tongue between his lips as he formed the letters. The ink glistened and dulled, drying on the page. Vipond looked up. Kemp still stared at the ceiling. Kitty leaned forward.

'Saul?' She waited until he tilted his head to look at her. 'How well do you know Marisa?'

Saul Kemp blushed, the blood rushing up his neck. He chewed his lip as he planted his elbows on the desk. His forearms were bare, golden hairs rising from tanned skin.

'We were friends.' He looked straight ahead, watching some scene play out in his mind. The tip of Vipond's pen hovered above his pad.

'It's a funny place,' said Kemp. 'That house.' He shook his head. He looked at Kitty. 'Different.'

Vipond made a note.

'Can you tell us about that?' said Kitty.

'I've worked for all sorts.' His voice trailed off.

'Tell us how you started working for the Lyndons?'

She felt Vipond bridle. She had crossed a line.

'I started back in March.'

'What was the garden like?' said Kitty. 'When you arrived?'

'A right tip!'

Kitty nodded, willing him on with a smile, knowing the best route was not always a straight line.

'No bugger raked the leaves for years. Paths covered in moss. Lawns yay high!' Kemp levelled his hand, a yard above the floor.

Kitty smiled. 'So there was plenty to do?'

'Aye!'

'And you like that?'

'Of course!' He rubbed his fingers together, as if fingering cash. 'I gave 'em an estimate to tidy the place. Worked a day - a long day. Lyndon swans over and pulls out a wad of notes and peels them off.' Kemp mimed the peeling. 'Marisa's there, watching. She says 'It's a pity we can't have you regular.'

Kitty sensed Vipond had relaxed. He leaned back, letting her take the lead.

'Lyndon gives in. Straight away. We come to an arrangement. One day a week. Lyndon says he's happy. 'I haven't got green fingers, Saul,' he says. 'You're not bloody joking,' I thought!'

'So it was Marisa's idea? That you work there?'

Kemp nodded. 'And Mr Lyndon was happy about that?'

Saul Kemp bit his lip. Kitty watched his pupils narrow. 'I'm just trying to understand the arrangement you had with the couple, Saul.'

Kemp glanced at Vanita Mistry, who nodded. After a moment Kemp went on. 'She was the boss. Marisa decided what she wanted doing. Lyndon paid.'

Kitty nodded, noting it was 'Marisa and *Lyndon*,' rather than 'Marisa and *Jack*.'

'She liked what you did with her garden?'

Kemp nodded. 'She had an eye for it. Knew what worked.'

'It sounds like you got on well?'

'We got on fine.'

Vipond leaned forward. 'What does that *mean, Saul*?' There

was an edge to his voice. Kemp glared back. Kitty sensed the pair hated each other. She spoke, anxious to reconnect.

'You liked Marisa. You got on well. Had a good working relationship?' Kemp nodded. 'But Jack was different?' Kitty spoke softly, easing Kemp back to the path.

'Some people think money makes them special. People look up to Lyndon. Because he's got this...' Kemp rubbed his finger and thumb together. 'They think he floats above the rest of the world. *Scum* floats! Jack Lyndon's no better than me.'

'Tell me about the moment when you fell out?'

Saul Kemp sighed. He sucked his lips between his teeth, leaning back, rubbing his palms over his knees.

'I didn't like him. I don't want to say more.'

Vipond opened a buff folder. He placed some photographs on the desk, leaving them face down. 'Marisa Lyndon suffered a brutal attack.' Vipond turned over one of the photos. It was a head shot, a close up. 'She was struck with a axe.' He turned another photo. Another close up, the wound to the side of Marisa's head. The drying blood, thick and matted in the blond hair, spreading from the wound. 'She may well die.'

Kemp nodded, allowing that he understood. Vipond went on, his voice soft. 'The axe that inflicted this...has your name on it.' He turned another photograph. Kemp glanced at the image, then looked away. '*Your* axe, Saul.'

'I would never hurt her.' Tears spilled from his eyes. 'I want to speak to Wendy. '

Kitty leaned closer. 'Saul?' Maybe you can help us out here? ' Kemp glared at her. 'You say she was bleeding when you found her. You arrive, with your bag of tools, and you see she's been hurt. If it turns out that Marisa *was* attacked with that weapon, we need to know how that axe, with your name on, got there. Before you did...'

Saul Kemp rubbed his face. Ignoring Vipond, he spoke only to Kitty. 'I don't know. I have no idea.'

Kitty had dealt with many men who were convincing liars. Saul Kemp was not one of those. She was sure he was telling the truth.

'Thanks.' Vipond stood. 'We'll take a little break.' He announced the time and switched off the recorder. 'I need a word with my colleague. Back in five.'

Vipond left the room. Kitty followed, running to keep up. He sat on a low wall outside and lit a cigarette. Kitty hovered nearby. Vipond patted the brickwork. She sat beside him. Vipond found his lighter, put a cigarette between his lips and lit up. Kitty found a muesli bar in her pocket and peeled the wrapper.

'What did I say?'

Kitty nibbled her bar. 'I don't recall, sir.'

'Eyes open...?'

'Right. 'Mouth shut'?'

'We work together.' He jabbed his lit cigarette towards her face. A flake of ash fell from the tip. 'Together or not at all. In a team you work with people above you and below you. It's a chain of command.' Vipond blew a plume of smoke into the air. 'You probably think I'm a bully.' Kitty stretched her legs, tapped her toes on the tarmac.

'I don't know you well enough. Sir.'

'As senior investigating officer I lead the interview. There's room for input. I *welcome* input. But *I* steer the ship.'

'Sir.'

'You went off on your own...'

'He's hardly Mr Chatty, is he?' Her throat tightened. 'I thought I might warm him up, get him talking. Then you'd come back in.' Kitty heard a shrill edge in her voice. 'With the awkward questions.'

Vipond stared across the car park.

'You're working on the other case, sir. I need to be involved.'

'They told me you were pushy.'

'Who did?'

He tapped his cigarette. When the ash fell he scuffed it with his shoe. 'Finish this, then we'll go back.'

'Whenever you're ready, sir.'

They sat in awkward silence for two minutes. Vipond stubbed out his cigarette and flicked it into the hawthorns at the edge of the car park. He paused at the door. Without turning to look at her, he spoke.

'When we go back inside, if a question comes to mind, speak up.'

'Sir.'

'Speak up. Don't bloody take over.'

She followed him inside.

CHAPTER TWENTY ONE

'GOT MY PRESENT?'

Something twisted inside Molly, a wire curling as it tightened. 'No.'

Lorelle came closer. Molly could smell the girl, her sweet fragrance. 'I haven't had a chance.'

Lorelle rested her hand on Molly's shoulder. 'You better hurry up.' Running her fingers up the curve of Molly's neck, she pinched her earlobe, twisting the flesh. Molly heard laughter. She curled her fingers into a fist. When she looked up at Lorelle it was the first time she was able to hold her gaze. Molly saw a glimmer of doubt. After a moment, Lorelle Ferrier blinked. She called over her shoulder to the Witches.

'You there?' There was a new tone in her voice, a hint of uncertainty. 'Next time,' she hissed.

Molly watched her hurry away.

Vanita Mistry was whispering in Kemp's ear when they returned.

'Need a minute?' asked Vipond.

'Mr Vipond? My client has told you all he knows. I'd be grateful if we bring this to a conclusion?'

'We're getting there.' Vipond's smile was cool. Vanita Mistry tapped her laptop, unscrewed her Mont Blanc fountain pen and leaned back. Vipond switched on the tape, leaning his bony elbows on the table.

'Saul. You say your relationship with Marisa Lyndon was a sexual one?'

Kemp glanced at Mistry, then nodded.

'For the tape, Mr Kemp nodded.'

'So let's be clear about this, Saul. Your relationship with Marisa Lyndon was intimate. It was of a sexual nature?'

Another glance at his brief.

'At one time, yes.'

The plastic chair squeaked as Tony Vipond leaned back.

'Would you like to tell us about that?'

Marisa knew it was a mistake. She was attracted to Saul from the first moment. It was something to do with the tanned skin, the shape of his back. When he went out to look at the garden, Marisa followed him. She sat by the pool, watching him as he looked up at the dark wall of Leylandii. He paced back and forth, squinting in the sun, shaking his head. Saul snapped a twig from the hedge and held it to his nose.

'It's an ugly thing, isn't it?' she said.

'A wall of death.' He smiled. 'I have no idea why people plant them. It does the job, I s'pose. Blocks out everything.'

'It was here when we arrived.'

'A beech hedge can be a beautiful thing. Firethorn too. They breathe. They don't kill the light. But this...'

His shoulders were broad. It was that bear thing - she wanted to be wrapped in his arms. Held.

'So what do you advise, doctor?'

She peered at him over her sunglasses. He looped his arm through the step ladder and half turned. 'Surgery! Chop 'em down and plant something else. For now, let's cut it down to a civilized height. Seven foot? That way you've got privacy but we get some light in this side of the garden. Long term, you need to rip it out, condition the soil and start again. I could plant beech? You'd have that fresh green in the summer, the copper leaves the rest of the time.'

Marisa watched him twist the cutting in his hands. He tossed it away and put his hands on his hips as he looked up at the hedge.

'Have you got a longer ladder? I need to get up there.'

She led him to the garage. As he reached to unhook the steel ladders she watched the way his body moved. They were laughing as they carried the ladder into the garden. He propped it against the hedge and started to climb. She watched his arms flex, the contours of his thighs as he climbed.

'Be careful!'

'I'm always careful, Mrs Lyndon.'

'Marisa.'

He smiled at her over his shoulder. 'Marisa.'

Saul parted the leaves, peering in to the dark interior of the hedge.

'It's a monster!'

He gripped the rim of the ladder with the insteps of his boots and slid to the ground, dusting his hands. 'I'm Saul.' She took his calloused, sap stained hand.

'Hello, Saul.' She felt the warmth of his tanned skin. It seemed to carry a scent, cucumber or horse chestnut. Marisa felt a rush of desire, dark wings fluttering. She called for Cathy, asking her to bring them tea. They sat by the pool.

'Your husband says you're the boss.'

'Out here, in the garden.'

Saul stretched his arm towards the line of trees that bordered the river.

'Those are native species. Oak, Beech, Alder, Hawthorn, Holly. We need to work with that backdrop.'

Some tradesman simply added a nought to their usual price when they worked an address on the Callerton Chase estate. Saul was different. Like her, he did not seem to care about money. He made her laugh.

'So I make arrangements with you?' She looked at Saul's face and knew what would happen. She sensed the danger from the start. That's the illusion we have about a love affair - that it can be started and stopped at will. We forget we're dealing with another human being, with their desires, their way of seeing the world.

'Want the long answer, Locky? Or the short?' Leapy's voice wheezed like a pedal organ. The pollen count was high and rising.

'I thought you said a week?'

'I don't hang about.'

'Something I can understand would be nice,' said Kitty. She stood in the corridor outside Interview Room 3.

'OK. I processed the axe using the M-VAC system. I collected the resulting liquid in 50 mill conical tubes. Ran them through the centrifuge. The resulting cell pellets were transferred to a microcentrifuge tube for organic extraction. With me so far?'

'Ish...'

'So I bigged up the resulting DNA with the YFiler YSTR amplification kit.'

'You know what, Leapy? The short answer will do.'

'This *is* the short answer. We got a smidgeon of male DNA from the handle - around 140pg of male DNA. We got 850ng of female DNA, which makes a ratio of six thousand to one, female to male.'

'And that's Marisa Lyndon's DNA?'

'Yup. Despite limited male DNA, a partial Yfiler profile from a single male contributor was obtained, after we'd amped up the male component. We tested all the investigators and crime scene personnel, the daily, what's her name?'

'Cathy.'

'Her and the paramedics and Uncle Tom Cobley.' She heard a rustle of paper. 'So the profile we got indicated Saul Kemp's DNA on the axe.' The phone hissed in her ear.

'That's it? It's *his* axe.'

'Yup.'

'So you're telling me Saul's axe had Saul's DNA on it. As well as Marisa Lyndon's?'

'Shock result, eh?'

'So you're telling me nothing I don't already know?' She heard a honk as Leapy blew his nose.

'Don't shoot the messenger, Locky. DNA testing doesn't tell us *when* material was deposited. With small quantities like this it's so tricky. But there's one positive you can take. We only found two traces - the victim and the suspect.'

Kitty closed her eyes. She wanted certainty. She needed to know that she was wrong and Vipond was right - that way she could live with what they were about to do.

'There's no alien DNA on the weapon,' said Leapy. 'No DNA from *outside* the group we tested - the cops, the medics.'

'So the axe was used by someone within that group? Which in effect, means Saul Kemp?'

'Not quite. If someone else used the axe - someone other than Kemp - the DNA was washed away. Or maybe they wore gloves. Or the contact was faint, or very brief.'

'I thought every contact left a trace.'

'In theory...'

'Cheer me up?'

'The axe caused Marisa Lyndon's wound. If you can prove Kemp swung it, you're laughing...'

Kitty passed Vipond a note about her chat with Leapy Lee. Vipond blinked and tucked the note into his pad. He fixed his gaze on Saul Kemp - Kitty marvelled at his poker face.

'You liked her? Marisa? She was your type?'

Kitty wondered if the reply would ever come.

'We have all day,' he said. Vanita Mistry smirked and made a show of glancing at her watch. The truth was they had less than an hour to charge Saul Kemp. If not, they would have to let him go.

'She was easy to talk to. Knew about plants. She listened.' He glanced at Kitty, who nodded.

'You work for her. When did your relationship change?'

'The second week.' Kemp shrugged. 'I was working on the hedge. Cutting it back. Marisa was by the pool. She was making phone calls. I was making a racket with the cutters.'

In the corner of the Interview Room a Daddy Long Legs was dashing spindly legs against the breezeblock wall.

'What happened?'

Saul tapped his lip with his finger. Kitty knew that it was a 'tell'- a subconscious tic that revealed his thoughts. The usual interpretation was that there was something left unsaid which the speaker hesitated to reveal.

'I turned around. She was holding out a glass of lemonade.' He fell silent.

Marisa enjoyed the attention. Most afternoons at home were spent alone. Having a man there, someone who felt like a friend, felt good. The house was empty. Cathy had gone home at lunchtime. Marisa knew they were alone. She made the running.

Their fingers touched as he took the glass. The lemonade was ice cold, frosting the glass. A droplet ran over her skin, onto his. They talked about the garden, though it meant nothing. When they finished their drinks she said, 'Are you going to start up that bloody machine again?'

Everything became a blur. His fingers were in her hair, cradling her head, pulling her closer. She led him upstairs.

Knowing that Saul was married added to his appeal. A married man would not become dependent. A married man wouldn't tell.

'We talked about everything.' Saul Kemp shrugged. Kitty

guessed that Saul Kemp was like many men - more expressive with his lover than with his wife. It was easier to talk to a relative stranger than to Wendy, the woman with whom he spent his life.

'How often did you sleep together?'

Saul shrugged. 'I didn't keep count.'

'Was it often?'

He shook his head.

'Three? Four times? Cathy was there a lot of the time, so... Then *he* started turning up, odd times of the day.'

'Jack?'

'He would go to work, then we'd hear his car coming back into the drive. After a while he was there every time I was.'

'So he knew what was going on?'

Saul Kemp shrugged.

'Did he act jealous?'

'We were never going to be best buddies!'

'He was distant? Cool?'

Saul nodded.

'So...it fizzled out?'

Saul Kemp rubbed a nail over his stubble. Kitty noticed the callouses, the thin seam of dirt beneath his nails.

'She wanted it that way.'

He knew how to touch her. It was as simple as that. Marisa cared for Saul but she was not 'in love' with him. The illusion of control was just that, of course. In love, there is no control.

For her, it was just a fling. For him, it was more. When Marisa whispered 'I love you,' it during was a moment of fondness. For that moment, it was true. A kiss, a caress - no more. Saul was lovable, but she was not in love with him. He reminded her of old boyfriends, the men she had dated in her teens. If she was sixteen, she might have fallen. They would not spend their lives together. She could not imagine sharing a table with him, let alone her life. But when Saul whispered, 'I love you,' she knew that he meant it. It scared her too.

They took another break. Their 24 hours was ticking down to zero. Kitty sat on the wall while Vipond paced around the car park, sucking on his cigarette.

'You're quiet, Locky.' His face was wreathed in smoke.

'Just thinking.'

He smirked in the way she was starting to hate. 'Thinking it's shaky? Wobbly as a clown's bike?'

'He said Marisa was lying on the ground, bleeding, when he arrived.'

'His axe. Her head.' He wafted the DNA report. 'No trace of anyone else.'

'Why attack her in the first place?'

'She *dumped* him!' Vipond thrust out his chin, stretching his turkey neck. 'Posh bird dumps her bit of rough.'

'This was a violent, sudden attack. Done out of rage. A raging, furious assault.'

'That's why jealousy is a perfect fit, Locky. As is Saul Kemp.'

'Or her husband. For instance.'

He snorted, shaking his head. 'Jack Lyndon's not the type.'

'How do you *know* that, sir?'

Vipond glared at her. 'Jack's firm, when he needs to be. But he's a pussycat. Even his bloody staff like him.'

Vipond's cigarette smoke drifted across her face.

'Maybe he arranged to have it done. To put an end to a problem.'

'Then why not finish the job?'

Kitty looked towards the horizon. The hills were bathed in sunlight. 'Why cover her face with a towel?'

He sighed. 'An attack like that is a dynamic situation. There's no logic! They're living in the moment. It's adrenaline. Instinct.'

'I don't buy that. We reveal ourselves in the way we do things.'

'Oh. Do 'we'?' Vipond dragged on his cigarette.

'Tell me a lie.'

'We haven't got time to piss about, Lockwood! We have thirty minutes to charge him or let him walk.'

'Tell me a lie!'

'OK.' He glanced at his watch then looked up, his eyes flicking back and forth. 'My wife left me, because I collect stamps...'

'You looked up and to the right. It's a tell. It's what right handed people do when they tell porkies. Sir.'

'Bollocks! And your point is?'

'Saul Kemp did none of the usual things people do when they lie. No blinking. No head shaking. Whereas Jack Lyndon...'

'Jack doesn't fit, Lockwood. The lad in Interview Room Three does...'

'Maybe.'

'Jack's not the type. I've played golf with the guy. He's sound.'

Kitty bit her tongue. Jack Lyndon might bludgeon his wife, but his etiquette on the green was immaculate.

'I know the Callerton Lodge,' he said. 'I can't afford to live there, but I know it. Every morning the Daddies climb into their Audis and Hummers and drive to Town. Then this army of men drives in. Blokes who build extensions and plumb bathrooms and clean hot tubs.'

'And what do the wives do?'

Vipond narrowed his eyes, blowing smoke. He shrugged. 'You tell me. You're supposed to be a woman.' It was clear he loved getting under her skin.

'I guess they work, sir. And if not...maybe they buy shoes online. Go for quicktans. Make plans for charity functions. Maybe.' She pursed her lips. 'Perhaps they leaf through a box of old love letters. Look out of the window, wondering if they made the right choice.'

Vipond tapped the ash from his cigarette.

'I guess they get bored, sir. Being perfect must get dull, after a while.'

'Which is why,' he pointed his cigarette towards the station, 'Marisa started shagging the gardener. And why, when she dumped him, she got whacked.'

Kitty knotted the wrapper of her bar and pushed it into her pocket. 'Maybe you're right.' She needed time away from Vipond, away from the job. 'I wouldn't live there if you paid me.'

'Everyone wants to live there, don't they? Those houses are fantastic! Don't be daft! Everyone wants more. It's human nature.'

'The more you have, the more you fear someone will take it all away.'

Vipond sighed, shaking his head. 'They told me you were a bit of a shrink too.'

'That was long time ago.'

Another life.

Vipond stood, swatting brick dust from his trousers. 'Sounds like socialist bollocks to me.'

Looking at his pale, vulpine face, Kitty knew he'd made up his mind.

'I don't think he did it,' she said, dusting her hands. 'I don't know why. But I don't think Saul Kemp did it.'

Keep your job. Button your lip.

'Fair play. You're wrong, of course.'

'...I just feel there was more to this than Saul being dumped.'

Vipond yawned and stretched, his arms uncoiling into the air. 'Maybe you should take a look on the PNC, then.'

The Police National Computer was the database of criminal activity across the country. 'Saul Kemp is on the Names File.'

The ground beneath Kitty's feet shifted. 'What for?'

'He was cautioned, six years ago.'

'Right...' Kitty looked at the ground, seeing the ridges and bobbles in the tarmac. Whatever was coming would be the clincher.

'He split up with his girlfriend. She started seeing someone else. Saul gets pissed one night. She wakes up and he's sitting on her bed with scissors, snipping her hair.'

The fight left her. She stared straight ahead. It was easier to agree, easier to take the big slide sideways and go along with the boss.

'Not so good.'

'You have a talent for understatement, Lockwood. You're right. That's not so good.' He flicked his cigarette butt into the shrubbery. 'Ponder that while I go inside to charge the sod you think is pure as the driven...'

CHAPTER TWENTY TWO

'YOU ARE CHARGED with the Attempted murder of Marisa Lyndon, under the Criminal Attempts Act 1981, section 4.'

Kitty felt no elation as Vipond spoke the words. Kemp stared at his hands, shaking his head as the waves of legal jargon broke over him. Kitty sensed Vanita Mistry's anger, so fixed her gaze on the surface of the table. She felt no triumph. As Kemp was led away she heard him shout his innocence all the way to the cells.

'One less villain,' murmured Vipond, glancing at his watch. 'Got to be somewhere else.'

'Would you like me to drive?'

'Thanks, but no.' Vipond scratched his cheek. 'Look - I'm starting on the Liu case first thing. Can I leave you to do the housework on this, Locky?'

Kitty tidied the papers, tapping the edges on the desk.

'Call the Crown Prosecution Service. Oppose bail - danger to victim blah blah. Let Kemp's wife know the lad's been charged and won't be home for his tea. Not for ten years, anyhow.'

'Sir.'

'Cheer up, Locky. A result!' He leaned towards her. 'I'll be in the Dog around ten. If you fancy a drink.'

'Thanks. I need to get back. For Molly.'

'Of course.'

Vipond filled the silence by scooping the paperwork into files and stuffing them into a cardboard box.

'I have a couple of days leave due, sir.'

'Lucky you.' His voice was flat.

'My daughter wants to visit her dad. In Paris.'

Vipond nodded, leafing through the sheets.

'She's still a kid, though she thinks different. I wondered. Would it be OK for me to take her there?'

'As long as it fits in with the hearings,' he shrugged. 'It's your time off.'

'Marisa Lyndon is still in hospital...'

'We can step that down. The Chief will be happy! We've removed the threat, so there's no need. Is there?' It was a challenge, rather than a question.

'I'll be back at work on Monday.'

'She's safe now, wouldn't you say, Lockwood? Now that we've got the villain in a cell?'

Kitty ran the tip of her tongue along her lip. 'Maybe we should keep the vigil going? In case she comes round?'

'That can't be open ended. The longer she's in a coma, the less likely she is to wake up. It's a hard fact. Would you keep it going six months? A year? I mean...we ain't got the money.' He raised his eyebrows. 'We've charged Kemp. The threat has gone.'

Kitty nodded. He relaxed.

'So you pop off to Paris!' His smile did not reach those blue grey eyes. 'What I *do* need you to do, Locky, is to box up everything at Mrs Lyndon's bedside.'

'Sir?'

'The stuff in her bedside cabinet. Handbag. Purse. Chequebook. Cards. Letters. I took a look at everything, but now the vigil's ending we need it all secured.'

'You mean now?'

'Why not? You're not coming to the bloody pub, are you!'

Saul Kemp paced the cell in a tight circle. Kitty called his name. After a moment he padded over to the door. She expected to see defeat in his eyes but saw defiance.

'I've called your wife. She'll be over as soon as she can.'

He placed a hand on either side of the doorway and leaned his head close.

'I didn't do it.'

Kitty had no answer to that. It was hard to meet his gaze.

'Get some rest, Saul.'

When she closed the slit she could hear the sound of his footsteps as he began to pace.

The ward was emptying as visiting time ended. Relatives rinsed their hands in alcohol gel and struggled to open the electronic doors. Kitty entered the Intensive Therapy Unit. Her heart sank as she saw Jayde behind the desk.

'Hi, Jayde. Don't you ever have time off? Any change in Mrs Lyndon's condition?'

'Nope.' Jayde shook her head. 'To both questions.'

Kitty held up a cardboard box. 'I have to take Marisa's stuff. Not her toiletries but anything that may be counted as evidence.' She unfolded the papers and passed them across the desk. 'Would you like to watch?'

'Just go ahead.'

'I'll give you a list of what I take.'

'As I say...'

Nothing in the room had changed. The bed was tightly sheeted, as before. The monitor pulsed with the same icy bleep.

Kitty boxed up the contents of the bedside cabinet. She searched among the bottles of water, tissues and wet wipes. There was a Tom Ford lipstick, a stainless steel fountain pen lying on top of a writing pad. The barrel was inscribed '*All my love - Jack.*' Some caring soul had brought these things in for Marisa. Cathy Fletcher, Kitty guessed.

She found little that would be of use as evidence. There were a couple of paperbacks, which Cathy must have brought from Marisa's bedside - *Sculpture since 1945* and a thriller by George Pelecanos. She wondered if Marisa would ever finish them. She listed and boxed each item.

At the bottom of the pile lay a small notebook. Kitty eased it out. It was an A5 tan leather journal, tied with slender thong of leather. Kitty flipped the corner and glimpsed the tidy, neat handwriting and the occasional sketch which filled the pages. She glanced at the door. She was alone. Marisa Lyndon slept on. Kitty loosed the leather thong and opened the notebook. She read one sentence. It seemed to make little sense.

'*Beautiful evening. Atticsalt - Han St. Cas on b/behaviour. Exhib autumn?*'

Kitty dropped the journal into the box. She was about to enter the notebook in the list of contents when something stopped her. She slipped the notebook into her bag. It was an almost unconscious decision. She walked to the Nurses Station and handed over the list.

Her heart skipped as Jayde checked the list against the contents of the box. For a moment, the nurse looked puzzled, then shook her head.

'Is it OK if I keep this list?'

'Of course,' smiled Kitty. She walked towards the door.

'Hang on a sec?' Kitty turned to see Jayde walking towards her. Jayde took the box from her hands.

'Now you can do your duty.' Kitty felt her jaw drop. She blushed, searching for some excuse for leaving the notebook off the list. Then she understood. Jayde was nodding towards the bio-wash dispenser.

'Nobody escapes the gunk,' said Jayde.

'Of course.' Kitty smiled.

She hurried to her car. Only an idiot 'borrows' evidence. Someone who wants to lose their job. When she returned to the station she would photocopy the journal and put the original in the box. She would change the list and make everything right.

Back at her desk in Etal Lane Kitty called Jayde and did just that. She explained she'd found a leather journal in the box.

'Did I include that in the list?'

'I can't seem to find it.'

'Sorry about that,' said Kitty. 'Can you write a note at the bottom? Saying I called and...'

'No problem.'

Kitty ended the call. The photocopier groaned and clattered into life. As the sheets went through Kitty recalled a story she once read to Molly.

So the fairy cast a spell; and everyone that lived in the castle fell into a deep sleep.

'*Now,' thought the fairy, 'when the Princess wakes up, they too will awaken. And life will go on.*'

CHAPTER TWENTY THREE

THE DOORBELL CHIMED as she was struggling with the zip on her case. A cone of evening sunlight shone through the window on the stairs. As she reached the bottom step she glimpsed a red car parked outside her house. The deeply contoured lines and spindle grille of a Lexus RC glinted in the evening sun. The moment she opened the door, she remembered who owned such a ridiculous car. Tony Vipond stood on her doorstep, a bottle of wine under his arm.

'You're in!' His voice was slurred, the words tumbling into each other. 'A peace offering?' He waggled the bottle.

'I'm in the middle of packing.' Kitty tried to keep the edge from her voice.

'One glass won't hurt,' he said, putting his foot on the threshold. 'It's tradition!' She realised he must have driven the twenty miles to her house while drunk. 'Ask me in, Locky, for fuck's sake!' She moved to allow him in. He made a show of looking around, whistling in admiration. 'What a beautiful place!'

'You're easily impressed. It's magnolia.'

'Bottle opener?' His voice was too loud. Vipond strode into the kitchen, plonked the bottle on the surface and yanked open a drawer. Cutlery clattered across the floor. It seemed easier to have a drink while she worked on a plan to get rid of him.

One glass.

As she leaned over the drawer looking for the corkscrew she felt his hot, boozy breath on her neck. She shoved the corkscrew into his hand. As she watched him fiddle with bottle her anger grew. Vipond poured himself a generous slug, a larger one for her. He raised his glass.

'A good result!'

Kitty sipped her drink. 'Yup. Result.'

The texts arrived all day.
'Ugly slut. Yool get it.'

Now the witches were waiting behind the village hall. Lorelle Ferrier hung back, content to watch Midge and Becky. Molly sensed her fear. Becky, the gangly, fair haired girl, leaned on Molly's shoulder, steering her to the bench where Lorelle sat, pretending to watch a cricket match on the green.

'I asked you to get something for me. I've been very patient.' She looked at Becky, who nodded. 'Where is it?'

Molly had reached that point beyond fear. She no longer cared what happened. 'I don't have it.'

'Why not?'

'I won't do that. Not for you. Not for anyone.'

Lorelle watched the men in white run after the ball. 'Then you know what's going to happen.' Lorelle stood. She strolled along the side of the green, towards the woods. Molly's wrists were held by Midge and Becky. All she could do was follow.

'I wish I cared. Wish I cared like you,' said Tony Vipond.

'Yes. I'm sure you do.' Kitty's voice had the patient, weary tone she used while talking down any drunk. She was listening but thinking of other things. How her ceiling needed painting. Why the mixer tap always dripped, no matter how hard she turned the handle. She sipped her drink.

'I *did* have that. Once upon a time. Now it's just a roundabout. We arrest the same people for the same things.'

'Yes.' Kitty could think of nothing to say. She wondered how she could get him out. She was feeling a little drunk herself. One glass had become three.

'Let me call you a taxi. I need to finish this packing.' She glanced at her watch.

Where's Molly?

Vipond stood, his chair screeching as he pushed it back.

'Not yet.'

She felt his breath in her ear. He gripped her neck with one hand, while the other fumbled with her top. She leaned back, then fell, crashing to the floor. He was a shadow, grinding away, somewhere above her, his shoulder sliding over her mouth. There was a distant roar in her ears.

'*No!* Get *OFF!*'

He lay on top of her, motionless. She opened her eyes and

peeped out from beneath his shoulder. She looked at the shadow the lamp threw on the curtain. Vipond was quiet, his chest rising and falling. She wondered if he had gone to sleep. When her eyelash flicked against his cheek he moaned and rolled off her. He lay still, his cheek pressed into the carpet, his lips glistening with saliva. They lay on the floor, side by side.

That was the moment Kitty heard the front door open.

They pushed Molly onto a bench in the riverside park. It was dusk now, the sun sinking behind the hills. Midge and Becky sat on either side, holding her wrists. Lorelle strutted in front of a fallen tree, her hands thrust deep in her pockets.

'You're even more stupid than you look.' Becky twisted Molly's arm.

'I won't do it,' said Molly, biting her lip.

Lorelle leaned close, her lips an inch from Molly's eyes.

'If I tell you to do something, you DO IT!' Lorelle paced again, kicking a stone along the path. She gathered the stone in her fingers. She drew her arm back and grinned at Molly. She feinted, whipping her arm forward, pretending to hurl the stone at Molly's face. Molly flinched.

'Do what you're told, Minger!' Lorelle's eyes glittered - she was excited by her power.

Get it over with.

'No. Because it pisses you off.'

The stone whistled past Molly's cheek. There was a moment of silence. Then she wrenched her wrists free and lashed out, slapping Midge's face with the back of her hand. Midge fell in the mud, a pink welt scarring her face. Molly swung at Becky. Her finger nail scraped Becky's eyeball and the girl screamed, clutching her face. Blood leaked through her fingers. Lorelle was nowhere to be seen. A shadow ran through the trees, clambering up the bank. Fury blinded Molly to any danger. As Molly closed in, Lorelle stumbled. She scrambled to her feet then doubled over, her hands on her knees. Molly grabbed a fistful of Lorelle's hair, twisting her head. She slapped her face again and again. Lorelle whimpered, begging her to stop. Eyeball to eyeball they gasped for breath. Lorelle closed her eyes and Molly whispered in her ear.

'Who's the minger now? Say it...'

It was dark when she reached Cloud Street. Light shone from open windows as she walked up the lane and into the tiny garden. She barely noticed the Lexus parked outside. As she walked up the pebbled path she was thinking about what she would say to her mother.

Molly opened the door. Passing the mirror by the door she dragged her fingers through tangled hair. Tugging her cuffs over her bruised wrists she stepped into the kitchen. Dirty glasses lay on the table. A bottle lay on its side, dripping red wine onto the floor. A man stood in the corner, turning away as he tugged at his zipper. Molly watched her mother stagger to her feet. Kitty leaned on the table.

'This is not what it looks like,' she said.

'I have something for you.'

Bryson was mesmerised by Greta's voice. He took her call while he sat at the kitchen table, eating his tea. He thumbed a drop of baked bean sauce from his chin and glanced at the door. Maureen was in the next room, watching a programme about the white rhino. Bryson closed the door with his foot and pressed the phone to his ear.

'Falcon's Nest? Tomorrow at twelve? How would that be?'

'See you there,' Bryson whispered. He rang off. He tapped the phone against his lip.

'Who was that?' Maureen called.

'Work,' he said, rolling his eyes and waggling the phone.

She turned back to watch the rhinos, while Bryson's mind wandered elsewhere.

Molly stared at them, a look of horror on her face. Kitty pushed past Tony Vipond, took Molly by the elbow and steered her into the hall. 'Upstairs. I'll be up in a minute.'

Molly took the stairs two at a time. Kitty closed her eyes, bracing herself. The clash of Molly's bedroom door shook the walls. Vipond buttoned his jacket. As he headed for the door he leaned on her.

'Wanted it though. Didn't you?'

Kitty shoved him outside and locked the door. She called a cab, telling them to pick up the man in Cloud Street. She gave Vipond's name, rather than her own. As she walked upstairs she had no idea what she would say. She knocked on Molly's door but there was only silence. She turned the handle but the door was locked from the inside. She knocked again, half hoping there would be no response.

'What?' A single word loaded with so much anger.

'He turned up on the doorstep.' Kitty's voice trailed away. 'He's my boss.'

'So?'

'I had to let him in.'

'Why?'

Kitty sat on the top stair and put her head in her hands.

Good question.

Kitty stared at the carpet. The pile lay flat, crushed by ten thousand footsteps.

'Sometimes you have to do things you don't like.'

They sat in silence, separated by the door.

'Is doing *that* in your job description?'

Kitty smiled as she brushed the sparkle from her eye.

How sharper than a serpent's tooth it is, to have a thankless child.

CHAPTER TWENTY FOUR

THE MANNER IN which Whitey landed his three stretch was sheer bad luck.

Davy Clark kept on about this old bonded warehouse on the Quayside. It was a Victorian job, timber and brick, eight floors high. When it was built they used it to store grain and barrels of sherry. In the seventies it was filled with Norwegian wood, in the eighties Scandinavian flat packs. Since the turn of the century the only thing it kept safe was fresh air. So a friend of a friend of the owner got in touch with Davy Clark, who phoned Whitey.

Davy Clark said the warehouse was a listed building, though Whitey had no idea what that meant and cared less.

'The site's worth millions but the building's worthless. A waste of fucking brick,' said Davy Clark. The owner put in five planning applications to develop the place into loft apartments but every plan was blocked.

'They need to lose the warehouse,' said Davy Clark. 'Get me?' Then the developer could start again, put up his loft apartments for young single professionals on the empty plot.

So the friend of a friend offered Davy Clark ten grand to set a fire. 'The blaze has to be fucking discreet, right? Nowt blatant, just big enough to make sure the dump falls down.'

Davy Clark told Whitey he'd been offered three grand to do the job. There was fifteen hundred in it for Whitey, if he did the business. Whitey agreed. He trusted Davy Clark. The pair had settled their beef when they met up in Aycliffe. Coming from the same street, in the same city, Kirk White and Davy Clark had a lot in common. The other cons were Mancs or Scallies and so Whitey and Davy Clark stuck together. In Aycliffe Davy Clark was Whitey's only friend. The other kids thought he was weird. Davy helped him out. When Davy talked, Whitey listened.

'A little drop of turps gans a long way,' he advised. 'Cannot stress it enough, Whitey. This job has to be discreet. Fuck'n' discreet.'

Whitey nodded. Once the money was mentioned, he could

think about nothing else.

'Get ya ratio right, man! Too much and you'll blow your face off. Which would be an improvement in your case! But if the place stinks of turps, the sniffer dogs will pick it up. So, your ratio is a little drop of turps and a shed load of wood, right? Set it in the cellar. Once you've set the fucker, light up. Watch and wait. Let it take hold.' He clicked his fingers as if nothing could be simpler - 'Just walk away!'

They settled on a Monday night for the deed, late in the month. By then the kids are spent up because payday was way back. There were never many drinkers on a Monday. The clubs are shut, the Quayside is quiet.

So Whitey tips up at half one in the morning, toting two placky bags. One is rammed with wood shavings and smashed up orange crates. The other contains a torch, a packet of Swan Vestas and some turpentine. He'd emptied the turps into a bottle of Fanta in case he was stopped by some caked up bizzy wagon.

Getting inside was a piece of piss. He found a rotten door around the back. Whitey dropped his bags on the pavement and kicked open the door. His torch between his teeth, Whitey trotted downstairs to the basement. The place spooked him. It was clay cold and there was something alive in there, something scratching and scuttling in the dark. But Whitey kept his eyes on the prize - that fifteen hundred quid.

In the basement he piled his tinder by one of the doors. He drenched the shavings in turps, then stacked pallets around the pile. He sat there in the dark for a while, flashing his torch at the rats. He wrapped his sleeve around his face because the stench of turps burned his throat.

After ten minutes Whitey struck a match and flicked it onto the shavings. Smoke curled through the beam of his torch. There was a '*phoof*' and the room lit up, bright as Guy Fawkes night. He watched the fire take hold. By then he was buzzing, his old man getting stiff as he watched the flames lick around the wooden pallets and flicker on the ceiling. Smoke caught his throat but he hung on, waiting until he was sure. Then he ran up the stairs, boots clattering the wooden stairs. He kicked the door and ran into the lane, sucking the cool night air. Fire licked the shuttered windows. It all looked sweet. That was when he got unlucky.

Walking backwards up the lane, admiring his work, he bumped into some random old bloke who was out walking his dog.

'You're not supposed to be in there, son. What you up to?'

'Fuck off,' said Whitey, pushing past. If the old fucker had left it at that everyone would be happy. That's when the sodding collie bit him, sinking her white teeth into his calf muscle. Whitey howled. The dog snagged her fangs on his tracky bottoms and shook her head. Whitey's fist slammed into the dog's eye. The collie whined and cringed, rubbing a paw over her snout. But the old tosser went radgy. He screamed at Whitey, saying he was calling the bizzies. He took out his mobile. Whitey knew Radgy Tosser had clocked his face. So he reached for Stanley.

Stan the Man.

Stanley the Manly.

Whitey cut an extra pair of lips in the Radgy Tosser's face. And then he ran, legging it up Lombard Street, sprinting along Akenside Hill, his ears cocked for the siren on the bizzy wagon. He ran all the way to Davy Clark's flat in the Swamp. He hammered on the door until Davy let him in. Whitey was buzzing.

'Nin*jaaa* warrior!'

'The B&Q samurai,' laughed Davy Clark. 'Stanley knife for hire.' He cracked a tin of White Lightning. Whitey refused the cider but took a hit on a joint. He had not smoked for a while. His heart was clanging like a hammer and he needed a soft landing. He stared into the gas fire as the skunk hit. Then he told Davy Clark everything that had happened. He lied about the size of the Radgy Tosser and said the dog was a Rotty. Apart from that he stuck to the facts. They fell quiet. The gas fire hissed.

'Where's me money?'

Davy Clark reached into his pocket and tossed a brown envelope into his friend's lap. Whitey's eyes glittered as he flicked through the wad. He had never seen so much. 'Ah've got mair lowey than *yee*! I'm fuckin' minted!' He stood and stuffed half the wad into his tracky pants. For a laugh he began to dance, spreading the tenners like a fan, rubbing them on the crotch of his trackies. He laughed, for the first time in a long while. All the tension, all the fear just melted away. He felt safe. Davy Clark grinned.

That was the moment the front door flew across the room. There was a crash as the 'Big Key' shattered the wood and the bizzies swarmed in. Whitey dropped the money, the tenners fluttering to the floor. He and Davy Clark were wide eyed and silent as they were cuffed and cautioned.

Sheer bad luck is what it was.

Kitty spent the morning writing up the Lyndon job. Wendy Kemp knew that Saul had been charged, but Kitty wanted to talk to her in person.

The Kemps' home was a neat little doll's house on a brand new estate called Deer Park, north of the city. Deer Park was a Happy Shopper version of the Callerton Chase. Only a narrow gap separated each house from its neighbour. Silver birch and rowan trees had been planted to soften the newness of the street.

The Kemp house was a prim little box in stone shaded brick. The windows were 'cottage' style, tight white grids of PVC which gleamed in the noonday sun. The lawn looked as if it had been unrolled from a spindle of Astroturf that morning. Kitty walked up the gravel path and pulled a bell handle. 'Ode to Joy' echoed through the house. There was movement behind the frosted glass panel. The door was opened by a plump young woman with straight, dark hair, cut in a lopsided bob. She wore a pastel cardigan and dark new jeans. She passed her thumb over a ring in her brow, lifting the edge of her fringe.

'Yes?'

Wendy Kemp frowned, her dark eyes narrowing.

'Hi. Are you Mrs Kemp? Saul's wife?'

They each sat on the twin floral sofas in the front room. A bowl of ceramic eggs sat in the centre of the glass topped coffee table. Above the fire a piece of African art - a herd of water buffalo in marble - glittered like sugar. The air smelled as if it had been dry cleaned.

'When are you letting him out?'

'I'm sorry, Wendy, I don't know. There's a preliminary hearing on Monday. The magistrate will hear representations about bail. But don't expect him home. Bail will be opposed.'

'He's done nothing wrong!'

'A woman suffered a very serious assault. She's in a coma.'

'Slut!' A sheen glistened on her brow. '*I* would kill her if I had the chance!' Wendy sat back, sinking into the folds of the couch.

She closed her eyes. 'I'm sorry.' She shook her head, taking a moment to before she spoke again. 'Saul isn't violent. He's soft as clarts!'

Kitty decided not to mention Saul's caution for stalking.

'And dim!' said Wendy. Kemp had seemed anything but. 'He kept mentioning her. When he started to work over there. How he was going to do this, plant that. '*Oh, Marisa does this, Marisa wears that. Marisa loves what I did with the rockery!*'

'A bad case of mentionitis?' said Kitty, her voice soft.

'I *knew* there was a rabbit off.'

'What did you think of Marisa Lyndon?'

'Never met her!' Wendy's laugh was like the yap of a terrier. 'Not allowed! They had some sort of garden party. A few weeks ago. Saul mentioned it, said we were invited.'

'You wanted to go?'

'Of course! Saul put his heart into that job, for bugger all money!'

'You wanted to meet Marisa?'

'I wanted to clap eyes on this gorgeous creature, this superwoman!' Wendy plucked a ball of tissue from the hem of her sleeve and dabbed the corner of her eye. 'He was never sure of the time, the date. You know? Stalling tactics! He kept changing his mind. We were going, then we weren't. When he stopped mentioning it, I thought he'd decided not to go.' Wendy Kemp rocked, shifting in her seat. 'The date came and went. Then I found out he'd gone there! On his own!'

'How did you discover that?'

Another snort of laughter. 'Silly bitch is on Facey B, isn't she? Posts pictures of her posh do. There he was - Saul - decked out like a kipper, suit and tie. Which *I* bought him, pulled tight around his neck. He's surrounded by all these women. '*Cocktails on the fucking terrace, darling.*' Pardon my French.'

'He confessed?'

'He told me he was going fishing. Saturday morning he loads his tackle in the pick up and off he toddles. Must have hidden his suit in the cab, driven off, changed on the way.' She dabbed away more tears. 'You see what I mean? He's not violent - just a bloody idiot!'

Her mobile buzzed. Wendy Kemp glanced at the screen, then

pushed it aside.

'Why do you think he did that?'

'Men have two emotions - hungry or horny. Can I eat it? Can I screw it!' Wendy folded her arms beneath her breasts. 'They don't think beyond that!' She dabbed her eyes. 'Why won't Saul get bail?'

'I don't know if Saul told you. He has a caution for stalking a previous girlfriend.'

'He was a kid! That was nothing! *Really!*'

'The magistrates may not see it that way.'

Wendy saw Kitty to the door. 'The truth is, that he's ashamed of me.' Her voice was small. 'He didn't want to be seen with me. His fat frump! There you go.'

As Kitty drove through the maze that was the Deer Park Estate, she wondered about Mandy Kemp's hatred for Marisa Lyndon.

Merlin greeted Kitty on the doorstep, twining smoky fur around her ankles. Kitty dropped her bags on the kitchen table.

'Molly?'

The house was silent but Kitty heard music coming from upstairs. Merlin's mewling rose a couple of notches. Kitty cut her thumb on the edge of the cat food tin and sucked the wound. She glared at her cat.

When you die kiddo, that's it! No more pets.

She stood in the stairwell and yelled.

'*Molly!*'

Her daughter appeared at the top of the stairs, tousled hair flopping over her face.

'I'm *here!*'

'What do you want for tea?'

At seven they were in the sitting room. The television burbled in the corner. Kitty nodded off for a few minutes. Her naps were becoming a regular thing, sometimes accompanied by a flashback. She dreamed she was back in the burning cellar at West Neuk Farm, a gun to her head. She woke with her heart in her throat.

'Bad dreams, mother?'

Kitty detected the ghost of a smile. She wiped her mouth with the back of her hand.

'Just the usual. I'm in that cellar and can't find my way out.' She rubbed her face and padded to the dining table and tapped the laptop. 'Your half term is Friday 23rd May until the 2nd June?'

'Yes.' Molly's voice was loaded with suspicion.

'Then we're going. Train to King's Cross. Then the Eurostar to Gare du Nord. I'll stay one night and hand you over to his lordship the next day.'

'Hand me over?'

'Your father wanted me to stay but I need to get back.'

Molly yelped and wrapped her arms around her mother's neck, squeezing until Kitty saw stars. Hot tears ran down Kitty's neck.

'Listen. OK?' Molly nodded, her eyes glistening. 'You've built your dad up to be this wonderful, saintly man. He's just a human being.'

'I know that.'

'And if you have problems at school, or whatever, you have to tell me about them.'

'Yup.'

'You've always been an oyster, Molly. Everyone has secrets. But if you're in trouble, I need to know. Right?'

Molly hugged her mother.

'How are things at the moment?' Her face was hidden in Kitty's hair.

'It's all sorted.'

'Really?' But Molly was running to her room to tell her friends the news.

Kitty booked tickets and e-mailed Gerard telling him when they would arrive. She reserved a double room in a small hotel on rue Beautreillis, in the Marais. Feeling weak at the hammering her credit card was taking, she kicked off her shoes and lay on the couch to drink a glass of Merlot. She closed her eyes and let the sound of *The Mandé Variations*, by Toumani Diabaté, wash over her. The kora chimed throughout the house, the notes falling in cascades of sunlight and sadness.

Images from the last few days drifted through her mind. Molly's tears. Vipond blowing cigarette smoke in a tight column, the smoke unfurling as it climbed into the air. The face of Saul Kemp as he was led to the cells. Tears running between the fingers of Wendy Kemp, a woman filled with rage at her foolish husband and her beautiful rival. Everything came back to that woman, to Marisa Lyndon.

Kitty swung her legs off the couch and fetched the laptop.

She searched for Marisa Lyndon. Of the half dozen choices, it was easy to find 'her' Marisa. The avatar showed an attractive woman with blond hair and a confident smile. Kitty had only seen that face bruised and bloody, so it was odd to see her as a happy woman, clearly enjoying her life.

She read the bio. '*Marisa Lyndon: Gosforth Grammar School: worked at Fenwicks Limited: married to Jack Lyndon. Love art. Love creativity.*'

Kitty scrolled through Marisa's past and worked her way towards the present. There were posts about bees, about badgers in the wood, about her plans for the garden. As she worked her way to the present day there were photographs of art that Marisa admired. One was of a piece in twisted, rusting metal entitled *Kiss the Jailor*. Her comment read 'Work by Caspar Greene. He has an intricate yet natural approach to creating beauty. Love it!'

Kitty scrolled through Marisa's photographs. The latest showed a garden party, clearly held in early spring. She guessed these were from the party Wendy Kemp mentioned. The trees in the background were in leaf, the foliage a fresh, vivid green. She counted over thirty guests in the images. The women wore summer dresses, butterflies around the pool where Marisa would be attacked. She could almost hear the laughter, the clink of glasses. The male guests looked restive - their smiles fixed, their bodies tense.

Saul Kemp stared at the camera, his collar tight around his bull neck. His knuckles white as he gripped a bottle of beer. Jack Lyndon stood in the background, his white shirt open at the collar, smiling as he held a tray of drinks. Lyndon and his wife never appeared in the same photograph. At the centre of another shot stood a young man in his mid twenties. Ringlets of copper hair snaked to his shoulders. He wore Converse trainers with a Moschino two-button suit in dark, shiny blue. He held two women around the waist - Marisa Lyndon and another, a little older, her head in profile as she talked to someone out of shot. Kitty guessed this was Honor Blackett. Marisa had tagged the photo 'Caspar'.

So this is Caspar Greene.

Marisa was clearly happy in the company of this young man. Her fingers rested on the hand that circled her waist. Her smile was broad as she leaned in for the photo.

Kitty studied the image. Who knew what really happened at a party? Perhaps Jack Lyndon had brought in his own staff. But Kitty suspected the clearing up had been done by Cathy Fletcher.

CHAPTER TWENTY FIVE

EVERY FEW MINUTES Molly hopped to her feet, tugging things from her bag - her water, her headphones, her book. Kitty smiled to herself. They should have done this when Molly was younger. One reason Kitty avoided contact with Gerard was that she Kitty did not trust herself.

'How long does it take?'

'Under the sea? About twenty minutes.'

'Will they let us know?'

'Probably not. If someone suffered from claustrophobia they might have a wobbler... *You* don't do you?'

'Soon find out,' grinned Molly.

Molly found a seat in the departure lounge and flicked through her magazine. Kitty watched the crowds of people who swept through the station, wondering at the way it brought strangers together by chance. A school party poured into the lounge, the kids hanging together, anxious and excited. The boys mooched around on their own while the girls stuck together, in pairs or tight groups. They pushed their heads together, bitching and laughing. Their friendships seemed so intense.

Who is Marisa Lyndon's best friend?

For such a well connected woman there were few visitors to her bedside. The stack of get well cards was thin.

The Eurostar pulled out and they rattled through the Kent countryside. The train slowed and entered the tunnel.

'We're under it now!' hissed Molly. Kitty watched the tunnel lights pass by, a steady pulse of light in the darkness. It reminded her of the rhythm of the machines at Marisa Lyndon's bedside. Kitty took out her photo copy of Marisa's journal. The first sentence was not promising.

'Very little in the world is not made better with toast.' Much of the writing was banal, almost childish. 'Read a brilliant article about a Thread Wrapping Machine in *Wallpaper*.'

'What's this?' said Molly. She grabbed the journal and flicked through the pages.

'It's work. Just work.' Kitty prised the sheets from Molly's grasp. 'It's a diary. By that woman that was attacked.'

Molly frowned. 'You need to think about your work/life balance, mother.'

'I thought there might be something there.' But Molly was pushing headphones into her ears. Kitty skimmed the pages but there were no easy answers. After a few pages she turned to watch the flat terrain of northern France flash by. She glimpsed petrol stations, rusting tractors and barns. Small farms with flat, dreary fields. Here and there lay a relic of the past - a windmill without sails, a stone bridge too narrow for trucks. This was Georges Simenon territory - a place where ordinary people lived, hiding their passion, their frustration until it burst out in a torrent of rage and violence. She returned to Marisa Lyndon's journal.

This is Me; she read. *A slim frame, though toned and shapeful with strong bone structure. A pale, soft and clear complexion, with bright blue-green eyes.*

What sort of woman used the word 'shapeful' when writing about herself? The entry continued for three pages. Marisa Lyndon was a grown woman, yet as self absorbed as a teenage girl.

'*We stayed in Amanruya, amid the olive groves and pines on a slope above Mandalya Bay, near Bodrum. The sky so blue, reflected in the sea below. The sand so white it's blinding. The hills are covered with pines, the scent drifting over the water. Jack makes everything possible. Such a sweet, kind man.*'

Other jaunts were described in detail : two weeks at Cap EstelÊon the Côte d'Azur, ten days at the Hotel du Cap-Eden-Roc, near Antibes. Marisa wrote of Jack's promise to take her to Necker, on the island of Calivigny in the Caribbean - '*the most expensive holiday in the world!*'

They rolled into the Gare du Nord at five. Kitty stuffed the journal into her bag. Molly was wide eyed, drinking in the sights and sounds of a new city. She dragged Kitty to the metro. As if on cue, a man with an accordion boarded the carriage and began to play. By the time they reached their room in a small hotel on Rue Beautreillis, in the Marais, Kitty was drowsy. She fell onto the bed and closed her eyes.

When she heard Molly in the shower she splashed cold water

on her face. For a while Kitty stood at the window, watching the rush hour traffic on the Rue Saint Antoine. Kitty dragged a chair onto the balcony and opened Marisa Lyndon's journal. Resting her bare feet on the balustrade she began to read. A warm breeze drifted up the street. The bustle of the traffic around Place de La Bastille faded into the background. Kitty flicked through to the end of the diary. The sentence she read surprised her. The entry was starred and seemed to be written in shorthand.

' *w/ C to MalMai. Room 216, overlooking river. Glass of bubbly. C manoeuvred me to the bed, said 'You are beautiful' - in his calm, sly way. For a moment, I did feel beautiful.'*

Kitty read the entry again. The man who manoeuvred Marisa to the bed could not be her husband. Nor did it fit Saul Kemp. This was someone else - another lover, perhaps. When Jack Lyndon talked in the hospital he said 'Marisa's a child - which I love.' To Jack perhaps that is all she seemed. Kitty knew that nobody is one, single person. To the 'C' of her journal, Marisa was a passionate lover, a woman he was eager to bed. She read more.

'Some men bark orders. Unconnected thoughts. C is different. He touches my skin, he touches my soul. He looks into my eyes and knows what I'm thinking. He knows how to touch me. J has no idea! C's hands are rough: cut and scarred. J has soft hands, like a woman. I cannot bear to be touched by him. His hands are like fish, slithering over my skin. But C understands how I want to be held.'

Kitty looked up. For a while she watched the strangers pass on the street below. Most people lead three lives, she knew. A public life. A private life. A secret life. Marisa Lyndon had a secret life : the key to the mystery lay there.

In the room behind her Molly was trying on different outfits, experimenting with her hair. To Kitty she was a daughter. To her schoolfriends she was someone else - a bully, a victim, a clown.

We show different faces to different people.

The concentration camp guard goes home to be a gentle father.

Doubling. We're all many people, many personalities.

One of Marisa's personas was that of a lover. The stats showed that if a married woman was attacked in her own home, the most likely perpetrator was her husband. Had Jack discovered the truth? How many Jack Lyndons were hiding behind that charming face?

They ate breakfast in a cafe on the Rue Saint Antoine, then wandered the streets of the Marais. In the Rue Saint-Paul they stumbled upon Aux Comptoirs du Chineur, a junk shop where a heap of colourful tat from the sixties had washed up. Winklepicker shoes, fringed buckskin jackets, hats and ray-guns, flicker film books, kitsch album sleeves and a juke box straight from an Elvis flick were piled to the ceiling. Molly found the place fascinating, squealing with delight as she found another treasure.

At noon they found a table in a cafe in the Place des Vosges. A vaulted arcade ran around the edge of the square. In the centre, beyond iron railings, lay a small park. The trees were in full bloom. Sunlight glinted off the blue slate roofs. A chaffinch hopped between the table legs, searching for the crumbs that Molly flicked across the flagstones.

'What's happening at school? With Lorelle?'

'I've told you. Nothing.' Molly's eyes were fixed on the bird.

'You're friends?'

'I could never be friends with her.' Molly sipped her lemonade. 'Girls can be mean, mother.'

'But it's stopped now?'

'I stopped it.'

'How?'

'I slapped her.'

Kitty placed her cup on the saucer. 'Right...'

'She asked me to steal something for her.' Molly saw her mother's frown and laughed. 'I wouldn't. So they took me to the Riverside Park.'

'Who?'

'Lorelle and her friends, The witches. But I fought back. I hit them. It's what you have to do.'

'I don't think Lorelle Ferrier has a very happy life.'

'So it's OK to bully me?'

'Some people bully because they're unhappy. Or inadequate. It gives them a feeling they're in control.'

Molly looked away, flicking her hair over her shoulder. Life for her was black and white. She sipped her lemonade, then placed the glass on the table.

'You're too kind, mum. Too nice. She's just a little cow!'

Molly grabbed a piece of bread and walked through the gate

into the park. She stood in the shade beneath the Linden trees, scattering bread for the birds who flocked around her feet.

Kitty met Gerard at York while they were both studying Psychology. When she fell pregnant with Molly, that was the end of her degree. Gerard vanished, leaving a note on her pillow. Though loath to admit it, Kitty was curious to meet him after all the time that had passed.

He was late, as ever. She spotted his tall figure, rake thin, loping beneath the arches towards the cafe. His hair was thinning, though he still had a faded elegance, his leather coat well cut but battered. He arrived just as Molly returned from the park. He beamed at both of them. He hugged Kitty, holding out his hand for Molly. She blushed as she took it, looking up into his face in her solemn, watchful way. Gerard released Kitty and folded his daughter in his arms. They were laughing and weeping at the same time. 'You are beautiful.' He held her at arm's length for a moment. 'As beautiful as your mother.'

He ordered a glass of bottled water and asked about the journey. From the corner of her eye Kitty watched Molly drink in every word. His mineral water arrived. Watching him swallow the water, seeing the way his neck moved, Kitty felt a flutter of desire.

They crossed the Seine to walk along the Quai Saint-Bernard. Molly and her father seemed so easy with each other, chatting and laughing as they walked side by side. While Molly took pictures of the monkeys in the Jardin des Plantes, Kitty and Gerard sat in the shade of a horse chestnut tree, eating ice cream.

'My father is ill. I want him to meet Molly. To understand my life has not been a complete waste!' He brushed the back of her hand with his fingertips. 'What does she think of me?'

'She thinks you're perfect. Of course. A gentleman.'

'That is a nice idea. Très attirant.' He watched Molly, who was taking a photograph of the capucins tumbling over each other. 'A gentleman is just a patient wolf.'

'A wolf.' Kitty tried to keep the sarcasm out of her voice.

'Like wolves, what we want is straightforward.'

'A full belly and empty bollocks?' said Kitty.

He grinned. 'Perhaps.'

'Whereas, women?'

'Women are more cruel. More devious.'

'You think?'

'Love is a bloodsport for women,' he said. He leaned close. 'Women are the hunters. Pitiless. If their anger is roused. Or in pursuit of what they want.'

'Maybe *you* shouldn't lecture *me* on that subject.'

His head drooped, falling on his chest. For a moment she thought he was ill. 'I was young.' He looked up, into her eyes. Despite herself, her heart skipped. 'Young people do stupid things. I was a bit of a...a cock?'

She laughed. The sparkle in her eyes was a tear. Kitty fixed her gaze on the people walking along the pebble path. An old man, shuffling along, a newspaper tucked beneath his arm, his straggly yellowing beard. A woman in her sixties, wearing shades, still chic, a dachshund trotting at her feet. It was easier to watch these strangers than look at Gerard.

She hurried inside the cafe. She took off her shades and fixed her face in the mirror. When she returned to the bench Gerard was watching a young, dark haired woman jog along the gravel path.

'I should make a move,' she said. 'I'll miss the train!'

He stood and took her in his arms. He put his lips to her ear. 'I was very scared.'

'Me too.'

'I will take care of her.'

'You better!'

He kissed Kitty on both cheeks, squeezing her hand. She walked over to Molly. 'I'm going to scoot!'

'Already?' Molly slung her camera across her shoulder.

'Yes. Now. Hug.' They wrapped their arms around each other.

'Don't give your dad an excuse to say I've brought you up wrong!'

'My '*dad*.' That sounds weird.'

'Doesn't it just?' She kissed Molly. 'See you next week.'

Knowing that both were watching, she fluttered her fingers above her shoulder as she walked away, knowing that if she looked back, tears would betray her.

The Eurostar swayed through the southern suburbs of Calais. Kitty dropped Marisa's journal on the table. She looked at the factories and houses, the quarry pools and canals, the water spangled by the setting sun. It would be strange for Molly, meeting a new family. Would she write home: send postcards to her friends?

Who was Marisa's best friend?

The question vexed her.

Who knows her secrets?

The train took a wide sweep around the pink and white sprawl of Vieux Coquelles, then ran between sloping grassed banks. Kitty mused that, while she might trust her friends with her life, female friendship could be double edged. The keeper of your secrets knew how to inflict the deepest wound. Best friends held such power. They might give love and support, yet knew the dirty secrets too.

The entry to the tunnel was sudden, the train swallowed by a concrete maw. Kitty reached into her bag and spread the photocopy of Marisa Lyndon's journal on the table. The writing filled every line, running like coiled wire across the page.

Sat 2nd/Sun 3rd April

Lazy Sunday lie in. Jack sleeping beside me - exhausted after last night, the build up, the prep and the party itself. All went well.

Two hundred guests. Press - arts bods from the nationals. Jack sent for extra bubbly! Met a strange little pixie called Caspar - sculptor - blagged his way in and persuaded Jack to buy his work! Only blemish was when the Half turned up, with her flock of interns - Amanda, Daisy - posh, dim, big hair, big teeth. The Half Witch looking daggers, as usual. Helen Brooker said she has 'a face like a witch doctor's rattle.' Cruel. Untrue. Made me laugh!

Kitty riffled through pages of shopping trips and 'fabulous' meals. At least Kitty knew that Marisa had a friend - or a colleague - Helen Brooker. Another lead to check out when Kitty reached home. After four pages the writing stopped. There were a couple of half finished sentences then a page of sketching and doodles. Then two pages were blank, though the date had been written at the top. April the 20th and 21st. When the narrative resumed, on the 25th, something had changed. Her gushing gave way to more reflective comments. Even the writing changed, the line becoming faint, the tone uncertain.

'A strange day. It feels like the end of something. The next stage is beginning - whatever that may be! I'm Jack's wife - but my dreams are my own.'

Kitty reached the section in which 'C' was mentioned. That oblique entry was the only mention she made of him. It seemed likely that 'C' was Caspar, the pixie from the party. Marisa was describing a visit to a beach. This was not a return to her holiday brochure style. The entry was starred and was as cryptic as the last.

'Our picnic - champagne, olives, bread, eaten on the bedroom floor. Dressed and walked on the beach. It's real. This time, it's real!'

All around the carriage passengers stirred, reaching for bags and coats as the train slowed. They glided through London. As Kitty read the passage again the significance became clear.

None of us ever see the world quite as others do - ego always gets in the way. Our view is filtered through our hopes and dreams and prejudices. The moment Marisa fucked Caspar, her world changed. Her view of it was distorted, skewed by sex, by her desire for a man she barely knew. Marisa had fallen in love. And when we're in love, we see everything anew. To Marisa, Caspar Greene was a beautiful, clever, talented lover. To her, the world looked magical.

CHAPTER TWENTY SIX

KITTY ARRIVED HOME at midnight. In a moment her eyes closed too. She fed the cat and lay on the bed. She heard nothing until seven o'clock the next morning when her eyes sprung wide. She was awake in a moment, certain that she had heard a noise.

'Molly?' She tilted her head, listening for a reply. Then she remembered that her daughter was still in Paris. She moved from room to room. Merlin lay asleep on her bed but the house was empty.

She splashed cold water over her face, dressed and swallowed a mouthful of tea. The traffic was light. She yawned as she drove to work. It would be mid morning in Paris, the heat steadily rising. Taking Molly there had been right : she needed to get to know her father. As the car took a rise Kitty imagined her own father was sitting behind her. She glanced in the mirror, expecting to see his smile. The dead rarely appear in the back seat of a Saab.

At the office there would be an avalanche of paperwork - dozens of messages to chase up - fragments of something and nothing. They mattered, but did not engage her. In her mind she moved through the Lyndon house, floating through the front door, gliding up the stairs, drifting into every room. What had really happened there?

The break allowed Kitty to see everything a little more clearly. It was time to change tactics. She made a mental list of who to call, now that she was running the investigation. The first name was Jack Lyndon. Vipond seemed to lack curiosity about his role. She wondered about Lyndon's link to Honor Blackett - they 'went back a long way.' She needed to speak to the elusive Helen Brooker - Marisa's colleague. And she needed to hunt down Caspar Greene - the man she suspected was the 'C' of Marisa's journal. Perhaps Saul Kemp might yield something new, if she spoke to him without Vipond present. Kemp would be hostile, though he might talk if, as he claimed, he was innocent.

Saul has a nasty side - that does not mean he's guilty.

As she parked the Saab she had a vision of her desk, the surface covered in Post-It notes. More notes fluttered down from above, pink and yellow paper, falling like snow, gathering in drifts, covering her desk and then her face. It was time to play dirty. Instead of going inside the station she crept back to her car. She called Reception.

'It's Kitty Lockwood. I need to leave a message for Tony Vipond?'

'Want to speak to him?' said the voice. 'He's just walked down the corridor.'

'No! Just leave him a note? Say I'll be in later. I'm calling at the hospital first. To check on Marisa Lyndon. Then I'm dropping in on Cath Fletcher. I need a signature from her.' Before the voice could reply, Kitty broke the connection.

Since her last visit the wound on the side of Marisa's head had faded to a lemony yellow. Kitty wondered if the inside of her head was healing in the same way. Now that Marisa's would-be killer was in custody, there was nobody guarding her. Kitty returned to the desk.

Honor Blackett was at the nurses' station. Honor leaned over the counter, chatting to a couple of nurses. There was laughter as the nurses opened a box of chocolates. Honor turned her dazzling smile in Kitty's direction.

'Kitty?' She waggled the box. 'Want one?' There was a rustle of paper, a glimmer of purple and gold.

'Thanks. I'll leave it.'

'Go on! They're slimming!'

'Really?'

Honor threw back her head and laughed. 'Of course not!' She popped a chocolate between her lips. 'How's the patient?'

'Mrs Lyndon's looking better, don't you think?' This was aimed at the nurses, who both nodded.

'Still very serious, I guess?' Honor frowned.

'Doctor Hobart could give you details. I'm pleased you're here,' said Kitty. 'Any chance of a chat?'

'May I take a peep at poor Marisa first? Just for a moment?'

Whitey had never forgotten what he did to his father. The last time he saw him was the night Whitey slit open his cheek. They never spoke again. When Whitey was doing his three stretch the governor called him in to the news. Peter White had a heart attack, brought on by the booze. The governor pushed the letter across his desk.

'Of course, we'll give you compassionate leave. To attend the funeral.'

Whitey stared at the paper. He knew they were waiting for him to say something.

'Can I go now, boss?'

Whenever he recalled his father, he felt an odd mixture of emotions. There were fragments of happiness - times when they laughed together. Whitey would never admit it, but he missed him. His father was the only family he knew.

The last three months of Whitey's sentence was spent in adult prison. In the weeks before they shipped him out Whitey grew anxious. Some of the screws delighted in scaring the young men in their care. There was sly, knowing laughter about what would happen in the showers. Whitey hid a shiv in his bed but the screws found it. They shipped him out first chance they had.

In Acklington, the adult prison, Whitey spent the first week avoiding the other cons. His plan was to stay low until he sussed how the gaol worked. They padded him up with an older man. The bloke was overweight but well built, over six foot with broad shoulders and a shaved head. He said little, rolling over to sleep when Whitey moved in.

On the third day it all kicked off. The cons were on 'association.' The doors to all the pads were open and the lads mingled, watching telly or playing games. Officers leaned against the wall and gossiped, only half an eye on the room.

Whitey stayed in his pad and read 'Anatomy of the SS State'. He dozed off, half hearing the click of the pool balls and the hum of chatter outside. He woke to find a figure by his bed. Blinking his eyes he saw a shape, in denims and grey jumper, stinking of tobacco. He felt a hand on his crotch. The old bastard was grinning down at him. Whitey was about to shout when a knuckled fist cracked the side of the man's head. He hit the floor, groaning as he crouched on hands and knees. Whitey's cellmate kicked the old con in the kidneys. The con howled and curled into a ball. By then

Whitey was on his feet and they both hoofed the old bastard as he crawled from the cell.

Whitey mumbled his thanks. His cellmate flopped onto his bunk. Then he closed his eyes and rolled over.

'They call me Whitey.'

'I know,' said his cellmate.

'Clive.' In a few seconds Clive's breathing slowed. It was not long before Whitey heard the deep, rhythmic snort as his protector began to snore.

Honor stared at Marisa, watching her chest rise and fall. Kitty glanced at her companion. The glow from the bedside lamp shone on the side of Honor's face. Every detail of her appearance was perfect. Her hair was immaculate, each strand falling into place. As ever, her outfit was immaculate - her clothes perfectly cut and chosen with care. The tailored suit was black, the earrings silver. A silver bangle gleamed at her wrist.

'Poor kid.' Honor dabbed a tear from her cheek.

'You take the chair,' said Kitty. Honor sat by the bed.

'I just wanted to see her. There's no change.' This almost a whisper, as if Honor was talking to herself. Kitty had become so used to the sigh of the ventilator that she had forgotten Marisa Lyndon was a living person. Her life had stopped, though she was not yet dead.

'Fancy a coffee?' said Honor, arching her eyebrows.

They faced each other across the table. As Honor pushed her spoon through the muddy liquid, Kitty studied her face.

Must take hours.

The grooming seemed to be a kind of armour, a carapace that she wore to fend off the world. Only the faint lines at the corner of her eyes betrayed her age.

'Poor Jack.'

'You know him well, don't you?'

Honor took off her gloves and placed them on the table, by her cup. 'We've been friends a long time. We're from the same town.'

'In Cumbria?'

Kitty detected a wariness. 'It's just you have a similar accent.'

Honor smiled. 'Of course.'

'You mentioned Caspar Greene. On that first night.'

'Did I?'

'You said Caspar would be devastated.'

'It hit me like a train. All of us. Everyone who knew her.'

'But there was a reason it affected Caspar in particular?'

Honor lifted her face, meeting Kitty's eyes. She laughed then put her hand to her mouth. 'What a *terrible* thing! I've a confession. I've forgotten your name!'

'Kitty. Kitty Lockwood.'

'Of course!' Honor wafted a hand, mocking her own ditziness. 'I'm *so* sorry, Kitty! What an idiot! I meet so many people! Sometimes I forget. It's easier to call everyone 'darling.'

Kitty blinked as she tried to work out what had just happened.

'What were you saying, darling?'

'Caspar?'

'Well - they were close, at one time. Marisa was going to make him a star!' Honor's eyes twinkled as she studied Kitty over the rim of her cup.

Kitty recalled the search items on Marisa's Mac. 'They planned to go to New York, didn't they?' She was fishing now.

'New York?' Honor shrugged. 'I really have no idea.' Her smile was a little too bright. 'Is that so?'

Kitty placed her cup on its saucer.

Count to five...One...two...

'That would never work,' said Honor. 'Caspar doesn't let anyone 'help' him for very long.'

'You were giving him advice, weren't you? For a while?'

'For about five minutes, yes!'

'What happened?'

Honor rested her fingers on Kitty's wrist. 'I'm the star of PR, darling - not artist management. That's a very different game. To be honest I just didn't know what I was doing! That world - art - it's foreign to me. Different rules. Fortunately, we drifted apart before I signed a contract. Caspar's too hard to handle.'

'In what way?'

'He pretends to listen to advice - then does whatever he feels like. It's like talking to the wind!' Honor looked at Kitty for a moment, as if making up her mind. 'As it happens, I have offered to step in. For now. Just while Marisa is...unwell.'

'That's kind.'

'It's the least I can do! I don't do anything, actually. I have one of the girls - Daisy - handle his diary. I keep well out of it. Caspar is quite, quite crazy, I'm afraid.'

'You mean a little eccentric?'

'It comes with the creative thing, doesn't it? You know, he'll spend months working on a piece then set fire to it! Or you spend a week arranging an interview for the little sod then he'll not turn up! Or I admire Marisa for taking him on.'

'He's unstable?'

Honor looked down, tapping her fingernail on the table. She turned her sparkling eyes on Kitty.

'He's charming, in many ways. But he is quite capable of violence.' She held Kitty's gaze. 'Yes. I'd say. Quite capable of that.' Honor gathered her things together, pulling her gloves tight, smoothing the fingers. 'It's been lovely to meet you again! Even if it was not in the sweetest of circumstances!' Her fingers rippled along Kitty's forearm. 'Now, I must fly!'

They rode the lift down to the car park. Above the faint whiff of Cutan Handwash, Kitty caught the scent of something more exotic. 'That's a beautiful perfume.'

'Scent,' said Honor. 'Sorry!' She shook her head. 'That sounded awful! The training runs deep.'

Kitty said nothing.

'I used to sell the stuff. A long time ago!' She twisted her face. '*Call it scent ladies, never perfume!*' She held out her wrist. Kitty put her nose to Honor's skin and inhaled. 'What is it?'

'It's called '*Whoso List To Hunt.*'

'Right,' said Kitty. 'Whoso list to hunt *what*?'

'A deer, I believe. It's from a poem. Sir Thomas Wyatt. Pretentious! It's made by *Black Phoenix Alchemy Lab*. I love all their stuff but this is sex in a bottle!'

Kitty imagined her sales technique, rocking back on a spike heel, scoping every passing customer.

'I get all sorts of freebies, in my line! It's funny. I used to work their concession. On my feet, all day long on for eighty quid. Now I arrange the launch parties. I get thirty times that. I'll find you some, if you like?'

'Thank you,' said Kitty. She rarely used scent, yet she needed to connect with this woman. As the lift doors opened Honor turned and kissed Kitty on both cheeks.

'This is a terrible business! We must do what we can to make it right.' The door clunked. Kitty rapped on the glass and the window purred open.

'I'd like a longer chat, at some point.'

'We're so busy at the moment. Deadlines!'

'I wouldn't ask if it wasn't important.'

Honor handed her a card. Kitty noticed there was no mobile number. 'Shall I call your mobile?'

'Got rid of mine years ago. There's no escape with a moby, darling! If you want to arrange a date call the agency - speak to Daisy. Or Amanda. The girls will get the message to me.'

'I'll do that - thanks. Is your home address on here?'

'I'm in town during the week.' Honor tapped her card. 'This address is my apartment. At weekends I have my bolt hole - out in the wilds. Just me and Spike. The dog, in case you're wondering!'

The Maserati Gran Cabrio rolled down the ramp, tyres squealing as they took each bend. Kitty walked towards her own car, tapping Honor's card against her lip. It carried her scent. Kitty knew she had encountered it before.

Though Honor Blackett claimed Marisa was little more than an acquaintance, she knew Jack Lyndon well. If she had witnessed even a single instance of violence, that would be worth hearing about. She knew Caspar Greene too, of course. Her choice of words was odd, Kitty reflected. Honor said that she and Caspar had 'drifted apart.' Perhaps she had intended to say 'parted company.'

Kitty neared home she remembered where she had encountered Honor's strange, haunting scent. It was in the hall of Marisa Lyndon's home, on the morning that she was attacked.

Kitty searched her phone for Cathy Fletcher's address. She knew the Fletchers lived in an upstairs flat somewhere in the west end of the city. Canning Street was part of a tight grid of Victorian terraces which sloped down to the river. Cobblestones peeked through holes in the crumbling tarmac. Kitty parked outside number 71. The door was painted in a subtle shade of green - Bryson would know the name, no doubt. The doors on either side were covered in dust, their paint chipped and flaking.

Kitty clocked the front step of the Fletcher house, the stone scrubbed clean. The brass letterbox gleamed in the afternoon sun. She looked up and down the street. While many of the flats had shabby nets Cath Fletcher's blinds were a spotless white. Across the road a bunch of Bangla kids played cricket against the wall. 'Shabash!' they shouted at each other, laughing as they chased the tape ball. The leafy avenues of the Callerton Chase estate were a world away.

Kitty lifted the brass knocker, then stopped. All she needed to do was drive back to the office and send the case files to the Crown Prosecution Service. Once she went inside the Fletcher house, she was on her own. She opened her fingers and let the knocker fall. She heard footsteps. The door inched open and Cathy Fletcher peeped out.

'Hi Cathy.'

Cath Fletcher looked over Kitty's shoulder. It was clear that to be seen talking to the police was the last thing she wanted.

'We need to talk about Marisa.'

Cathy slipped the security chain and stood back, allowing Kitty inside.

'Sorry. Would you mind taking off your shoes?'

It was a moment before Kitty understood.

'Of course! No problem.' Kitty shucked off her shoes and they climbed the stairs to the flat. The air was scented with cut flowers and leather polish. Kitty crossed the sitting room to stand in the bay window. Down below the Bangla kids screamed with laughter. The walls were oatmeal, the pile on the cream coloured carpet ankle deep. A reproduction of Monet's *Sunrise* hung above the coal effect gas fire, the sky and lake shimmering in soft blue and beige.

'Mike's on a late. He won't be back till midnight.'

'What does Mike do?'

A beat before Cathy replied. 'He's on the cabs.'

'That's hard work!' said Kitty.

'He loves it!' Cathy Fletcher perched on the edge of a seat. She shook her head. 'I heard about Saul. Can't believe it!'

'Can't believe he was involved?'

Cathy Fletcher shook her head. 'Any of it! This whole thing's like a nightmare.' She ran her fingers through her hair. Her face was wan, pale shadows beneath her eyes.

'I don't suppose you've got a cup of tea, Cathy?'

'Just bags.'

'Teabags are fine. Milk. No sugar.'

Cathy disappeared into the kitchen. Kitty wandered around the room. She peered at the painting above the fireplace. *Sunrise* was a landscape, two dark blue boats crossing the water at dawn, orange light glittering on silver blue water. Kitty peered at framed photos on the wall - Cathy and a beefy looking man - husband Mike, she guessed. They were tanned, smiling, somewhere hot and sandy. There were no pictures of children. A photo of Cathy and Marisa, smiling, their arms around each other, hung on the wall. Two blond women, Marisa younger by a few years. Cathy looked similar, in many ways, though her face was more lined.

'I'm trying to find Marisa's friends.' Getting no reply, Kitty wandered through to the kitchen. 'Wow!' Her surprise was genuine. Cathy's kitchen was immaculate. A Thermador oven, a Smeg fridge, a Fisher & Paykel dishwasher had been wedged into the tiny room. Such luxury seemed surprising in a tiny flat in a poor area of the city.

'It's Mike's pride and joy. He does all the cooking. I get fed up with kitchens! Cleaning them all day.'

'I can imagine!' Kitty wondered how they could afford it. 'I'd like to ask you a couple of questions about Marisa.'

Cathy stirred milk into the tea. 'Shall we go into the front room?'

Kitty shook her head. 'Here's fine.' They faced each other across the kitchen table.

'Did you ever help out at the Lyndon's parties?'

Cathy blew across the surface of her drink. She placed the drink on the table. 'Sometimes.'

'I'm wondering about a garden party? A few weeks ago?'

Cathy clutched her drink. When she set it down on the table, the liquid slopped onto the surface. She sprang to her feet and ripped a sheet of paper towel from the dispenser. 'I thought this was all sorted out?' She mopped up the liquid, dabbing at the surface, catching every drop. 'You've charged Saul.' It did not take much to unsettle her. Kitty held her gaze until Cathy could stand it no longer. 'Marisa asks me to help out. If there's a party.'

'This was a garden party. Late April. What was the occasion?'

'I can't remember.' Cathy shrugged.

'Was it business?'

'I have *no* idea!'

'Who were the guests?'

She glared at Kitty. 'What's this about?'

Kitty put her hands on the table, stretched her fingers.

'It's about finding the person who hurt Marisa.'

Cathy Fletcher dropped the sodden kitchen roll in the bin. The lid shut with a clang.

'There must have been about fifty, sixty people.' Her brow furrowed. 'It was a lovely day. Sunny. A Friday afternoon. April the thirteenth, I think. Or the fifteenth? Middle of the month, anyway. It was still chilly outside but everyone wanted to be in the sun. I was run off my feet. Dishing out the food. Serving. Sorting. Getting drinks. Scuttling around with trays.'

'Was it some special celebration?'

'I don't know. *I'm* not socialising! I just fetch and carry!'

'Was it mostly friends?'

'When Jack and Marisa have a party... ' Her brow creased and Cathy looked around her kitchen. 'I mean, if *I* had a party it would be my friends. My family. But with Marisa and Jack it's more about meeting people. Making connections.'

'It's business?'

Cathy nodded her head. 'That's why they're lonely, aren't they? Those sort of people. It's all about making money.'

Kitty was surprised at the glint of defiance in Cathy Fletcher's eyes.

'Was Marisa lonely? Lonely enough to cheat on Jack?'

Cathy turned to look through the window. It seemed she had said too much.

'What sort of people were there?'

'All kinds! Footballers. Business people. Models. You know! Pretty people...'

'How did Saul Kemp fit in?'

Cathy shook her head. 'He stood on the edge of the pool, by himself. He was holding his glass in those great hands, trying to eat canapes. Huge fingers wrapped around these fiddly bits of food.'

'Did you speak?'

'I gave him a wink. You know?'

'Tell me about the other people.'

Cathy shook her head. Kitty took out her phone. 'This might help.' She found Marisa's Facebook page and scrolled through the photographs. She turned the phone for Cathy to see. It was the picture of the puckish, red haired man, his arm around Marisa and the woman with ash blond hair. He looked like the cat with all the cream.

'What can you tell me about him?'

Cathy wrinkled her nose. 'Caspar Something... Fell in love with the mirror, that one...'

'A bit full of himself?'

'Full of shit! Sorry.'

'Marisa's beside him here?'

'She was helping him.'

'Helping with what? His art?'

Cathy snorted. 'That's one way of putting it!'

'Tell me about him.' Kitty saw the shutters fall. Cathy Fletcher had said too much. 'Come on, Cathy.'

'He gets people to do what he wants, that one. That's all I'm saying.'

'He manipulates people?'

'Helen wouldn't have anything to do with him.'

'Helen Brooker?'

'She and Mrs Lyndon work together. She has this gallery in town. She's sharp. Helen saw right through the little toerag. But he had Marisa running around, making phone calls, introducing him to folk. People who would help his career.'

'Maybe I should talk to Helen?' But Cathy wasn't listening. She was peering at the tiny screen on Kitty's phone.

'Her too.'

Cathy tapped the screen at the woman on the other side of Caspar Greene. 'She was another one running around after him.'

'Honor Blackett?'

Kitty studied the image on her phone. 'Of course. Honor and Jack were old friends, weren't they?' Cathy gave her the hard stare, her lips tight. She was not so easily duped.

'She was the little bleeder's agent. Or manager. Whatever you want to call it.'

'How did the party go? Everybody looks happy.'

'It went fine...' She let the sentence hang, staring at Kitty for a moment. She shook her head. 'It's not my place. Tittle tattle.'

'Cathy. You know how serious this is...'

Cathy Fletcher sighed. She twisted her wedding ring around her finger. 'I heard them. There was an almighty row. I don't like to think about it. I kept myself busy, made a lot of noise when I was washing the glasses...'

'This was Marisa and her husband?' Cathy twisted the ring, moving it around her pale, thin finger.

'You've been very helpful.'

'Have I?' Cathy looked alarmed.

'Have you any idea where I might find Caspar Greene?'

CHAPTER TWENTY SEVEN

IT WAS AS if Marisa was able to partition her mind, hiding her secret while she lived the rest of her life. Now and then, when she felt safe, she unlocked the box to take a peek. That morning was such a moment.

On Thursday evening Jack would leave for the club at six, as always. His routine never wavered. It gave him the illusion of control. Half an hour later, when she was sure that he was not returning, her taxi would arrive. She would take one bag, that was all. Everything else she would forget. None of it mattered - it belonged to her Old Life. Fifteen minutes to the airport, checking in as late as possible. Once she was airside there would be no turning back. That would be the moment her new life began. She had regrets, of course. Jack had done nothing to deserve the pain he would feel.

On that night he would return home from work, in the small hours. By then she would be five miles high over the Atlantic. He would open the envelope, read her words. Whenever she thought of that moment, she wobbled. Jack's only desire was to make her happy. That was the problem. He tried too hard. He loved her: she was fond of him. That was it. She would never love him. 'NEXT WEEK' was for the best, for both their sakes.

She had doubts about the marriage from the start. Jack was good looking. He was rich and so attentive. But Marisa had drifted into the marriage. She had settled, too soon, for the wrong man. It would have been better if they had never met. She and Jack were not meant to be. In a way, she was doing her husband a kindness. If the break was sharp and clean, it would soon heal. Jack was still good looking, still rich. There would be other women. It was quite possible that one of them would be at his side before Marisa touched down at La Guardia.

Marisa enjoyed the warmth of the sun on her skin. Her thoughts drifted as she fell into the music in her ears. That was the reason she did not hear the doorbell.

She loosened the yellow halter top to drip oil on her skin. Her fingers ran down her stomach, touching the edge of her bikini. Saul might arrive at any moment. It was awkward having him still about the place, mooning at her with his big cow eyes. Needy was never sexy.

Marisa closed her eyes and hummed along to the song. The sunlight through her eyelids darkened, orange to carmine red. She shivered, the hairs on her skin rising as the shadow fell across her body. She opened her eyes and experienced a flicker of recognition. The axe arced through the air and struck the side of her head. The flat of the blade slammed into her skull near the eye socket, shattering the bone. The force of the blow threw her to the ground. She lay beside the pool, her fingers clawing the tiles as she sank into a deep, velvet darkness.

There would be no midnight flight over the Atlantic. No cabin by the lake in Williamstown, upstate New York. No openings at the Tibor de Nagy gallery on Fifth Avenue. No new life.

NEXT WEEK was cancelled.

CHAPTER TWENTY EIGHT

KITTY WAS SLIDING the breakfast dishes into the sink when the doorbell chimed. She opened the door to find a man in a beige overall. He turned and thrust out a package.

'Autograph please?' He held out an electronic pad. The pen skidded over the glass surface.

'This is exciting. Any idea what it is?'

'Not a clue, darling.' He turned away. Kitty held the box to her ear and rattled it. She tore at the box like a kid on Christmas morning. Inside a nest of pastel coloured tissue lay a bottle of scent - '*Whoso List to Hunt*.' She sprayed it on her wrist. It smelled nice, though it was hardly sex in a bottle.

'You smell nice! What *is* that?'

Kitty and Elayne Hawes faced each other across the melamine table. It was mid afternoon and the canteen was almost empty. 'Gift from an admirer?'

Kitty shook her head. 'A freebie.'

'Knew you were too tight to shell out! What's it called?'

'*How to Hunt,* or something.'

Elayne dropped a lump of crystal sugar into her cup. She tapped her spoon on the rim and rested her chin on her hands.

'Does anyone like Vipond?'

'His mum. His wife, I expect. At one time.'

'Divorced,' said Elayne.

'She escaped then?'

Elayne Hawes glanced around, checking that nobody was in earshot. She leaned over the table, dropping her voice still lower.

'Vipond is a double bagger.'

Kitty frowned.

'Imagine someone so sleazy you couldn't imagine shagging him unless he was zipped inside a body bag?'

'Right...'

'With Tony Vipond you wouldn't even want to touch the *bag*

he's in. So he's a...'
'...double bagger!'

For a while Kitty sat at her desk, working her way through the Post-it notes. It was almost eleven o'clock when she brewed a mug of tea and wandered outside to sit on the car park wall. The door opened and Tony Vipond emerged, blinking in the sunlight. When he saw her his face fell but it was too late to go back. He forced a smile.

'Locky! Nice break?'

'Fine, thanks.'

He sat on the wall, leaving a space between them. He lit his cigarette. 'It's time I gave these up.'

'You must be the last smoker in the building.'

'I dunno about that!'

Kitty turned her face to the sun.

'Are we OK?' Vipond shot her an anxious glance. 'I should never drink on an empty stomach. Not clever.'

Kitty stayed silent, letting him stew a little. Then she nodded. The agreement to forget what happened was mutual. He blew smoke. Another minute passed in silence.

'Well. I should get back...' He stood, tapping his cigarette on the wall. 'How's the Lyndon job?'

'Just tidying up the details.'

'You're not still talking to witnesses?' She heard the tension in his voice.

'Nothing major.'

'Good.' Vipond nodded. 'That's good.'

Two 'goods.' That's a first.

As the door closed behind Vipond she walked to her car. Vipond felt guilty. While he immersed himself in his new case she had a period of grace.

Helen Brooker's gallery was housed in an old pallet factory near the river. The building was a bright white cube, the original beams peeping through the plaster. The receptionist read Kitty's id.

'The director's upstairs right now.' 'Supervising a hanging.'

'A member of staff?'

The receptionist's stare was cool.

'Woodcuts.'

Kitty took the stairs. She heard Helen Brooker before she saw her.

'That's out of whack, Steve!' The voice echoed around the gallery. 'This one and the horse one clash. And not in a good way!' As Kitty reached the top stair she saw two figures at the far end of a long gallery. A striking woman in her early thirties raked her fingers through dark red hair. She wore black jeans and boots and rocked back and forth on the heel, tapping the toe on the panelled floor. She stood with one hand on her hip as she scanned the walls. A workman in overalls was holding a framed print. An electric drill lay at his feet. He looked like he was having a bad day.

'I want them like this...' The woman scythed the air with the edge of her hand. 'Bang bang bang!' Helen Brooker became aware they were not alone and turned, looking Kitty up and down.

'Hello?'

Kitty flashed her id. 'Are you Helen Brooker?'

'What's this about?'

'I believe Marisa Lyndon's a friend of yours. Is there somewhere we can talk?'

Helen Brooker turned to her workman. 'Get yourself a coffee Steve. Back in fifteen?' Steve looked grateful as he rested the picture against the wall and ambled down stairs.

'Follow me.' Brooker strode towards the back of the gallery. She marched through a steel door, along a corridor and into a large, well lit office in the corner of the building. Framed pictures lay stacked against the office walls. The desk was bare, save for an earthenware jar filled with pencils, their sharpened points like a bed of nails. Helen Brooker sat behind her desk and pointed to a small chair at the other side.

'I thought all this was wrapped up?' She leaned forward, resting her elbows on the surface. 'I thought you had arrested somebody?'

'We need more information.'

'How is Marisa?'

'There's no change, I'm afraid.'

Helen Brooker flicked her hair behind her shoulder. 'It's awful! *Everyone* loves Marisa! We've all been terribly worried.'

'Have you visited her?'

'I'm up to here at the moment.' She glanced at Kitty then looked away. 'From what everyone is saying there seems little point. She's hardly up for a chat, is she? Sorry if that sounds callous.'

Kitty smiled in her lop sided way.

'*Everyone loves Marisa.* So I'm told. But finding her friends seems more difficult.'

'I haven't been hiding anywhere.'

Faced with Kitty's level gaze Helen Brooker looked ill at ease.

'I need to talk to someone who knows Marisa well. We all confide in *someone*.'

Helen Brooker frowned. She turned her face to the window. Kitty studied her profile - the strong nose, the dark brown eyes which flicked back and forth.

'We were close. Once upon a time.' Helen Brooker's smile was sad. 'I'll tell you something about Marisa. When she first becomes your friend she's all over you. It's very intense. She calls every ten minutes, there are gifts, she tells you her secrets. It's a girl crush. Everything is there. The sun is shining, but only on you?'

Kitty nodded.

'That doesn't last. It just burns out. There was no fight. We're still friends. But she moves on, to the next person. Particularly if there's a man involved.'

'Were there many of those?'

'Some.'

Kitty pursed her lips, searching for the word. 'She's fickle?'

Helen wrinkled her nose. 'She's restless. There's some part of her that is never still. She's always looking for something. I dunno, this sounds like psychobabble but it's like she's not complete. Not the finished article, or something. Like she's fifteen or something. Not a grown up. Does that make sense?'

'She was unhappy with her life? *Is* unhappy...' It was hard to avoid speaking about Marisa in the past tense.

'You have to wonder what happened when she was a kid. She's tight about that.'

'But she has a beautiful home. She has people to take care of the boring stuff - cleaning, cooking, the garden. She has an attentive, wealthy husband...'

'You don't get it? Neither do I! Jack's lovely! Not the sharpest knife in the drawer but he's kind. He's devoted to Marisa. He's a good man.'

'That wasn't enough?'

'She *loved* him. But she isn't IN love with him.'

'Who were the men?'

'People she met through work. Neighbours. You know! It happens. It doesn't *mean* anything...'

'Did it get serious? With anyone?'

Helen Brooker glanced at her watch. 'Perhaps.'

'I need names. She's in a coma. But this may become a murder inquiry.' Helen Brooker stared at the surface of her desk, nodding.

'She had a fling with her gardener. I expect you know about that. Marisa wasn't in love with him. He's too dim.'

'Anyone else?'

'We 'discovered' this sculptor. By discovered, I mean we turned over a rock and there he was.'

'Caspar?'

Helen stared. Kitty feared she had broken the spell. Sometimes it was better to pretend not to know the truth. After a moment, Helen nodded. 'There's no reason artists have to be 'nice' people. They're like everyone else. Some are lovely. Some I wouldn't wipe my boots on.'

'And Caspar Greene?'

'His stuff is...ambitious. Execution. Craft. He's got that. There's nothing much behind it. Don't waste your time looking for any 'meaning.' It's the sort of stuff they plonk in the reception lobby of a bank or a hotel foyer, if they're trying to be 'edgy.' It's cold. Empty. But it sells. Caspar's taken a little talent and ridden it a long way.'

'What's he like?'

'He's...' Helen Brooker plucked a pencil from her jar and twisted it between her fingers. 'He's a manipulative, self centred, lying little toe rag.' She looked up and beamed at Kitty. 'That do for you?'

'Was Marisa Lyndon being taken for a ride?'

'Worse than that. She'd fallen for him. I worry that she was planning to leave Jack and run away with the little sod.'

CHAPTER TWENTY NINE

KITTY SAT IN the car park at Etal Lane flicking through messages on her phone. One was a picture from Molly. She posed with her father in front of a gallery of dinosaur bones in the Musée d'Histoire Naturelle. They were making scary faces, their teeth bared, fingers curled into claws.

The next was from an unknown caller. Kitty listened to an odd, asthmatic wheezing before the recording clicked off. There were three missed calls from Tony Vipond, asking her to make contact. As she sat at her desk he appeared at her side.

'A word.'

Vipond strode towards his office. She followed, her head held high.

'Where have you been for the last two hours?'

'Working.'

'At what, exactly?'

'I went to see Helen Brooker. A friend of Marisa Lyndon.'

'You've a mountain of work here. '

'Also I spoke to Cathy Fletcher about working for the Lyndons. About a garden party, in April. There was an artist there. Named Caspar Greene.'

'So what?'

'He was involved with Marisa Lyndon.' Kitty nibbled the inside of her lip. She was moving into deeper water. 'Cathy suggested I talk to a friend of Marisa's - Helen Brooker. They worked together. Helen told me that Marisa Lyndon was having sex with this man, this Caspar Greene. She was in love with him. And he was conning her.'

'Gossip.'

'We've never spoken to these people! Helen Brooker. Caspar Greene. One was a close friend. The other she was having sex with.'

'We can't question everyone. What's the point? Saul Kemp has a motive. Owns the weapon. Has form for stalking. He's in custody. All you need to do is submit to the CPS. All this other stuff is irrelevant!' Vipond rocked in his chair. Kitty twisted her fingers into a knot. She looked up. Her voice was soft.

'Let me follow it through.'

He looked away, shaking his head.

'Why not?'

'No one's dead, Kitty.' It was the first time he had used her name. 'This is not a murder. We don't have that luxury. We've a man in custody. Good evidence. Leave it.'

She looked Vipond in the eye. 'You owe me this.'

His eyes widened. Her meaning was clear.

'That's blackmail. You little fucking...'

Kitty walked out and returned to her desk. She moved papers around, tapped at the keyboard. Every now and then she looked up, watching Tony Vipond through the plate glass of his office window. As the afternoon wore on, she would see him looking back at her.

Time passes and it gets easier to push what happened to the back of your mind. There is no hand on your shoulder. No knock at the door. Life goes on. Everything continues as usual. People smile, talk to you in the same way.

Surely they can tell?

But it is as if that morning never happened. You have learned to live a double life. Each day you get up and do what needs to be done. You push those images back inside their box. Life goes on.

The Arrivals board flickered, orange pixels flipping in the pale blue light of the terminus. Flight DLH962 from Charles de Gaulle had landed two minutes earlier. Kitty bought a cup of tea from Greggs and sat down to wait. The whistle and hum of the cooling ducts was oddly soothing. Her muscles softened and she stared at the floor, thoughts slipping between the flecks of marble, blue and grey and white. Somewhere the attacker was living their life, hanging on to a guilty secret that would surely overwhelm most people.

The Arrivals door opened and a middle aged couple in pastel leisure wear emerged. They blinked, eyes sweeping the hall, seeking a familiar face. The rumble of suitcase wheels grew louder as the trickle of passengers became a flood. Molly emerged, pale faced and sleepy eyed. It had been only a few days, yet her daughter seemed older. She ran towards Kitty.

'How was your flight?'

'Fantastic! I *loved* it!'

They said little until they had cleared the airport car park. Kitty probed for details but Molly was as careful as ever. The road darkened as the airport was left behind.

'I was wondering…'

'Go on.'

'Dad asked me to ask you something.' Molly looked at the side of Kitty's face. 'Would it be OK for me to go back?'

'Of course! I mean, I'm sure…'

'For longer.'

Kitty felt a stab of jealousy, at the same moment hating herself for it.

'How long?'

'I don't know. A month?'

They drove in silence for a while, deeper into the darkness of the countryside. Guilt mixed with jealousy in Kitty's mind. Letting go was a process, not an event. She thought of how it might be, living a month without her daughter. There was a mixture of excitement and anxiety. Returning home to an empty house for thirty days, thirty nights. Yet she had to learn to let go.

'A month.'

'Thanks mum.'

In the darkness, Kitty smiled to herself.

'No problem. I'll have a wild old time!'

'You're right, you know.'

'About what?'

'Dad. I *do* love him. But he's the same as everyone else…'

CHAPTER THIRTY

'WHAT IS IT you *do* here, Mr Greene? Exactly...'

The shadows were split by a shaft of sunlight which shone through a crack in the roof. Caspar Greene shuffled through the thatch of rust, swarf and metal flake which littered the floor of his workshop. His stained white overall was open to the waist, revealing that he was naked underneath. Caspar reached inside and raked his stomach with long, grubby fingernails.

'I take drugs and masturbate.'

Kitty, picking through the debris with the point of her boot, looked up, thinking she had misheard. 'I'm sorry?'

'That's OK,' he grinned.

'Keeps you out of trouble, does it? All this drug taking and masturbation?'

Caspar affected a lisping whine.' I was lying. I make toys for all the ickle children in Africa.'

Sheets of torn and rusting metal littered the space. The workbench was pitted and gouged like the surface of a dark, distant planet. A mask dangled from an oxy acetylene welding kit.

'Mr Greene, I don't believe a word you say.'

Caspar Greene tore a swatch of cotton waste from a bobbin. Plunging his right hand into a tin of Gunk, he stared at Kitty while his fingers made slurping noises in the goo. He held his fingers close to his nose and sniffed.

'I'm a sculptor, officer. An artist.' He wiped his hands as he sauntered towards her. 'I make real the diaphanous structure of the world.'

'That must be tremendous fun.'

Caspar crushed the cotton into a ball and played keepy uppy before kicking it high. It arced through the air and landed in the bin.

'Yes.' For a moment he looked unsettled. 'It is. Such *tremendous* fun.'

Kitty picked up a car spring, a coil of thick, twisted steel, turning it between her fingers.

'My work is the only thing that matters,' he said. 'I've been labelled a minimalist - which I can live with. And a conceptualist - which I can't.'

'How awful for you.' Kitty picked her way across the floor. 'Do you call this a workshop, or a studio, Mr Greene?'

He spread his arms wide. 'I call it home.'

Kitty moved to take a closer look at the piece in the centre of the floor. A tangle of cylinders and coils fuzed into a human figure, the head thrown back, the mouth wide, eyes turned to the heavens.

'Interesting!' Kitty tapped the metal with her nail. 'It's quite beautiful!'

He soaked up the praise while, at the same moment, dismissing it. 'Beauty isn't relevant. You need to separate art from aesthetics, darling. *Guernica*? The Chapmans' stuff? It's about dissonance. Provocation. Laughter!' He jabbed his finger against his temple. Realising she had pricked a nerve, Kitty decided to goad him further.

'What does this mean then?'

'Nothing! It's what it is. It *defies* meaning!' He spat the word. 'There are no hidden *ideas* there! My work doesn't come from fucking *ideas*.' He grabbed his crotch. 'It comes from desire. From the guts. From the cock!'

'How lovely.'

'We live in a linguistic culture, darling. People don't understand anything unless you've *explained* it! I *never* explain my work. Just as I *never* apologise.'

'Never apologize. Never explain - it's a sign of weakness.'

'I don't know what the fuck you're talking about.'

'You and me both. And by the way, I'm not your darling.'

Though the rant seemed a rehearsed routine, Kitty noticed that Caspar was breathing heavily. He reached out and touched the spring she was holding, tracing his fingertips around the curved metal. 'Sculpture is alchemy.' His hand moved closer, his fingers brushing hers. 'It's mathematics, made flesh.'

He ran his finger over her hand, along her forearm. His fingertips were warm, his hands marked and pitted with cuts and burns. A thin seam of dirt lay beneath each nail. Kitty stood still, as if a snake were crawling up her arm.

'It's a bit like being God,' whispered Caspar.

She bit her lip, fighting laughter. Looking up she saw his eyes blaze. Rage never seemed far from the surface. She moved away, breaking the contact.

'As you know, Mr Greene, Marisa Lyndon is in Intensive Care.' He tore another piece of cotton waste from the roll. 'I was wondering if you could shed any light on what happened?'

'You mean, did I do it?'

Kitty blinked.

'*Did* you?'

Caspar flicked the ball of stained cotton into the bin. '*Why* would I do that?'

Kitty shook her head. 'I have no idea. Why would *anyone* do that?'

'You don't understand why people might become violent? No idea why they might lash out? In passion? Rage? Why do you do this job then?'

'Because I want to understand. I'm curious.'

'Curiosity killed the cat.'

'You were sleeping with Marisa Lyndon?'

'*Very* curious!'

Now it was her turn to close in. She kept her eyes on his until they were inches apart. Caspar looked down, smearing the red stain onto his overall. The pulse in his neck ticked, the skin shiny with sweat.

'Were you?'

'That's all we can expect from life, isn't it?' he said. 'A few good fucks along the way?'

'Mr Greene?'

'Amongst the various things we do to pass the time until we die, sex is one of the best. Don't you think?'

'We're not talking about me.'

He licked his upper lip. 'Call me Caspar. Tell me your name?'

'Lockwood. I showed you my id.'

'Your first name?'

She blinked.

Don't.

'Kitty. My name is Kitty.'

'Kitty. What was your question, Kitty? I'm sorry.'
You're never sorry.
'Were you sleeping with Marisa?'
'Yes.' He leaned close, so that Kitty could feel his breath on her cheek. 'I was fucking her. That doesn't put me in a very exclusive club. Everyone loved Marisa.'

Kitty nodded, one dip of the chin. How many times had she heard that, though never delivered with a sneer, as now.

'Did her husband know?'

He shrugged. 'No idea! We never talked about him.'

'You planned a future together?'

'That sounds sweet! I don't plan anything, Kitty. Life's not like that.' He looked away, biting his lip. 'My parents were killed. In an accident. They went out one morning and...' He shrugged.

'I'm sorry.' She suspected another lie.

'That's why I never plan anything.'

'Did Mrs Lyndon understand that?'

'Again. No idea!'

'So she might have been planning your future together?'

'Well, that rather proves my point. Doesn't it? Planning is a waste of time. Something else always happens.' He leaned across her to tear another hank of cotton. Was this callousness or bravado, Kitty wondered. Caspar Greene seemed indifferent to the fate of his lover. He displayed some of the traits of an antisocial personality disorder - the lies, the aggression, the desire to provoke.

'How long had you been seeing her?'

Caspar shrugged.

'I'd been fucking her for a month. Six weeks?'

'You knew she was married. Why did you keep the relationship going? Sex? Or was it the money?'

'Money?'

'I understand that Mrs Lyndon helped you financially.'

'Whatever success I enjoy is down to me. To my talent. My hard work.' He raised his eyebrows, challenging her to disagree.

'You're saying she didn't help you out?'

'She was a good fuck, Kitty. That was a help. A good fuck.'

'So for you it was just sex?'

'There's an Italian saying. 'Cunt hair is stronger than rope.' Heard that one?'

'Delightful.'

'True, isn't it?'

'Does that mean you wanted to end it, but you couldn't?'

'I don't know. Does it? I told you, I don't make plans.'

Kitty's looked around the workshop. There were tools of all kinds dangling from butcher's hooks - grinders and cutters, routers and rasps, chisels and mallets and hammers. On the wall were outlines of tools had been sprayed in car aerosol paint, the colour of rust. Of course, she reflected, that was of no interest now. The weapon was bagged and tagged in the evidence store. The weapon belonged to Saul Kemp. The known stalker, Saul Kemp, Marisa's spurned lover.

'So Marisa wasn't your manager, or agent?'

'I leave all that to professionals.'

'Who's that? Honor Blackett?'

Caspar Greene nodded.

'She's the one. Now. Unless you want to get undressed, I need to get back to work.'

'Thanks. But I'll leave you to it, Mr Greene.'

'No problem. Darling...'

As she drove home, Kitty laughed, shaking her head. She had not had sex for months, yet had been propositioned by two men in the last week. Apart from that, her progress had been slow. She knew that Vipond would shred her if he discovered what she had been doing. Had Caspar Greene tired of his adoring sponsor and tried to kill her? There was some mystery there. While Caspar claimed that Honor was his manager, she had been eager to state that her unstable client was quite capable of violence. And Jack and Marisa had fought after their garden party. The statistics suggested someone close to Marisa was the attacker. She decided wander a little further down this intriguing path.

And then, just as it all seemed safe, you find the little bitch sniffing about, turning over the stones. Getting so very close. It had to stop. Time to pull in some favours. The secret, in all such matters, was delegation. Find the right man and give them freedom to finish the job.

He knew the lads laughed about him and the old man. Whitey heard the whispers. But they never said a word while Clive was in earshot. On Association, in the exercise yard, when he was working on the kitchens, they all kept their distance. Whitey had heard of Clive Lumley, knew of his reputation. They said that people who crossed Clive disappeared. To some, the protection of someone like Clive was a dream. But Whitey did not see it that way. Life had taught him that there was always a price to pay. He worried that Clive would exact that price. He feared not knowing what the price would be. So he had mixed feelings when Clive told him his news.

'They're shipping me out.'

Clive sat on his cot, rubbing his eyes. Whitey stood by the bed, a brew in each hand. It was as if the floor opened up. 'When?'

'Could be any time. I'm not supposed to know. Keep it under your hat.'

Clive took a sip and screwed his face. 'You put sugar in that?'

'Two. Big spoons.'

'Must be the water.' Clive grimaced as he took another mouthful. 'Where will they send you?'

'Acklington. Then early release.'

Whitey struggled to keep the disappointment from his face.

'Never been inside before,' said Clive. 'First custodial.'

Whitey's jaw dropped. 'Straight? You've never been inside?'

'I don't get caught, son,' Clive grinned. He rubbed his thumb and forefinger together. 'And if I do, that's not the end of the story.'

They sat on his cot, sipping their drinks. Outside there was a buzz of chat as the lads watched the match on telly. Whitey wasn't bothered about football. He wanted to tell Clive he would miss him. He felt anxious, wondering if he would survive without his protector. But he said none of those things.

Clive, read his mind. 'You'll be OK,' he said. 'I'll put the word out.' They clinked mugs in a toast. Whitey felt tears welling so gulped his tea. This man had become his father - a better dad than the real one. He mumbled his thanks.

'It's OK. You remind me of someone.'

Whitey nodded, though he did not understand. He owed Clive. One day he would be happy to pay back the debt.

CHAPTER THIRTY ONE

IT WAS UNUSUAL for Bryson Prudhoe to be late. Inside the cafe Kitty had found the heat oppressive, the clatter of dishes too jarring. She wafted away the first wasp of the summer. Bryson emerged from the crowd and sauntered towards her table.

He's lost weight.

The suit hung loosely about his frame. Bryson would never be thin, but his cheeks were not so plump, his neck seemed easily contained in the collar of his blue shirt.

'Locky!'

He kissed her cheek.

'You've lost weight, Bryson. Hitting the gym?'

'Stress. I've had Harris on my back. Now you've kindly passed Vipond on to me.'

'My pleasure.'

A waitress arrived. Bryson ordered tea and a scone.

'Off your grub?'

'Just eating sensibly.' She saw the shadows beneath his eyes.

'What's up?'

'I have a source.' He looked down, tried again. 'Someone I'm using on this Horror Hotel job.'

A breeze blew along Nelson Street, pushing dust into the air.

'I'm guessing it's about drugs?' Sweet wrappers tumbled along the gutter.

'We don't know. Don't know very much at all. There's nothing on the victim except that he was questioned, as a witness, to a street brawl in Manchester. A bit of late night argy bargy. Members of the Wo Shing Wo taking lumps out of each other.'

He fell silent. Kitty studied his face - the sunken cheeks, the haunted look in his eyes. It came to her in a rush.

'Hang on...Your source?' She leaned forward, dropping her voice another notch. 'It's not Greta is it, by any chance?'

Bryson ran a fingertip along his moustache. Kitty rocked back, her fingers on her lips. The man had such a gift for getting himself into trouble.

'I'm in too deep.' Bryson sipped his drink.

They sat in silence for a few moments, watching the shoppers pass by.

'Do you need me to do anything?'

Bryson shook his head. 'I'll sort it. One way or another. How's the Lyndon job?'

For a moment she said nothing, tapping her lips as she watched his face. She wondered if Bryson was the kind of man who might harm himself. When she spoke again it was in a more measured tone.

'The Viper thinks it's the gardener - Saul Kemp.'

Bryson grinned. 'He's 'The Viper' now?'

'Marisa had a fling then dumped him.'

'Strong motive...'

'He didn't do it! But Vipond doesn't care. There are loose ends he just ignores.'

'Such as?'

'Marisa Lyndon was seeing this artist.'

'Seeing him?'

'Shagging him.' She finished her tea, swirling the leaves around, looking for a pattern. 'And I think she may have been planning to run away with him.'

Bryson's lips formed a tight circle.

'So that puts the husband back in the picture. Insurance?'

'Jack Lyndon's minted.' She shook her head. 'No. Really. He *is*. I've checked the company accounts. The latest figures show a turnover of eleven million, with a profit of three.'

Bryson slit open his scone and smeared a thin seam of butter over the surface. 'So. It's sex. Jealousy?'

Kitty nodded. 'The Lyndons had a huge row about Caspar Greene. The daily told me. Greene admitted to me he was sleeping with her. Her journal confirms that and suggests she was planning to run away with Caspar.'

'She kept a journal? How quaint.' Bryson chomped his scone.

'I think it's Jack Lyndon. A jealous husband about to lose his wife. She's been sleeping with two blokes. All the stats point that way.'

'You need more than statistics.'

'He's sketchy about their CCTV - it was switched off because the foxes were waking him up. Allegedly. I'll admit there's a problem with the timing. But maybe he hired someone to do it. He hires people for everything else!'

Bryson wiped his fingers with his napkin. 'Maybe it's someone else completely. Maybe the victim was being stalked. Someone from her past?'

Kitty turned down her lips, allowing that it might be so.

'Were there any threats by this Saul Kemp?'

'Nope.'

He pushed his hands between his knees and rubbed them together. 'That you know of.'

'There's no complaint. Nothing recorded. The daily, Cathy Fletcher, didn't mention any problems with Kemp. And there's no mention of anything like that in her diary. She barely mentions the gardener. Whatever was going on with him wasn't important to her.'

'She wasn't the wounded party...'

'But she bangs on and on about this artist.' She glanced around the other tables, aware that her voice was turning heads.

'Maybe it wasn't important to her. That doesn't mean it meant nothing to this Kemp. A love affair,' said Bryson. 'is a car with two drivers.'

'Maybe. But I just don't...' Kitty stopped, shaking her head as she saw Bryson's grin.

'You were going to say you just don't *feel* it was him.'

She was grinning now. 'OK. It could be the artist. Could be Kemp's wife. Could be Kemp. Happy?'

'And it could be a burglar.' Bryson licked butter from his fingers. 'And what do you want *me* to say?'

'What I *want* you to say is that I'm right about Jack Lyndon. But I can see I'll wait a long time for that.'

Bryson reached inside his jacket and pulled out his sunglasses. 'No-one wants advice, Kitty. We only want to be told that what we've decided is right.' Bryson cleaned the shades with his tie. 'The best way to give advice is to find out what someone wants to do, then tell them to do it.' He slid his sunglasses onto his face. 'So. What do you want to do?'

'Dig around some more. Build a case against Jack Lyndon.'

Bryson pushed his sunglasses up the bridge of his nose. He grinned. 'Brilliant idea! You should do just that.'

'Really?'

'Nothing I say would stop you, would it?'

'Nope.'

'Happy to be of service.' He picked up the last morsel of scone and pushed it between his lips. 'Look for connections. Sex and money. Who has a stake in this artist? Who was sleeping with him?'

Before she could answer his phone buzzed. His smile faded.

'Sorry. Got to get this.'

She watched him wander away, down the street, his mobile pressed to his ear.

A glass of Merlot rested on the coaster. Kitty placed Honor's card on the laptop keys. She tapped in the *Honor Bryte* address. The graphics on the webpage were tasteful, the colours vivid.

'*Honor Bryte* - The Nutshell Version: We are a creative agency We offer an array of services, expertise and connections in PR, event production and content origination We work across a range of brand-sectors: design, fashion, film, food & drink, beauty, travel, restaurants and music.'

It was the usual blether. 'We track sentiment, sniffing the wind of social media. We deliver actionable counsel based on our findings.'

When Kitty tapped *About Us*, it came as no surprise that a shot of Honor Blackett appeared. Honor's smile was bright and wide. Her teeth were immaculate. Viking blue eyes peered back, sharp and sparkling blue. Her hair was blond, enhanced to a dazzling white. Hers was a hard beauty, all surface sheen and shine.

Kitty read the bio. 'At eighteen, Honor moved to Paris to work as an interpreter, but instead joined Benetton. She moved to London to become a buyer for the company. This led to a buying position at Selfridges, where she remained for five years before settling on a career in PR.' There was a quote from Honor. 'You have to cast a vibe and tell a story - if you don't, it's just stuff...'

The text was the usual soufflé, vapid boasts about understanding the media 'mindset' and branding the image into the mind of a target audience. The clients were more impressive - a list of national and international names, garnished with logos and brands. Kitty sipped her wine as she trawled the blog. When she tapped 'Older Posts' it began to get interesting. Here was an item about Caspar Greene. 'Caspar is interested in blurring what is and what is not present. 'My work is about passion - not ideas. It is more about the skin, the heart, sex and desire than thought. It's about the struggle between lightness and darkness.' Honor Bryte PR is delighted to promote this super-talented and controversial sculptor.'

It was headed by an image of Honor and Caspar at a party. Honor's smile looked sincere, while his eyes were glazed, looking elsewhere. She leaned towards Caspar, her right hand near his side, as if reaching for him. Honor, as ever, trying just a little too hard. Kitty sent an e-mail, asking for a convenient time to call by.

Tony Vipond and Colin Harris faced each other across a desk in a side office. Vipond was reading a report Harris had written to get the new SIO up to speed. Vipond enjoyed feeling the anxiety in the other man. Now and then he nodded, moving quickly to the next sheet as he dropped the last on his desk. He had no intention of making it easy. He reached the last page and tossed it onto the pile.

'So you think it was a professional job?'

Harris ran his hand over his buzz cut hair. 'The violence was excessive. Far more than needed. But it cannot be an impulse thing. And the message seemed to be - 'Don't fuck with me!' Or us.'

'You've got the Fat Policeman on the team? The Bison?'

'Yes.' Harris smiled, eager to divert Vipond's fire from himself. 'Prudhoe has his own theories, of course.'

'Which are?'

'Who the fuck knows?' said Harris. 'He's following his own line at the moment. I can't say we're greatly missing his input. He knows he's hanging onto his job by a thread.'

'Thank you for coming to see me, Mrs Lockwood.'

'I'm not married.'

Mrs Loveridge appeared not to hear. Her office was tiny, little more than a cupboard with windows. Kitty's knees were almost touching those of the Deputy Head. The desk was covered with a pile of blue exercise books.

'It's about an incident which has just come to light.'

Kitty braced herself.

'I've had a word about the shoplifting. Molly has assured me it won't happen again. It is totally out of character.'

'It's not about the shoplifting. It's about the fight in the Riverside Park.'

Mrs Loveridge pushed aside the exercise books and picked up a sheet of paper. 'I've had a complaint from the parents of Lorelle Ferrier. Molly attacked their daughter and two of her friends. One of the girls had to be taken to Casualty. A scratched cornea.'

'Really?'

Loveridge leaned forward. She assumed what was meant to be a sympathetic smile. 'Molly has never shown any sign of violence before. She's usually very quiet. But...Girls are worse than boys in this, I'm afraid. Girls just don't have the concept of a fair fight. Do they?'

All Kitty could do was to nod in agreement.

'With boys, they hit each other and then it blows over,' said Loveridge. 'It stops as quickly as it starts. But with girls, it's all or nothing. Girls may be reluctant to fight - but when they start, nothing can stop them. It's a fight to the death!'

As she drove away from her meeting with the Deputy Head her feelings were mixed. She felt embarrassment at Molly's behaviour. Anger that she had been bullied. Pride that she had fought back.

She pulled into a gateway on a country road, not far from the airport. The sun glinted on the bonnet. A gentle breeze swayed the tops of the ash trees. On the far side of the valley the rape had turned the fields a buttery yellow.

Kitty had stepped in to several fights between women. They were fuelled by alcohol and jealousy in most cases. She had not expected violence from her own daughter. It was one of those moments which made her look at the world in a new way. She took out her phone and checked her e-mails. There was no reply from Honor/Bryte. She found Honor's black and silver business card and punched the numbers.

'You're listening to the voice of Honor Blackett at Honor/Bryte. None of us are here right now. Leave a message and we'll get right back.'

'Hello, Honor. It's Kitty Lockwood here.' She paused. 'I hate to talking to machines. I sent you an e-mail asking to meet but haven't heard back. I was wondering if you were free for a chat?' Kitty hoped that Honor was listening in and would pick up. 'You know - what I'm going to do is swing by your flat and give you a knock. I'm nearby,' she lied. 'Be with you in ten minutes.'

She ended the call. Honor had been involved with Jack Lyndon. She claimed to be a friend of Marisa. She had glossed over her connections to Caspar Greene. Kitty had put off this conversation for too long.

Such a wonderful day. A client leaves a message, saying how happy they are. You play the recording a couple of times, to see if they mean it. Sales have spiked, they say. They want to extend your contract for another year.

You open the papers and it's all there : you read the coverage for the brand in all the locals and a couple of nationals. There's a splash in the *Independent* and a photo spread in *Living North*.

Around five you get another call. This is something different. Icy fingers curl around your heart. They want to take you down. They want to drag you back into that hole.

That can't happen.

CHAPTER THIRTY TWO

BRYSON WAITED IN the beer garden with a tumbler of fizzy water, watching droplets slide down the glass and soak into the dry wood. Somewhere in the sky above a skylark sang - an innocent sound that belied the events below. Bryson shielded his eyes as he looked into the blue sky, searching for the tiny bird.

He caught her scent. Greta smiled, her eyes hidden behind sunglasses as she crossed the lawn. She wore a white dress with slim, spaghetti straps. Her skin glowed, tanned to light caramel.

'Let me get you a drink.'

The barmaid raised an eyebrow as he approached. He guessed she had marked them down as a cheating couple. He wanted to explain, to tell her that it was more complicated than that.

I'm police. She's married to a drugs king. This is about a businessman who was murdered. You're young. Things are never black and white.

Instead, he asked for a pint of Wylam Bitter and a white wine spritzer. As he placed the drinks on the table Greta was fixing her lips. He watched her smear the rich goo on her mouth. She smiled, clicked the compact and slipped it into her bag.

'Vanity.'

'Plenty to be vain about...'

Inside, Bryson cringed at his clumsy compliment. But Greta smiled. He glimpsed danger there. Was she playing him because it amused her? Or was it because it was handy to have a cop in your pocket when your business is dealing drugs?

The Phoenix Building was a converted office block which overlooked the waterfront. The lift rose with a gentle sigh, oiled wheels spinning in the darkness. Kitty soared from the Quayside to the tenth floor in seconds. She glimpsed the river below, the afternoon sun glittering on cola coloured water. The door hissed open and she found herself in a dimly lit corridor. Honor Blackett stood at the open door of her apartment, hands extended in welcome.

'Hooray! You found me!'

Honor pulled Kitty into a lingering hug. If she was angry she made a good fist of hiding it. Kitty was wrong footed, unsure when a police visit had become a social call. It felt odd to walk into a loft apartment she recognised from a magazine article. The room was vast, the brick walls framed by steel girders, the floor polished cedar.

'Drink? Tea? Coffee? Wine? I've just opened a bottle?' Honor spreads her hands wide. 'It's Friday evening!'

In a moment the glass was in Kitty's hand. The wine touched her lips and she felt the buzz. 'Thanks for seeing me. I wanted to ask you...'

'You just caught me, to be honest. Friday evenings I head out to the country. I was just on my way.'

'Sorry! I won't keep you...'

'Come.' Honor took Kitty's hand and steered her to the window. The afternoon sun glittered on the river below. The breeze whipped foam into ragged lines along the surface.

'This is what I work for,' said Honor. She stretched an arm along Kitty's shoulders. 'Well, one reason...' 'What was it you wanted to ask me about?' Her voice was soft, a purr. The wine was working and it took Kitty a moment to gather her thoughts. Honor's arm was warm, softly curling around her neck. Kitty enjoyed the sensation. It had been some time since anyone had touched her in that way.

'I just wanted to know...' Kitty's mind was feathers. Why *had* she wanted this meeting? When Honor turned her pale blue eyes towards Kitty, she tried again. 'We're following up the interviews with Marisa's friends.'

A tiny furrow appeared at the bridge of Honor's nose. Kitty sensed her concern was faked. 'Has there been any change? Is Marisa OK?'

Kitty ignored the question. 'Tell me about Jack Lyndon.'

'Jack?' Honor's stare was glassy.

There's something...

'How well do you know him?'

Honor gazed at the river. 'I feel awkward talking about personal matters, Kitty. When my friend lies in a coma.'

The shutters were up. Kitty tried a more oblique approach. She sipped her wine, made a point of looking around the apartment. 'It's so quiet up here!'

'Any place I live has to be calm, Kitty. Tranquil.'

'Did you get the e-mail I sent?'

'I avoid screens at the weekend, Kitty. There's an answerphone. Anyone who wants to reach me can! How many ways do we NEED to stay in touch with the same people, for heaven's sake? There's something cheap about being available 24/7. Don't you think?'

'You must lose business?'

'I have more business than I can handle, darling! Look - *I* decide where and when I work. If I don't like a client, *ptoof!*' She blew across her pursed fingers. 'Gone! The girls in the office are diamonds. I'd trust Daisy with my life! Hire the right people for the job! That's the secret. Delegate!'

She took Kitty's glass. Kitty looked down at the river, hearing the wine glooping into her glass.

'You have no idea how *sexy* being unavailable is, Kitty! Trust me!'

Never trust anyone who says 'trust me.'

'I'm bored with PR, to be honest.' Honor handed Kitty her wine. 'This might sound wanky, I suppose, but what I do these days is fortune telling. Not tarot cards and tea leaves but looking into the future. Business needs to know what's going to happen in five, seven years. They're so slow to adapt! They pay me to predict trends. That sort of knowledge is gold!'

'What sort of things do you tell them?'

'Well...There's a backlash coming against the net, for example. It eats the brain. Trust me! We're becoming aware of this monster we created. Technology should be our servant, not our master.'

'It makes my job easier.'

Honor tipped her glass in a salute.

'Well it would! Exactly! It's all about surveillance. Consumption. Slavery, not sensuality!' She sipped her wine. Kitty watched the way her throat moved, the line of her neck, her lipstick on the glass. Honor moved closer. 'The future lies in the sensual world.' She touched Kitty's arm. 'Not the virtual one.' Her voice was low. 'What beautiful skin.'

Honor caressed her arm with the backs of her fingers. Kitty

watched the hand slide over her skin. It seemed that movement was impossible. Honor's fingers moved onto her shoulder, slipping around her neck. She was pulled into a soft, warm kiss. She tasted wine, felt the tongue dancing along her lips. Then Kitty's mobile chirped. The kiss ended. Honor Blackett was gazing into her eyes.

'You see? *That* was real. You'll remember that moment for the rest of your life...' Her smile was warm. '...whether you enjoyed it, or not! How many e-mails will you remember? It's the touch of another person. That is what matters. Touch is real.'

Kitty was surprised to find that she still held her glass. How it had survived the kiss was a mystery. The phone nagged on, chiming the '*I Fought the Law*' ringtone. With a sardonic smile, Honor relieved her of her glass. She tipped her head towards the phone. 'No escape. Tethered goat...'

Kitty did not recognise the caller id. The ringtone stopped and the red light indicated she had a message. Moving to the window she put the phone to her ear. As she listened, her lips parted.

'Hi. Hope that's Kitty Lockwood? It's Caroline Hobart. Doctor Hobart. At the Infirmary? It's about Marisa Lyndon.'

Kitty listened to the rest of the message, then closed her phone. Honor Blackett was watching her.

'Why don't you come to my place in the country? Now. Tonight!'

Kitty tapped her phone against her lip.

'You'll love it!' said Honor. 'Seriously! It's like an eagle's nest. I can see for miles! See everything very clearly. See my enemies coming.' Honor drew closer. 'You look like you've had a shock.'

'That was the Infirmary.'

Honor Blackett's smile was frozen.

'Marisa Lyndon.'

'Oh yes?'

'It seems she's woken up.'

CHAPTER THIRTY THREE

THE TUBES OF the nasal cannula were in place. The monitors pulsed to their steady rhythm. Marisa Lyndon's eyes were closed but the bruising on her head had faded to a pale yellow.

It might be better to stay out...

Caroline Hobart stood at Kitty's side. Together they looked down at the woman in the bed.

'Has she said anything?'

Hobart beckoned Kitty to follow her to the corridor. 'She said quite a bit, though none of it makes much sense. She drifts in and out. It'll be like that for a while. Her body has a lot of repair work to do.'

'Has her husband been in?'

'Yes. I made sure there was someone here all the time.'

'It would be good if it could stay that way.'

'But I thought you had arrested someone?'

'A man called Kemp. He worked for Mrs Lyndon. All the same I'd be grateful if she's not left on her own. Especially with visitors. *Any* visitors.'

'If you want her watched round the clock, that's not possible.' Doctor Hobart turned to leave. 'And if she starts talking, please don't wear her out with questions.'

Kitty pulled a chair to the bedside. Marisa's eyes were closed but her pulse was regular. For a while she watched the monitor, trying to work out the meaning of the figures and lines. Then she pulled *The Red and the Black* from her bag. She managed three pages. When she looked up Marisa's green eyes were fixed on her.

'Hi. I'm one of the officers who found you.'

Marisa tugged the oxygen tubes from her face. 'I need some water. My throat's so dry!'

Kitty poured a glass from the jug on the bedside cabinet. She held it to Marisa's mouth. A drop ran down her chin. 'How did I get here?'

'By ambulance.'

'Who are you?'

'A police officer.'

Marisa licked her lips. 'Did I have an accident?'

'Sort of. Someone attacked you. You were in your garden. By the pool.'

Marisa closed her eyes.

'It was on the morning of the 23rd of May. A Friday. Two weeks ago.'

'I've been asleep for *two weeks*?'

'Do you remember that morning?'

Marisa frowned. 'What's the date now?' Her voice was tight.

'Today's the 7th. Friday the 7th of June.'

Marisa closed her eyes. Her face twisted as she began to cry. 'But he'll be...' She shook her head, a look of distress on her face. She clawed at the sheets, struggling to pull them off. Kitty stood, seeing that Marisa was trying to climb from the bed.

'It's OK! Everything's fine. Your husband has been here every day.' Kitty reached for Marisa's hand. She leaned over the bed, smoothing the sheets. 'Jack knows all about it.' As Kitty leaned over Marisa recoiled, pushing her head back.

'What's that?' Her eyes were wide with fear.

'What? What's the matter?'

Marisa struggled, pushing herself away as if trying to escape. The monitor bleeped as Marisa's pulse rate soared, tripping an alarm. Kitty heard the sound of someone running towards the room. Caroline Hobart rushed in and forced Marisa back into the bed, tucking the sheets in as if to restrain her. 'You need rest, Mrs Lyndon.' The doctor fitted the nasal cannula to Marisa's face. She took her hand. 'You've been through the wars. You need peace and quiet.'

Kitty moved to the door, reluctant to leave.

'Get her out of here,' said Marisa. She opened her eyes and looked straight at Kitty. 'Stay away. I don't want you here.

That three stretch changed Whitey. When he was released he vowed that nobody would ever disrespect him again. Not even his friends. He had been a kid - too soft, too trusting. That was done.

Inside he was on Education and met a teacher. She was fit, but old. When they were doing classes, writing or whatever, she would play music.

'This will help you relax, Mr White. Music helps you think.' He wanted to please her, so he listened. It was classical music. Some of it mashed his brain, but it soothed him, like a woman's hand on the back of his neck. The sound made everything better. Everything washed away - his mother, his father, the tricks people played. He felt cleansed. The music made everything sweet. 'Happy sad,' he called that feeling.

His favourite was a piece by some gadgy called Scarlatti. A sonata the teacher said. The lads laughed when he said 'I'm not listening to fucking Sinatra!'

It was music that rippled down his spine like a good hit of skunk. He liked the sound and he liked the name. It sounded Italian, Mafia maybe. Whitey decided he would call himself Scarlatti. That didn't work, of course. It doesn't matter what you call yourself if everyone still calls you Whitey. But inside, in his own mind, he became Scarlatti.

On the out, Whitey steered clear of trouble for the first few weeks. He went back to laying carpets and all of that shit. He kept his head down and was a good boy. But now and then he would treat himself to a little extra. He would call a cab for Mr Scarlatti. He would ask the driver to take him to a sketchy part of town. His favourite spot was a car park on Skinnerburn Road, right beside the river. When the driver held out his hand to collect the fare, Mr Scarlatti would pull out Stan and cut him, just to show he meant business. To show he wasn't fucking about.

After the driver handed over his night's takings Mr Scarlatti would take out Stanley. Then he would drag the driver by the hair and push him into the boot. He'd slam the lid and put his head close to the metal, just to hear the man crying.

'I'm going to drive the car into the river and watch you drown, mate.' Then he'd rev the engine and listen to the howls. It was a lot of fun. And Stanley was Mr Scarlatti's calling card. His USP, you might say.

CHAPTER THIRTY FOUR

KITTY AND ELAYNE Hawes wandered through the mayhem.

'How much will this cost?'

'The drink's are on me, Elayne. You're only here to give me cover.'

'Thanks!'

'That didn't come out like I meant it...'

The streets were filled with young men and women. They poured into town from the villages and the suburbs, jamming the bars and clubs along the Diamond Strip. They stumbled from taxis, laughing as they rushed towards the evening's fun. Midnight's bitter tears lay several hours in the future.

Behind each bar the bottles were ranged in line like soldiers on parade. Soft light gleamed on polished glass. The staff stood at the ready. This end of the evening their uniforms are crisp, their smiles bright. The scent of soap and fresh cologne filled the air. Another Saturday night.

There were big women in tiny frocks and tiny women in dresses like wedding cakes. They shimmered like exotic sweets, sparkled in silk and tinsel. Young women teetered in dangerous shoes, flashing creamy shoulders and bare legs. Beside the women the men seemed drab, monochrome in white shirts and black pants, the only colour the ruddy skin of their freshly shaved faces.

Kitty and Elayne threaded their way along the Strip, passing *Madame Koo*, *Baby Lynch* and *Perdu*. Garish light spilled across the pavement. The evening air buzzed with chatter and laughter. Taxi horns honked as they moved through the throng, dropping new arrivals, picking up others.

Kitty and Elayne walked around a young woman in a silk frock who was kneeling in the gutter, trying to push her feet back into her heels. Her friends hauled her upright. The woman wobbled, lunged at her closest friend, then vomited into her shoes.

All along the Strip negotiations of a carnal nature were taking place. Men peeled sweat seamed collars from their sticky necks, while the women hunted in pairs. They sat on stone steps and slipped off their shoes, laughing at the lads who tried to chat them up. Kitty tugged at her skirt and pushed through the crowd. She felt guilty for dragging Elayne into this. The queue moved and the doormen allowed them inside. Elayne leaned closer to a mirror. She pinned up her dark hair and stood back, squinting at her work.

'I feel under dressed.' They pushed their way to the bar. A young, bearded barman clocked them and winked.

'With you in a moment, ladies.'

'Tasty,' murmured Elayne. 'But hairy.'

The bar was on heavy rotation - as soon as one customer left with drinks his space was filled. A flurry of notes crossed the bar. Kitty bought two Purple Lace cocktails and they made their way to the wall. A crowd of young men surrounded them.

While some were on the lookout for a Premiership footballer, Kitty had only one man in mind. Her eyes flicked around the room as she sought her quarry. It did not take long. Jack Lyndon stood in the shadows behind the bar. Despite the heat he wore a dark suit and a blue silk shirt, open at the neck. His clothes were impeccable, yet he faded into the background. He seemed content to lurk in the gloom, a puppeteer controlling his young, good looking staff. He was totally involved - scoping the crowd, fielding calls on his mobile. Now and then he tapped a barmaid on the shoulder to whisper a word of advice.

'That's him?' said Elayne, peering over the rim of her glass. Kitty nodded. 'His wife's just out of a coma?' Elayne shook her head. 'That's cold!'

Kitty sipped her cocktail as she watched him.

A haunted man.

Jack Lyndon spotted her. He frowned then half smiled, nodding a greeting. Kitty raised her glass. Lyndon whispered to his barman and made his way through the crowd.

'Didn't recognise you there,' he said. 'You look fabulous!' He kissed Kitty on both cheeks. 'Beautiful! Both of you.' He stepped back, looking them up and down. Kitty smiled, in spite of herself.

'This is my friend, Elayne.'

'You're both in the same business?'

'Is it that obvious?' Elayne was smiling now, her resistance melting.

'Can I get you a drink? I'm celebrating.'

'Celebrating?' said Elayne.

'Marisa!' His eyes sparkled. 'Isn't it incredible?' Jack Lyndon opened a door behind the bar and beckoned them to follow. The women exchanged a look, then Kitty nodded and they followed Jack up the staircase. Kitty expected sticky carpet and striplights but the backstage ambience at the *Orchid Noir* was surprisingly chic. The wallpaper was a fruity swirl of purple and dark green. Spiky metal uplighters gave the corridor a strange, Gothic glamour. Their heels made no sound on the deep, rich carpet. The door to Lyndon's office was oak, the handle a phallus in dark bronze.

'That's interesting,' laughed Elayne.

'Do you like it?'

'It's different!'

'It was made by this artist. A friend. Caspar Greene? Have you heard of him?'

'I think so,' said Kitty.

'I like to support artists. When I can.'

Jack swung the door open to reveal an office the size of a tennis court. The far wall had three semi circular windows which reached from the cedarwood floor to the vaulted ceiling. The lights of the city twinkled as the summer sun went down. Elayne Hawes whistled, her eyes wide as she appraised the view.

'I've been very fortunate,' said Jack. 'Time to put a little back.'

To the right there a bank of CCTV monitors took up the entire wall. The camera revealed the various rooms in the *Orchid Noir,* as well as the street outside.

'I can see what's going on downstairs. There are feeds from all my other clubs too. I like to know what's going on.'

'No problem with foxes here, then?' said Kitty.

Jack Lyndon's smile never wavered. There was a discreet knock. The bearded barman entered with a tray, three crystal glasses and a bottle of champagne. 'Thanks, Jago,' said Lyndon. Jago left, closing the door with a soft click. Lyndon poured the drinks.

'I'm surprised to see you at work,' said Kitty.

'I didn't know you were checking up on me,' said Jack, handing her the champagne. 'All I've done for the last two weeks is visit Marisa then come here. Work helps me forget.'

'You must be relieved.'

'You cannot know how relieved!' As he placed his champagne glass on the desk his hand trembled. 'I'm sorry I was so rude that morning. Marisa is everything to me.' He thumbed a tear from the corner of his eye. Elayne glanced at Kitty, raising her eyebrows. 'I just want our life back again.'

'I've been talking to one of Marisa's friends...' She shook her head. Lyndon watched her over the rim of his glass as he sipped the wine. She clicked her fingers. 'Honor? You remember - you saw her at the hospital? '

She watched Lyndon place his glass on the edge of his desk.

'Honor Blackett? She says she's an old friend of yours? '

He nodded. 'Honor's an old friend. We grew up in the same town.'

'That must be a comfort? Having someone like that?'

Lyndon tilted his head. The silence stretched. 'Yes. I suppose. Honor's a good friend - to both of us, in fact.'

In the silence that followed Kitty heard the sound of the crowd in the bar below - a faint, insect buzz.

'The most important thing is you got the bastard!' Jack raised his glass. 'You got Kemp. That's what matters.'

Kitty and Jack Lyndon regarded each other for a moment.

'We have Saul Kemp in custody.' She raised her glass and drank. It seemed clear Jack Lyndon shared none of her doubts about the identity of the attacker.

'I've been lucky, you know. All my life. I sell people what they want. I hire the right people to deliver it. There's no mystery to success in business. It's delegation.' Kitty watched his face, recalling where she had heard this before. 'But this...this has been the worst thing that has ever happened to me. Till now I've lived a charmed life.'

'Saul Kemp dropped a few hints.'

Jack Lyndon folded his handkerchief, halving, then quartering the silk before tucking it away.

'Hints? About what?'

'About the way things were. In your house.' This drew a glance from Elayne Hawes. Kitty was entering dangerous ground. 'That your marriage wasn't always happy.'

'Whose is?' Lyndon sipped his champagne. 'Who enjoys a marriage that is *always* happy?'

'He hinted that you weren't always faithful.'

'I wasn't.' Lyndon shrugged. 'I don't know many men who are. No! Let me qualify that. I don't know many *people* who are completely faithful - men or women. Straight or gay. Do you? 'Look at them!' He jabbed a finger towards the screens which took up one wall of his office. 'Do you think all of those people are single? Half of them are married. Why do you think they're here? They want more. It's human nature.' He raised his chin, stretching his neck. Kitty read the signs, the tics, the little 'tells' that showed Jack Lyndon was struggling to contain his anger. 'So what?'

'So things like that throw light on an investigation.'

'Your investigation is over. You have your man.'

They stared at each other. At last Kitty nodded, a cool smile on her lips. Jack Lyndon drained his glass. 'Have you read anything by Michel de Montaigne, Kitty?'

'Who?' said Elayne. Lyndon ignored her, his eyes fixed on Kitty.

'He wrote about how to live. Let me read you something.' Jack Lyndon reached into a drawer in his desk and pulled out a fat paperback. Yellow Post-It notes were stuck to some of the pages. Kitty knew Elayne Hawes was watching her. Lyndon began to read.

"We must cling tooth and claw to the pleasures of this life which the advancing years, one after another, rip from our grasp."

Jack Lyndon closed the book. 'Cling tooth and claw.' We're all dying. But we must never surrender. 'Tooth and claw.' He tapped the book on the edge of his desk. 'I keep a room at the Copthorne Hotel. It's only a moment away from here. Perhaps Kitty, you and your friend here, might accompany me there?'

Elayne Hawes laughed. Her eyebrows lifted as she glanced at Kitty. 'He's joking!' said Elayne, shaking her head. Jack Lyndon turned to her, his face a mask. 'I've heard it all now!' said Elayne. 'God loves a tryer.'

A smile spread across Jack Lyndon's face. They began to laugh. 'Of course I am.' He winked. 'But I had you for a moment, there, Elayne, didn't I?'

Kitty's taxi home cost thirty quid. She watched the red digits on the meter flick over as they sped through the darkened lanes. She swayed in her seat, discovering that champagne did not mix well with cocktails. Jack Lyndon was an enigma. He had switched from tears to seduction in a moments. Perhaps he used sex as a sedative.

It could be that the charming joker was his default persona - she had never met him other than as the grieving husband. Yet his wife still lay in a hospital bed. The man was a mystery.

CHAPTER THIRTY FIVE

TWO NIGHTS EARLIER, in a different part of the city, a different kind of party took place. The Assembly Rooms was packed with an early evening crowd. The hum of conversation rose to a low roar as the free champagne kicked in. This was the sound of people who had convinced themselves they were there to do good. They did not aspire to glamour: they were the real thing.

The Assembly Rooms was the perfect venue for such a distinguished assembly - Palladian arches in dove grey, Doric columns coated with fine white stucco - an ideal backdrop for the chic hairstyles and the designer teeth. Built in 1776, the place belonged to another time, though the world then was like our own in this respect - the rich could get away with murder.

Tony Vipond watched the guests drift around beneath the crystal chandeliers, balancing canapes and glasses of Brut Millésime. This was a party was to raise cash for Olympians of the future. Most Friday nights found Vipond in front of Sky Sports with a takeaway curry but this was the kind of event he loved. The famous guests and the free booze were just too tempting.

He had lived alone for two years. Jan, his ex, was shacked up with her hairdresser in Whitley Bay. They lived in a caravan on the Links. His pride was hurt when she left but it eased his pain to know she was miserable. He still lived in the house they shared for seventeen years. A woman came in twice a week to clean and do his washing. Most nights he ate out so the house was as neat and sterile as a show home.

At first he found social occasions a trial : now he saw the advantages of being the lone wolf. He could drink, cruise for skirt, then disappear whenever he fancied. Vipond's blue grey eyes took in everything and everyone, a faint smile on his lips as he worked the room. An imposing figure, he stood at the edge of a group, smiling and nodding until all eyes turned to him.

When he recognised a familiar face he nodded and smiled. Celebrity did not impress Tony Vipond. He could see beyond the shiny mask the sports stars and business leaders presented to the world. He was privy to their the grubby little secrets. He nodded at a church leader whose weakness was blow jobs from young Chinese boys. He smiled at the senior barrister with the serious coke habit. It pleased him that they were the same as everyone else - they had their guilty secrets, their little weaknesses. He knew enough to embarrass most of them : enough to put others inside. Tony Vipond's secret gold card was that he had access to criminal records. He could open any case file he wanted. In return for silence, they let him into their world. He had a free pass. Money goes to money. Power knows power.

But Vipond was not without his own flaw. A working class boy from Walker, he found it hard to resist women he thought were 'above' him. Tony Vipond had a weakness for 'posh totty'.

He saw Honor Blackett's smile widen as she moved through the crowd, heading in his direction. Vipond often encountered Honor at such events. There was, he was sure, some chemistry between them. She was available, if he wanted. He was certain of that. She wove her way towards him, stepping lightly, a panther shimmying down a branch. The silk Oscar de la Renta dress revealed her shoulders, the skin on her back, toned and firm.

'Tony!' She laid a hand on Vipond's wrist, her fingernails raking his skin. 'Darling!' Heads turned as they kissed. Her lashes fluttered against his cheek. He breathed in her perfume, the tang of chypre. As the kiss ended she looked straight into his eyes. He mumbled something about the evening being in aid of a good cause. She smiled up at him, her fingers still circling his wrist.

It was said that Honor Blackett knew everyone. Her black book contained the contact details of five thousand 'friends'. She was well connected. Yet she valued her privacy, he knew. At weekends she went 'off the grid,' holing up in her country cottage alone, or with a close friend. As the soft light gleamed on her shoulders, the nape of her neck, her slender throat, Vipond wondered if he might be among the chosen few. A waiter passed and he plucked two glasses from the tray, passing one to her. Honor winked as she opened her mouth to drink.

'Tony, there's something I need to talk about. A private word. Is there a chance we could go somewhere?' Her voice was low, sweet as honey.

'Of course.' Vipond placed his hand on the small of her back, steering her through the throng. He led her up the broad Georgian staircase. They reached a deserted landing. The sound from the room below was a soft babble, waves of words and laughter, rising and breaking. They crossed the landing to sit at a window seat. As Honor looked down on the street below, Vipond admired her neck, the line stretching from below her ear to her collar bone. He imagined running his tongue up the skin. He watched the way her throat moved as she swallowed her wine. Honor possessed glamour, in the real sense of that word. She bewitched : she was a shapeshifter.

'Thank you, Tony. It's about poor Marisa.'

Vipond's heart sank, but his smile stayed in place.

'A nasty business.' For a moment, his urge to smoke trumped his desire. He patted his pockets, searching for the comfort of a fag packet. 'But you can be sure I'll convict the man responsible.'

'The one you arrested?'

'Sorry. I can't discuss the details.'

'Of course.' She looked away, gazing out of the window. He was losing her.

'We did a lot of work for Jack. In the early days.'

He sensed there was some half secret here. A moment later that thought slipped from his mind. 'We still do. Jack and I are friends. We look out for each other.'

'Right...' He tapped the pack of cigarettes in his pocket.

'I'm sorry to bother you but I've spoken to your colleague.'

'Who's that?'

'I forget her name. Reddish brown hair.' She raised her hand to her head. 'Tousled. Like she'd just fallen out of bed. Kim, or something?'

'Lockwood? Kitty Lockwood?'

'That's her! Quite attractive. In a rough and ready sort of way.'

'Why did you speak to her?'

'I bumped into her in the hospital. I went to drop off some flowers. The girls at the agency have a soft spot for Jack. '

'Right...'

'Since then this Kitty has been...How can I put it? On my case? She came round to my flat.'

'Really? Why?'

'She seemed to be almost accusing me.'

'She was harassing you?'

'That's a bit strong. She is *very*...insistent, though.'

He shook his head. 'That's not acceptable.' He wanted to protect Honor, to show he cared. He watched her lips, the way they glistened. As her mouth opened and closed, he imagined himself in that softness. As she leaned in a lock of hair touched his cheek. 'Do you think she's up to the job? I don't want to be unkind but... She seems a little dim?'

'Leave it with me.'

She kissed him, lightly, on each cheek.

'I knew you'd understand.'

She sat back. As he leaned in, aiming to kiss her, there was movement on the stairs. An elderly, booze flushed man tottered to the top of the stairs and looked about, seeking the bar. As he waddled towards the window Honor slipped away, her silk dress rustling as she skipped down the stairs.

It was a month after he left prison that Clive Lumley got the visit. Two Chinese men, in their mid twenties, arrived at his office above the floor of the warehouse. They were well dressed in their charcoal business suits from WW Chan, of Kowloon, their silk shirts by Ascot Chang. Shuffling around the office in his stained grey trackies, Clive Lumley felt like a tramp beside these elegant young men. Their manners were as faultless as their clothes.

'We have heard of you for many years, Mister Lumley.'

'Call me Clive. Can I get you a drink?' He trudged towards a gilt tray on wheels in the corner of the office. They smiled and shook their heads. 'So.' He spread his hands wide. 'What can I do for you, gents?'

Mr Liu explained that he and his colleague were from the Wo Shing Wo.

'What's that?' Clive bared his teeth in a smile. 'A new Chinky restaurant?' Clive always masked his anxiety with a joke. He was wishing he was not alone in the office, trying to recall if he had a weapon stashed close to hand. Because Clive knew all about the Wo Shing Wo. They were his suppliers.

'No.' Mr Liu's smile was gracious. 'Though we have prepared a dish we hope you will enjoy.' His colleague, who sat a little to the rear, clicked open the briefcase which rested on his knee. 'You are famous, Mr Lumley. Your reputation is known all over the world,' said Mr Liu. Clive was both flattered and unsettled by the lie. Over the next ten minutes the two men told Clive Lumley how much they liked his work. They were sincere. They told him how much they respected him and how they admired the way he had grown his business. Then they got to the point.

'We understand that you have experienced problems recently.'

'I was inside.' Clive shrugged. 'Prison! Can you believe it? In a civilised country?' He shook his head sadly, as if the world was going to the bad. 'But it's not a problem. My wife did a great job while I've been away. The problems are over.' He grinned at them. They smiled in return. The world turned.

'We all get old,' said the one called Liu.

'I expect.'

'In time, all grow old. Each and every one of us. Time comes when we must pass on what we have built. Change is inevitable.'

'When the time comes, Mr Liu, no doubt I'll think about that. Until then...' Clive spread his hands. 'Business is good. Life is sweet.'

So they told him how it would be. They would take over. They would compensate him - they were honourable men, not vagabonds.

'I should like to offer you this much. For your retirement.' Mr Liu pulled a Mont Blanc pen from an inside pocket. He wrote a figure in a notebook and passed it across the desk. Clive looked at the figure. Had he wanted to sell up and retire, he would have been tempted. He could bank the cash and walk away. He might buy a place in the sun and never trouble himself with work again.

'That's a very generous offer.' He told them he would think about it. Mr Liu shook his hand.

'We'll speak again soon. I hope.'

After they left, Clive stood at the window, watching the sun glint on the copper dome above the Bruce Building. He felt uneasy. If he had been feeling good about himself, perhaps it might have been different. If he was twenty years younger. If he and Greta were getting on. But Clive was feeling low. He thought about the money they offered and he was tempted. But he felt a little spark of pride too, an ember burning and smouldering inside. His anger grew, brighter and hotter, red to white, as he thought about what they had said.

'Cheeky Chinky bollocks!' Clive pulled out his mobile and swiped through his contacts. It was time to call in a favour.

CHAPTER THIRTY SIX

'YOU MUST BE relieved. Knowing that Marisa is on the mend."

'Yes.' Cathy Fletcher placed the tray of drinks on a side table. 'Help yourself,' she said.

'Thanks for seeing me again. There's just a couple of things...'

'I think I told you everything the last time.'

Kitty peered at the framed photos on the wall of Cathy Fletcher's sitting room. In the centre was the photo of Cathy and Marisa, smiling, their arms around each other. Two blond women, Marisa younger by a few years. Green eyes. A similar build. Cathy entered carrying a tray.

'That's a lovely picture! You look like sisters. Marisa must be lonely, at times? On her own in that huge house. Does she ever confide in you?'

'How do you mean?'

'You spend a lot of time in each other's company.'

Cathy nodded.

'So she confides in you?'

'She's like a kid, really. Does things that are just crazy.'

'What kind of things?'

'Please don't say anything to Jack.'

'I won't.'

'She just, I don't know. She *oozes* sex.' She stretched the word, honey dripping from a spoon. 'She doesn't realise. Mike was over there fixing a skirting board. I knew she was getting him hot and bothered. It's not that she *does* anything. She doesn't have to...'

'That bothers Mr Lyndon?'

'He tries to pretend it doesn't matter but...He loves her. He would kill anyone who stole her away.'

'What was the atmosphere like in the house? In the days before the attack?'

'I don't get what you mean?'

'I think you do.'

Cathy Fletcher placed her cup squarely on the coaster.

'There was something funny going on.'

'After the row?' Cathy nodded.

'Just odd things.'

Kitty waited.

'Deliveries at the house. Taxis turning up at all hours. No-one had ordered them. One morning a lorry turned up with a skip. They were just about to dump it in the drive!'

'What was the name on the order?'

'Lyndon. But Marisa hadn't ordered it - she phoned Jack - it was nothing to do with him.'

'Anything else?'

'Someone delivered a platter of fish. They left it in the garage. It stank the place out. We had funny phone calls.'

'What kind of calls?'

'Silent.'

'This was reported?'

'To the police? No.'

'Jack knew?'

'He couldn't *not*! They talked about it.'

'And how did that conversation go?'

'Jack said it was most likely kids.'

'Did Marisa have any ideas?'

'She was spooked. She said 'It's the Half Witch.''

'She said this to Jack?'

'To me.'

'Who's the half witch? What does that mean?'

'I don't know. She just said 'It's the half witch', then she clammed up.'

The door of Greta's white Range Rover Discovery closed with a *thunk*. She had parked in a wooded side road on the edge of town. Bryson glanced in the wing mirror, then at Greta. He was cautious when meeting any source, but this was more than routine. The added element was his own guilt. He found it hard to meet Greta's eyes. The car was filled with her scent - a lemony, tangy perfume that worked its way deep inside.

'Morning, officer,' she said. Something about the situation amused her. 'How are you today?'

'Good. Thanks.' A flush crept up his neck.

'I'm told he flew in from Amsterdam on the seventeenth. Don't know the flight number. Maybe you could find his name on a passenger list.'

'What's his name?'

'Chien.'

'How do you spell it?' Bryson pulled a tiny black pad from the pocket of his jacket. She watched him, a wry smile on her lips. 'Chien. Is that a surname?'

Greta shrugged. Her driving gloves creaked as she ran her hands around the leather wheel. 'Who hired him?' Bryson licked the stub of a pencil and scribbled his notes.

'Someone in Wo Shing Wo.'

'The Triads?'

'That's what I'm told.'

'Who told you?'

'Come on Bryson,' she smiled.

'Worth a try!' he said. 'Why did they cut off his head?'

'He was skimming the take. Chocolate Rock.'

When Bryson frowned, she explained. 'Heroin and crack.'

'Right.' Bryson knew that Wo Shing Wo was the largest Triad in the country. 'Where is he now? This 'Chien?''

'I suspect he's flown home. Don't you?'

Bryson looked across the park. At least he had something to give Vipond. It might be a Dead Sea Apple, good looking but worthless but it was more than anyone else had found. Enough to stop the whispers: enough to save his skin, perhaps. He thrust his hand into his pocket. Bryson Prudhoe always carried a column of £2 coins in his pocket which he played with when stressed. They were like worry beads. He let the coins fall through his fingers.

'What's that?'

'What?'

'That chinking sound?'

Bryson blushed. He pulled the coins from his pocket and opened his fingers to let her see.

'And I thought you were pleased to see me...'

Bryson popped the coins back inside his pocket. Greta watched him, a curious smile on her face. He turned to her.

'Thank you.'

'My pleasure.' Birdsong drifted through the open window. 'So,

Bryson. That's it?'

Bryson shifted in his seat.

'I'm very grateful.'

'Are you?'

'Of course.'

Greta nodded, her eyes on the horizon. Something amused her. She leaned over, her lips grazed his ear.

'Will you miss me?'

On instinct, he glanced at the wing mirror. Her gloved hand rested on his knee. Her hair brushed his cheek as she turned her face. The world became a blur, melting at the edges. Her hand slid up his thigh. Deep down, low in his throat, in his chest, he moaned. As he leaned to kiss her, she moved back, her eyes locked on his as she slipped her fingers between the buttons. He made a final, feeble protest.

'Greta...' It was a sound rather than a word. Her fingers moved over his skin. Each time he moved closer, trying for her lips, she moved, pulling back, teasing him, the ghost of a smile on her lips. When he came his head jerked forward then back, hitting the seat. He lay still, eyes closed.

Sitting back in her seat, Greta fixed her face in the mirror. It was a while before he opened his eyes. Even before he did, he understood how he had been played.

CHAPTER THIRTY SEVEN

'SIT.'

FOR A minute or so Vipond scribbled on a pad. Then he closed the notebook and placed his pen squarely on top. She sensed he was trying to keep a lid on his rage.

'You've been sniffing around. Asking questions.'

'Who told you that?'

'Never mind who told me.'

'It's a dynamic situation, sir. Now Marisa Lyndon's awake. Things are still moving.'

'Do you enjoy making work for me?'

'I'm doing my job. Asking questions. Finding the truth.'

'All I want is you to do is to tidy up the details. Wrap this up in a pretty bow and we can all move on.'

'Between forty and seventy per cent of female murder victims are killed by their partners or former partners. I'd like to talk to Jack Lyndon. To ask one more question.'

He ran the tip of his finger along the edge of his desk.

'I want you to drop it.' His voice was dead.

'But I won't, sir. Will I...'

It felt odd to be back in Jack Lyndon's office, sitting in the same leather chair. Lyndon sat behind the oak desk. Behind him the windows opened onto a view of the city. As Kitty and Tony Vipond walked across the blue carpet their feet made no sound.

'Thanks for this, Jack,' said Tony Vipond.

Jack looked up, nodded then signed another sheet. He capped his pen and leaned back. Vipond was uneasy, his pale cheeks flushed, like a schoolboy dragged in to see the Head.

'There's just a detail we need to clear up.'

Jack Lyndon spread his hands. 'Whatever you want. As long as it helps convict Kemp.'

'My colleague here,' Vipond tipped his head towards Kitty, 'has a question.'

'It's about the CCTV, Mr Lyndon. The neighbourhood where you live is a target for crime?' Her voice echoed around the vast room.

'It is. The papers call it Millionaire's Row.'

'That's why you had security cameras fitted?'

Lyndon smiled. 'Have you two been transferred to Crime Prevention?' He winked at Vipond.

'The cameras are linked to a hard drive,' said Kitty. 'And your Mac?'

Jack Lyndon sighed. 'We have eight Genie GS550 High Resolution surveillance cameras, with Day/Night vision. The images are stored on an eight way DVR H.264 hard drive connected to my lap top and to the machines at home. The reason I know all this crap is that I paid a fortune for the damn things! I did my research. '

'But they were switched off? At the time of the attack?'

'Yup. I told you that.'

Kitty unfolded a piece of paper. She slid it across the desk.

'This is a warrant to seize your hard drive and laptop.'

Lyndon's gaze remained on Kitty. He did not look at the paper. So. What is this 'question' you have? Or did I miss it?'

'Would you like to change anything you told us?'

'Luckily, I'm feeling mellow. I spoke to Marisa this morning. She's looking great. We sorted things out.' He reached into his desk and pulled a laptop from the drawer. He turned it to face Kitty's chair.

'I'll play you some footage. Then you can decide if you want to pursue this any further.'

'So the cameras were switched on? That's not what you said earlier.'

'This dates from early May. Around a fortnight before Marisa was attacked.' He turned to Vipond. 'You and I can talk downstairs, Tony. We can leave your colleague to watch in privacy.'

Jack Lyndon hit a key and waited a moment, to check that the footage was playing. 'I've seen it. I never want to see it again.'

Lyndon and Vipond left the room. The first thirty seconds of footage revealed different shots of the front of the house on 'Millionaire's Row'. One shot looked down at the front door. The next sequence of shots showed the edge of the garden, from a camera mounted in the trees. The next revealed the rear of the house. The footage was bleached, the shadows deep. Kitty looked at the clock, the counter flicking numbers in the corner of the screen. The footage was dated on the 7th of May, at seven minutes past eleven.

Marisa lay on a lounger by her pool. Another figure, a man, was swimming. He climbed from the water and grabbed a towel, which he slung across his shoulders. Though the footage had no sound, it was clear that Marisa and the man were talking. He moved to stand beside the lounger. The man said something which made Marisa laugh. It was strange to see this young woman laughing.

Marisa reached out and ran her fingers up the man's thigh. She pulled him closer. Kitty groaned and put her hand to her face. She watched the scene between her fingers. Marisa opened the man's bathing shorts and began to fellate the man. Saul Kemp closed his eyes and threw back his head.

The footage froze on that image. Kitty sat for a while, tapping her fingers against her lips. The door opened. Jack Lyndon carried a tray holding a bottle of brandy and two glasses. He placed the tray on the desk and powered down the laptop. He poured a small measure of brandy into each glass. He slid one drink in front of Kitty.

'You understand why I switched off the cameras?'

Kitty ran her hand over the surface of the desk, stroking the veneer of dark blue leather.

'I love my wife. Perhaps she doesn't love me in the same way. That's just something I live with. Tony's waiting for you in the car.'

Kitty stood. As she reached the door Lyndon spoke again.

'I don't want anything to change. I want our life to go on in the usual way. And it will.'

'Happy now? That was a fucking shambles!'

'Sir.'

It was a new experience to be in a car with Vipond and not be behind the wheel. They headed up Westgate Road, through the afternoon traffic. Women in saris and headscarves pushed buggies, trailing toddlers in their wake.

Vipond's Lexus RC rolled like a boat as they followed the long, straight road. At the bottom of the hill a little stub of the Roman

Wall poked through the grass at the side of the road. It seemed as if the clouds lifted as she left the city behind. She was heading towards home. They drove in silence. They hit the A69 and the Lexus picked up speed. Vipond's hands moved over the wheel.

'Are you hungry?'

Kitty thought she had misheard.

'I...'

'Don't piss about Lockwood. Could you eat?'

'I suppose.'

'I blame myself.'

'Sir?'

'It's *all* my fault.'

Kitty was surprised by this new, reflective side.

'You showed initiative in putting forward ideas and...' He ran his tongue along his teeth as he sought the right word. '...*theories* about this case. That's to your credit.'

'Where are we going?'

'For a bite to eat.'

They entered a village, a clutch of stone built houses gathered around a green. The Lexus swung into the car park of the Black Bull. The beer garden was decorated with huge hanging baskets, blowsy fountains of colour and scent. Kitty sat at a table at the front of the pub, sheltered from the afternoon sun by an umbrella. A group of men glanced over from the next table, watching as she took a seat. They wore green boiler suits and peaked caps, as if they had just stepped down from a tractor.

'Beautiful day,' said one. Kitty agreed. Their interest dived when Vipond arrived with a drink. She smiled across at them, in some regret. An afternoon drinking cider in the sun would have been very sweet.

'I ordered the pâté,' said Vipond. 'My treat.'

Kitty was taken aback. This was turning into some kind of awkward date. Why had he brought her here? Was this another attempt at seduction? It would take a lot more than a glass of Pimms and some pâté. The food arrived. Vipond looked across the green, eyelids creasing into his thousand yard stare.

'Do you like your life?'

'How do you mean?' She feared this was going to be a confession of loneliness.

'Just what I say.' His tone was clipped. Kitty put down her toast. 'You have a good life?'

'Yes.'

'You have a job.' He seemed to have no interest in her answer. 'Your friends. Jacqui. Elayne. Good friends. You have your little house, in Cloud Street.'

Kitty felt uneasy. This was beyond awkward.

'Your mother lives just around the corner, doesn't she? In Hencotes Lane? And Molly...Molly's a growing girl. A good kid. Despite her recent troubles...'

The men at the next table drained their glasses and headed inside the pub. Kitty and Vipond were alone.

'You have your kickboxing. Your little holidays.' He swallowed a mouthful of his drink, his Adam's Apple bulging. 'Your pension pot's growing, I expect.' He stared at her, as if gauging how this was going down. As she sipped her Pimms she was aware her hand was trembling, the ice tinkling against the glass. 'It's all good, isn't it? All sweet?'

She found herself nodding.

'It would be terrible if all that were to stop.'

'Why should it stop?' Her voice sounded far away.

'There are people you should not cross.'

'What do you mean, sir?'

'Just what I say, Lockwood. Drop it. Walk away. Enjoy your life.'

CHAPTER THIRTY EIGHT

ELAYNE HAWES WAS waiting for her when Kitty returned to her desk.

'Saul Kemp wants to talk to you.'

'Fancy a little jaunt?' Though shaken by her conversation with Vipond, Kitty's curiosity won out.

'What's he want, do you think?' said Elayne, as they hit the Durham road.

'Maybe he wants to confess,' said Kitty. 'Which would make life a little easier.' She overtook a line of trucks. Vipond's words churned around in her head. Even if she shrugged off the threat to herself, his mention of her family was disturbing.

'You know Locky, we have a speed limit in this country?'

The wind whistled through the razorwire, even on a warm summer day. They blanked the usual catcalls they got from men behind the barred windows.

The meeting room was tatty - green carpet stained with dark splodges, the scuffed walls a grubby yellow. The sound of shouting and clanging doors echoed down the landings.

'They've got this looking nice,' said Elayne. 'What shade would you call that? Fagnolia?' The door opened and Saul Kemp shambled towards the table. He wasn't in irons, but walked as if he was. The screw sat on a chair by the wall and pulled out a paperback.

'How's it going, Saul?' said Kitty.

'I've remembered something.'

Elayne gave Kitty a knowing look.

'What have you remembered?'

'The day before, before it happened, we'd had a row.'

'Who are we talking about here, Saul?'

'Marisa and me.'

'Right.'

'She said they wouldn't be needing me so often.'

Kitty's gaze was fixed on Saul's face.

'She said it was awkward. Me working there.'

'Do you remember her exact words?'

Saul rubbed his thumb in his eye, working it until Kitty heard a cracking, squelching sound. 'She said 'You've done a fantastic job. I'm very fond of you. But it's awkward...'' He paused, staring at the grey table top.. ''I think it's better if we go down to just once a month.''

'That was it?'

'I knew what she meant. It wasn't the garden.' He jabbed his thumb into his chest. 'I lost it. A little bit.'

Kitty waited.

'I was shouting at her. I know it was wrong.' A tear gathered at the corner of his eye. 'I would have done anything for...'

They were quiet, watching his shoulders shake. When Saul recovered himself Kitty spoke.

'Then what?'

'I was furious. Like I'd been played for a sucker.'

Kitty nodded.

'That was it! I grabbed my tools and went. As I grabbed my bag a load of stuff fell out. I heard it clatter on the stones. I didn't stop, just grabbed the bag, hoyed it into the pickup and went.'

'You're saying you dropped the axe?'

'I don't know! I didn't stop to look. It would have looked stupid to pick it up. I must have done!'

Kitty glanced at Elayne Hawes.

'How come it took you until now to recall this?' said Elayne.

'I've been going over it. Night after night. There's plenty of time to think, in here.'

Elayne Hawes leaned forward in her chair.

'Time to make up stuff, too...'

They hit the evening traffic. The sun turned the Angel of the North's' wings a rusty amber. Kitty drummed her fingers on the wheel as they sat in the tailback.

'Did you buy that? said Elayne.'

'I don't know.'

'You say Marisa dumped him,' said Elayne. 'So he's got an 'excuse'. He's full of righteous fury.'

'I know it doesn't look good.' The traffic eased and they trundled across the bridge. 'My axe fell out of my bag, miss. A big boy found it. He done it and ran away...' Kitty smiled.

'But I did, sort of. Believe him.'

'Just because you're a bit thick, have a record and a motive, it doesn't *necessarily* mean you done it...'

'No. But if not, who does that leave?'

When Whitey was doing his time in Swinfen Hall, Davy Clark was in Her Majesty's Prison Castington. He took a course on Car Maintenance, taking an old banger apart then building it again. When the two young lads got out, five months later, they would meet up every weekend, nick a car and go for a drive. Whitey loved that. He didn't drive - just couldn't do it, somehow. So they would steal a car and Davy would drive all night. Around five in the morning he drove them home and they would torch the car.

Davy had this neat trick when they were bimbling through the darkened lanes. When he came to a cross roads he would put his foot to the floor. When they reached eighty he switched off the headlights. The first time he did it, Whitey screamed. But Davy wasn't stupid. If he saw light, he knew there was a car on the other road, so he'd slow down. If it was completely dark, he knew the road was empty. So he'd go faster still. It took Whitey a while to twig this. It was so useful. Having a mate who could drive.

'Thanks for coming in. I appreciate this.'

Honor Blackett smiled. 'Anything to help.'

Always smiling. Always charming.

'I'll keep it brief, Ms Blackett.'

'*Honor*, Please, Kitty.' She arched her brow. 'We know each other well enough, don't we?'

'I need to tie up a few loose ends.'

'No problem.'

'Tell me about Caspar Greene.'

Honor shook her head and turned towards the window, her smile as wide as ever. It was the face of an indulgent, exasperated parent. Kitty studied her profile, wondering when that smile might slip. Honor turned to look at Kitty. 'What would you like to know?'

'You were his manager?'

'Briefly. I did what I could to help.'

'As did Marisa Lyndon?'

'You really need to ask her.'

'I will.'

Honor Blackett sat back, her head rocking as she absorbed this news. It seemed the smile had stretched as far as it could.

'Really? How is she?'

'On the mend.'

'That's wonderful! That is such good news!'

'Isn't it?' Kitty watched her prey, looking for a tell. 'Can I get you a drink, Honor?'

'No. Thank you.' Her voice seemed to come from somewhere far away. Kitty knew the moment had come. She trotted out her little lie. 'The best news though, is that Marisa is starting to remember things. It seems her memory of that morning is returning.'

'Good.' Honor nodded. 'That's so good.' Kitty watched the smile falter. 'What sort of things?'

'Sounds. Shapes.' Kitty waited, stretching the moment, savouring it. 'Smells.'

'Smells?' Honor shook her head, as if baffled.

'Yes. Something in your experience, I suppose. The sense of smell is so important. She thinks she may be able to identify the fragrance the attacker wore. Or scent.'

'Really? The after shave? Some of them are so pungent.'

'She's thinking it was a scent. A fragrance.'

'Really?'

Kitty nodded. 'Yes. She has a quite specific memory of that,' she said, compounding the lie. The door opened. Tony Vipond was there, in his shirtsleeves, a sheet of paper in his hand. He looked from one to the other, puzzled.

'Tony. Lovely to see you!' Honor flashed her best smile, flicked the swatch of blond hair over her shoulder. There was an awkward moment in which Vipond bent to kiss her. He seemed caught, stranded between his two personalities, the social animal and working copper.

Doubling.

'Lovely. Yes. Must get on.' He glared at Kitty. 'A word, the moment you're free.' He closed the door. Honor turned to Kitty, the smile on full beam. 'Now. What was it you wanted to know?'

CHAPTER THIRTY NINE

HONOR WASN'T SATISFIED. It seemed clear that her chat with Tony Vipond had failed, as she suspected it would. For all his posturing, Vipond was weak. So the little bitch was still snapping at her heels, yelping and sniffing around. Honor refused to be dragged down. They would never drag her down. She was not the kind of person who allowed that to happen.

She opened her little black book, scrolling down to W.

Take control. Feel the fear and do it. Just do it.

She became a burden. They all did, sooner or later. They wanted more than he could give. None of them saw the world the way he did. She wanted him to move in, become half of a couple. That was so predictable. But Caspar loved his freedom. He liked to step lightly through the world, to glide without friction, to slip, eel like, through the mesh of life.

It was sweet for a while, of course. Honor was older. Well preserved and chic, she possessed true glamour, the ability to attract, to persuade others. She had connections. Honor 'raised his profile.' For the first time he started to make real money. He could forget the teaching and ditch the community arts shit. No more begging letters to charities and arts bodies. Honor did that, leaving him to do what he was put on earth to do. 'I drink,' he told her. 'I fuck. I bash metal. That's it.'

The sex was good. Honor was so wild it scared him at times. She lacked an off switch - she would do anything, push him to the edge. But he grew tired of being touted as 'my artist,' paraded around like Porky the Prize Pig.

She took him to Menton : they shared an apartment there in March. She had a couple of moments - episodes - when he stayed out all night. He was drinking, that was all. Drinking, sleeping on the beach. He did it to make a point. She freaked. When he came back at dawn she was waiting for him. Crockery flew as she raged at him. He sat on the couch, rolling a spliff as she tipped a cactus over the balcony. The neighbours started shouting and 'les flics' arrived. Honor changed in an instant, all sweetness and smiles. For a while it seemed they thought he'd done the damage but she confessed she was to blame. Charmed them, you see? Once the cops were on their way they went to bed and made up.

In April they flew back to England. She wanted him to move his things into her place. He felt trapped. He loathed Spike, her stinking dog. He guessed she thought of him in the same way and he hated being petted and leashed. It got old, very quickly. *Next!*

Marisa was closer to his own age. She seemed reluctant, which was a spur, of course. But she quickly got on his tits.

They all become a burden.

Within a week Marisa bored him. She talked about his work in that naive way, like a kid tugging on his sleeve, whinnying about his 'oeuvre' and his 'body of work.' She didn't understand his work. She didn't understand him, though she put in the hours, God knows. It set him on edge when she stood behind him, her fingers on his neck, teasing out the curls. He took the piss but she didn't stand up to him. She cried. At least the old one gave as good as she got. This one seemed to love him and something about that just boiled his piss. He hated sentimentality. He despised weakness. Marisa was attractive. And she got him some money, serious cash. She had her uses. But he was bored.

In the end, they all become a burden.

Honor parked the Maserati near the stadium. She had taken particular care of the way she looked - a white summer dress, Louboutins and her shades. She glanced in the shop windows on Blackett Street, checking the details. It was a warm day, she loosened the wrap around her shoulders.

Clive Lumley owned an office opposite the Bruce Building. It was the registered office for Powerdram, his shell company whose business was importing gym equipment and dietary supplements. Years back, when Clive started the company, she'd organised the launch - a champagne and canape bash in the Centenary Suite.

She rode the cage to the top floor. The lift creaked as it rose. Honor looked up at the oiled cable, grinding away in the gloom. She dabbed perfume on her wrists, by way of a distraction. The cage clanged and jerked to a stop. She waited until it stopped swaying before she opened the door and walked down the corridor. Her heels clicked on the tiles, echoing through the deserted block. The door lay open. Clive stood at the window, his mobile pressed to his ear. He smiled at her and rolled his eyes, miming shooting the phone. She looked around the tatty office. There were calendars of gym kit and boxes of supplements, Almond Butter and Protein Smoothies. The room smelled of coffee and floor polish.

Clive ended the call. They kissed on both cheeks. Clive whistled, admiring the way she looked.

'You're not looking so bad yourself!' she said.

'Yeah,' he patted his belly. 'I let things slide for a bit. But I'm on top of it.' For a minute they danced around like a pair of bees discussing pollen, talking of people they knew. He poured her a filter coffee from the machine in the corner. She sipped her coffee and raised her eyebrows.

'Delicious!'

Then they got to it.

'So. Just tell me how I can help?'

'It's a police officer.'

'Isn't it always?' He narrowed his eyes.

'Her name is Lockwood. Kitty Lockwood.'

'I know the name,' said Clive Lumley.

Whitey was fitting a roll of Timeless Luxury Chartreuse when he got her call.

'Is that Mr White?'

Whitey rasped the blade across the pad of his thumb. 'Who's this?' He made himself comfortable on the floor, his back to the wall.

'You don't know me, Mr White. We'll keep it like that. Strictly professional.' Whitey liked the idea.

Professional.

The client had stripped the room. The house was empty - just the carpet, Whitey, and the dust in the sunbeams. He watched dust swirl and sparkle in the sun.

'A friend gave me your number.'

'Which friend?'

'You shared a room with him.'

It took Whitey a moment. 'Right.'

'I have some work for you, Mr White.' She sounded posh. His cock twitched as he wondered what she looked like. 'There's a car park by the Crown Court. A multi storey. I'll be on the third floor. Tomorrow morning. At ten.'

'I've got a job on tomorrow.'

'I'll pay for your time. So. Multi storey. Third floor. Ten o'clock tomorrow morning.'

He heard a click as the call ended and the purring in his ear, so knew it was made from a landline. He dialled 1471 but the number was blocked. Whitey tapped Stanley against his lip. He watched the dust turning, twisting and falling. He yawned, the skin on his pale cheeks taut, stretching like parchment over bone. Whitey nudged the Luxury Chartreuse with his knees, tucking it snug against the skirting. He opened Stanley and slit the overlap. The blade slipped through the backing. Whitey dropped the sliver of carpet on the floor and watched it uncoil.

'You're well enough to go home?'

Marisa Lyndon was dressed in a pair of Big Star jeans, a white T and a fawn cardigan. It was the first time Kitty had seen her out of a hospital gown.

'I can't wait!' Marisa clipped a pearl stud in her ear. 'I can't stand this place! Jack had a quiet word and I'm free. He can be very persuasive.'

I bet.

'What do you plan to do?'

'I just want to go home. To rest.'

Kitty wanted to admit that she knew all about Caspar.

'There are questions I have to ask, Marisa. But I don't want to rush you.'

'Ask away.' Marisa sat on the edge of the bed. 'Jack says it was Saul who attacked me. He says you have him in custody.'

'What do you think about that?'

'I didn't see who did it. I don't remember anything about that day.'

'For the moment, I'd like you to keep that to yourself.'

Marisa Lyndon nodded. 'OK.' She touched her wound with the tip of her fingers and teased out a strand of hair to hide the scar.

Whitey jogged along the Quayside, squinting against the dazzle of the sun on the river. He'd always found sunlight a problem. It came with his pale skin. He didn't own a car because he couldn't drive but if anyone asked about that he gave a different reason - he wasn't paying those Jew prices. Whitey knew - for a fact - that all car parks were owned by Jews. All Jews carried money in their hats. Once he had told Davy Clark that.

'Those cowboy hats they wear, the reason they wear them, right, is to carry their money around.' Davy Clark looked at him and shook his head, biting his cheek to stop the laughter. Whitey saw this. Sometimes he wanted to cut Davy, even though he was his only friend.

Whitey trotted up the ramp of the multi-storey car park. The place was clean, the walls bright yellow, the concrete floor gleaming. He looked at the numbers of each space. All the spaces on this floor were reserved, some with gold stars. He guessed those spaces belonged to Jews. Gold was a Jewish name, he knew. Gold. Diamond. Silver - all Jewish names.

He reached the third floor. Instinct made him glance at the CCTV. He saw cameras everywhere, so he flipped up the hood on his trackie. His hand went to his pocket and he clicked Stanley's button, opening and closing the blade, flicking it like the tongue of a snake. Most of the bays were empty. He heard cars enter and leave on the floors below, rubber wheels squealing on the shiny floor. A black Maserati Gran Cabrio was parked by the far wall. A blond woman sat in the driving seat, watching him. She was old, but Whitey liked the look of her. He walked around the car. She opened the door on the passenger side and he slipped inside.

'You're late.'

Rage glimmered in Whitey. He wondered if she was a Jew. He pushed his hands down his thighs, smoothing his tracky bottoms against the skin.

'I'm here now. What's the job?'

'The job, as you call it, is a person.'

Whitey's lips fell open. He stared at her, trying to work it out.

'You want a carpet fitted to a person?'

The woman laughed, throwing back her head. Her teeth were white, the inside of her mouth pink. He liked the way her neck looked, lit by the sun. What Whitey didn't like was being laughed at. He never enjoyed that.

'You did a job for Clive. Yes?' Whitey stared at her. 'Yes?' Her voice was harder this time. He nodded. 'I need something similar. He said you were the man for the job.'

She opened her bag and plucked an envelope from the stuff inside. A scent reached his nostrils - musky, not sweet. The bag looked expensive - soft leather, silk lining. He looked at her legs in that tight skirt. She wore driving gloves - black leather, with silver zips on the back. She opened the flap to reveal a wad of notes. He could do her, right here. In this car. Do her, then take the money.

Do her right now.

But there was something about this woman that put him on his guard. Though he would never admit it, even to himself, he was a little uneasy. She counted the money and he heard the crisp rustle of new notes.

'So.' She held out the money. His fingers closed over the wad but she tugged it from his grasp. 'One. This meeting never took place.' She waited until he nodded. 'Two. The address is 7 Cloud Street. The postcode is NE48 2BU. Can you remember that?' She made him repeat the code.

'Good.' She held out the notes. 'Three. Her name is Lockwood. Kitty Lockwood.'

'Lockwood.'

'Four. The message is this. 'Drop it.' I want her scared. Not hurt. Do you understand?'

Whitey nodded. The woman held out the wad and let him ease them from her fingers.

'You can go,' she said. Whitey climbed out of the car. The engine came to life and he watched her car disappear down the ramp.

CHAPTER FORTY

'I'M INTRIGUED, BRYSON.'

Bryson Prudhoe shrugged his shoulders. It was hard to avoid Tony Vipond's eyes.

'The source is reliable.'

Vipond turned away to look out of the window. 'Care to share the her name?' His voice was soft, the purr of a tiger.

Bryson thrust his chin out and ran the tip of his finger around his shirt collar. 'Sorry. I don't have that sort of relationship.'

''Relationship'?' Vipond raised his eyebrows, taking the piss. Bryson smoothed his hands along his thighs but said nothing, a kid waiting for the next kick from the school bully.

'Well. I'm glad to know your relationship with this source is so important.'

He knows.

Bryson gave him nothing. After a moment Vipond stood up. He moved to the window. Bryson studied his back, the way his suit jacket hung loosely on his shoulders.

'Right. I want you sitting next to me at the press conference. We need to throw them a bone. Otherwise they'll realise we know sod all. Run me through what's safe to say.'

Bryson looked at the press release he had prepared.

'We believe was some dispute about money between the victim, Mr Liu, and his criminal bosses in China. Our enquiries suggest someone was sent over to teach him a lesson.'

Vipond smiled. He caught hold of the cord which dangled from the window blind, twisting it around his fingers. 'And we think things got out of hand?'

'Yup. We keep it short and to the point. Otherwise they'll unpick it.'

Vipond grinned. 'Do you have a name for the killer?' He loosed the cord and watched it bounce against the glass.

'Chien.'

Vipond lifted the blind cord, let it fall again. 'Like the French for dog?' Vipond folded his arms and sat on the window sill. 'That's it?'

'He's Vietnamese. I'm told.'

'Couldn't they find someone local?'

Bryson shrugged. 'Maybe they wanted to farm it out. Keep their distance. So the trail didn't lead back to them.'

'You're guessing now, Bry.'

'Yes.'

The whole sodding thing is a guess.

A sigh escaped Vipond's lips. 'I'm not convinced, but...   And where do we think he is now?'

'Long gone, I expect. Long gone.'

Kitty's mobile pinged. She read the text then gathered her things.

'Marisa Lyndon says she's well enough to give a formal statement.'

'Going to tell Vipond?' said Elayne Hawes. Kitty shook her head.

'He'd beg me not to go.'

They signed out and headed for the car park.

'You know, he probably thinks we talk about him all the time.'

'People flap their gobs, Kitty. Whether they know anything, or not. They invent stuff and most of the time it's wrong.'

'Projection.'

'Oh yes? Projection. Which means? In English?'

Kitty had a fear of coming over as a swot. 'It's a Freudian thing. A kind of defense mechanism.'

'You've still got me...'

Elayne climbed into the passenger seat.

'A person unconsciously rejects their own faults by ascribing them to other people. A rude person accuses other people of being rude. A bigot accuses people of being narrow minded. That's projection. We all think that everyone shares our feelings. That they see the world through our eyes. But they don't.'

'Right.' They rolled out of the par park, heading north towards the Callerton Chase estate.

'So...nobody is ever what they claim to be?'

'Nope. And the interesting bit is the gap between the face they show the world and the person they really are.'

'You're wasted in this job, Lockwood. You know that?'

They drove past the airport. Kitty noticed a silver BMW M5 in her mirror, though she didn't give it a second thought. The police never imagine they are under surveillance.

'So our line is... This was a dispute between villains from the Far East. Our enquiries lead us to believe the murder was committed by a foreign national. A tragic and brutal killing but nothing to do with this city. We are pursuing inquiries with the relevant authorities. Full co-operation with our Chinese colleagues, blah blah. You OK with that?'

Bryson nodded. He tucked his file beneath his arm and followed Tony Vipond to the Media Room. Vipond swaggered onto the dais and blinked in the glare of the television lights. The room was almost full. Two dozen journalists and camera crew had gathered on the blue padded chairs. Bryson sat beside Vipond. Behind them hung the familiar blue backdrop with the yellow logo. Vipond nodded and winked at his favourite hacks. Bryson poured himself a glass of water and prayed they would ignore him.

'Morning, ladies and gentlemen,' said Vipond. 'I want to bring you up to date on our progress on the investigation of the unfortunate incident at the Jury's Inn Hotel...'

Kitty's memories of the house were of the blood around the pool, the raised voices. Now there was no crime scene tape across the drive. The front door lay open. A sprinkler on the lawn turned in a lazy arc, the water sparkling in the sun. Cathy Fletcher answered the door, a yellow duster and a jar of beeswax polish in her hands.

'Cathy - this is my colleague, Elayne. Mrs Lyndon is expecting us?'

'Just come through.'

They followed her through the house. The scent of furniture polish hung in the air. Kitty was surprised to find Marisa Lyndon by the pool. The lounger was new but she lay in the very place where she had been attacked. She wore sunglasses and a jumpsuit, a floral pattern on an oxblood background. A book on Caravaggio lay in her lap, face down. The dressing on her wound was small, the hair above the wound shaved. She seemed to be dozing. Her eyes flicked open and Kitty saw fear.

'Hi. You gave me a start.'

'Sorry, Marisa. This is my colleague? Elayne Hawes.' They nodded at each other.

When Cathy Fletcher went inside Kitty spoke to Marisa.

'Do you feel safe here?'

'I'd sooner be at home. They say I need rest.'

'We could post an officer here?' Kitty knew that her request was likely to be turned down.

'Jack wants me to have protection. But I said no. He's worried I might run away.' She was smiling, though Kitty wondered if she had leaked the truth.

'Have you any memories of the attack?' said Elayne.

'Only that I was lying there,' she pointed to the pool, 'making plans for the day. To be honest, I don't know if I remember even that. That's what people tell me.'

'Who?'

'Jack. And Cathy.'

They talked for a while about what Marisa could remember, which was little. Kitty stood as they took their leave. looked down the garden, to the trees along the river. The trees were in full leaf, the rookery almost hidden.

'Someone bought me this scent.' She walked to the lounger. Kitty held her wrist to Marisa's face. 'What do you think? Marisa recoiled, her eyes wide.

'Not your cup of tea?

As they left Marisa Lyndon's home Kitty noticed a silver BMW parked on the other side of the road. A pair of young men sat in the front seats, deep in conversation. She thought nothing of it. A Beamer counted as little more than a teenager's runabout in Callerton Chase.

'What was that all about?' asked Elayne. 'The wrist thing?'

'I have been blind,' said Kitty. 'Now I can see.'

'Right.' They travelled a mile or so. 'The talking in riddles thing. Not really working, is it?'

'She can't recall seeing or hearing anything from the morning of the attack. But her sense of smell seems to be working perfectly.

'Let's pretend I know what you're on about.' Elayne buckled her seatbelt. 'It's easier.'

Kitty dropped Elayne Hawes at Etal Lane. She signed out and headed for home. As she drove along the Military Road the light was fading to grey. The Roman road stretched ahead like a slender ribbon. Her mind drifted. She barely noticed the car in the mirror, rising and falling with the road. It was almost dark when she reached home. Heavy cloud gathered over the hills, an inky smudge in the clear sky.

Merlin met Kitty halfway up the little cul-de-sac of Cloud Street, twining his body around her leg. She opened the door to her empty house. Molly was sleeping over at Emma Chan's house. As Kitty struggled to pull the key from the lock her feet crunched on something on the doormat. She bent down to see what it was. Little bars of silver gleamed in the darkness. She reached to pick one up, then swore as it pricked her thumb. She sucked the cut and tasted blood. The floor, she realised, was covered with slivers of steel. Blades from a box cutter.

Or a Stanley knife, perhaps.

CHAPTER FORTY ONE

HENDRICK'S IS YOUR favourite - a long, cool glass of Hendrick's with the tang of juniper berries. Before all this you were five years sober. 'White knuckle sobriety,' they call it, in the rooms. 'White knuckle' because you're fighting the drink through will power alone. It's a ride that could throw you off at any moment. The anger is still there, raging below, a fire that never dies.

Five years sober. Until the start of May. You've slipped a bit since then. Wine too, now. Until then you were doing well. You're surprised by your own strength. But the drink is stronger. Deep down, you know it. So a glass of Hendrick's is the sign that you are losing control. The lemon, the tonic, the ice tinkling against the glass. All you can do is resist that first glass. Beyond that first sip, you are lost. You drink because the memories won't quit. The sneers about your crazy mother, your father and his spawn.

Your mother, mad as a hedge, getting worse as the years slip by. Pigeon plump, doped with lithium carbonate and carbamazepine. She ended up in Rowanwood. You can't blame her - he drove her mad, leaving, then coming back the way he did. You rarely visit because you can't stand to see her like that, wobble eyed, whispering to herself. 'Which one are you?' The taint of sweat and medication hangs about her. The smell on the wards, the cries of all those sad, crazy people. Misery hangs over some families like a thunderhead cloud. It lingers, moving from one generation to the next, passed on, like blue eyes or brown skin.

You wanted out. You made a new life. Once you made that decision, it was easy. You pulled yourself out of the mire.

As time passed the memories dulled. Life was sweet, or sweeter, at least. There was money. There were 'compensations'. And there was love. No-one stayed forever, but you didn't expect that. Only children expect love to last forever. In the end, everyone you love goes away.

But you met new people and some of them loved you. Most of them remained friends. That was a skill, was it not? Life was good until that little bitch turned up. She wanted to live your life. Tried to steal it. You would never let anybody take it away.

Cool, clear Hendricks. Gin lets you see the world in a different way. The sad thing is that every time you touch the stuff, things get a little strange.

Kitty was cooking pasta when she heard the knock. She licked sauce from her fingers before opening the door. Cloud Street was deserted but she heard a car rattle over the cobbles at the far end of the lane. The box lay on the ground. A white cardboard cube, big enough to hold a wedding cake. Blank, white, anonymous. There was no delivery note taped to the side, no writing at all. The hairs on her neck rose.

Kitty picked up the box and closed the door with her foot. A bitter odour hit her nostrils, a coppery scent like the taste of pennies. Her fingers stuck to the cardboard as she hurried to the kitchen. Molly yanked the neck of her top over her mouth.

'That stinks!'

'Spread that newspaper. Quickly!'

Kitty felt something seep through the seam and run down her fingers. She dropped the box on the kitchen table. Molly stood at her side. Brown, viscous liquid oozed into the newspaper, the stain spreading. The air was loaded with the coppery stench. Kitty gulped air through her mouth and buried her face in her shoulder.

'Open the door!' Kitty hurled the whole mess into the back garden. She dry retched into the sink, gagging, white flashes in her eyes as she rinsed her hands. Molly grabbed a carving knife from the block and slit the tape that sealed the box.

'Don't!' shouted Kitty. 'Leave it!' Gulping air she tore at the flaps. Merlin lay inside, his face pushed into a corner, his whiskers curling where they pressed against the cardboard. The cat's mouth was half open, ancient teeth peeping between the lips. His grey fur was matted with the blood which seeped from the wound in his neck. Something was scratched on the cardboard beside his body.

'*Drop it. Or your next.*'

Kitty tried to close the box but it was too late. By then Molly was howling.

When you return home after school your mother sits at the

kitchen table. There's a cup in her hand, a tea cup, but you know what's inside is something else. You drop your school bag on the floor.

'He's gone,' she says. 'For good.' Spain, she thinks. And half of you thinks that's fine and the other half is breaking apart, because he's your father, however bad he is. The police have been and gone. He's spent everyone's money, pissed it away on his Spanish whore. There's nothing left. You can forget the riding lessons, the holiday.

'We're on our own from now on. Just you and me,' she says. You sit beside her for a while. She takes a swig from the cup, her hand trembling as she brings it to her mouth. She shouldn't drink with the tablets. You think your mother might hurl the cup at the wall but she puts it down, the rim clicking the table top. She stares straight ahead.

'I'll say this for you Lockwood. You never give up.' Vipond perched on the edge of his desk. 'That's not a compliment, by the way.' He twisted his lighter in his fingers. 'You seem incapable of working in a team.' He flicked the switch and watched the flame.

'You were right, sir.' Kitty took advantage of his silence. 'I thought it was Jack Lyndon. I was wrong. You think it's Saul Kemp. You're wrong too.'

'I don't give a tuppenny toss what you think, Lockwood. I should have suspended you the first time. Your attempt at 'persuading' me shows the kind of person you are. You have five minutes to clear your desk. If you're not gone by then I'll have you chucked out.'

Her shoulders lifted. The relief was like a glass of cool water after a walk in the desert.

'And if you have any thoughts about trying to blackmail me, go ahead. Say whatever you like. Nobody in their right mind would ever think I tried it on with you, of all people. It would be your word against mine. I think we both know how that would play out.'

The water was too hot. Kitty replayed her conversation with Vipond for the twentieth time. His mind was made up. He had called her bluff. There was nothing to be done. She had known the risk.

Rain spattered the bathroom window, the wind tugging at the willows in the garden. She wanted to sleep. Her muscles stretched, uncoiled. A drop of sweat ran over her lip and fell on her neck. In her dream Merlin padded across the floor towards her. Blood dripped from his neck. She woke to hear the downstairs phone ringing.

Heather Lockwood, her mother, was her only regular caller on the landline. 'I don't like paying those mobile prices, Kathryn. He charges you a fortune!'

'Who does?'

'That Beardy Branson!'

One more ring and I'll answer it.

Kitty launched herself from the water and grabbed a towel. She ran down the stairs, a trail of drips falling on the carpet. She grabbed the phone. There was a crackle, the hiss of static. The phone was halfway back to the cradle when she heard a scratchy squawk.

'Kitty?' A man's voice.

'Speaking...' she said, softening her tone. This was not a call centre. She wedged the phone between her ear and shoulder as she secured the towel, tucking the corner tight. She heard a rhythmic sigh, a gritty, keening whine in the background.

'I'm coming.' His tone was amused, though there was no warmth there. 'I'm on my way.'

Her throat tightened. 'Who is this?'

He laughed. 'Laters.'

Kitty slammed the phone onto the cradle. She stared at the receiver as if she expected the mystery to be revealed. She dialled 1471. '*You were called today at 14.37 hours. The caller withheld their number...*'

A pool of water gathered around her toes. At the top of the stairs she paused, giddy, her knuckles white as she gripped the banister. She slumped onto the top stair, her eyes closed. She recognised the sound she had heard. The keening whine of a blade being sharpened on a whetstone.

'Daddy's back.'

You stare at her, your lips open. You take the stairs two at a time. He's in the bedroom, your mother's room, smoking a cigarette. He blows smoke through the open window. But he's not alone. There's a child on the floor, looking up at you. Blond hair, she wobbles towards you, wide eyed, holding out her arms. She wants to be cuddled. You want to hug your father but she's in the way.

Daddy flicks his cigarette out of the window. It falls, spraying sparks, like a firework. He kneels behind this child. He's smiling at you, his hands on the girl's shoulders.

'Say hello, Honor! Say hello to your little sister.'

Molly wandered down Hencote, a song floating around her head. Her schoolbag hung from her shoulder, the leather grazing the ground as it swung back and forth. She wandered into the cobbled ginnel that led towards the bus station. A figure entered from the far end, walking towards her through the gloom.

'Molly?'

She looked up into his face, half hidden by the hood.

'Are you Molly?'

'Yes?'

He put a hand on her shoulder. She could feel the warmth of his fingers as he squeezes her flesh.

'Tell your mam to watch herself, yeah? Chop chop!'

Molly shrugged off his hand and ran. As she hurried towards the bus stand her heart hammered in her chest.

CHAPTER FORTY TWO

'HONOR/BRYTE PR,' trilled the voice.

'Hi,' said Kitty.

'Daisy here. So...how can I help?'

'I need to see Honor Blackett. It's urgent. Is she there?'

'OK. So Honor's not here right now. She's meeting a client. To whom am I speaking?'

'That's a shame. I have these...' Kitty's searched for a plausible lie. 'I have these proofs which she really needs to see. To approve them.'

'Cool. So, OK, I can get a message to her. Who shall I say called?'

'Daisy.'

'Coolio! You're a Daisy too?

'Yup. That's me,' said Kitty. 'Daisy.'

'Brilliant! OK. Well, I can show them to her later. So would you like to ping them over? She's back in a couple of hours.'

Kitty took a chance. 'I'm meeting Caspar Greene this afternoon. Perhaps I can see her there? At the studio?'

'Of course. So...if you're going to Caspar's now, you should catch her...' Daisy's voice trailed off. On some level, she realised she had been duped.

'Who did you say you work for?'

'Thanks Daisy.' Kitty ended the call.

An hour earlier Molly had burst into the house, white faced and crying as she recounted her encounter. Now she sat beside Kitty as the Saab pulled up outside Caspar Greene's studio.

Kitty pushed open the steel door. At the far end of his studio Caspar Greene lolled on a stool. As before, his stained overalls gaped wide, open to the waist. Honor Blackett stood in front of him, her fingers on his chest. She half turned as she heard Kitty enter. The air in the room was an odd blend of scent and WD40. Kitty picked her way across the floor between chains hanging from the rafters.

'I have couple of questions.'

'Really?' Honor's smile wobbled.

'If you wrote down what we said, in your lickle notebook,' said Caspar, miming licking a pencil. 'Then you wouldn't forget.'

'Was it me you wanted to speak to? Or Caspar?'

'You'll do.' Kitty's heart pounded. She made a conscious effort to slow her breathing. Losing it now would be a disaster.

Aim between the eyes.

She fixed her gaze on the bridge of Honor's nose. 'One question.'

'We've a plane to catch,' said Caspar. At the edge of her vision, Kitty saw the white of his teeth as he grinned. Honor stepped closer.

Hit her.

'Friday the 24th May. Can you tell me where were you that morning?'

'I couldn't possibly say.' Honor rocked on her heel. 'I'd need to look at my diary. I could check with Daisy and get back to you?'

'Do that.'

'And when I know what I was doing that morning, do I pass that information to you? Or to Tony...?'

Kitty took a step forward. Their faces were inches apart. Honor's scent cloyed, catching in Kitty's throat.

'It's just I heard you'd been sacked. I'm sorry about that.' Honor's smile was teasing. 'Life's just not fair, is it? I hope you find the strength to deal with that.'

'Thank you.' Kitty's nose was an inch from Honor's face. 'I just did.'

As the studio door slammed Honor's smile vanished.

'That was exciting,' Caspar said. He murmured in her ear and slipped a grimy hand between her legs. She pushed him away. Caspar flopped onto the stool, shaking his head.

Honor hurried to her car. It took her several minutes to find a working phone box. She heaved the door wide and clamped her hand to her face. The box stank of piss. She held the phone away from her ear as she punched the buttons. The call connected.

'See me at the usual place. In an hour.'

Whitey watched the air above the line of cars shimmer. He

was steaming inside his tracky - sweat slipped down his back, gathering into a cool trickle between his buttocks. He yanked the cap from his head and scratched the ginger stubble which covered his skull. Something shifted at the edge of his vision. Above the entrance to the multi-storey a camera swivelled in his direction. Whitey pulled his cap low, tucked his chin onto his chest as he hurried into the gloom.

Her Maserati was parked in the same slot as before. Honor did not look at him as he approached. He opened the door and slid inside. The car was filled with her scent. They sat in silence. She looked straight ahead while he listened to the tick of the dashboard clock. She opened her bag and handed him a brown envelope. He did not have the courage to open it, though he could feel the thick wad of notes inside.

Something bad.

'My friend is still causing problems.'

He nodded.

Very bad.

'I need you to make this problem go away.' She waited a moment before she went on, her voice low and slow. 'I need a man to do that.'

Whitey swallowed. She looked in the mirror, touching her hair. Her scent was stronger now. He looked at her neck, the line emerging from the silk shirt. 'I'd do anything,' she said. 'For that.'

CHAPTER FORTY THREE

'BUSY DAY?'

THE words seemed innocent, yet the hair prickled on Greta's skin. Her keys chinked as she dropped them on the hall table. Clive lay on the sofa, as usual, his eyes fixed on the racing. She sensed there was something different about him.

'Fine. Good! A good day.' She touched his shoulder as she passed, careful not to come too close. In the bathroom she dropped her clothes into the laundry basket, intending to wash them as soon as she was clean. She stepped into the shower. Closing her eyes, she felt the warm needles prick her skin. The spray hit her face. She thought about Bryson. She felt an unexpected fondness for him.

A click. A body against hers. Lips on her neck, fingers in her hair. Her eyes opened then closed, stung by the gel. Whispered words in her ear, a hand on her shoulder, pushing her face against the tiled wall. Her cheek slammed against the tiles. He seized a hank of hair and moved behind her, then inside her. Clive mumbled in her ear, a low, animal grunt. The words were muffled but she sensed their cruelty. What followed was brutal, a blur of images, a torrent of pain.

At last he groaned and his head slumped forward, his brow resting between her shoulder blades. They were like that for a while, the water running over their skin. He pushed open the door and left the shower. She was aware of a shape, a blur beyond the frosted glass. The bathroom door slammed. Water hissed down, streamed over her skin, a rushing white noise. She leaned against the tiles. She looked down, watching the water circle as it slipped away. Her knees were shaking and for a moment she thought she might tumble to her knees. She reached for the tap and switched off the water. In the silence she heard the *ploink ploink* of droplets falling into the water, the curling, swirling pink around her feet.

She dabbed her skin with a towel, knotted her robe and walked into the kitchen. The marble top, the range, the familiar bright gleaming surfaces all looked just the same. She saw her reflection in the surface of the kettle. A wisp of steam trailed from the spout. She inhaled the lemony tang of the surface cleaner. The burble of the racing commentary drifted through from the next room. Everything was the same, yet everything had changed. She stared at the knife block, six black handles sprouting from the blond wood. Her fingers closed over the smallest knife. She pulled it from the block and looked at the gleaming blade. Greta slipped it into her pocket. She walked into the sitting room, where Clive lay on the sofa, his mouth open as he watched the 3.10 from Chepstow.

You were running the Coudray concession. You had a good run but by then, you'd had enough. You were on your way, in spirit, though the flesh was still obliged to turn up nine to five, Sundays and Mondays excepted.

It was a Friday morning when she turned up. It was one minute after nine. The store was barely open. You had yet to have your caffeine kick. It took a moment to recover.

'Hey!' You worked up a smile. She put her arms around you and pulled you close. You patted shoulders.

'What are *you* doing here?'

'Working!'

'Not here?' Your heart sank. 'Really?'

'It gets worse!' She moved forward, into your space. 'On this counter.'

'That's...'

'Yeah! Dad had a word. He knows the regional rep.'

'Does he? That's fantastic!'

'Isn't it? He knew you were working here. So, you know...I think he thought you could look out for me, or something. This could be so much fun!

She produced the paperwork. You read the letter. You folded the letter and handed it back. She was the same as she had always been. Full of life and laughter. Her skin honey tanned and flawless. She was you, but younger.

'You had no idea?'

You shook your head.

'That's a bit naughty! Maybe he wanted to keep it as a surprise.'

Holding that smile in place was hurting.

'Where are you living?'

'I've got a room in a house. Off Acorn Road.'

'Nice,' you said, nodding. 'Good.'

There was a moment of silence while she looked up at you, waiting. Smiling.

'What do you know about scent?'

'I just love *Fleurissimo*. And *Vanderbilt* - they're my new favourites. '

'Really?' Her knowledge was unsettling.

'*Vanderbilt* is so refined!' she said. 'Kind of Oriental, don't you think?' She half closed those green eyes, pretending to swoon at the scent. 'Carnation, mimosa, rose. Spicy florals!' She was laughing. 'Think I'm some sort of 1970's throwback !' She twisted her blond mane into a loose knot and stabbed it with a hair stick.

'We don't sell *Fleurissimo* here,' you said. 'All of these fragrances are based on old formulas. *Vanille et Coco, Jacinthe et Rose, Givrine*.'

'Oh, I love the vintage thing,' said Marisa. 'You must love them too!'

Because I'm old?

But Marisa was oblivious. She was arranging the stock, moving a display, spiffing and primping.

'OK. You hold the fort? I need to make a couple of calls.'

You went upstairs, to the main office. They confirmed it. You were angry, though you were on your way. Sure enough, when you came back, the little cow had sold a hundred quid's worth of stock. You were sweet about it. Somehow you managed not to kill her right then.

Greta stood in front of the screen. Clive craned his neck to see the screen.

'Why?'

He gave a one shouldered shrug. 'You're my wife.' His eyes never left the screen. She knew the way Clive was but never believed he would use violence on her.

'To remind you.' He looked her in the eye.

'Of *what*?' Her voice was hoarse.

'That I'm still here.' He flicked the remote and switched off the television. 'You think Dusty Bính takes any notice of you?'

'What are you talking about?'

'He was on the phone to me before you started the car. It was a load of cock.'

'What? I don't understand. What are you talking about?'

'The Viet hit man.' He chuckled. '*Chien*'. All that shit.' He smirked as he tossed the remote onto the table. 'Dusty told me you wanted to know all about that business in the hotel. So I took a little time to find out why. Then I told Lê Van Bính to spin you the line about the Vietnamese hitman. I knew you'd feed that to Prudhoe. When it came on the news I knew I was right. I don't just watch the horses, you know.'

Greta's hand moved to her pocket. She turned the knife between her fingers.

'Clive. I thought it might help you.'

'Help me?'

'To have Bryson Prudhoe owe us.'

'Forget it Greta. I know everything. Stop digging, eh?'

He picked up the remote and switched the on button. He watched the screen, the horses loping around the paddock, the jockeys in their silks. Her fingers tightened around the handle of the knife.

'What happened in the hotel?'

'Why? Who are you going to tell?'

'Nobody.'

'The Chinkies got a bit ambitious. Taking the piss, weren't they? Lessons needed to be learned. There was this kid I was padded up with in Durham. He owed me. But he's a kid. He went a bit over the top. He's a bit over enthusiastic, Whitey. He was only supposed to frighten the little fucker...'

Davy Clark didn't want anything to do with it. He glanced at the wad of tenners in Whitey's hand and shook his head. Whitey shuffled the fifties like a deck of cards. It was more money than either one had ever seen.

'Nah.' Davy Clark shook his head. 'If they found out...'

'They won't.'

Davy shrugged and walked away. He took a wrench from the box and bent over the engine block, tapping and grunting. Whitey knew Davy was avoiding his eye so he clucked like a bantam. Davy Clark pushed his head further into the engine. 'Not worth it man.'

Whitey knew how to handle Davy Clark by now. Since three stretch, things had changed between them. Whitey was not prepared to take shit from anyone. Not even Davy. He waited a while, then picked up a piece of dowelling from the bench. With a click he opened Stanley. He leaned back against the bench and scraped a sliver of wood from the dowel, watching it curl and fall to the floor. He cut again, enjoying the way the blade skirred through the wood. Shavings gathered around his new Nikes. After five minutes Davy Clark sighed. Whitey pretended not to notice. Another slice feathered to the floor. Davy wiped his fingers on an oily rag which he threw on the floor.

'Fifty fifty.'

Whitey grinned. 'Sweet. So. We need to go shopping.'

CHAPTER FORTY FOUR

WICKES (ST JAMES Retail Park) Till: 011 Mandy 16:53
    Retractable trimming knife - £2.39
    Heavy Duty Trimming Knife Blades, Pack 5 - £1.99
    Self Adhesive Gaffa Tape 50MM X 45M (Pack 4) - £20.80
    Blue 6mm Multi-Purpose Polypropylene Rope 3000mm
    - £7.49
    Heavy Duty Rubble Sacks, Pack 30 - £7.99
    Sale TOTAL   £40.66

'I want to know who you're meeting.'

'I told you. Emily Chan.'

'And if you see Lorelle and her crew?'

'She steers clear of me, these days.'

'But if you do see her?'

'I walk away.' Molly tapped her fingers against the door handle, eager to escape.

'And no drinking. OK?'

Molly sighed. 'There's Chan.'

'Just be careful...'

The car door slammed and Molly was gone, running across the grass towards her friend. The two girls hugged. Kitty recalled when she and Jacqui were that age, their heads together, whispering as they plotted another scheme. Molly was laughing now, her arm on Emily Chan's shoulder as they walked towards the river. Kitty knew that Molly had changed since her return from Paris. The house was a little more peaceful but there was sadness too. Her daughter was no longer a child.

Kitty arrived early for the class. She began her stretches, alone in the empty hall. The door swung open as Raphael entered.

'We've missed you!'

'Work, you know? This and that.'

Raphael nodded. He dropped his bag in the corner and began his stretches. They pulled the mats into position as the class arrived in ones and twos. Kitty sparred with several partners, though she avoided young Neville, for both their sakes. After the class Raphael opened the side doors of the hall. Kitty sat with him, looking across the cricket pitch. It was a perfect June evening. Swallows swooped low, skimming the grass.

'How are things?'

'I'm suspended from work.'

'Not so good.'

'It's a relief, to be honest. I could walk away from all this. Do something different. Become a teacher, or work in Greggs. Whatever.' She shrugged. 'Risking losing my job was a bit stupid! I still have twenty years on the mortgage.'

'But you did the right thing?'

'I didn't have any choice in the matter. Maybe. The right thing. In the wrong way! My dad used to say I was too stubborn.'

They listened to the river, a whisper that echoed beneath the bridge. Raphael closed his eyes against the sun. 'Perhaps...'he said. She raised her hand to her brow, shielding her eyes against the dazzle. He cleared his throat and tried again. 'Would you consider...going out? Somewhere? With me? Perhaps?'

Kitty continued the pretence of gazing into the setting sun.

'Well, I don't know. I suppose I might.'

She drove home with a grin on her face, feeling as if she were sixteen again. She was still smiling as she swung her kit bag over her shoulder and headed along Cloud Street towards home.

They mooched up and down the river path for a while. Molly sat on their favourite bench. The sun glinted off the river.

'I can't wait to get away from this place!' After a while, she realised that Emily Chan was not listening, but was looking over Molly's shoulder, towards the trees that covered the higher part of the riverbank. 'Stop it! You're creeping me out, Chan!' Molly turned to look. Half hidden beneath the rowans that lined the bank stood two young men. They weren't dressed like village boys. This pair were in their twenties and they had an urban look - Nike trainers and Burberry jackets. The tall, thin one was staring back at the girls, while the fat lad was kicking something through the grass.

'Don't stare at them!' Molly whispered. The girls walked along the path towards Belfordham village. The young men watched, then followed. Molly bit her lip. Though anxious, she found it hard not to laugh. As they walked towards the bridge she sneaked sidelong glances at their admirers. The young men drifted ever closer.

'What do we do?' hissed Emily. Before Molly could answer, the boys hurried towards them. They stood on the dusty path, blocking the way to the village, and safety. One lad the tall one, wore a fixed smile and stared intently at her. The other youth, fatter, with a wispy beard, looked uneasy, avoiding their gaze. Molly recognised the boy from the ginnel.

'Hello girls!' he said. Tall and pale skinned, the youth looked down at Molly. 'Like to come for a ride?'

Kitty showered, singing as the water splashed her skin. She hummed a tune as she skipped around the kitchen in her robe. She smiled to herself as she made a drink and a sandwich. She was always hungry after a class. It was only as she sat down to eat that she noticed how silent the place was. It took her a moment to realise that she had the house to herself. Molly had not come home yet.

She checked her mobile but there were no messages. She rang Molly but the call went straight to answerphone. She took another bite of her sandwich, then pushed it away. Dusk was falling, the trees hardening into silhouettes against the golden sky. She tried Molly's phone again. Kitty's unease grew. Perhaps the girls had run into Lorelle and her crew.

She hurried to the car without locking the house. Bats flitted through the gloom. Dusk had fallen and the light in the narrow, sheltered land was dim. Kitty jumped into the Saab and started the motor. As the car rattled down Cloud Street she switched on her lights. She was about to turn into the car park by the river when she spoke aloud, voicing her worry for Molly. 'Where *are* you?'

'Here,' said the voice from the back seat. 'I'm right here.'

CHAPTER FORTY FIVE

WHEN THEY REACHED the sanctuary of the bridge they collapsed against the parapet wall, panting for breath. They felt safe here. There were drinkers outside the Lamb a few yards away, the tips of their cigarettes glowing in the dusk. Molly leaned against the wall, her chest heaving.

'I'm so unfit, Chan!'

'Where are they?'

The girls looked back across the bridge. The young men were nowhere to be seen.

'That was him.' said Molly.

'Who?'

'The one I told you about. The one who cornered me in the lane.'

The belt snaked around her neck, slapping as it tightened. Kitty cried out, jerking forward in reflex. The Saab shimmied, tyre rims scuffing the gravel at the edge of the road. His lips touched her ear. 'Straight on!' She glanced into the mirror to see a head beside her own. A black balaclava covered his face, one slit for the eyes, another for the mouth. A click and a blade glinted in the gloom. A moment later the sharp tip pricked the skin below her ear. She bit her lip, stifling a scream.

'Just drive.'

A few minutes later they were on the bypass and the adrenaline kicked in. Her legs shook, trembling as she tried to work the pedals of the Saab.

'I warned you. You should listen when people talk.'

She caught a whiff of foisty clothes and cheap cologne.

'What do you want?'

This earned a tug on the belt. The car wobbled as her hands jerked on the wheel. They rolled along the deserted road. She tried to understand why she had not seen him. The car had been unlocked, as always. There was little crime in Cloud Street, no car theft in Belfordham. Her mind had been elsewhere, with Raphael, with her date, the possibility of the future. That seemed unreal now, a cruel joke.

'Tell me what it is you want?'

Wet lips pressed against her skin. 'Shut up.' He tugged the belt again until she gagged. He twisted the belt and the world turned black. The Saab drifted towards the edge of the road. As the wheels bumped the verge he loosened his grip. Her eyes opened and she gulped air. They travelled the dark road in silence. She wanted to remember everything about him, to fix him in her mind - his accent, the cadence of his voice, his scent. The smell of him sickened her - the cheap cologne, the air freshener stink of his clothes. His gloves were black neoprene, like those in a wetsuit. His mask was stretch polyester, the fabric ribbed, with a gaiter which covered his neck. Kitty glimpsed pale blue eyes and the bridge of his nose, his pink skin sheeny with sweat.

'Next right.'

The road took her north, along the side of the valley, towards the moorland. The car climbed steadily towards the hills, the road a grey braid lit only by headlights. The hawthorn hedges gave way to dry stone walls as they reached the higher ground. After ten minutes he ordered her to slow down.

'Turn here.'

They rolled down a stony farm track, the grass and reeds scraping the exhaust.

'Switch off,' he said, his voice husky as he leaned towards her.

Molly sensed the house was empty even before she pushed at the unlocked door. The lane was empty with no sign of her mother's Saab. She hoped her mother had not gone to the park to collect her. Molly's shout echoed around the darkened rooms. She called her mother's mobile. Kitty would never answer her phone while driving. Molly heard the call click through to Answerphone.

'Hi, Mum. Just me.' She bit her lip. 'I'm home. OK? See you later?' She broke the connection and sat on the bottom stair in the darkness.

The wind rocked the car.

Talk to him.

'My name is Kitty.'

'I know your fucking name.'

'Of course you do.'

'I know everything about you. Where you live. What you do. I know where your daughter is right now. Which is more than you do, you cunt!'

'We can both walk away from this.'

'*We can both walk away from this*,' he whined, mimicking her.

'You could take the car.'

He yanked the belt so tight her feet lifted from the floor.

'And you could shut your hole!'

Kitty was on the edge of blacking out. She kicked out, her shoes scraping against the windscreen. Pink light flashed behind her eyes and she felt as if her head was about to explode. He released the belt and she coughed, gasping for breath. Tears flooded her eyes. The hooded man leaned back. As she caught her breath she watched him in the mirror. He moaned and shuddered, his eyes rolling into his skull. It was as if she were watching an animal, a different species. She wanted to destroy him.

A car passed on the main road. Kitty glimpsed the lights through gaps in the wall. When it was gone the darkness seemed more profound. The moorland merged with the night sky. Somewhere over the rise something was moving. Yellow eyes glinted in the darkness. A flock of blackface ewes coughed and bleated, calling their young.

The shadow hung over Molly, a premonition of disaster. She moved from room to room, switching on every light. But her anxiety would not quit. It was unusual for Kitty to leave without texting. Molly checked again, looking in all the usual places. She called her mother's phone once more but there was no reply. The likely explanation was that her mother had been called to work. She had no idea that Kitty had been suspended.

Kitty's phone rang, the galloping intro to Bobby Fuller's '*I Fought the Law*.'

'Give it here,' said the man in the mask. She raised the mobile, holding it in her fingertips. He switched off the phone and slipped it into his pocket. The silence stretched into minutes. The distant city threw a dim glow into the sky above the horizon. Kitty watched the stars appear, one by one. Ursa Minor took shape to the north, the tail of the Plough stretched overhead. Every few seconds she glanced in the mirror, watching the faceless silhouette.

'What's the plan?'

A car passed on the main road. The sound of the motor faded into the distance. She wondered about the time. Eleven, perhaps? Would she be missed?

'Are we staying here all night?'

Silence. Kitty would not let him forget that she was a human being, living and breathing.

'This is about Marisa Lyndon, isn't it?' She looked for his eyes, though the light was too dim. 'That's why you told me to drop it.' She stared at him, waiting for a nod, a sound. His wheezed a little, as if he was asthmatic. 'Do you mind telling me how much you got paid?'

'Shut your mouth.'

'What's the going rate? For this sort of thing?'

He turned to look out of the side window.

'Tell me about her.' She waited.

'Who?'

'The woman who hired you.'

He sighed. A car rattled along the back road. She watched it in her mirror, checking its progress by the glow of the headlights above the stone wall. The car slowed. Headlights lit the gateway, then swung around as the car headed down the track. Kitty's heart skipped. The cavalry were coming over the hill. Headlight beams strafed the moor as the car rocked and rolled towards them. The figure in the back turned to look. Revealed by a beam of light, he seemed smaller, his mask almost comical. The car halted behind them. The lights stayed on. Kitty heard a car door slam and the sound of footsteps. Fat knuckles rapped on the rear window. There was a sigh as the figure in the back fiddled with the door.

'It's stuck.'

'It's the child lock,' said Kitty.

'How do you open the window?'

Kitty watched his reflection struggle with the door.

'Would you like me to open the window?'

'Yes!'

'Please.'

'Please. Open the fucking window!'

She pressed the button. A pale face appeared in the gap, a young man with a plump face, his cheeks flushed. Bum fluff dusted his top lip.

'Mask!' hissed the man in the back. The pink face vanished. Kitty heard a rustling as the newcomer pulled out his mask and tugged it into place.

'You took your time,' hissed the man in the back. 'Where have you been?'

'I got LOST, man!'

The belt around Kitty's neck sagged. If she was to run, now was the moment.

'It all looks the same out here!'

'To a fuckin' divvy!'

Kitty raised her hands, sliding them over her breasts. Her fingertips touched the edge of the leather belt. If she could flip it over her head, open the door and run into the darkness, the fat lad would never catch her. The Masked Man would take five or six seconds to clamber from the car. By then she would be away, lost in the darkness. She hesitated and the belt jerked tight. Moist lips brushed her ear.

'Out!'

She opened the door. The Masked Man handed the belt to the Fat Lad.

'Got it?' The Fat Lad grunted.

'Hands behind your back.' The belt was jerked and she stumbled. She heard a crackle, then a screech as gaffa tape was peeled from a roll and wrapped around her wrists. She tried to separate her hands but they were trapped as the tape was pulled tight. Tape clagged her hair as he wound it around her head. She fought the panic as he taped her eyes. 'Wait.' He was still. 'Come closer,' she said, her voice low.

'Why?'

She waited, counting the seconds, stretching the silence as long as she dared. 'I want to tell you a secret.' She sensed him, felt his gaze as he looked down at her. He laid a hand on her shoulder. She heard the wheeze of his breath as he moved closer. Bristled skin brushed her cheek.

'What?' His voice was hoarse.

'She will be caught.'

'Fuck off.' He sniggered. Yet she heard doubt mixed with the contempt.

'She will be caught.'

'No fucking chance!' The stale scent of him filled her nostrils.

'And when they question her, they'll ask her why you killed me.'

She waited, willing herself to stay calm, to control the fear. The silence stretched. 'Do you know what she'll say?'

'No?' His voice was thick, the word sticking in his throat.

'She'll say it was your idea.' Kitty listened to him breathe, in and out. 'All your idea.'

The sound of his breathing faded as he straightened.

'You think she'll go down for it? She'll throw you under the bus. It will be you walking the floor of your pad every night, wondering why the rich get away with murder.'

His hand slipped from her shoulder. 'Hope she's worth it,' said Kitty. She tensed, expecting the next thing would be a blow to the head. Her eyes were flooded with darkness. The wind blew softly through the grass. 'Come on Whitey man!' She heard a rasping screech.

He taped her mouth and her nose. Someone kicked her from behind and she fell onto the grass. Dew soaked her face. One of the men straddled her. The tape screeched as they bound her ankles.

'Don't use all of it, divvy!'

'Fuck off, man!'

Kitty breathed through a slit below her nostrils. They stood above her, panting from their efforts.

'Boot,' said the Masked Man.

There was a pause, followed by scuffling and swearing. The car doors opened and were slammed.

'Where's the catch?' The sound of a car door opening. She imagined they had taken the keys and were trying to open the boot. Metal scratched metal.

'Leave it, man!'

'What about the keys?'

'Hoy them.'

She heard a swish as her keys arced through the air. They landed far away. In the silence that followed Kitty heard an odd sound, a click and whirr that reminded her of a grasshopper. They were taking pictures on a phone, she realised. Someone kneeled beside her. Another click. Close ups. The lips brushed her skin, nuzzling her neck.

'Nighty night.' A hand stroked the top of her head, ruffling her hair. She felt the beat of their footsteps in her cheekbone. Car doors slammed. The whine of the motor faded as they gunned the BMW up the track. The engine roared as they reached the main road. The sound of the car faded. A cool breeze blew through a gap in the tape around her neck. Alone at last, Kitty had time to think.

Molly searched the cloud of numbers scratched on the kitchen wall beside the phone. She called Bryson's mobile, counting seven rings before he answered.

'Mr Prudhoe?'

'Right. Is that you, Molly?' He sounded out of breath, as if he had been running.

'I'm sorry to bother you. I'm trying to find my mam.'

'Where is she? Sorry. Stupid question! Where are you?'

'At home. The house was empty when I got home. And dark. Mum dropped me at the park. I got home an hour ago.'

'You've tried her mobile? Obviously...'

'She's probably gone to work. It's just that she usually leaves a note.'

There was a pause, the hiss of dead air. Just as Molly thought he had rung off, he spoke again.

'I'll try her phone, Molly. But call the station now. Got the number? Tony Vipond might know. Someone should have some idea. OK?'

The BMW hit ninety five. Whitey tore the balaclava from his head and wiped the sweat from his face.

'Are ye fuckin' mental, or what, man?'

Davy Clark leaned over the steering wheel, his mask scrunched into a pile on top of his head. His eyes flicked between his companion and the road. The glow from the dash lit Davy's plump cheeks.

'Slow down, man! Fuck's sake! If the Bizzies stop us now, that's it! Finito!'

So Davy Clark cut his speed. Whitey found the pictures of Kitty and messaged them to his pc. He picked the SIM card from his phone. 'Open the window.' Cool night air filled the car. Whitey reached lobbed Kitty's phone into the darkness. The mobile clattered along the road, scattering plastic along the tarmac.

'I could've sold that, man!'

Whitey shook his head and sighed. 'They can trace an iPhone, you dick!' He clicked his fingers. 'Any fuckin' phone.' He waited a moment then flicked the SIM card into the bushes by the road. 'They're probably doin' that right now, you cocknocker!'

At one that morning Molly called the station at Etal Lane.

'She's not here,' said Tony Vipond. 'I wouldn't expect to see her. She's suspended.'

'Is she? What does that mean?'

'It means that you and your mother need to have a talk. Sorry. No idea where she is. Go to bed. I'm sure she'll be back in the morning.'

Vipond ended the call. Molly went upstairs and climbed into bed. For a moment she considered ringing her gran. But Heather Lockwood would be asleep and terrified to hear the phone ring at night. Molly switched off her light and lay on her back, her eyes wide, staring at the ceiling.

Kitty rubbed the heels of her hands against each other. The skin grew warm but the tape was tight and the movement it allowed was meager. She moved her hands in a steady rhythm, palm against palm. To keep her mind active she thought about the events of the last days. She had been too eager to assume that Jack Lyndon was behind the attack. Her certainty had blinded her to other possibilities. The truth had been in front of her all along.

After half an hour the glue on the tape had torn the fine hair from the skin around her wrists. Her arms were sore, her fingers swollen and prickling with trapped blood. The tape twisted into thin strands like cord. When waves of claustrophobia hit she tried to think about a place she had been happy. The Place des Vosges came to mind, the chaffinch beneath the table, Molly laughing. Kitty watched the little bird inside her head and the panic faded. Once again she flexed her hands, pushing them apart. She varied the action, moving them in a circle. The pain was worse, though the tape seemed to stretch and loosen.

She scrunched her fingers together, closing them like the petals of a tulip. When she tried to ease her hand free the gap was too narrow. She worked the tape for another ten minutes. When she tried again her hand slipped free. Her fingers felt like dead things. The flesh prickled as the blood began to flow. When feeling came back to the tips of her fingers she peeled the tape from her face, groaning with pain. One eye was freed, then her mouth. She lost her lashes and eyebrows but the relief of being able to see was exquisite. She picked strands of the tape from her skin.

In a few minutes she was free. She rubbed feeling into her limbs. Each minute the sky grew lighter. Her teeth chattered and she shivered, suddenly aware of the cold. Kitty unbuttoned her trousers and squatted by the car to piss. The relief was intense. She turned her face to the sky and grinned. She was free. Leaning against the car she looked around, hoping to glimpse her keys in the dew spangled grass. She began to pace the ground, moving out from the car in an ever widening spiral. The sheep watched her, keeping a wary eye open, moving away with their lambs if she came too close. When she was a hundred yards from the car she retraced her steps, spiralling in. She was about to give up when the rising sun glinted on metal. She clutched the keys and shouted with relief. Then she sat on the bonnet of her car and let the tears fall.

CHAPTER FORTY SIX

CIVILISATION IS A delicate, fragile creation. It falls apart so easily, like a suit of armour made from rice paper. No mobile, no car keys, no hot water and you're back in the Middle Ages in a moment. Kitty drove fifteen miles before she found a public phonebox. She called home.

'I was worried sick!' Molly burst into tears. 'Where have you *been*?'

'Everything's fine.' Kitty was aware of the irony - she had stayed out all night and was calling home like a guilty teenager. The mother/daughter dynamic seemed to have shifted. 'Call Bryson now. Call Elayne Hawes too. Tell them I'm on my way to see Honor Blackett. Can you do that? Honor Blackett. OK? I have to go, kiddo.'

Kitty broke the connection. She leaned her forehead against the glass door of the call box. The air inside stank of piss. A khaki coloured substance was smeared over the door and a gentleman called 'Makka' had spent hours etching his name into the perspex. She tried to remember Vipond's mobile number but it eluded her. After two wrong numbers she gave up. She stared at the phone for a moment before she understood what she must do next.

'It's me.'

Bryson recognised Greta's voice from those two words. He had replayed it in his mind every minute since they parted. From her tone he sensed her mood. She was scared, not playful.

'I know.'

He slipped from the bed. Maureen stirred, her eyes flickered, then closed.

'I'm sorry.' He heard Greta's voice break. In the front room a dustsheet lay on the carpet, step ladders leaned against the wall. In the morning light he could see that the shade he'd chosen was wrong. 'What I told you, Bryson. All that? It was a lie.'

Bryson dabbed his fingertip against the windowsill. The gloss was almost dry.

'I don't understand.'

'He lied to me. It was a test. He knows. There was no 'Chien.' It was some kid he met in Durham. Some nutty kid with a sword.'

'Greta?'

But the line was dead.

'Honor/Bryte PR.' The voice sounded sleepy.

'I need to speak to Honor.'

'Who is this?'

'It's...it's your old pal, Daisy.'

'I'm sorry.' She was wide awake now. 'I've been told not to speak to you.'

'Wait!' The line was still open. 'Do you know the penalty for obstructing a police officer?' The phone hissed softly. At least Daisy was still listening.

'No.'

'I need to know where she is, Daisy. That's all. In the city, or in the country?'

'She's packing. Her flight leaves in a couple of hours.'

'Where's she going?'

'New York.'

'With Caspar?'

'I think I've said enough. Don't you?' The line went dead.

Honor's card was tucked inside her purse. Kitty tapped the postcode for Shaftoe Hall, Honor's country retreat, into her satnav. The gentle Irish voice said 'Turn around, whenever possible.' She pointed the Saab to the north and drove. The satnav took a while to find the satellite. When it did the screen told her she was seven miles south of her destination. This was an ancient road, the cattle drovers' trail that led to Otterburn, through Kielder Forest and up to the Scottish Border. Most of the time it was little wider than a country lane which snaked between hills and woods, twisting and rising ever upwards. For centuries shepherds and drovers used this route, driving their beasts to fairs on both sides of the Border. A mile to the right the land rose in a steep ridge which ran parallel to the road. The morning sun shone golden light on the gorse and bracken. As the land rose the soft, green pasture gave way to moorland and scrub. White sandstone poked through the thin soil like bone. After five miles Kitty glimpsed a farmhouse clinging to the brow of the ridge. She cut her speed. Moving along the track was a car, a plume of dust in its wake.

Kitty looked for the opening to the track. A hefty metal gate blocked the entrance. She drove on and parked the Saab in a layby sheltered by a clump of Scots Pine. She rooted around in the glove compartment until she found a small pair of binoculars, a Christmas gift from Molly. She jogged back to the gateway and peered up at the ridge. Honor's Maserati was parked outside the farmhouse. An electronic gate blocked the entrance to the track. An intercom was mounted on the gatepost. Kitty's finger hovered over the button. Her hand fell to her side. Better to catch Honor unawares. She looked up at the ridge, gauging a route from the gate to the farm. The last quarter mile, up to the ridge itself, was very steep.

Kitty scrambled over the dry stone wall. Avoiding the dusty track she hurried across the scrub pasture, half crouching as she moved between the clumps of gorse.

You watch her climb the track. You feel anger - the irritation one feels at a yapping dog. Your flight leaves in three hours. But it is not entirely her fault, the yapping dog. What do you do if a supplier lets you down? You make contact. Give him a chance to put things right. He tells you he's on his way to finish the job. It is time to put an end to this.

The hill rose to meet her, as steep as a cliff. Kitty paused to catch her breath. The ridge towered above her and she had lost sight of the farmhouse. A huge boulder rested on the crest, seeming to hang in the air above her head. There was no way forward, apart from the track which ran through a notch in the cliff face. She wiped her brow and walked on, feeling the tug in her thighs as she climbed. After a while the track widened to reveal the farmhouse and the stone buildings to each side. Kitty stood and looked at the house. Shaftoe Hall was a square Georgian mansion of weathered grey stone. The white framed windows ranged along both floors in the regular, classical style, yet there was something a little rough, a touch ramshackle about the place. On the gravel drive that ran in front of the house sat Honor's black Maserati.

Her feet crunched the pea gravel. Kitty stepped softly, anxious to conceal her presence for as long as possible. As she lifted her head she saw Honor, watching from the doorway.

'I knew it would be you,' she said. Her smile was cool. She was dressed in a dark blue gilet, jeans and walking shoes. She held a shepherd's crook, resting both hands on the bone handle. Jabbing the point into the ground, she looked beyond Kitty, towards the road at the foot of the valley.

'It's good timing. I'm taking Spike for his walk. It's our routine - you don't mind, do you?'

Honor strode onto the path that followed the line of the ridge. The American bulldog, Spike, sniffed Kitty's hand. She looked down at the powerful jaws, the wary eyes, the broad chest above the beast's sturdy legs.

'Good boy!' Spike waddled ahead, trotting to catch his mistress. Honor strode on without looking back. Kitty fell into step.

'You found the place OK? What a clever woman you are!'

'The postcode is on your card, Honor. And I have a Satnav. I'm not Sherlock Holmes.'

'Perhaps 'clever' isn't the word, then. 'Persistent,' perhaps? Difficult to remove? Like a tick.'

'I'm sure you're right.'

Honor opened a kissing gate that led onto the moorland.

'Is this an official visit?'

'No.'

'I sort of knew that. Because you're suspended, aren't you?'

Kitty knew this was the last moment she could bail out with dignity intact. To go further was risky. But she had protected Marisa Lyndon and would not let that go. And she had nothing to lose.

'Yes. I have you to thank for that, don't I?'

Honor closed the gate and walked onto the moor. A fresh breeze pushed the clouds across the wide open sky. The grass was studded with boulders, the stone weathered and twisted into odd shapes. They walked along the ridge path, side by side.

'Where are we going, Honor?'

'In life? Or this afternoon?'

'Either.'

'This is our usual walk, isn't it Spike?' Honor clicked her tongue and the dog looked up, is slender tail beating a steady rhythm. 'We do this every day we're here. Spike doesn't handle change well. He likes everything to stay the same.' She tickled the bulldog under his chin. Kitty smiled to herself. Honor never forgot to charm and seduce.

'I spoke to Daisy.'

'Oh yes?'

'She says you have a plane to catch?'

Honor was looking ahead, along the path that ran by the edge of the ridge. Either she had not heard or she was choosing to ignore Kitty's question.

'This track is called Salter's Nick. They used to drive pack horses along here, years ago, when they smuggled salt over the Border. The return cargo was moonshine whisky.'

Honor picked up a stick and hurled it over the cliff. It tumbled end over end, vanishing into the trees below. Spike bounded after it, a blur of black and white. He found a way down the steep slope, loosing small avalanches of stones as he nosed his way through the scrub.

'Most of the time I walk here alone.'

'Don't you feel lonely?'

'I always feel lonely. Don't you?'

The two regarded each other for a moment. Now was the time.

'I know what you did, Honor.'

'Come here.' Honor grabbed Kitty's wrist. 'There's something I want to show you!' She dragged Kitty towards the rock, a vast, domed wedge which hung over the void, pointing into the air like a snout. Honor threw her crook onto the top of the where it landed with a clatter. She scrambled up the face, finding holds that were little more than notches in the stone. Within moments she was standing on top, hands on her hips, grinning down at Kitty. Spike mooched about in the shadows beneath the stone, gnawing at his stick.

'Come on!'

'I don't know if I can manage it.'

'Don't be such a coward!'

The holds were hard to find but Kitty was limber. She inched her way up the dome. Honor stared at her, an odd smile on her lips.

'Need a hand?'

'I'm good,' said Kitty, reaching for another hold then swinging her leg over the rim.

'Of course you are.'

In a moment Kitty crouched on the top of the stone. She stood to take in the view and wobbled, struck by a wave of vertigo. Beyond the edge the land fell away, a drop of a hundred feet or more. Kitty recovered her balance, fighting the urge to stay low as she moved towards the edge. She inched across the stone, fixing her eyes on the horizon, anxious not to look to either side, sensing the sheer drop to the valley below. The breeze tugged Honor's hair, whipping it across her face. She raised a hand to shield her eyes as she looked across the land. Kitty stood at her shoulder. It was as if they were flying above the valley. The landscape of moorland and forests stretched to the horizon, a hundred shades of green.

'That's quite a view,' said Kitty, her throat tight.

'All the way to the Simonside Hills. Must be forty miles!'

Kitty tapped her toes on the rock, so that she had an excuse to look down. 'What are we standing on?'

'It's gritstone. Very popular with climbers. Or boulderers, as they call themselves. This stone is the daddy. They love climbing it because of the overhang. It's like walking across the head of a huge dinosaur. It might spring to life at any moment!'

Honor reached inside her gilet and produced a small flask. She took a drink then offered it to Kitty, who shook her head. Honor peered over the edge, smiling, then waved her hands, pretending that she was falling. Kitty pointed to a hollow, a dished hole carved into the stone.

'That's the Devil's Punchbowl.' They kneeled down together, looking into the scooped dish. Kitty looked at their reflection in the rainwater gathered in the bowl. 'It was carved for a wedding in the seventeen hundreds.' Honor's voice was slurred, the words spilling from her lips.

'Have you ever drunk from it?' Kitty dipped her fingertips into the cold, clear water.

'A long time ago.'

'You and Jack?'

Honor affected not to hear. She took a drink from her flask and held it out for Kitty, who took a sip. The neat gin burned her throat. She coughed. Honor laughed. 'Not a Hendrick's girl?' A flock of whooper swans flew overhead, strung out in the sky in a ragged dart. Kitty heard the beat of their wings as they passed overhead.

'They marry for life.' Honor swigged another mouthful of gin. 'Idiots.' The note of self pity was new. Out of the corner of her eye, Kitty tried to gauge how high they were. The breeze shook the tops of trees, far below. Looking down on the canopy of Scot's Pine and oak was unsettling. The wind gusted as it swirled around the rock. The world tilted and her head swam. She crouched low, feeling for the rock surface with her fingertips. Honor watched this through half closed eyes. She took another sip, then placed the flask on the rock. *Tink.* She dabbed her lips with the back of her hand, kissing the skin. It was such a delicate, graceful gesture, though her self control seemed to be slipping away.

'I make a lot of money, Kitty.' She flicked her hair from her face. 'I mean, a LOT of money. I'm guessing, from that heap that you drive, that you don't?'

'Why did you do it?'

'One day, quite soon, your daughter will go to University. You could use a holiday. I can help you.'

'I don't think so.'

'I make more money in a week than you do in a year. I have beautiful houses. The cars I want. The lovers I want. I don't have any problems, darling.'

'But you have a problem with Marisa Lyndon.'

The ghost of a smile flickered on Honor's lips, an acknowledgement that Kitty had pricked her.

'I thought you were such good friends? You and Marisa?'

'Friends? With her?' Honor cackled as she took another drink. 'You know her name isn't Marisa, don't you?'

'I didn't.' The horizon seemed to tilt. 'No.'

'Marisa! It's Marie Sara. She changed it because she wanted to sound more interesting. I want to show you something else.' She moved towards the outer edge of the stone, the tip of the beak. Honor's tone was soothing now, coaxing. 'Here. Just here.' Honor knelt on one knee. With exaggerated care she placed her flask on the stone. 'Come see.' She crooked her finger. The surface of the rock was scarred with cuts and engravings, some ancient, some fresh, their edges hard and clean. Honor traced her fingertips over grooves in the stone, as if caressing the skin of a lover.

'We carved our names here. See?'

Kitty saw the letters, JL and HB, linked by a heart. 'The adventures I've had up here!' She smiled as she traced the letters on the rock with her fingertip. She uncorked the flask.

'This is where Jack and I first made love. On this rock. It was one of those perfect moments you always remember. You know? Here,' she tapped the rock with the tip of her crook. 'Right here. This is where we fucked.'

'I see.' Kitty closed her eyes, waiting for the swirling to stop.

'You're such a prissy little bitch, aren't you? '*I see*.' So dreary. So literal minded!'

Kitty opened her eyes to return Honor's glare. 'I spent last night tied up.'

Honor took another swig. 'Sounds intriguing.' The charming smile had returned.

'Some creep was hiding in the back seat of my car. That's going to be one of the nights *I* 'will always remember."

Honor threw back her head and laughed. 'I asked you to drop it.' Her smile faded. 'You really should have done that.' Her voice was flat. 'I can't let you take me back.'

'Why do you hate her?'

'She crossed me. All my life. 'Fool me once, shame on you. Fool me twice...' Her tone was soft, as if she were talking to herself. 'I asked you to drop this, Kitty. As a friend.'

'I don't think we're friends, Honor.'

'No?' Honor traced her finger tip over the rock. Kitty judged the distance between them. On flat ground, she might have taken a chance and rushed her. Glimpsing the drop behind Honor, she did not dare.

'My dad ran away. Went to Spain with his whore. He left me. Just went. I was just a kid. A child. And my mother went crazy. But we got by. Just the two of us. Then. One day. He came home. He'd come back to England with his whore and they had a fight. So he turned up. Just dropped by. The penitent husband...And she took him back! With this brat! Can you believe it?' She looked at Kitty, shaking her head.

'You're sisters.'

'Half sisters. I was six when he came back. With her.'

The Half Witch.

'Why did you want to hurt her?'

'I don't know. Doesn't everyone want to kill their sister? Now and then?'

'Jack said she has no family.' Kitty flashed her conversation with him on that first day.

'*So...Any brothers or sisters?*' she had asked.

'*Nobody.*' Jack had replied. '*She had no-one. Except for me.*'

'Jack and I were sweethearts, you see? Just kids. But he was the good thing in my life. The *only* thing.' She looked at Kitty. 'You know how that is? How intense that can be?'

Kitty saw the sun glint on a car passing along the main road. The car slowed as it approached the gate.

'Daddy drank himself to death. My mother got worse. They sectioned her. Time after time. Then Jack said he was leaving. He had a job in London. So I went with him.'

A figure got out of the passenger door and walked towards the gatepost. The gate opened. The black car drove in.

'I left everything behind. And we started all over again.' Honor sipped her gin.

The car was driving up the track, bumping and rolling up the steep climb towards the ridge. A cloud of dust rose behind it.

'Some people enter your life, and they leave, and they come back.' Honor raised a finger in the air, moving it in a lazy circle.

Now Kitty could hear the motor. The black BMW drove through the notch in the cliff face and disappeared.

'She wanted to *be* me. You see? Whenever I had something, she wanted it. She took everything.'

CHAPTER FORTY SEVEN

THE DAY ROOM had a unique scent, a cocktail of milky coffee, cheap biscuits and carpet shampoo. In the corner of the room a screen glowed, orange celebs on a yellow couch, gurning and grinning. For a minute Honor stood outside, watching her mother through the mesh glass door. Nothing had changed since her last visit. Her mother sat in the same chair, wearing the same cardigan. Honor took a deep breath and opened the door. 'Mum?' Her mother did not turn, though her eyes flicked to the side.

'Which one are you?' she sighed. 'Oh...It's you.' Honor took her mother's hand and squeezed. There was no response. The older woman's gaze was glued to the screen, where the presenters were cooing over a piece of jewellery. Honor looked at her mother, wondering where that pretty face had gone. The pills she took each morning kept her mind tethered to the earth, yet drained the life from her body. Her flesh was puffed, heavy, solid as damp sand.

The visit always followed the same pattern. Honor arrived every Wednesday morning. She was the only visitor. They never spoke. They sat, side by side, watching the screen until it was time for Honor's bus.

Today was different. Honor leaned over to kiss her mother's cheek for the last time.

'On my feet a hundred hours a week, selling scent for pennies. Marisa blagged a job for the same company. Then she turns up at one of my parties. And guess who's with her?' She laughed, taking another swig from the flask. 'My Jack. It's quite funny. Don't you think?'

'That's the reason you wanted to kill her?'

'That's the strange thing. I accepted that. I would be alone. That was my destiny. So I worked. That was all I did. I'm good at what I do. I got rich. I'm worth it.

Honor saw Jack the moment she entered the room. He sat at a

table by the window, hunched over a cup of coffee. He looked up, sprang to his feet and kissed her on both cheeks. A young waiter appeared at the table. That was always the way with Jack - he could make the world bend to his will. He ordered a whisky, asked if she wanted the same. 'Whoa, tiger! I've just had breakfast! In any case, I don't.'

'You don't what?'

'I don't drink.' Though for that second, you wanted to, more than anything.

He looked drawn. Honor sensed that this might not be the meeting she hoped for. She had dreamed he would say it had all been a mistake, that they should never have parted. But they were old friends, that was all.

'Thanks for this. I need a friend to talk to. We're friends, Honor. And, in a way, you're a party to all of this.'

'I can't stand the suspense, darling.'

'It's Marisa.'

'Right.' Honor nodded. Jack had no idea about tact or finesse. Never had.

'She's leaving me.'

Honor looked across the lawn to the university. Students lolled on the grass, soaking up the spring sunshine, their whole lives ahead of them. So happy, so full of hope.

'She's been sleeping with that client of yours.'

Those words tugged her back into the room. Everything became a little clear, a little more vivid.

'Client? Which client?'

'That little toe rag. The 'artist'. Caspar Greene.'

'I went round to see her. To have it out.'

'Tell me what you remember.'

'The anger.' Honor's eyes misted as she recalled the events of that morning. 'I remember the blood. Trying to stop it.' She shook her head. 'How did you know?'

''You covered Marisa's face. There was something about that. Some measure of pity, I think. And your scent. I remembered that from the house.'

Honor nodded. She looked towards the house, moving her head as if searching for something. 'No real proof, then?' Honor tightened her grip on her crook. 'It's all down to you?'

'I think you may be unwell.'

'I'm fine.'

'You seem to have many of the signifiers of BPD. Of Borderline Personality Disorder.'

'Ha! Mad you mean? Like my mother?'

'I have no idea.'

'Signifiers? Like what, exactly?'

'The feeling of being abandoned. Anger. Impulsive behaviour. These are all...'

'You know nothing about me.'

'No. But I know nobody has been killed. We can do something about this. That's all I'm saying.'

'I won't go back. You won't drag me down.'

Honor swung the stick in a flat arc. The stick hit Kitty's forearm with a sickening crack. She screamed and fell to the ground. The pain in her arm was electric, shooting sparks through the bone. Honor glared down at her and raised the stick.

'Don't! Please...' she begged. There was an impish smile on Honor's lips. There was a swoosh as Honor swung the stick at Kitty's head. She rolled to avoid the blow as the stick smacked the stone. She lay at the edge of the rock. Before she could rise Honor straddled her chest. Grasping the ends of her stick she pressed it on Kitty's throat. Her face flushed, turning dark. Kitty tucked her feet beneath her thighs and jerked her hips into the air. Honor flipped over, tumbling down the side of the rock. She screamed as she fell. Her body hit the ground at the foot of the rock. Kitty rolled onto her hands and knees, gasping for breath. She inched forward to peer over the edge. Honor lay on her back, her limbs twisted. After a moment Kitty scrambled down the rock. As she reached the ground she was aware of movement at the edge of her vision. She looked up to see a tall, pale skinned young man. Whitey held his samurai sword. Recognition came in an instant.

Kitty caught his scent, that mix of after shave and mustiness. She knew that it was the man in the mask. Seeing the sword she made the connection with the Horror Hotel killing. She sensed how dangerous he was.

He stared at her, open mouthed. She emptied her mind, entering the state which allowed her to be receptive to everything that was happening. She watched as one hand went to the handle of his sword while the other pulled the scabbard. The blade glittered as it emerged. Whitey tossed the scabbard aside and dropped into his fighting stance, his weight on both feet, the sword held parallel to the ground. Honor groaned as she woke. That gave Kitty a moment, just long enough. Clasping her broken arm to her chest she stepped towards him, screaming 'No!' His eyes widened and he stepped back, moving the sword behind his shoulder to strike. In Wado Ryu there is no attack, there is no defence. The two are simultaneous. Before he could swing she delivered the Mawashi, a roundhouse kick which struck him between the legs. Whitey doubled over on the ground, bellowing like a wounded bull. One move flowed into the next as Kitty stamped on his fingers until his grip on the sword loosened. She stood on Whitey's neck. His eyes bulged as he flailed around, desperate to throw her off. What happened next was to haunt her. She paused, looking down at his face. Then she drew back her foot and kicked him - hard - beneath the chin. His head snapped back, bone cracking like dry wood. His eyes rolled into his skull, the lids fluttering. She stepped back. Whitey's whole body shook, the convulsions moving through his limbs. Dark blood leaked from the corner of his mouth and fell on the grass. Then he was still. Kitty stared down at his body, breathing hard. She kneeled down. She could not take his pulse - she was in agony if she let go her broken arm. In any case, she could see there was no point.

That was the moment she became aware of the other man. He was plump, his cheeks covered with downy hair. Davy Clark watched from the gate, his lips parted. As Kitty caught sight of him he turned to run. She opened her top and slipped her arm inside. Then she picked up the sword with her good arm and followed. She did not run - the pain kicked in if she made a sudden move. She followed him, slowly and deliberately closing the distance. Davy Clark was trying to open the car door. As she arrived he turned. He said nothing, leaning against the car, trembling.

'Kneel down.'

'Please,' he begged. 'Please. I don't want any trouble...'

CHAPTER FORTY EIGHT

'SO...' CLIVE LUMLEY stood at the end of the bed. He held the fob of his car keys, tossing them from hand to hand. Greta looked up.

'I thought a little drive would be nice.'

'I'll get a jacket.'

'Good idea,' said Clive. 'I thought we'd drive to the reservoir. It can get chilly by the water.'

Greta ran her fingers though her hair.

'But it's nice up there,' he said as he locked the front door. 'Of an evening.' Clive smiled to himself as he turned the key. 'Very quiet.'

It seemed fitting that she lay in the ward where Marisa Lyndon had spent so much time. Kitty pulled her chair closer to the bedside and repeated her question.

'You wanted to kill Marisa?'

Honor raised an eyebrow.

'Did I? I don't recall saying that.'

It was clear she had no intention of making Kitty's job easy. Kitty glanced at Des Tucker, who lolled against the wall at the other side of the bed. Tucker scratched his nose and closed his eyes.

'Jack told you that Marisa was planning to run away with Caspar. So, you flipped?'

Another blank stare.

'It was Caspar's choice,' said Kitty. 'Don't you think he shares some of the blame?'

'He's hopeless.' Honor smiled to herself, like an indulgent parent forgiving her child.

'I hope he was worth it.'

Kitty rode the lift down to the car park. The secret of Honor Blackett's personality, she guessed, lay in the dark triad of narcissism, violence and a lack of empathy. Her father's abandonment of the family still resonated, after all those years. Her childhood anger at his desertion was unresolved. By attacking Marisa, the 'cuckoo in the nest,' she had been taking her revenge. Like many 'Borderlines,' Honor lacked control of her impulsive nature. When provoked by her sister, that lack of control spilled over into a rage which could only end in violence.

When Kitty walked into Tony Vipond's office he pretended to be signing some papers. After enduring her stare for a while he threw down his pen and sighed. He looked at her, clocking the cast on her arm.

'You're looking for some sort of apology?'

'No. I don't expect one.'

'Good. Because you'd expect for a very long time.'

He rocked back on his chair, then closed his eyes. It seemed he found it difficult to meet her gaze.

'How are you?'

'I didn't join to hurt anybody. Let alone...'

'No. Of course.' They were silent for a time. 'You may find this hard to believe but there's a lot of...understanding. You're not the first.'

'What happen's next?'

'It's been referred to Special Crime and Counter-Terrorism Division. York. They'll handle the investigation. If they decide you're criminally responsible for his death...' He shrugged.

'I've put in a for a transfer,' said Kitty.

'Where?'

'Anywhere you're not. Sir.'

He smiled.

'Did Honor Blackett confess? When you were out on the crags?'

'She did.'

'Has she repeated that confession since? In front of witnesses?'

'I'm afraid not.'

'Could be tricky. But she's not going anywhere. I'll keep on at her.'

'Bryson was right.'

'Prudhoe? What did he say?'

'The rich. He reckons they can get away with murder.'

CHAPTER FORTY NINE

EVERY MORNING SHE woke and felt that odd sensation, a strange hollowness before the memory rushed back. Kitty recalled the moment she stood above Kirk White, looking down at his face. Had she not defeated him he would have killed her. She had acted in self defence. She should feel no guilt. But something about the events of that morning haunted her, even after the charge was dropped and she was re-instated.

'I never intended for that to happen.'

'No,' said Bryson. 'Nobody would.'

'I was scared. Terrified, if I'm honest.'

'Of course. As anyone would be.' He seemed distracted, his thoughts elsewhere. Vipond blamed him for the 'Chien' affair and the humiliation in the press.

'I keep reliving that moment.'

Bryson Prudhoe peeled off his jacket and draped it over the back of his chair. 'You're cleared. When your cast is off you're back in business.'

Kitty nodded. She sipped her drink. 'You know, I thought, for a while, of going to the funeral.'

'Whose funeral?'

'Kirk White's.'

His eyes widened. 'You didn't?'

'No.'

Bryson was shaking his head, looking over her shoulder to see that nobody had heard.

'I knew there would be nobody there.'

'The press might have been sniffing around. It would look like you felt guilty.'

'But I do.'

'Well don't.'

'But there was a moment, you see? A moment where he was beaten and I was standing on him and maybe I should have stopped. Right then.'

'It happened in a moment, Kitty. You could spend your life thinking about it.'

'In the car, when he first got me, I wanted to destroy him. And I did.'

'My guess is that he was always headed there. It would have happened. Sooner or later. It was your bad luck you were involved.'

'I was naive, Bryson. I still am.' Kitty looked around the empty canteen as she stirred her tea. 'I remember you saying, 'When a woman goes bad, look for the man. And I was. Looking for the man. Looking too hard.'

'When women fight dirty...' said Bryson. 'The rules are off. We've got her. She'll crack.'

Kitty placed her spoon on the saucer.

'Honor's an intelligent woman. I don't think she's in love with Caspar Greene. Obsessed, perhaps. But it was the final insult, coming from a woman who had taken Jack Lyndon and, in a way, her dad.'

'Passion.'

'...makes fools of the wise.' Don't you always say?'

On the horizon the shadows of clouds raced over the Cheviot Hills.

'Kitty. I've got into a...' He looked down, at the table - squaring the cutlery, moving his cup. 'I've got into a situation.'

'Does this situation have dirty blond hair?'

He turned the knife square, then turned it back again.

'You're going to have to find a way to fight back, Bryson. Fight back.'

Her taxi stopped outside the Lyndons' house on 'Millionaire's Row.' Kitty noticed an electronic gate now sealed their property from the outside world.

'Nice place,' said the driver.

'You think?' She asked the driver to wait. 'I won't be long.'

She pressed the button and gave her name. The gates swung open. Kitty walked up the gravel drive. A red squirrel skittered along the beech hedge and disappeared. A sprinkler hissed on the lawn. As she looked up at the CCTV camera beneath the portico she saw the iris dilate as the lens found her face.

You're switched on now...

Cathy Fletcher opened the door. Her greeting was polite, though her look was guarded. She tucked a yellow duster into the lap pocket of her pinny.

'Have you hurt yourself?' She frowned at the cast on Kitty's arm.

'It's not an official call, Cathy. I was passing. I just wondered how Marisa was?'

Cathy narrowed her eyes. 'I've been told not to say anything.'

'Right. Well.' Kitty turned to walk away.

'Thing is, they're not here.'

'Well. Just say I called by, when you see her.'

'Mr Lyndon always promised to take her to Necker, you see. In the Caribbean.' Cathy's eyes glittered with vicarious pleasure. You see! It's the most expensive holiday in the world!'

The taxi carried Kitty to the west, towards home. As the sun dipped below the hills the sky was streaked with mackerel cloud, ripples of silver and blue. Kitty felt a comfortable weariness.

Honor Blackett was a driven woman. Ambitious, impulsive, yet so self-absorbed that she was blind to danger. It was that which allowed her to function in the world, to pass as safe, as charming, as 'one of us.' When she was growing up, Marisa had been the cuckoo in the nest. She had followed Honor, wanting to be loved and accepted, with little knowledge of the way her half sister saw her. Then Marisa had stolen Jack. Finally, she had humiliated Honor by stealing Caspar Greene. Honor's first humiliation was bad enough: for it to happen a second time was intolerable. People with a Borderline Personality Disorder can commit murder. It depends on the circumstances and how deep the pathology runs. They're capable of acting-out unresolved anger by inflicting harm on anyone who is close. Their lack of impulse control allows violent acts to happen. Rage was the spur for Honor. Her rage against her family was rooted in abandonment. Her anger centred on Marisa, who had destroyed her happiness not once, with Jack, but a second time with Caspar Greene.

As she walked up Cloud Street Kitty listed the things that made her happy:

Sunshine.
Friends and family.
The sea.

A nice cup of tea.
Laughter.
Love.

The house was empty when she got home. Tomorrow she would go to her self defence class and help out, watching the young ones. With her arm in plaster it would be a while before she was able to spar again. Afterwards, perhaps, she would share a drink with Raphael.

Kitty pictured the huge, billowing hedges, the green walls which surrounded every house on the Callerton Chase estate. She heard her father's voice, a soft, low murmur from the darkness.

'Happiness doesn't depend on how much you've got, Kitty.'

'No. Of course.'

'It's about connections with other people.'

'Yup.'

'Life is sad and beautiful, pet. The world is crazy. Sometimes you have to remind yourself of the beauty that is out there.'

'I'm sure you're right, dad.'

She switched on the light. The room was empty. She poured a glass of Merlot and watched the sun go down. A dark cloud bloomed in the sky, a drop of ink in clear water. Kitty knew she was lucky enough to have most of the things on her list. Some were harder to track down.

Those she would go on hoping to find.

Lightning Source UK Ltd.
Milton Keynes UK
UKOW04f0619101115

262426UK00002B/25/P